MAHĀBHĀRATA UNRAVELLED

MAHĀBHĀRATA UNRAVELLED

Lesser-Known Facets of a Well-Known History

AMI GANATRA

BLOOMSBURY
NEW DELHI • LONDON • OXFORD • NEW YORK • SYDNEY

BLOOMSBURY INDIA
Bloomsbury Publishing India Pvt. Ltd
Second Floor, LSC Building No. 4, DDA Complex, Pocket C – 6 & 7,
Vasant Kunj, New Delhi, 110070

BLOOMSBURY, BLOOMSBURY INDIA and the Diana logo
are trademarks of Bloomsbury Publishing Plc

First published in India 2021
This edition published 2021

ISBN: PB: 978-93-54351-27-3; eBook: 978-93-54351-33-4

11

Typeset in Adobe Caslon Pro by Manipal Technologies Limited
Printed and bound in India Gopsons Papers Pvt. Ltd., Noida

MIX
Paper | Supporting responsible forestry
FSC® C191020

To find out more about our authors and books visit www.bloomsbury.com and sign up for our newsletters

।। श्रीवेदव्यासाय नमः।।

नारायणं नमस्कृत्य नरं चैव नरोत्तमम्।
देवीं सरस्वतीं व्यासं ततो जयमुदीरयेत् ।।

CONTENTS

PREFACE

Indic knowledge systems clearly differentiate between mythology and history. The Mahābhārata and Rāmāyana have been called itihāsa (iti ha āsa: thus it has been), the history of our ancestors. Rāmāyana, as we know, is composed by Rishi Vālmiki, a contemporary of Shri Rāma. Mahābhārata has been immortalised for us by the man who was biologically related to the involved stakeholders—the Kạuravas and the Pāndavas—Rishi Veda Vyāsa. There cannot be a more unbiased source.

The Mahābhārata is also called the pancham Veda—the fifth Veda. By way of historical narration, it provides a framework for understanding and dealing with our own ethical dilemmas. The raw emotions and motivations, the dharma sankatas, faced by the people in the Mahābhārata are so relatable and real that even 5,000 years later, or 7,000 as per some recent estimates, it continues to inspire authors, artists, social scientists and us. The number of works in the mythological fiction genre that get written inspired by the Mahābhārata, even today, is a testimony to its relevance.

The popularity of the epic can be further gauged from off-the-charts viewership of a recent rerun of B.R. Chopra's *Mahabharat*, an old TV series with not-so-sophisticated production by current standards.

Even today, we have deep discussions regarding the people in the epic, their personalities and their actions. We have our favourite personalities. The level of our involvement with them is such that discussions often tend to get really passionate. We stand up for them like we would for our friends and relatives. And why not? It is a story of our ancestors, after all.

The original work is in Sanskrit and huge, spanning over 100,000 verses, making it practically impossible for mass consumption except by way of visual storytelling and abridged versions. There are some very good abridged versions but they too are rather big. There is only so much a story of such a large volume can be abridged. To some extent, this gap has been filled by TV series as well as numerous reimagined works based on the text. Even then, a mainstream TV series can't cover all of what is in there.

The adaptations and reimagined fictional works have an element of artistic liberty in different proportions. Sometimes, the artist's imaginations are so interesting that a reader begins to assume that as the real story. With the Mahābhārata, given its popularity, and many related works, some imagined stories seem to have become 'the truth'. Misplaced facts give rise to misplaced conclusions. That is why, for a story of such prominence and influence, it is even more important to know the facts as they were told by Veda Vyāsa, from the authentic sources available to us today.

That is the purpose of this book—to get to know the events and people as told to us by Vyāsa. By way of the book, I have attempted to shed light on some frequently asked questions, clarify some myths and add not-so-well-known nuances of personalities and relationships related to the Mahābhārata, based on the generally accepted authentic sources. Some questions which I have sought to seek answers to are:

> Who narrated the version of the Mahābhārata that is known to us today?
> Was South India in any way connected to the Mahābhārata?
> Was 'caste' the reason for Karna's downfall? Was he always discriminated against because of his caste?
> Why was Arjuna given so much limelight and love?
> Why was Yudhishthira called the Dharmarāja?
> Who was the best warrior of Kurukshetra?
> Why was Draupadi given such an important status in the Mahābhārata, more than any other queen? Do we know anything about her life as a queen?
> Were women in those days meek and submissive?
> What roles did the sons of the Pāndavas play?
> What happened after the war ended?
> ...so on and so forth!

The dialogues between the characters are so rich that they unravel the personality traits of the speakers and the essence of the relationship. I have endeavoured to translate and summarise the dialogues in a way to maintain its original intent, emotion, wisdom and nuance. As the idea was to convey the gist, the translation may not be verbatim. I have added notes in such places where I may have taken the liberty to translate words in more contemporary terms. Where needed, I have added a brief closing commentary to the story.

My introduction to the Mahābhārata was also through the TV series. It got me interested enough to read other works related to or based on the Mahābhārata later in life. The more I read, the more questions I had. The only way to satisfy my curiosity, I realised, was by going to the source and reading what Veda Vyāsa had to say. As I read, I made notes. In a way, the book is an outcome of those notes. There were just so many 'aha' moments that deciding what to add in here and what to keep for later was quite an exercise.

This book has been divided into several parts, beginning with an overall storyline and sequence of events in the Mahābhārata. This section gives a bullet-point summary of the core story and introduces the main characters. The objective is to bring up to speed a reader not familiar with the story and serve as revision/reference for readers aware of the story.

This is followed by Introduction, which is an essay on dharma, the underlying theme of the epic. There is no exact translation of the word in English. The objective of the essay is to explain the term to the readers in some detail.

The next part sets the context of the history—when was it narrated, who are the Bhāratas and what was the extent of the epic's geographical coverage.

This is followed by a section which features stories from the Mahābhārata, although not always in chronological order. I have picked and arranged stories to highlight personalities, relations and interactions. Some stories are not so well known, while others are generally known but have interesting details which may ordinarily not be known. Of course, for those Mahābhārata aficionados who have read the unabridged translations, all of these would be known. For them, the arrangement and choice of the stories might be of interest.

As the stories are not event-based, but more personality-based, there is repetition of the incidents where multiple people were involved. However, in every story, I have attempted to add personality-specific details, even if the incident is repeated.

The final part is the trivia section, highlighting associated legends about the scripting of the epic, names and descriptions of war formations mentioned in the text and a brief overview of the work happening in the area of dating of the Mahābhārata.

The primary reference used for the book is Gita Press' महाभारत, the edition with Sanskrit text and Hindi translation. I have also referred to the Pune-based Bhandarkar Oriental Research Institute's *Critical Edition of Mahabharata* (further referred to as BORI CE) and Kisari Mohan Ganguli's English translation *The Mahabharata of Krishna-Dwaipayana Vyasa* (further mentioned as KMG) to check certain verses and clarify meanings.

To convey the right pronunciation of names while keeping the text simple to read, I have used only the diacritic ā in Sanskrit nouns and names that have an 'aa' (आ) sound. The names ending in 'a' without the diatric have to be read as अ. For example, Arjuna is to be read as अर्जुन. Any unintended errors in the book are regretted. My sincere request to the readers to bring those to my notice so that they can be rectified in future reprints.

The beauty of the Mahābhārata is its honest portrayal of human psychology. However technologically advanced we may have become, the innate desires and psychological traits have remained identical over millennia. That is why, the story of our ancestors stirs us even today. In them, we can see our own selves.

It is only apt what the narrator Ugrashravā Sauti states in the beginning about the Mahābhārata. He says, 'By this radiant light of History, the shroud of ignorance is destroyed and the inner sanctum of our entire being is illumined with wisdom.'

इतिहासप्रदीपेन मोहावरणघातिना।
लोकगर्भगृहं कृत्स्नं यथावत् सम्प्रकाशितम् ।। (Ādi Parva 1.87)

I do hope the readers enjoy reading the book as much as I have loved writing it. Beyond that, I hope the book makes readers curious enough to read the original unabridged version for themselves.

Paush Shukla Shashthi,
Vikram Samvat, 2077 Ami Ganatra

ACKNOWLEDGEMENTS

To Veda Vyāsa and the sages of Bhāratavarsha, I bow in obeisance. Their effort has preserved this itihāsa and this wisdom for us. My gratitude to Gita Press, Gorakhpur, Bhandarkar Oriental Research Institute, Pune, and to all the artists and writers who have helped take the story of our ancestors to the people. I write this book today standing on their shoulders.

The idea of materialising my objective to bring out the stories of the Māhabhārata, as narrated by Vyāsa, not reimagined, in the form of a book was conceived by Shri Praveen Tiwari of Bloomsbury. For the idea and his trust in me, I will forever be grateful.

My heartfelt thank you to my friends Ajay Dave, Palak Ahuja and Shilpa Bohra—they took time out to read the draft and provided valuable inputs on the content; to my dear friend and Sanskrit go-to person Nityananda Misra for his encouragement and for always enthusiastically clarifying my doubts; and to the team at Bloomsbury—Shreya Chakraborti, Nitin Valecha and everyone else—who has played a role in giving this book a material avatār.

To my mother Kavita Ganatra, I can never thank enough. All I can say is that whatever I am today is the result of her sweat and blood. She believed, deeply so, that I should write. I began blogging due to her encouragement. My first book is a dedication to her, and to Krishna.

श्रीकृष्णार्पणमस्तु!

THE MAHĀBHĀRATA: SUMMARY OF STORYLINE AND THE SEQUENCE OF EVENTS

Oath of Bhishma

- Shāntanu, the king of Hastināpur, falls in love with Gangā.
- Gangā marries him on the condition that the king shouldn't ever question her.
- Gangā gives birth to seven sons but drowns them in the river.
- The eighth son is born. Gangā goes to drown the baby but is stopped by Shāntanu.
- As the condition is violated, Gangā leaves Shāntanu and takes the baby along, promising to return the prince when he is old enough.
- True to her promise, Gangā brings the young Devavrata to Hastināpur. He is made the crown prince.
- Shāntanu falls in love with Satyavati, daughter of Dāshrāja, the headman of the fishing community of Nishādas.
- Dāshrāja would only marry Satyavati to the king if the king promises to make her son his heir. Shāntanu refuses.

- Devavrata learns about this precondition and takes the oath of celibacy for life and pledges to serve the Hastināpur throne till the end of his life.
- Satyavati has a son from one past encounter with Rishi Parāshar. This son is Veda Vyāsa. He is brought up by his father in the forest.

Birth of Dhritarāshtra, Pāndu and Vidura

- Satyavati and Shāntanu get married. Vichitravirya and Chitrangad are born.
- Chitrangad dies young.
- Bhishma hijacks the swayamvara of the three princesses of Kāshi and gets them to Hastināpur to marry Vichitravirya. These princesses are Ambā, Ambikā and Ambālikā.
- Ambikā and Ambālikā marry the prince. Ambā objects due to her love for King Shālva, who rejects her because she was won by Bhishma. Extremely angry at her fate and holding Bhishma responsible for it, Ambā pledges to become the reason for Bhishma's death even if it takes her multiple lifetimes to make it happen.
- Vichitravirya dies soon after without leaving behind an heir.
- As per the custom of niyoga, Satyavati invites her eldest son Vyāsa to help conceive a child each through Ambikā and Ambālikā.
- When Vyāsa approaches Ambikā, she closes her eyes, frightened by his terrifying appearance. Dhritarāshtra, born of that union, is thus born blind.

- Ambālikā loses her colour on seeing Vyāsa. Pāndu is born of that union.
- Satyavati desires one more child, but the queens wish not to see Vyāsa again. Hence, they send a handmaiden of Ambikā's to Vyāsa. She serves him with joy and sincerity. Vidura is born of the union. He is a paragon of wisdom, like his biological father.

The Birth of the Kauravas and the Pāndavas

- When the three boys are old enough and well educated, Pāndu is crowned the king. Dhritarāshtra, though the eldest, has to forgo the throne due to his blindness.
- Dhritarāshtra is married to Gāndhāri. When Gāndhāri learns about her husband's lack of sight, she too blindfolds herself for life.
- Pāndu marries Kunti and Mādri. Vidura is married to Sulabhā.
- When she was still a young girl, Kunti was given a boon by Rishi Durvāsā by which she could call upon any deity and beget a son through them. Curious, she uses it to call Surya deva and has a son with him. Afraid of the reputation of her family, she gives up the kid at birth. Adhiratha, a friend of Dhritarāshtra, living in Anga desh, finds the baby and adopts him as his son. This son is Karna.
- Pāndu becomes a chakravarti king, defeating all other kings of Bhāratavarsha. He comes to be known as a powerful and just king.

- Once, while on a hunting expedition, he unintentionally kills a sage in communion with his wife. The sage pronounces a curse on Pāndu. According to the curse, the moment Pāndu comes close to his wife out of love, he will die.
- Dejected, Pāndu relinquishes his throne to Dhritarāshtra and goes to live in the forest to do penance. Kunti and Mādri follow him.
- Though living a celibate life, Pāndu desires to have children. Kunti uses the boon she was given by Durvāsā and gives birth to Yudhishthira, Bheema and Arjuna. Using the same boon, Mādri begets twins Nakula and Sahadeva. The five are known as the Pāndavas.
- In Hastināpur, Gāndhāri gives birth to a hundred sons and one daughter. Duryodhana is the eldest followed by Duhshāsana. The sister is Dushālā. Duryodhana is the same age as Bheema. Dhritarāshtra has one more son through one of Gāndhāri's maids. He is Yuyutsu. These 102 kids are the Kauravas.
- The Pāndavas grow up in the forest under the care of their father and two mothers. One day, Pāndu loses control and pulls Mādri close. The curse of the sage has its effect. Pāndu dies. Mādri does not wish to live and ends her life as well.

Training with Dronāchārya

- After Pāndu's death, Kunti returns to Hastināpur with the boys. The cousins meet for the first time.

- The Kauravas and the Pāndavas do not get along. Duryodhana is especially jealous and keeps scheming with his uncle Shakuni to harass the Pāndavas. He tries to poison and drown Bheema once, but the latter survives and emerges even stronger.
- Bhishma sends the young boys to Kripāchārya and then to Dronāchārya for education and training in warfare.
- Apart from the Kauravas and the Pāndavas, the princes of the Vrishni clan, Karna and other students also come to study at Dronāchārya's āshram.
- The princes become experts in different forms of warfare. Arjuna is a notch above all. He masters every form of warfare, with a special focus on archery.
- Karna learns the basics with Drona but leaves to go to Parashurāma when Drona refuses to teach him the deadly celestial weapon, Brahmāstra.
- After completion of the course, the princes display their skills in front of the citizens of Hastināpur.
- Karna comes uninvited and challenges Arjuna. Duryodhana is overjoyed to find a man willing to challenge Arjuna who is also a capable warrior. He befriends Karna and crowns him the king of Anga desh. Karna stays indebted to Duryodhana all his life.
- As gurudakshinā to their teacher Drona, the Pāndavas capture Drupada, the king of Pānchāla, and hand him to Dronāchārya. Drona takes away half of Drupada's kingdom and lets him go.

This was Drona's way of avenging his past humiliation at the hands of the latter.

- Drupada is furious and knows he cannot defeat Drona. Hence, he desires for a son who can kill Drona. Taking a sage's advice, he performs rituals to beget such a son. From that, Dhrishtadyumna and Draupadi are born.
- Drupada has another elder son by the name of Shikhandi. He was born a female but later became a man due to a boon bestowed by a Yaksha named Sthunākarna. In the previous life, Shikhandi was Ambā, the princess of Kāshi.

The Swayamvara of Draupadi

- By unanimous consensus, Yudhishthira is made the crown prince of Hastināpur.
- Duryodhana is livid. He convinces his father to send the Pāndavas and Kunti to Vāranāvata under the pretext of a celebration. In Vāranāvata, he arranges for Purochana to create an inflammable palace of lac, the lakshāgraha. They plan to burn alive the unsuspecting Pāndavas.
- Vidura learns of this devious plan and warns Yudhishthira. The Pāndavas play along with Purochana's plan. Meanwhile, Vidura sends a digger who creates a tunnel from under the palace to let the brothers and Kunti escape. When the tunnel is ready, the Pāndavas set fire to the palace and flee. The fire kills Purochana.

- News reaches Hastināpur. Everyone believes the Pāndavas are dead. Duryodhana is declared the crown prince.
- The Pāndavas spend a few months hiding in the Kāmyaka forest. There, Bheema kills a man-eating rākshasa, Hidimb, and marries his sister Hidimbā. They have a son named Ghatotkacha.
- The Pāndavas then spend a few days in Ekachakra Nagar in the house of a Brāhmin family. Here, Bheema kills the demon Bakāsura and liberates the villagers from his menace.
- On hearing about the swayamvara of Drupada's daughter Draupadi, the Pāndavas head to Kāmpilya. They find shelter in a potter's home, still in disguise.
- The swayamvara involves an archery challenge. Only a prince who hits the target can marry Draupadi.
- Warrior princes from all over Bhāratavarsha come to attend the swayamvara, desirous of making Draupadi their wife. But none succeed in hitting the target. Arjuna, dressed as a young Brāhmin, emerges from the audience, hits the target and wins over Draupadi.
- Though won by Arjuna, Draupadi is married to all the five Pāndavas brothers. She becomes their common wife and a bond that binds them.
- Krishna recognises the Pāndavas in the assembly of Kāmpilya. He follows them to the potter's hut. Kunti is Krishna's father's elder sister. By that relation, he is a maternal cousin of the Pāndavas.

- Arjuna and Krishna are of the same age and take an instant liking to each other. They become the best of friends in the times to come. Krishna plays the role of an advisor and well-wisher of the Pāndavas from then on.
- The news of the survival of the Pāndavas reaches Hastināpur.

The Game of Dice

- Dhritarāshtra is embarrassed. Hence, taking suggestions from the elders and Vidura, he invites the Pāndavas home and divides the kingdom. Duryodhana keeps Hastināpur while the Pāndavas get Khāndavaprastha. The Pāndavas toil and establish a flourishing kingdom of Indraprastha there.
- All is well till one day, for breaching a code of conduct laid down regarding the privacy of the brothers with Draupadi, Arjuna leaves to spend twelve years in the forest and do pilgrimages.
- He travels around Bhāratavarsha and marries Uloopi and Chitrāngadā. With them, he begets two sons, Irāvan and Babruvāhana respectively. Towards the end of the journey, he visits Dwārkā and marries Krishna's sister Subhadrā. She gives him a son named Abhimanyu.
- In Indraprastha, Draupadi also gives birth to five boys. Prativindhya, Sutasoma, Shatānika, Shrutakarma and Shrutakirti.
- To satisfy the request of Agni deva, Krishna and Arjuna let him burn the Khāndava forest. Maya,

an architect of the Dānava tribe, pleads with them to let him escape the fire and promises to build the most beautiful palace for the Pāndavas. He builds for them the 'palace of illusions—the Māyā sabhā'. From Agni, Krishna gets his Sudarshan Chakra and Arjuna, his Gāndiva and quiver of inexhaustible arrows.

- Yudhishthira conducts the Rājasuya Yajna.
- Over a row on who should be the first person to be revered during the Yajna, Shishupāla insults Bhishma and Krishna. Shishupāla is Krishna's maternal aunt's son. Krishna lets him hurl a hundred insults before severing his head with his Sudarshan Chakra.
- Duryodhana burns with jealousy seeing the prosperity of the Pāndavas in Indraprastha and begins plotting with his uncle Shakuni, friend Karna and brother Duhshāsana to bring them down.
- Shakuni is an expert in the game of dice (dyuta kridā). He is adept in deceitfully defeating the opponents. He suggests organising a game with the Pāndavas. After some vacillations, Dhritarāshtra gives in. Yudhishthira agrees to come.
- Yudhishthira stakes and loses everything—his kingdom, wealth, brothers, himself and Draupadi.
- Duhshāsana drags Draupadi to the Hastināpur assembly by her hair. Duryodhana and Karna humiliate her calling her a slave along with her husbands, and incite Duhshāsana to disrobe her. Except Vidura and Vikarna, one of Duryodhana's brothers, everybody just keeps mum and looks on

at the humiliation being meted out to Draupadi and the Pāndavas.

- Duhshāsana does not succeed in disrobing Draupadi. Eventually, sense prevails. Dhritarāshtra frees the Pāndavas from slavery as requested by Draupadi. But on Duryodhana's insistence, he orders for another round of the game of dice. The Pāndavas lose again and are banished to the forest for thirteen years (vanvās). Of these, twelve are to be spent in the forest and one year in hiding (agyātvās). Per the clause, if the Pāndavas are identified during the year of disguise, they will have to go to the forest for another thirteen years. If not, they are to get their kingdom back.

Years in the Forests

- The Pāndavas spend twelve years in the forests in the company of sages and do pilgrimages.
- Meanwhile, on the advice of Veda Vyāsa and Yudhishthira, Arjuna goes to gather celestial weapons in preparation of a probable war with their cousins; if Duryodhana doesn't give their kingdom back after thirteen years, a war would be inevitable. He spends five years of the twelve in this expedition.
- One day, Duryodhana and Karna, along with their women and other Kauravas, go on an expedition to the forest where the Pāndavas are camped. They desire to flaunt their riches before the Pāndavas

and make them feel miserable over their pitiable state.

- However, even before their tents are pitched, they get into a tussle with the Gandharvas in the forest. The Kauravas are defeated and captured by the powerful Gandharvas. Karna runs away to save his own life.
- Some soldiers escape and seek help from Yudhishthira. The eldest Pāndava sends the four brothers to rescue them. The Kaurava party goes back to Hastināpur, thoroughly embarrassed.
- One day, when the Pāndavas had gone hunting, bewitched by Draupadi's beauty, Jayadratha, the husband of Dushālā, attempts to kidnap her. The brothers return in time to rescue Draupadi and capture Jayadratha. Due to the consideration of Dushālā, their cousin sister, Yudhishthira lets him go with only a small humiliation as punishment.
- The Pāndavas spend the last year in disguise in Matsya desh, ruled by King Virāta. Yudhishthira becomes a courtier; Bheema, a royal chef; Arjuna disguised as a eunuch becomes a dance and music teacher for the royal women; Nakula becomes a stable keeper and Sahadeva, a cattle keeper. Draupadi finds work as the handmaiden of Queen Sudeshnā, Virāta's wife.
- Keechak, Sudeshnā's brother, was the commander of Virāta's forces. Once, in Sudeshnā's palace, Keechak sees Draupadi. He is immediately infatuated and desires her at any cost.
- Bheema kills Keechak for his indecent propositioning of Draupadi.

- After Keechak's death, suspicious that the killer might be Bheema, the Kauravas along with the Trigartas attack Matsya. Arjuna, disguised as the eunuch Brihannalā, defeats the entire Kaurava army consisting of Bhishma, Drona, Kripa, Ashwatthāmā, Duryodhana, Duhshāsana and Karna, among others.
- After the battle, the Pāndavas come out of hiding having successfully completed their agyātvās.
- Virāta marries his daughter, Uttarā, to Arjuna's son Abhimanyu.

Peace Negotiations

- The Pāndavas and their allies gather in Upaplavya, a city in Matsya desh, and send a messenger to Hastināpur to demand their kingdom back.
- Messengers go to and fro to no avail. Instigated by Karna, Duryodhana refuses to give back anything. Yudhishthira demands for just five villages in lieu of Indraprastha to avoid the war. That too is not agreeable to Duryodhana.
- As a final measure, Krishna goes to negotiate. Duryodhana doesn't agree. Instead, he tries to imprison Krishna.
- Before returning, Krishna informs Karna about the truth of his birth, disclosing that Karna is the eldest son of Kunti and a brother of the Pāndavas. He tries to convince Karna to join hands with the Pāndavas. Later, Kunti reaches out to him too. But Karna decides to stay with Duryodhana.

- War is now inevitable. The armies assemble in Kurukshetra.

The War of Kurukshetra

- Bhishma becomes the commander of the Kauravas, Dhrishtadyumna of the Pāndavas.
- Following an ego tussle with Bhishma, Karna decides to stay out of the war till Bhishma is the commander.
- Arjuna is deluded at the thought of killing his own people. Krishna narrates the Bhagavad Gita.
- Battle begins.
- Bhishma falls on the tenth day of the war. He is laid on the bed of arrows by Arjuna. Dronāchārya becomes the commander. Karna enters the battlefield.
- On the thirteenth day, when Arjuna is away fighting the Trigartas, Drona makes the Chakra Vyuha. Abhimanyu enters the formation but is killed by six warriors together.
- The next day, Arjuna kills Jayadratha. Karna kills Ghatotkacha on the same day with his Indrāstra, the weapon he wanted to use to kill Arjuna.
- Dronāchārya is killed on the fifteenth day. Karna becomes the commander.
- Arjuna kills Karna on the seventeenth day. Bheema kills Duryodhana on the eighteenth day. That night, Ashwatthāmā attacks the sleeping Pāndava camp and kills Draupadi's sons and brothers.

- Ashwatthāmā attempts to destroy the child in Abhimanyu's young wife Uttarā's womb but fails.
- The battle ends. Only eleven warriors survive, including the five Pāndavas.
- Gāndhāri curses Krishna, saying that his Yādava clan will kill each other and perish, just like the Kauravas.
- Parikshita is born to Uttarā.

The Years of Peace

- Yudhishthira is dejected with the destruction caused by the war. He wishes to renounce the throne and lead a life of an ascetic. After a lot of convincing, he agrees to stay back and is crowned the king.
- Bhishma decides it is time to leave his body and accepts death.
- A few years later, Yudhishthira conducts the Ashwamedha Yajna.
- After spending some years in the care of the Pāndavas, Dhritarāshtra, Gāndhāri, Kunti, Vidura and Sanjay head to the forest to spend their remaining years.
- Dhritarāshtra, Gāndhāri and Kunti die in a forest fire.

End of an Epoch

- Thirty-six years after the war, the powerful Yādavas of Dwārkā kill each other in a feud.

- Krishna dies subsequently.
- Crowning Parikshita the king of Hastināpur, the Pāndavas along with Draupadi leave for their final journey.

Introduction: What Is Dharma?

The Mahābhārata is the history of the descendants of Bharata, a great sovereign king of Bhāratavarsha. Throughout the story, one theme stands out—that of dharma. The war between the cousins—the Kauravas and the Pāndavas—which forms the core of the epic is called dharma yuddha, the war for dharma. One of the most sacred texts for Hindus, the Bhagavad Gitā, has its provenance in the Mahābhārata. It captures the conversation between Krishna and Arjuna before the commencement of the Kurukshetra war when the latter was gripped with confusion over the merit of the war and his responsibility. The text talks extensively about dharma and swa-dharma. Bhishma gives a discourse to Yudhishthira on Rāja Dharma from his deathbed. Vidura advises Dhritarāshtra of his dharma as the king and the patriarch of the family. Draupadi and Kunti exhort Yudhishthira to follow his dharma. So, what exactly is dharma?

Dharma is routinely translated as religion, or sometimes as law. These words, while not completely wrong, are not appropriate in explaining dharma. Merriam-Webster defines religion as follows:

> The belief in a god or in a group of gods: an organized system of beliefs, ceremonies, and rules used to worship a god or a group of gods: an interest,

a belief, or an activity that is very important to a person or group.

Dharma, on the other hand, is a much more encompassing and profound concept. This Sanskrit word comes from the root word धृ–धारणे, which means to support, to uphold, to sustain. Dharma is, therefore, defined as धारयति इति धर्मः (Dhārayati iti dharmah)—that which upholds or sustains when imbibed is dharma. In the Mahābhārata, Krishna explains dharma as धारणाद्धर्ममित्याहुर्धर्मो धारयति प्रजाः (Dhāranāt dharma iti āhuh, dharmo dhārayati prajāh)—due to sustenance, it is called dharma; dharma sustains life.

In this sense, dharma is that which is needed for life to go on.

Sri Aurobindo defines dharma as follows:

> It is the whole government of all the relations of man with other beings, with Nature, with God, considered from the point of view of a divine principle working itself out in forms and laws of action, forms of the inner and the outer life, orderings of relations of every kind in the world. Dharma is both that which we hold to and that which holds together our inner and outer activities.[1]

A society can sustain when all the different elements and stakeholders behave in a mutually symbiotic manner. There is life on earth because it is at a certain distance from the sun and moves in a certain way. Other planets known to us do not have life-conducive circumstances. As long as the sun and the earth behave in a manner that allows nature to survive and thrive, life will sprout and sustain, else not. That which governs this life-sustaining cosmic order is dharma.

Likewise, for a country, community, family or even a professional unit to sustain, there are certain norms, behaviours and considerations that are expected of the stakeholders. The norms and the systems have to be such that nourish the involved entities. The overarching governing principle of such units of interdependent entities that helps define the norms, behaviours, duties and codes of conduct for interaction and ensures their symbiotic existence is called dharma.

When seen in the context of an individual with respect to their surroundings—family, state, profession, etc.—it becomes swa-dharma. When applied to governments, kings, administrators in relation to their state and subjects, it becomes Rāja Dharma. When applied to relations, it is Putra Dharma, Pati Dharma, Patni Dharma and so on.

At any point, we are a part of various social and professional units. As an involved stakeholder in those, we have various roles to play. Many times, the dharma associated with these different roles comes into conflict with each other. This conflict is what we call dharma sankata or ethical dilemma. That is what Arjuna faced before the Kurukshetra war—to prioritise family or justice; what Bhishma dealt with while trying to dissuade Duryodhana and Dhritarāshtra from being unjust to the Pāndavas—to play the role of a Kuru patriarch and compel Dhritarāshtra to follow the rule of law or toe the orders of the king as a loyal employee would; what Yudhishthira faced when accepting the invitation to play the game of dice—to be a good warrior and son by obeying his uncle's order or stake his reputation by refusing to play and protecting his self-interest; Dhritarāshtra was forever struggling with it—to be a king or a father; Kunti faced it while giving up Karna and then again while revealing the truth to Karna when he came back in her life. Like it was in the Mahābhārata, so it is in our personal lives—we are always faced with such conflicts. What should we do in situations? How do we prioritise?

Vidura recommends the prioritisation of the greater good. 'Sacrifice your son to protect the village and sacrifice the village to protect your nation. But to protect your own ātmā, be ready to give up everything,' he says. One's conscience is supreme. A guiltless conscience is what brings peace within. Hence, while advising Dhritarāshtra, Vidura reinforces his message—'Do what is beneficial for all, most of all for your ātmā, driven by pure intellect.' There are no straightforward context-free answers about dealing with ethical dilemmas. But interestingly enough, if we really listen to that intuition within us, we will know what is the appropriate approach in a specific situation.

A value or a conduct that sustains and fosters dharma is a virtue and one that hinders it is a vice. Hence, truth, non-violence, compassion and generosity are encouraged because these qualities tend to nurture the mutually beneficial set-ups, whereas speaking untruths, committing an act of violence, hoarding, cheating, indulgences and addictions tend to be destructive and are discouraged. The role and responsibility of an administrator is to protect the stakeholders from those within and outside the set-up who refuse to live by the set norms, thus posing an existential threat to the stability of the system at large.

While these virtues and vices are to be generally adhered to, one has to be aware of their context-sensitive nature as well. If in specific situations, or over time, the norms start hindering the sustenance of the stakeholders, they too need to change and evolve. This is the inherent flexibility of dharma. The end goal—that of sustenance and growth—is what matters. While explaining the meaning of dharma, Krishna categorically states, 'यः स्यात् धारणसंयुक्तः स धर्म इति निश्चयः' (Yah syāt dhāranasamyuktah sa dharma iti nishchayah)—only that which promotes sustenance is dharma.

The flexibility, however, is for longevity, not convenience. The virtues and norms should be adhered to as much as possible. To know when to transgress a norm, and when not to, also requires intuition and wisdom. Krishna insists on developing 'yogastha buddhi', stable and clear wisdom, to foster objective and unbiased decision-making. This is the gist of the Bhagavad Gitā.

Every stakeholder has the responsibility to abide by the dharma of the unit of which they are a part for their nourishment and sustenance. A system is as good as the stakeholders. When violation becomes a norm, the system collapses, destroying the stakeholders as well. That is why Vyāsa says multiple times throughout the Mahābhārata: 'धर्म एव हतो हन्ति धर्मो रक्षति रक्षित' (Dharma eva hato hanti Dharmo rakshati rakshitaha)—Dharma destroys those who destroy it and protects those who protect it.

Strive to understand the nuances of dharma. Strive to uphold dharma. Through dharma, uplift yourself. That is the essence of the Mahābhārata—and of life.

ॐ ψ ॐ

Part 1

Context of the Mahābhārata

I

Janamejaya's Revenge on the Nāgas and the Narration of the Mahābhārata

The Kurukshetra war had ended. Though victorious, Yudhishthira was a devastated man. This had been an unprecedented war. Most kings of the Bhāratavarsha[1] were party to it. At the end of the eighteen days of the war, it is said Bhāratavarsha was left devoid of warrior kings. Duryodhana had smirked just before dying, 'I have lived a luxurious life and will unite with my brethren in death, you can live and mourn over all that is lost.'[2] Yudhishthira was indeed going to be the monarch of a kingdom full of widows.

Devastation was alike on both sides, for the loser and the victor. The second generation of the Pāndavas had perished. Abhimanyu and Irāvan, the sons of Arjuna from Subhadrā and Uloopi respectively; Ghatotkacha, the son of Bheema from Hidimbā; and the five sons of Draupadi; all had succumbed to the war. Only Babruvāhana, Arjuna's son from Chitrāngadā, had survived. That too because he had not participated in the war.

The only hope of the Pāndavas was hinged on the unborn child of Uttarā and Abhimanyu. This child who was to carry forward the lineage of the Kurus would have also perished due to the treachery of Ashwatthāmā, who had directed the Brahmāstra at Uttarā's womb and had nearly killed the yet-to-be-born baby. It was only Krishna's grace that saved the child. Krishna named him Parikshita[3]—the one who was born when the Kuru lineage was almost extinct.

Thirty-six years after the fated war, Yudhishthira, along with his brothers and Draupadi, renounced the kingdom and proceeded to the Himālayas to spend their last days. Parikshita was crowned the king of Hastināpur. Yuyutsu, the foster brother of Duryodhana and cousin of the Pāndavas was appointed to guide Parikshita.

Living up to the reputation of his ancestors, Parikshita was a just and popular king. An expert in both administration and economics, the kingdom flourished under his rule. He reigned peacefully for twenty-four years before falling prey to an unfortunate turn of events. Once, while on a hunting expedition, a lost and tired Parikshita approached Rishi Shamik's āshram. Unaware of the rishi's vow of silence, Parikshita asked him the whereabouts of an animal he was hunting. On not receiving a reply, in a fit of anger, he picked up a dead snake lying nearby, threw it around the rishi's neck and left. When Rishi Shamik's son, Rishi Shringi, returned to the āshram later that day, he saw his father in deep tapasyā with a dead snake hanging around his neck. Enraged, he showered a curse on the perpetrator. 'Whoever has slighted my father, may he be bitten dead by dreadful Nāga Takshaka in seven days,' he thundered. A siddha rishi's curse couldn't have gone in vain. As was foretold, Takshaka bypassed all the security arrangements made for Parikshita and bit him dead exactly on the seventh day after the unfortunate incident in Rishi Shamik's āshram. After Parikshita's demise, Janamejaya, his son, took over the reins of Hastināpur.

The Narration of *Shrimad Bhāgavata Purāna*

When Parikshita was informed he had only seven days to live, he didn't flinch. Instead, he crowned Janamejaya the king of Hastināpur and proceeded to banks of the Gangā to spend the seven days in the company of sages, fasting and meditating. He posed a question to the sages around about the duties of the man who is about to die. Just then, Rishi Shukadeva, the son of Veda Vyāsa, came to his camp by the Gangā. Rishi Shukadeva was an accomplished ascetic although only sixteen years old. Parikshita welcomed him and posed the same question to him. 'What activities should he who is about to die be engaged in to achieve peace and contentment. What should he do? What should he chant and whom should he meditate upon?' In response, Rishi Shukadeva goes on to narrate the stories and leelās of Shri Krishna to Parikshita. This narration is immortalised as *Shrimad Bhāgavata Purāna*, one of the most important religious texts for the Hindus in general and Vaishnavas in particular.

Janamejaya had just returned from a campaign in Takshashilā when a rishi named Uttank came to his court. He wanted Janamejaya to teach Takshaka a lesson. Takshaka had become a menace. He would trouble innocent people even though they posed no threat to him. Once Takshaka stole the earrings that Uttank had procured for his guru-mother, without any provocation. Only by divine intervention and his guru's grace did Uttank manage to retrieve the earrings and gift them at the ordained time. Uttank, narrating his own story of Takshaka's harassment, reminded Janamejaya of how the snake[4] had killed his innocent father. He provoked Janamejaya to avenge Parikshita's death by conducting the ritual of snake sacrifice, the Sarpa Satra. The idea appealed to Janamejaya. He took Uttank's suggestion and soon initiated the Sarpa Yajna. This ritual sacrifice was so potent that on completion, it would have annihilated all the Nāgas from earth.

Yajna

A yajna, especially one conducted by a king, used to be a grand social spectacle involving fire rituals, chanting of Vedic mantras and giving away generous donations to rishis, brāhmins, common citizens and guests. Royal yajnas were typically undertaken to fulfil a desire or mark the fulfilment of a resolve. Distributing wealth was one of the motives of grand yajnas. Such charities were said to accrue significant virtues to the host. Students, ascetics, monks, performers and even common people from all walks of life would come to partake in the bounties of the yajna. To keep everyone entertained and intellectually engaged between the rituals, rishis would narrate stories of the past and the present. There would also be dances and dramatic performances enacting stories from the scriptures and epics.

In a way, these grand yajnas also helped boost the economy of the kingdom. The organisation of such an event involved employing hundreds of workers, sculptors, architects, artists, priests and traders among others.

In the Mahābhārata, there are four major yajna ceremonies mentioned.

1. Rājasuya Yajna by Yudhishthira in Indraprastha,
2. Vaishnava Yajna by Duryodhana in Hastināpur when the Pāndavas were in exile,
3. Ashwamedha Yajna by Yudhishthira after the Kurukshetra war and
4. Sarpa Satra by Janamejaya during which the Mahābhārata was narrated by Rishi Vaishampāyana.

Janamejaya's yajna was as lavish as one would expect from the king of Hastināpur, the great-grandson of Yudhishthira. Distinguished rishis, brāhmins, kings and their ministers from across Bhāratavarsha assembled to witness the one-of-its-kind yajna. The most revered Rishi Krishna Dwaipāyana Vyāsa, also known as Veda Vyāsa, came with his students to bless the king.

By the time of the Sarpa Yajna, Vyāsa Muni had already composed the itihāsa[5] of the Kurukshetra war and the circumstances that led to its eventual unfolding.

He was the most neutral as well as a contemporary observer of the war and of the life and times of the Kauravas and the Pāndavas. Firstly, he was an accomplished rishi who had transcended the emotions of attachment and anger. Secondly, he was equally connected to both sets of cousins by blood. Vyāsa Muni was the grandfather of Janamejaya's great-grandfather, Arjuna. It was through him that the Kuru lineage was saved from extinction two generations before Parikshita. Veda Vyāsa was the biological father of Dhritarāshtra, Pāndu and Vidura.

Extremely pleased at his arrival, Janamejaya paid his obeisance to the rishi. Once he was settled with his students, Janamejaya made a request. 'You have seen the war of the Kauravas and the Pāndavas as it happened. I hear my great-grandfathers were men of great virtue and restraint. What then led them to fight such a disastrous war? I wish to know about this story in detail.'

Veda Vyāsa happily obliged. Vyāsa Muni asked his student Vaishampāyana to narrate the history of the Bharata vamsha[6]—the Mahābhārata. Vaishampāyana began reciting the great story of the Bhāratas, as was instructed to him by his guru.

Janamejaya's Sarpa Satra thus became the first instance of the public rendering of the Mahābhārata. It was not a monologous recitation but a conversation between Janamejaya and Vaishampāyana. Janamejaya asked and Vaishyampāyana expounded.

Another rishi by name of Ugrashravā Sauti, of the Suta community, was amongst the guests who heard the rendering of the Mahābhārata on this occasion. Ugrashravā was a storyteller, a kathā vāchaka, who travelled around janapadas and forests narrating stories from the shāstras as well as histories of ancient kings and kingdoms. On his way back from the yajna, he stopped at the āshram of Rishi Shaunak in Naimishāranya[7]. There, at the request of Shaunak Muni and his students, Ugrashavā recounted the story of the narration of the Mahābhārata by Vaishampāyana to Janamejaya, as composed by Krishna Dwaipāyana Vyāsa.

The Mahābhārata we read today is an account of the narration of Ugrashravā Sauti's account of Rishi Vaishampāyana's narration of Rishi Krishna Dwaipāyana Vyāsa's composition of the history of the Bhāratas.

The End of Sarpa Satra and the Redemption of the Nāgas

As Janamejaya's Sarpa Satra progressed, the effect of the fire rituals and chanting became increasingly potent, the entire Nāga kingdom was consumed by fear. The snakes started getting increasingly restless. As if driven by an unknown power, they began to come out of their hiding and started dropping into the burning yajna kunda. Hordes and hordes of snakes were being reduced to ashes. It was a matter of time before the entire race would have been wiped out.

The main culprit, however, was still elusive. Takshaka had still not fallen into the fire. He sought refuge in his friend Indra. But as soon as the priests officiating the rituals called upon Takshaka, the snake became completely powerless. The impact of yajna was so strong that Indra too couldn't be of much help. Takshaka appeared in the sky. Like a leaf being swept off by a gust of wind, oblivious to its own will, he was being pulled down into the yajna kunda.

Just then, a young Brāhmin boy named Āstik entered the mandapa where the rituals were on. He started singing paeans to Janamejaya and all the priests and luminaries present there. Janamejaya was impressed. Already joyous that his Sarpa Satra was coming along well, he offered to fulfil any wish that the young boy had. 'Seek and it shall be given. Gems, jewellery, cows, you name it. Anything as long as this snake sacrifice continues,' beamed Janamejaya.

Āstik replied, 'I seek not gems, jewellery neither cows from you. All I wish for is the end of this Sarpa Satra and well-being of my mother's family.' Āstik was the nephew of Vāsuki, the king of the Nāgas. His mother Jaratkāru was Vāsuki's sister.

Janamejaya urged Āstik to change his mind and ask for other gifts. But Āstik was firm on his wish. Other rishis and guests too voiced their support in favour of Āstik and requested Janamejaya to end the ritual and spare the surviving snakes. 'So be it,' said Janamejaya and called for the closing of the yajna, much to the pleasure of the Nāgas and all the esteemed guests.

This way Āstik saved the day for the Nāgas and ensured their survival.

Who Were the Sutas

The narrator of the Mahābhārata as we know it is Rishi Ugrashravā Sauti. He was the son of Rishi Lomaharshan and belonged to the Suta community. Hence, the appellation 'Sauti'. The community was considered a 'mixed jāti'[8] of offsprings of a Brāhmin mother and Kshatriya father. Sutas were considered expert sārthis[9]. The role of the charioteer was significant in ancient India. Charioteers were usually those who were close friends and confidants of the person they worked with. Their role became even more important in a war. They were to not just steer the chariot but also ensure the warrior they were driving stayed safe and motivated. They acted as guides in the war. The importance of a charioteer becomes evident from the fact that Arjuna asked Krishna to be his charioteer. To match Krishna, Karna asked Shalya, the old king of Madra, to drive his chariot.

In addition, Sutas were engaged as storytellers, history keepers and ministers in royal courts. Many were also warriors and commanders.

Famous Sutas in the Mahābhārata are:

1. Sanjay, the narrator of the Bhagavad Gitā and the Kurukshetra war to Dhritarāshtra. He played the role of charioteer, friend, trusted messenger and mentor to Dhritarāshtra.
2. Sudeshnā, the queen of King Virāta of Matsya desh, Uttarā's mother and Abhimanyu's mother-in-law. She was the maternal grandmother of Parikshita.
3. Keechak, the commander of King Virāta of Matsya desh. He was the brother of Sudeshnā and amongst the most powerful men in Matsya.

4. Karna, though born to Kunti, was raised in a Suta family of Adhiratha and Rādhā. He married women from the Suta community and his children were brought up as Sutas. Duryodhana crowned him the King of Anga desh. A great warrior, considered equal to Arjuna in archery, he was the commander of the Kaurava army after the death of Dronāchārya. Not only Karna but the sons of his foster parents were also trained warriors. They had participated in the Mahābhārata war on the side of the Kauravas.
5. Rishi Bandi, a great sage whose story is narrated in the Vana Parva of the Mahābhārata.

In the Rāmāyana, one of the closest confidants and an important minister of King Dashratha of Ayodhyā is Sumantra, who belonged to the Suta community.

2

The Bharata Vamsha Family Tree

'Respected Sir, I wish to hear about the great kings of the Puru dynasty. How were they? How courageous were they? I believe my ancestors were men of great virtue,' said Janamejaya.

Vaishampāyana proceeded to lay out before Janamejaya the family tree[1] of the Puru dynasty, listing its major branches. He narrated the stories of great kings born in the lineage and how it came to be known by multiple names—Pauravas (from Puru), Bhāratas (from Bharata), Kauravas (from Kuru).

Puru was the youngest son of a great ancient king Yayāti, the son of another renowned king Nahusha and great-grandson of Pururavā. Pururavā was the son of Ilā and grandson of Manu. Manu was the son of Vivasvān. Vivasvān was born of Daksha's daughter Aditi and Rishi Kashyap.

Yayāti had two wives, Devyāni and Sharmishthā. He had two sons with Devyāni—Yadu and Turvasu. And three with Sharmishthā—Druhyu, Anu and Puru. The descendants of the five came to be known as Yādavas from Yadu, Yavanas from Turvasu, Bhojas from Druhyu, Mlecchas from Anu and Pauravas from Puru. Janamejaya was born into the Puru lineage while Krishna and Balarāma were Yadu's descendants.

Dushyanta was born into the lineage of Puru generations before Janamejaya. By way of his union with Shakuntalā, Bharata was born. Bharata was as noble as he was brave. He is said to have ruled the earth like Indra ruled heaven. He established himself as a chakravarti—the sovereign emperor of the land. It is King Bharata from whom this land came to be known as Bhārat[2] and his descendants came to be known as Bhāratas.

Bharata had nine sons through his three wives. But he did not find any of his sons fit enough to be his successor. He conducted many grand yajnas for begetting a worthy son. Eventually, with the blessings of Rishi Bharadwāja, Bharata obtained a son through his wife Sunanda. This son was Bhumanyu[3]. He ascended the throne after Bharata.

Bhumanyu's grandson was Hasti, who established the city of Hastināpur. Ajamidha was the grandson of Hasti and had many children. The descendants of his sons Dushyanta and Parameshthi came to be known as Pānchālas. His son Riksha[4] and grandson Samvarna carried forward the Puru–Bharata lineage.

The much-revered King Kuru was Samvarna's son. It is through him that Kurukshetra gets its name. Kuru, through his efforts and tapasyā, purified the land on which stood five lakes filled with the blood of the Kshatriyas shed by Parashurāma. The land came to be known as Kurujāngal, his lineage was called as the Kuru vamsha and his descendants as Kauravas.[5]

Shāntanu, the father of Devavrata Bhishma, was an eighth-generation Kuru. He had two brothers. Devāpi, the elder one, took the path of sanyās[6] and renounced the kingdom. Shāntanu became the successor to the throne after his father Pratipa. Bāhlika, the youngest brother, became the king of Bāhlika desh. Bhurishravā, the son of Somadatta and grandson of Bāhlika, was one of the foremost warriors on Duryodhana's side in the Kurukshetra war.

Shāntanu was a noble king. It is said about Shāntanu that he was so soft and gentle that by his mere touch, the old and feeble would feel energised and calm. Thus, he was called Shāntanu, the one who brought joy and tranquillity to all.

Devavrata was Shāntanu's son with Gangā. After he was crowned the prince of Hastināpur and declared Shāntanu's successor, Shāntanu fell in love again with Satyavati, the daughter of Dāshrāja, a fisherman. Dāshrāja would marry Satyavati to Shāntanu only if he promised that Satyavati's son would be the successor to the throne. To fulfil this condition and get the father his love, Devavrata took the vow of celibacy and relinquished his claim to the Hastināpur throne forever. That is how he got the name Bhishma—the one who took a terrible vow.

Before Satyavati married Shāntanu, she had a son through a union with Rishi Parāshar. This son was Krishna Dwaipāyana. Rishi Parāshar took away the boy with him and imparted to him the wisdom of the Vedas. Krishna Dwaipāyana was to play a pivotal role in continuation of his mother's family. He came to be known in the world as Veda Vyāsa.

With Satyavati, Shāntanu had two sons, Vichitravirya and Chitrangad. Chitrangad was the elder one but died young. Vichitravirya married two princesses of Kāshi, Ambikā and Ambālikā. He too died young without a progeny. There were only two options to revive the Kuru lineage—either through Bhishma's marriage or through the process of Ambikā and Ambālikā's niyoga. Bhishma wouldn't break his vow. Hence, Satyavati's first-born, Krishna Dwaipāyana, was called upon to help the princesses conceive. By that union, Dhritarāshtra was born of Ambikā, Pāndu of Ambālikā and Vidura of Ambikā's maid.

Niyoga

Per scriptures, in cases where a husband died without leaving a progeny or was impotent, the lady could call upon a revered male with the permission of her husband or her in-laws, in case the husband had died, to help her conceive a child. This practice was called niyoga. However, there were very strict rules around how and when it could be practised. It was not meant for sexual pleasure, rather only for begetting a child. There were restrictions regarding how many times niyoga could be practised by a woman. The biological father was to not seek any relation with the child born through this route. The child would get the names of the actual mother and her legal husband in whose name niyoga was done.

Dhritarāshtra married Gāndhāri who bore him a hundred sons and a daughter. Duryodhana, Duhshāsana, Vikarna, Vivamshati were prominent amongst the siblings. Dushālā was their daughter who was married to Jayadratha of Sindhu desh. Yuyutsu was Duryodhana's stepbrother born of Dhritarāshtra and Gāndhāri's Vaishya maid. In the Kurukshetra war, Yuyutsu fought on the side of the Pāndavas.

Pāndu married Kunti and Mādri. Kunti was the daughter of Shurasena of the Yādava clan. She was Vasudeva's sister and Krishna's paternal aunt. Mādri was the sister of Shalya, the king of Madra desh. Pāndu was unable to consummate his marriage with his wives due to a curse cast on him by a rishi. Pāndu and his wives resorted to niyoga to beget children. Yudhishthira, Bheema, Arjuna were born of Kunti through Dharmarāja, Vayu deva and Indra respectively. Nakula and Sahadeva were born of Mādri and the Ashwini Kumars. The five sons came to be known as the Pāndavas.

Karna was Kunti's son with Surya deva, born when she was yet unmarried. Afraid of begetting a child before marriage, Kunti gave him up at birth. Karna was brought up by Adhiratha and Rādhā of the Suta clan. Adhiratha was Dhritarāshtra's close friend. Karna became the closest ally and friend of Duryodhana.

The Pāndavas married Draupadi, the daughter of Drupada, the king of Pānchāla, and twin sister of Dhrishtadyumna. She bore the Pāndavas one son each. Prativindhya with Yudhishthira, Sutasoma with Bheema, Shrutakirti with Arjuna, Shatānika with Nakula and Shrutakarma with Sahadeva.

The Pāndavas had other wives too. Yudhishthira married Devikā, the daughter of the Shaibya king Govāsan. He had a son with her named Yaudheya. Bheema had two other wives, Hidimbā of the rākshasa tribe, and the princess of Kāshi, Valandharā. Ghatotkacha was Bheema's son with Hidimbā. With Valandharā, he had a son named Savarga.

Arjuna married a Nāga princess Uloopi, Chitrāngadā, the princess of a southern coastal kingdom of Manipur[7] and Krishna's sister Subhadrā. With them, he had a son each, Irāvan, Babruvāhana and Abhimanyu. Nakula married Karenumati of Chedi and had a son with her named Nirāmitra. Sahadeva married Vijayā, the daughter of King Dyutimān of Madra desh. Suhotra was Sahadeva's son through her.

Of these sons of the Pāndavas, Abhimanyu carried forward the Kuru lineage. He was married to Uttarā, the daughter of King Virāta and Sudeshnā of Matsya. Parikshita was their son.

'Parikshita married your mother Madrāvati and you, Janamejaya, were born. You married Vapushtamā and have two sons with her, Shatānika and Shankukarna. Shatānika has a son named Ashwammedhadatta with the princess of Videha. Thus, I have narrated to you the genealogy of the Puru vamsha, as I have learnt from my Guru Veda Vyāsa,' said Vaishampāyana.

Folklore suggests Draupadi and Yudhishthira had a daughter as well, by the name of Suthanu. She was married to Krishna and Satyabhāmā's son Bhānu after the war. But the Mahābhārata has no mention of Draupadi's daughter.

The Mahābhārata makes a specific mention of only one son of Duryodhana, Lakshman. The *Shrimad Bhāgavata Purāna*, however, has an account of Duryodhana's daughter Lakshmanā, sister of Lakshman, who married Krishna's son Sāmbā.[8]

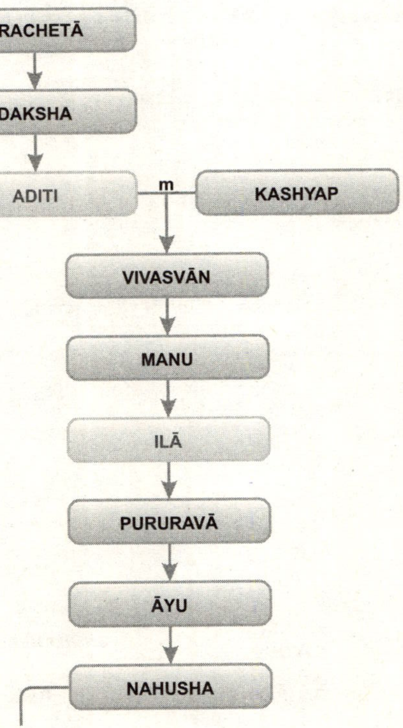
PRACHETĀ
DAKSHA
ADITI
m
KASHYAP
VIVASVĀN
MANU
ILĀ
PURURAVĀ
ĀYU
NAHUSHA

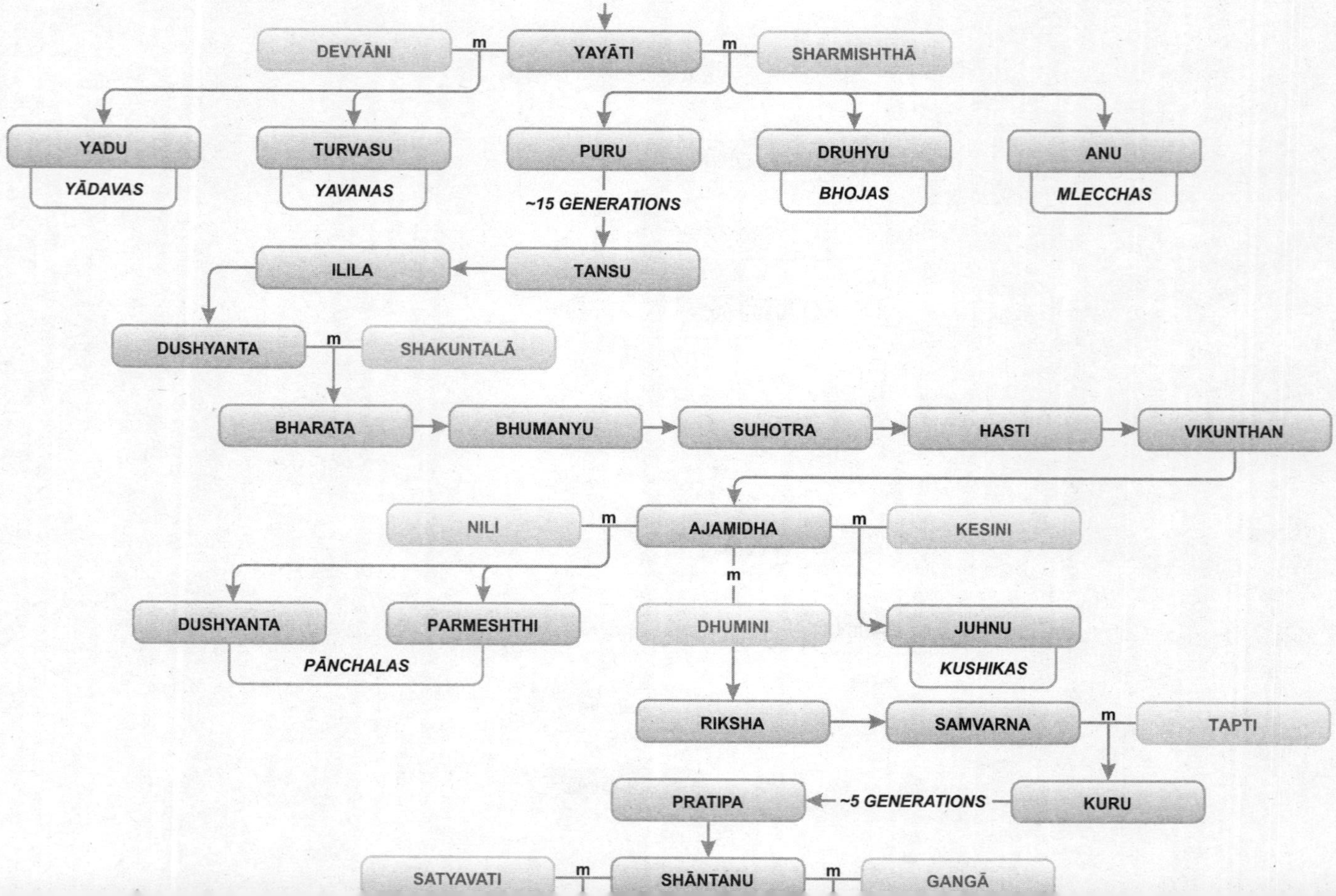

DEVYĀNI
m
YAYĀTI
m
SHARMISHTHĀ
YADU
YĀDAVAS
TURVASU
YAVANAS
PURU
DRUHYU
BHOJAS
ANU
MLECCHAS
~15 GENERATIONS
TANSU
ILILA
DUSHYANTA
m
SHAKUNTALĀ
BHARATA
BHUMANYU
SUHOTRA
HASTI
VIKUNTHAN
NILI
m
AJAMIDHA
m
KESINI
m
DUSHYANTA
PARMESHTHI
PĀNCHALAS
DHUMINI
JUHNU
KUSHIKAS
RIKSHA
SAMVARNA
m
TAPTI
PRATIPA
~5 GENERATIONS
KURU
SATYAVATI
m
SHĀNTANU
m
GANGĀ

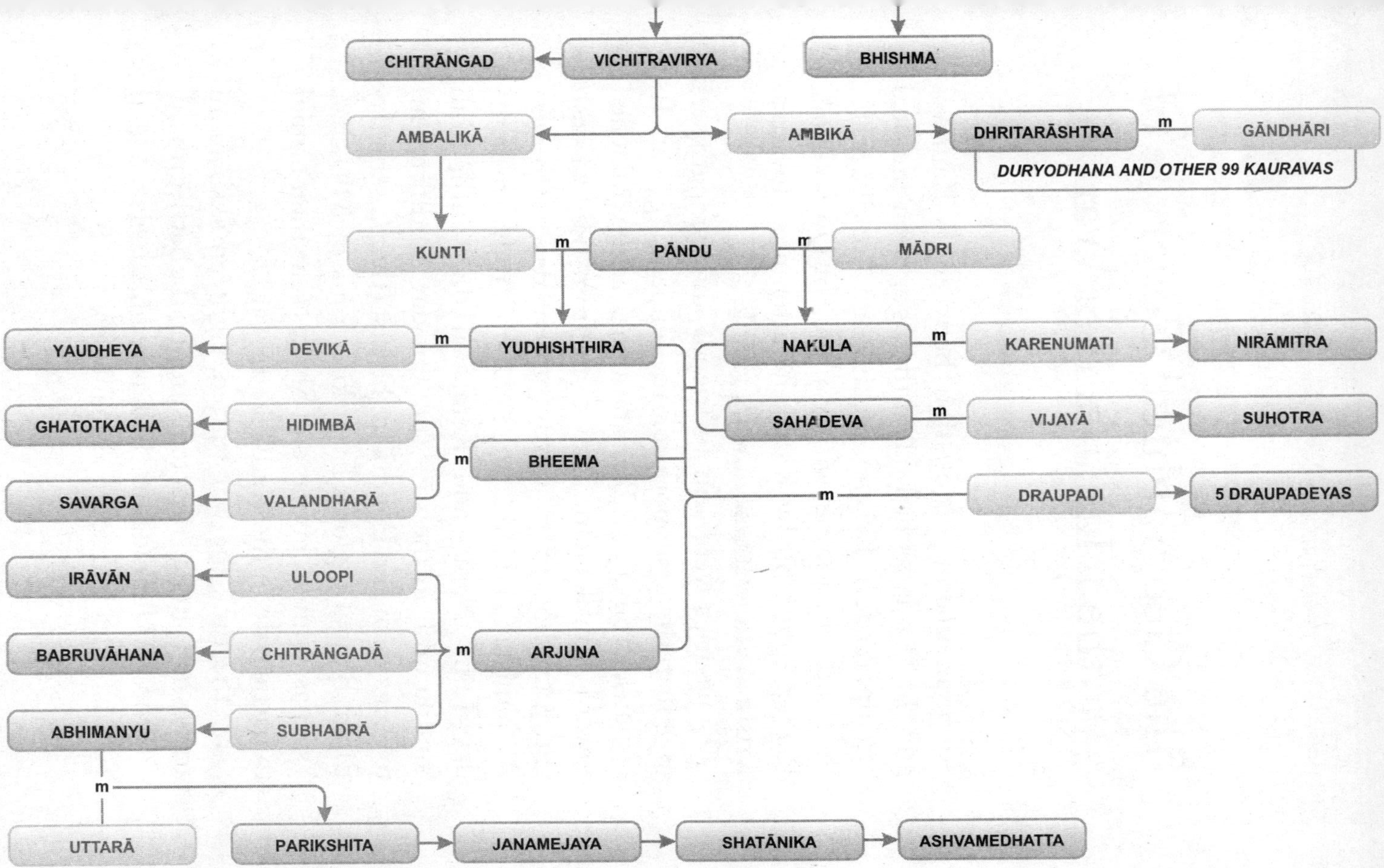
CHITRĀNGAD
VICHITRAVIRYA
BHISHMA
AMBALIKĀ
AMBIKĀ
DHRITARĀSHTRA
m
GĀNDHĀRI
DURYODHANA AND OTHER 99 KAURAVAS
KUNTI
m
PĀNDU
m
MĀDRI
YAUDHEYA
DEVIKĀ
m
YUDHISHTHIRA
NAKULA
m
KARENUMATI
NIRĀMITRA
GHATOTKACHA
HIDIMBĀ
SAHADEVA
m
VIJAYĀ
SUHOTRA
m
BHEEMA
SAVARGA
VALANDHARĀ
m
DRAUPADI
5 DRAUPADEYAS
IRĀVĀN
ULOOPI
BABRUVĀHANA
CHITRĀNGADĀ
m
ARJUNA
ABHIMANYU
SUBHADRĀ
m
UTTARĀ
PARIKSHITA
JANAMEJAYA
SHATĀNIKA
ASHVAMEDHATTA

3

The Geographical Coverage of the Mahābhārata War

All peace-making negotiations between the Kauravas and the Pāndavas had fallen through. Even the final attempt made by Krishna, seeking only five villages for the Pāndavas, was met with contempt by Duryodhana. Rather, egged on by Karna, he attempted to arrest Krishna. The war was now inevitable.

Emissaries were sent to friends and sympathisers to enlist their support for the impending war. In response, from across Bhāratavarsha,[1] armies marched towards Kurukshetra. They came from Bāhlika desh and Kāmbhoja in the north (present-day north-west Afghanistan and Pakistan region) to Pāndya (present-day Tamil Nadu) and Kerala in the south, from Sindhu desh in the west (present-day Sindh region) to Anga desh and Pundra in the east (the present-day Bihar-Bengal region). Even kingdoms of Mlecchas, Yavanas, Chinas, Hunas and Shakas sent their armies to participate in the Kurukshetra war.

By the time the war started, eighteen akshauhini armies had pitched their tents around the battleground. Of these, Duryodhana had assembled eleven and Yudhishthira had seven akshauhinis.

How Big Is One Akshauhini?

An akshauhini army consists of 109,350 foot soldiers, 21,870 chariots, 21,870 elephants and 65,610 horses. Assuming one charioteer per chariot and one mahout per elephant in addition to the warriors, one akshauhini has 2.6 lakh people (260,000). Both sides put together had 18 akshauhinis. By that, one can infer at least *47 lakh people* from across ancient India participated in the Kurukshetra war.

Major Allies of the Kauravas and the Pāndavas in the War[2]

	The Kauravas	The Pāndavas
East	✦ Karna from Anga desh ✦ Brihadbal from Kosal (descendant of Rama from the Kush lineage)	✦ Drupada, Dhrishtadyumna, Shikhandi from Pānchāla ✦ Dhrishtaketu and Chekitan from Chedi ✦ Jayatsena and Sahadeva from Magadha
West	✦ Kritavarmā, a Yādava commander ✦ Jayadratha from Sindhu desh along with other kings from Sauvira ✦ Shalya from Madra ✦ Susharmā and his brothers from Trigarta	✦ Yuyudhān Sātyaki, a Yādava commander

	The Kauravas	The Pāndavas
North	✦ Bhurishravā, Somadatta from Bāhlika ✦ Sudakshin from Kāmbhoja along with Yavanas and Sakas ✦ Shakuni from Gāndhār ✦ Ruling Kekaya brother ✦ Bhagadatta from Prāgjyotisha[3] with warriors from Kirāta and China	✦ Banished Kekaya brothers
Central and South	✦ Vinda, Anuvinda from Avanti ✦ Neela of Māhishmati ✦ Kalingas along with Dravidas and Āndhras	✦ Virāta and his sons from Matsya ✦ Kuntibhoja from Kunti ✦ Malayadhwaja from the coastal kingdom of Pāndya along with armies from Cholas and Keralas

In addition, both sides also had support of the Rākshasa tribes. Ghatotkacha and his warriors were on the side of the Pāndavas while Alambush and his men sided with Duryodhana and the Kauravas.

The commanders of each of the seven akshauhinis of the Pāndavas were Drupada, Virāta, Dhrishtadyumna, Shikandi, Sātyaki, Chekitan and Bheema[4]. On the Kaurava side, the commanders of their eleven akshauhini armies were Dronāchārya, Kripāchārya, Ashwatthāmā, Shalya, Jayadratha, Sudakshin,

Kritavarmā, Bhurishravā, Shakuni, Bāhlika and Bhishma. Karna took the position of Bhishma after the fall of the old Kuru.[5]

After eighteen days of the Kurukshetra war, only eleven of the participating warriors survived. Eight on the side of the Pāndavas, namely, Krishna, the five Pāndavas, Sātyaki and Yuyutsu, and three on the side of Kauravas, namely, Ashwatthāmā, Kritavarmā and Kripāchārya. No part of Bhāratavarsha was left untouched by the wailings of the widows of the dead warriors. East lost as much as west and north lost as much as south.

The Only Warriors Who Did Not Participate in the Kurukshetra

Balarāma: Both Duryodhana and Bheema were his students. Hence, he did not want to take sides. Balarāma took off on a pilgrimage instead of being a party to the war.

Rukmi: Rukmi was the prince of Vidarbha and brother of Rukmini, Krishna's wife. Rukmi was defeated by Krishna when the former tried to stop him from eloping with Rukmini. Before the war began, Rukmi came to the Pāndavas and boasted about his prowess. 'With my help, you will surely win,' boasted Rukmi. Arjuna laughed it off and turned down his offer. Rukmi then approached Duryodhana and again boasted of his prowess. Duryodhana too was not impressed and refused to enlist Rukmi on his side. Rukmi was forced to return to Vidarbha.

Vidura did not participate in the war either but he is not known to be a warrior in the text. In fact, there is no instance of Vidura participating in any war.

There is a folklore about the king of Udupi not participating but providing food to both armies during the war. The story does not appear in any known edition of the Mahābhārata, including Gita Press, BORI CE, KMG.

The Kurukshetra war was not the only time that the kingdoms of Bhāratavarsha had come together. The Mahābhārata elaborately mentions the participation of kings from all over Bhāratavarsha in Draupadi's swayamvara as well. Then again, they attended the Rājasuya Yajna conducted by Yudhishthira in Indraprastha, bringing elaborate gifts. Even Lanka sent gifts for the yajna. The Mahābhārata mentions the conquests made by the four Pāndavas—Arjuna, Bheema, Nakula and Sahadeva—in the four directions of Bhāratavarsha. Before the Rājasuya, the Pāndavas had undertaken a successful campaign to seek the allegiance of the various kingdoms of Bhāratavarsha towards Yudhishthira. All kingdoms had come on board, some through show of strength, some through diplomacy.

The names of some of the kingdoms won over by the brothers are:

1. Arjuna, North[6]: Kulindas, Kalakuta, Shāakaldwipa, Prāgjyotisha, Ulluka, Puru, Kāshmir, Bāhlika, Kāmbhoja, Darada, Loha, Rishika, Kimpurusha[7], Hātak, Uttar Kuru (via Lake Mānsarovar) and other kingdoms along the Himālayas.

2. Bheema, East[8]: Pānchāla, Videha, Gandaka, Chedi, Kosal, Mallarshtra, Kirāta, Magadha, Anga, Vanga, Pundra and Lauhitya.
3. Nakula, West[9]: Marubhumi (Marwad), Shibi, Trigarta, Dashārna, Mālav, Panchanada (Punjab), Dwārkā and Madra.
4. Sahadeva, South[10]: Matsya, Avanti, Māhishmati, Surāshtra, Vidarbha, Pāndya, Kerala, Dravida, Āndhra, Kalinga and Lanka.

Rather, the very reason the kingdoms from all across participated in the war was because they were all closely connected, either through marriage, lineage, allegiance or simply through friendship.

Sanjay's Description of Bhāratavarsha

In Chapter 9 of the Bhishma Parva, Sanjay describes Bhāratavarsha to Dhritarāshtra. In that, he lists out about 150 rivers, including Sindhu (Indus), Vitastā (Jhelum), Gangā, Saraswati, Yamunā, Sarayu, Mahānadi, Chandrabhāga, Kāveri and Lohitya (Brahmaputra).

Sanjay also lists out about 220 janapadas (provinces and kingdoms) in Bhāratavarsha, including those that are situated in the north and the south. He also makes a mention of janapadas ruled by non-Kshatriya tribes. Northern kingdoms include Kāmbhoja, China, Yavana, Kuntala, Huna and the provinces of other Mleccha (non-Vedic) tribes. The southern region includes kingdoms of Pāndya, Chola, Kerala, Konkan, Vindhya, Dravida among others. Some non-Kshatriya kingdoms mentioned are Kāshmir, Kalinga and Pahlava.

Bhāratvarsha during Mahābhārata Times

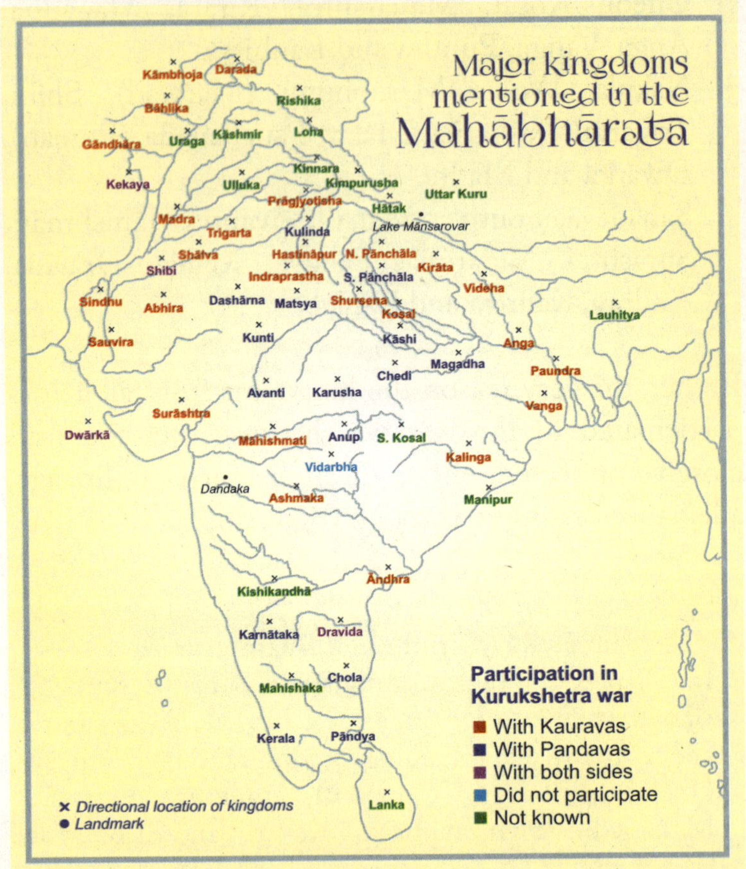

Note: The map has been recreated using references from the Mahabharata as well as some older maps, such as the 'Map of India in the Age of the Mahabharata' from the World Digital Library (https://www.wdl.org/en/item/144/); 'Map of the Alliances for the Kurukshetra War in the Mahabharata' from https://imgur.com/a/Bx6b5; and geographical information available on http://ancientvoice.wikidot.com/.

Illustration: Syed Dilshad Ali.

ॐ ψ ॐ

4

Sanjay's Narration of the Kurukshetra War

The happenings of the Kurukshetra war are known to us through Sanjay's narration. Sanjay was a friend, confidant and sārthi of Dhritarāshtra. He was entrusted to give regular updates of the war to the king. The narration, however, is not live as it is sometimes believed. Sanjay was out there on the battlefield, participating in the war on the Kaurava side, and he made mental records of the happenings to update Dhritarāshtra later.

Before the war began, Vyāsa went to see Dhritarāshtra and offered him divya drishti—the divine sight, to see the war. The latter, however, declined. He didn't wish to see the war but he still wanted to know all that had transpired on the battlefield. So Veda Vyāsa conferred that vision upon Sanjay. 'When on the field, Sanjay will be able to see all that is happening and hear all that is being spoken. He will also know things which are not spoken but are in the thoughts of the warriors. No weapon shall kill him, nor will exhaustion take over him. Sanjay will survive this war,' Vyāsa said.[1]

Sanjay gave the first update of the war to Dhritarāshtra on the tenth day of the war. He returned from Kurukshetra to inform the king of the fall of Bhishma.[2] Dhritarāshtra wanted to know the details. He wanted a day-wise update. Sanjay served him an elaborate description and then went back to the battlefield. He then returned to inform Dhritarāshtra about the death of Drona. He came again to tell the king about the killing of Karna and finally came after the death of Duryodhana.[3] Vaishampāyana tells Janamejaya that Sanjay had horses that galloped like the wind.[4]

The first verse of the Bhagavad Gitā is a question from Dhritarāshtra. He asks, 'What did my and Pāndu's sons, who had gathered in Kurukshetra, there desirous of the war, do?'[5] The question is asked in the past tense, indicating the event had already happened.

Sanjay also told Dhritasrāshtra how he fell into the hands of the opponents and would have died if Veda Vyāsa had not intervened and ensured his release. That incident occurred on the seventeenth day of the war. The fighting continued late into the evening, even after Karna's death. The Pāndava army was in high spirits and thrashed everyone and everything that came in its way. Sanjay was out in the field along with Kripāchārya, when Dhrishtadyumna attacked them. Sanjay managed to escape Dhrishtadyumna but fell into the hands of Sātyaki. The Yādava warrior captured him alive[6] and was planning to kill him when Vyāsa appeared and stopped him.

On the eighteenth morning, Sanjay saw Duryodhana just before the latter entered the Dwaipāyana pool[7]. They even had a conversation. Then again, Sanjay met Duryodhana one last time after the latter was defeated by Bheema. With the death of Duryodhana, Sanjay lost the divya drishti.[8]

After the war, Sanjay and Vidura continued to be close companions of Dhritarāshtra. Sanjay accompanied the blind couple and Kunti to the forest along with Vidura and stayed till the very end. Only when they were caught in a forest fire did Sanjay escape, at the insistence of Dhritarāshtra, and saved his life. Dhritarāshtra, Gāndhāri and Kunti stayed on and eventually let the fire engulf their material bodies.

The Legend of Barbarik

An often-quoted story related to the Mahābhārata war is about Barbarik. It is believed that Barbarik was the son of Ghatotkacha. He is considered to be the only other person apart from Sanjay who witnessed the war in real time from atop a hill. As per the story, Barbarik had a boon that he could destroy the opponents in an instant. But there was also a condition that he could fight only on the side of the weaker opponent. Hence, he came to support the Pāndavas who had only seven akshauhinis compared to the Kauravas' eleven.

But Krishna was quick to realise the danger of this condition. Whichever side Barbarik fought on would become stronger and he would have to keep switching sides, ultimately destroying everything. Hence, to stop him from participating in the war, Krishna asked for his head as a dakshina.[9] Barbarik was willing to do so but requested Krishna to enable him to see the war. Krishna agreed. He severed Barbarik's head and mounted it on a hilltop. Sitting there, Barbarik witnessed the war. After the war ended, he was asked to narrate what he saw. Barbarik replied he saw Krishna and only Krishna. Krishna was the one who killed and Krishna was the one who got killed.

This story, however, is not from Vyāsa's Mahābhārata. It comes from *Skanda Purāna* and is part of the folklore from Rajasthan and Gujarat. Vyāsa's Mahābhārata has no mention of Barbarik. It does talk about Ghatotkacha's son Anjanaparvā who was killed by Ashwatthāmā on the fourteenth day of the war.

ॐ ψ ॐ

Part 2

People, Personalities and Happenings

5

Shakuntalā's Grit

Dushyanta was born into the Puru family tree to a king named Ilila. Like his ancestors, he was a just and popular king. He expanded the boundaries of his kingdom up to the country of the Mlecchas. His subjects were happy and prosperous in his rule. His rivals too regarded him with respect. One day, he went hunting with his soldiers and friends into a dense forest near his capital city. While pursuing his game, he got separated from his army and ventured deep into the jungle.[1]

The game escaped and Dushyanta lost his way. Exhausted and famished, he began looking for a semblance of human settlement in the forest. The search took him to a place adorned by āshrams[2] of sages. The trees were bulging with the bloom of flowers and fruits. The surroundings were alive with sounds of the birds and insects. A refreshingly cool breeze took away the weight of exhaustion from Dushyanta's body and mind. A soft, delicious fragrance permeating the air softly tickled his senses.

He noticed that this part of the forest was situated by the bank of the river Mālini. Looking up the bank, his eyes fell on a beautiful āshram. Dushyanta recognised it as the hermitage of Rishi Kanva, a great sage living in his kingdom. Wishing to seek the sage's darshan[3], Dushyanta took off the jewellery and insignia that indicated his royalty and entered the āshram disguised as an ordinary citizen, so as to not attract the attention of the people around. The place was brimming with activity. He saw some rishis and students singing the mantras from the *Sama Veda*,[4] while some others were busy with the fire rituals. But Rishi Kanva was not to be seen. He ventured further inside where there weren't any other people. 'Is there anyone here,' he asked aloud. A lady of divine beauty emerged from one of the huts. She introduced herself as Shakuntalā, daughter of Rishi Kanva.

'Rishi Kanva is a lifelong celibate, as far as I have known. How can he have a daughter?' asked Dushyanta, perplexed. His heart was already bewitched by the beautiful damsel. 'Let me tell you what I heard from my father regarding my birth,' said Shakuntalā narrating the story of her life.[5]

Rishi Vishvāmitra was engaged in rigorous tapasyā[6]. The severity of the austerities made Indra insecure. Indra thought that the successful completion of Vishvāmitra's resolve might make the sage more powerful than himself. Therefore, he sent Menakā, a celestial nymph of unparalleled charm, to distract Vishvāmitra and impede his mission.

Menakā went to the place where Vishvāmitra was performing the austerities. Like a young girl, intoxicated by her own youth, she played in the river and among the trees. All this while, she ensured she was within the line of sight of the rishi. Inevitably, Vishvāmitra's eyes fell on Menakā. The symmetry of her body, the perfection of her features and her youthfulness in full bloom beguiled the rishi. Vishvāmitra had acquired a lot of power through his tapasyā. But he had not yet overcome his anger and desire. Consumed by lust, he called Menakā near him. They revelled in each other's company and spent many pleasurable days together.

Vishvāmitra's resolve was broken. Through their union, Shakuntalā was born. Menakā had achieved her objective. It was time for her to go back. Thus, leaving the new baby by the bank of river Mālini, Menakā returned to her abode. This abandoned baby girl was taken care of by a group of birds (shakunta[7]). They covered the baby with their wings to protect her from becoming food for the wild animals in the forest. Just then, Rishi Kanva arrived at the river bank for his regular ablutions and worship. The birds communicated to him the story of the baby's birth. Kanva Muni had the ability to decipher the language of birds. Hence, filled with compassion, he took the baby and brought her to his āshram.

Hindu scriptures consider three types of men as fathers—the one who gives birth, the one who rescues from danger and thus saves life and the one who feeds. By that injunction, Kanva became the father to the baby. Because the child was protected by the shakuntas, she came to be known as Shakuntalā.[8]

After Shakuntalā had narrated her story, Dushyanta was convinced she was worthy of becoming his wife. He proposed to her for marriage. 'I pledge to you my entire kingdom. Marry me and become my wife. Let us get married by way of Gāndharva Vivāh right now. The scriptures consider such a marriage to be the most superior,' he appealed. Shakuntalā hesitated. This was a big decision. She wished to seek her father's permission before committing. 'My father will be back soon. Please wait till he returns. I am sure he will himself offer my hand to you,' she said.

'While your decency and virtue are commendable, do know that I am waiting here only for you. You are capable of giving yourself to me by your own accord. A marriage solemnised by the bride and groom's selection is recommended for us Kshatriyas.[9] Our ātmā[10] is our friend and our guide. You will be doing nothing wrong by taking your own decision. As a king, I could even force you to marry me, but I wish for you to accept me if you so desire too,' he said, trying to convince Shakuntalā to accept his proposal immediately.

Shakuntalā, too, was smitten by the graceful and handsome Dushyanta. After some thought, she responded, 'If it is indeed sanctioned by scriptures that I can make my own choice and offer myself, then I am ready to marry you by this route of Gāndharva Vivāh, but you must promise that only my son conceived through you will be the heir to your kingdom.'

'It shall be as you say,' promised Dushyanta. So desperate was he that he made this commitment without any thought. They accepted each other and consummated the marriage.

'I will return soon with my army and take you to my city and palace,' assured Dushyanta and left.[11]

Different Types of Marriages Mentioned in Hindu Scriptures

1. **Brāhma:** A marriage where the daughter, adorned with clothes and jewellery, from a family is married to a suitably learned man of another family. In this form of marriage, the groom's family approaches the bride's family after the son has finished his studies. There is no other demand from the groom's family except for the girl. No financial transaction is involved.
2. **Daiva:** In this case, the daughter is married to an officiating priest by the family for which the ritual is being done. Here, it is the bride's family that seeks the alliance.
3. **Ārsha:** A marriage in which the daughter is married to a sage. The sage, in return, gives a pair of cattle to the bride's family. In this, the alliance could be sought by either side.
4. **Prājāpatya:** A marriage in which the bride and groom are married with the clear intention of performing religious and social duties as equal partners and begetting children. In this, the alliance is sought by the girl's family.
5. **Gāndharva:** In this case, the boy and girl get married by mutual consent. Such a marriage was not encouraged for Brāhmins but was acceptable for the others, especially Kshatriyas.
6. **Āsura:** A marriage in which a price is paid in the form of shulka (cash or kind) to the bride's

family by the groom and his family. Such a form of marriage was not prescribed for Brāhmin and Kshatriya communities.

7. **Rākshasa:** A marriage in which the girl is taken by force, by a show of strength and defeating the girl's kin in a battle. This kind of marriage was permissible only for Kshatriyas.
8. **Pishācha:** A marriage where the groom gets the girl by stealth and deception. This is the most unacceptable form of marriage and prohibited for all.

The first four forms are considered most suitable and the last two the least suitable for society, per the seers and commentators of Hindu scriptures.

When Rishi Kanva learnt of the marriage of Shakuntalā and Dushyanta, he was happy. Shakuntalā had made a worthy choice. She was still in her father's āshram but had started living by the norms of a wedded wife, waiting for Dushyanta to call for her. Their encounter that day in the āshram had got her pregnant. After a few months, she delivered a healthy and bright baby boy, who she named Sarvadaman. The boy was tall for his age, had well-toned limbs, broad shoulders and a big forehead. By the time the boy was six, he could wrestle with tigers, lions, boars and elephants dwelling in the forest. By twelve years of age, he had become well versed in the Vedas and other scriptures. One day Rishi Kanva told Shakuntalā that her son was ready to be crowned the heir of Dushyanta.[12]

The call from Dushyanta was still elusive. Kanva suggested they should themselves go and hand Dushyanta his son and wife. Thus, Shakuntalā and her son left the āshram along with a group of priests and reached his palace. Entering the king's assembly, Shakuntalā declared openly and assertively, 'Mahārāja, this is your son from our marriage in the āshram of Rishi Kanva. Please accept him and per your promise, make him the crown prince.' Dushyanta had recognised Shakuntalā but he behaved as if he hadn't and said, 'Vile lady! What are you talking about? I have no memory of any such marriage!'

Shakuntalā was taken aback and highly embarrassed at Dushyanta's refusal. Her eyes were red with anger and shame but she did not react. Keeping her emotions in check by the power of her self-discipline, she asserted, 'In spite of being well aware of the truth, why do you lie like an ignoble person? Your heart knows the truth. Why do you wish to degrade your own soul? A man who pretends to be something that he is not is as sinful as a thief because he has stolen his own integrity. Or is it that you are thinking we were alone that day and nobody has seen us? Forget not, the witness is not outside, it resides in our hearts and knows our sins and virtues. All the elements of nature are witness to all our actions. Hence, he who thinks no one knows is surely mistaken. He has to bear the consequences of his actions.'[13]

With even more firmness, Shakuntalā added, 'I am your wife. I have lived all these years committed to you. I deserve to be treated with respect. You shouldn't disregard me. Why are you insulting me in this assembly full of people, like a lowly man? A wife is a woman who loves her husband like her own life. She is a wife who bears the man his children and takes care of his household. A wife is the better half of the husband, a wife is a man's best friend, a wife is instrumental in the successful fulfilment of a householder's duties. Only through a wife does a man become a true householder. Only a man with a wife is truly happy and prosperous. That is why people desire to have a worthy wife. She is his only partner in this world and the next. And more so, once the wife becomes the mother of his kids, it behoves the man to respect her as he would his mother.'

Then, pointing at her son, she said, 'Look at this son of yours. He looks expectantly at you wishing you would lovingly make him sit in your lap. Even ants take care of their eggs. Why don't you take the responsibility of nurturing your child? There is nothing more pleasurable to a man than an affectionate hug of his child. And this child is even more special. When he was born, I was told by the seers that he will conduct a hundred grand yajnas and rule this land. He is born of your seed. If you do not accept me, I will return to my father's āshram but why do you wish to give up this child?'[14]

Dushyanta, however, refused to yield, 'I do not know this son of yours. Women are anyway known to lie. Moreover, your own mother Menakā is of questionable character. She cruelly abandoned you when you were a baby. Your father, though considered a great sage, was overpowered by lust upon seeing Menakā. Your words are not trustworthy. Are you not ashamed to speak such lies? And this boy looks too big for his age. How has he grown so tall so swiftly? I do not agree with anything you have said about us. Neither do I know you nor do I wish to know you. You may please leave,' said he, adding further insult to injury.[15]

Shakuntalā was not the kind of woman to be flustered. She responded with her pride intact. 'You are great at finding fault with others without seeing the ones within yourself. You are born of humans. My mother on the other hand is a divine nymph. To be frank, there is no comparison in the nobilities of our families. You are like a mustard seed in front of the Sumeru[16]-like family of mine. There is a famous saying often quoted, "An ugly man considers himself as the most handsome among all until he is made to see the mirror." Like pigs who prefer rot over everything else, stupid men only look out for flaws in others and feel content. There is nothing more laughable than a crook calling a gentleman a crook. A man who lies is anyway a dangerous being. Do remember, if one disrespects a worthy son, he will have his wealth destroyed by the gods. Hence, I urge you, do not give up on your son and do not carry the weight of untruth in your heart. Truth is more valuable than virtues accrued through very many pilgrimages and yajnas. Truth is paramount. However, if you are so attached to your untruth, I will go away myself. I do not wish to concern myself with such an unrighteous man. But before I go, I will tell you this much: even without your support, my son will reign this whole earth. That I am confident of.'[17]

Saying so, Shakuntalā began to walk away. Just then, a celestial voice reverberated throughout the court.

'Dushyanta, Shakuntalā is your wedded wife and this boy is your son. Accept them both and assume responsibility of nourishing and nurturing your son. We command you to do so. Going forward, your son will be known to all as Bharata—the one who was nourished as advised by us gods.'[18] Dushyanta was delighted upon hearing these divine words. He looked at his ministers and said, 'I have known of their identity and who they are ever since they arrived here. Shakuntalā speaks the truth. But had I accepted the boy just based on Shakuntalā's words, people would have doubted the legitimacy of it. Now, I hope no questions remain!'

Dushyanta accepted both Shakuntalā and Bharata. He gave them their due right and respect. Some years later, Dushyanta renounced his throne and went to the forest to spend his last days. Bharata succeeded Dushyanta to the throne. By his valour, he became the sovereign king of Bhāratavarsha. The land he ruled came to be known as Bhāratavarsha—the land of Bharata.

The story of the Mahābhārata is the history of Bharata's descendants. Kuru, Shāntanu, Bhishma, Dhritarāshtra, Duryodhana, Yudhishthira and other Kauravas and Pāndavas belong to this illustrious lineage. Shakuntalā is, therefore, the mother of Bharata vamsha.

Kalidāsa's Shakuntalā

One of the most well-known 'reimagined' dramatisations of this episode of Bhārata's history has been done by Mahākavi Kalidāsa in his work *Abhigyān Shākuntalam*. It is considered as one of the most melodious Sanskrit works. Kalidāsa's Shakuntalā is not as feisty and a lot more mellow than the original characterisation of hers as mentioned in Vyāsa's Mahābhārata.

Kalidāsa has added a lot more emotion to the poetry to bring out nuances of the relationship between Kanva and Shakuntalā. There is a lot of romance and yearning in *Abhigyān Shākuntalam*. A storyline attributing Dushyanta's non-recognition of his wife and son due to the curse of Rishi Durvāsā has been added. Shakuntalā unintentionally ignores the coming of Rishi Durvāsā, lost in the thoughts of Dushyanta. Angered at this, rishi curses her that whoever she was thinking of will forget her.

The *Padma Purāna* also has this historical episode. But the general view is that the original story is the one mentioned in Vyāsa's Mahābhārata.

ॐ ψ ॐ

6

The Foundational Years

The five sons of Pāndu were born in a forest on a mountain called Shatashrunga and were born a year apart. Their initial years were spent amongst the rishis and tribes living there along with their mothers and father. Their study of weapons, astra vidya, began under the guidance of Rāja Shuka,[1] a renowned king of the Sharayāti dynasty who was also living the life of an ascetic on the Shatashrunga mountains. Among the five brothers, Arjuna had an inclination towards archery, Bheema for the gadā,[2] Yudhishthira for the javelin and the twins began mastering the sword.

Arjuna was fourteen[3] at the time of Pāndu's death. A guilt-ridden Mādri, too, had given up her life at Pāndu's pyre, leaving the five boys in the care of Kunti alone. At the time, the rishis of Shatashrunga discussed the future of the young family and concluded that it was indeed the right time for Kunti and the boys to return to their ancestral home, the capital city of Pāndu's kingdom—Hastināpur. When Kunti and the Pāndavas arrived in Hastināpur, the citizens emerged to see them. They had heard stories about the princes and were eager to get a glimpse of the young boys. Bhishma, Dhritarāshtra, Satyavati and others welcomed them with open arms. This was going to be the first tryst of the Pāndavas with palace life. They settled in quite well.

Here in Hastināpur, Duryodhana, the eldest child of Dhritarāshtra and Gāndhāri, was also their most pampered son. He was strong, generous and, at times, overbearing. But the king's heart resided in his son's happiness, so no one ever objected to anything he did, not even the parents. Everyone did his bidding. Till then, Duryodhana had firmly believed he was the sole heir to the Hastināpur throne. With the arrival of the Pāndavas, things changed drastically. Duryodhana was no longer the eldest, neither was he the strongest: Bheema was as strong, if not more; Arjuna was a lot more talented and Yudhishthira was not only the eldest but also polite and wise. The Pāndavas were winning everyone's hearts by their demeanour and attitude.

Amongst the Pāndavas, Duryodhana most despised Bheema, who was mischievous and loved flaunting his strength. Though not done maliciously, his mischief-making was sometimes rash. The younger Kauravas were scared of him. Duryodhana was already envious and this behaviour riled him up further—so much so that he attempted killing Bheema by poisoning his food, not once but twice.[4] The first time, Bheema was saved and his strength was further fortified by an old Nāga, Āryaka, who recognised young Bheema. He was the maternal grandfather of Kunti's father Shurasena, and by that relationship, Bheema's great-great-grandfather[5]. The second time he was forewarned of Duryodhana's devious plan by Yuyutsu, Duryodhana's stepbrother.

Bheema and Duryodhana were of the same age. Both were physically very strong. Both had anger issues and could be reckless. But there was one big difference: Bheema's rage was reined in by Yudhishthira, Kunti and the other Pāndavas. Duryodhana's rage was encouraged by his maternal uncle Shakuni, his father Dhritarāshtra, and willing younger brothers and friends like Karna. His uncontrolled rage would eventually lead to the doom of the Kauravas and all associated with them.

Shortly after the arrival of the Pāndavas, both the Kaurava and the Pāndava princes began training under Rishi Kripāchārya, the royal priest of the Kuru family. One day, Dronāchārya came to Hastināpur. A student of Maharshi Agnivesh and Parashurāma, he was an expert in the science of warfare. He was considered one of the best warrior-teachers in Bhāratavarsha. Drona was also Kripāchārya's brother-in-law; his wife was Kripi, Kripāchārya's sister, with whom he had a son, Ashwatthāmā.

In Rishi Agnivesh's āshram, Drona had become friends with Drupada, the prince of Pānchāla. Once, Drupada promised Drona that when he became the king of Pānchāla, he would share his luxuries and comforts with him. Time went by and soon the friends went their separate ways. Drupada became the king and Drona was relegated to live a poverty-stricken life. Remembering the promise of his friend, Drona approached Drupada. All he wanted was a cow so that his son could drink real milk. However, when Drona addressed Drupada as a friend and reminded him of the promise, the king of Pānchāla flatly refused to acknowledge the friendship. 'Friendship can only be among equals. Do not harp on that. If you have come as a seeker, I can feed you for the night,' he said dismissively.

Enraged, Dronāchārya left, resolving to humble Drupada at an opportune time. He was looking to get students who could be helpful in fulfilling his resolve. His search brought him to Hastināpur. Bhishma was happy when he heard about Drona's arrival. He, too, was on the lookout for an appropriate teacher for the advance training of his grandsons in the art of warfare and weaponry, and Drona was amongst the best. Bhishma thus approached Drona with a request to reside in Hastināpur and teach the Kauravas and the Pāndavas. Drona was waiting for just this opportunity. He readily agreed. Thus began the next phase of the education of the Kuru princes.

Hearing of Drona's fame, many students from across Bhāratavarsha came to study with him. Boys from the Vrishni and Andhak clans, princes from Sindhu desh and many others made Drona their teacher. Adhiratha, Dhritarāshtra's friend, a renowned figure of the Suta community of Anga desh, also sent his son Karna to train under Drona. Karna spent his initial training years alongside the Kauravas and the Pāndavas studying under Drona before heading to Parashurāma to gain the knowledge of powerful celestial weapons such as the Brahmāstra.[6]

Arjuna

Like all other princes, Arjuna was in awe of Dronāchārya since their first meeting. Once, before Drona became their teacher, the boys had dropped their ball in a well while playing. Drona, then a stranger to the kids, pulled out the ball from the well using just long blades of grass. It was after this incident that Bhishma got to know of Drona's arrival.

A few months after the training of the princes had begun, Dronāchārya called them and asked, 'When you boys finish your training, I will need you to fulfil a wish of mine. What do you think of that?' The Kauravas kept quiet, so did four of the Pāndava brothers, not knowing what the wish entailed. Only Arjuna instantly stood up. Without a second's thought, he promised to fulfil whatever wish the teacher had. Dronāchārya was profusely happy. He affectionately kissed Arjuna's forehead. By this one gesture, Arjuna had expressed his deep commitment and faith in his guru.

Amongst Drona's students, Arjuna excelled in archery. His thirst for knowledge and dedication to learning was unmatched. The Kauravas envied Arjuna. Karna was especially jealous. His inclination was also towards archery and he was proud of his skill. He considered Arjuna as his biggest competitor. Karna's jealousy, coupled with pride, made him forever contemptuous towards Arjuna in particular and the Pāndavas in general.[7] Arjuna, however, had little care or concern for things apart from his study and practice.

Drona was forced to acknowledge that Arjuna's grasp of the subject, his speed and his dedication were exemplary. Arjuna proved time and again that he was a notch above the others, not consciously but by his response to situations.

Dronāchārya had given the students a narrow-mouthed pot to fill water for their use. To his son, Ashwatthāmā, he gave a broad-mouthed pot. This helped Ashwatthāmā finish the task faster than the others and gain time. In the time that was saved, Dronāchārya would teach Ashwatthāmā additional techniques of using weapons. Arjuna realised that he was losing out on the learning that Ashwatthāmā was getting because he took much longer to get his work done. To expedite the water-filling task, Arjuna devised a smarter way. By using the Varunāstra to fill his pot, Arjuna would finish his chores faster and get ready for the additional class along with Ashwatthāmā. Drona couldn't refuse. Thus, Arjuna ensured he would not miss out on any lesson taught by the āchārya.[8]

Arjuna's passion and hunger for knowledge had left Drona bewildered and cautious. Once, Drona instructed the cook to never serve any food to Arjuna in the dark. Arjuna was not to be told of such an instruction either, lest he become suspicious. However, it so happened that one evening, when Arjuna was having his food, strong gusts of wind blew the lamps out. It was completely dark, so much that Arjuna couldn't see his hands.

Arjuna noticed something interesting. Even though it was dark, his hand would reach his mouth without any difficulty. Arjuna was wonderstruck. He quickly realised this was possible due to the sheer practice of eating every day. 'With practice, everything can be achieved,' he concluded to himself. Since then, while other princes rested at night, Arjuna started practising archery in the pitch dark. He wanted to perfect the art of hitting the target even in the dark, without being able to see it.

One night, Dronāchārya heard the twang of Arjuna's bow when other students were fast asleep. He immediately understood the reason. Arjuna's focus, quest for perfection and complete devotion had won over Drona. He had to acknowledge that Arjuna was a student like none other. Overwhelmed, Drona made a promise to Arjuna, 'I will do all I can to make you an archer without a parallel in the world.'[9]

As the training of the princes neared completion, Drona was desirous of testing their skill and focus. He got a stuffed toy bird and perched it on a tree. He then asked the boys to take aim at the bird and describe what they saw. All of them responded saying they saw the bird, the branch, the trees and also the people around. When Arjuna's turn came, he replied, 'I see nothing but the head of the bird.' Pleased, Drona asked him to shoot. He did and off flew the neck of the toy bird.[10] Such was Arjuna's single-minded focus.

One other time, Dronāchārya, along with his pupils, went to take a dip in the river Gangā. Suddenly, Drona screamed aloud. A crocodile had caught his ankle from under the surface of the water. He called out for his students to save him. While others were still trying to figure out what to do because the crocodile was not to be seen, Arjuna immediately steadied his bow and shot five arrows at where he perceived the invisible crocodile was. The crocodile was instantly cut into pieces and killed. Mightily impressed with Arjuna's presence of mind, alacrity in action and archery skills, Dronāchārya gifted him the unique and powerful Brahmasheera weapon. 'Use this powerful weapon, Arjuna, with utmost care and control. Use it to destroy only a non-human enemy who harasses you.' Drona exhorted and proclaimed once again, 'No other man in the world will be able to match you in archery.'[11]

By the end of their training, Duryodhana and Bheema had become adept in the use of the mace. They were ever ready to compete with one another. Nakula and Sahadeva made their mark in fighting with the sword. Yudhishthira became an expert at fighting from the chariot. Arjuna had mastered every form of warfare.[12]

Few days after the princes had demonstrated their skills before the citizens of Hastināpur after having finished their training, Drona revealed to them the gurudakshinā he expected of them. He asked the princes to challenge Drupada in a war and capture him alive. The Kaurava brothers along with Karna[13] went first, but could not face the force of Drupada's retaliation. They retreated. The five Pāndavas went next. Displaying exemplary valour and skill, they successfully captured Drupada and handed him over to Dronāchārya, whose resolve was finally fulfilled. Taking half of Drupada's kingdom, he let his friend free. 'Now we are equals,' smirked Drona to the embarrassed Drupada.[14]

Arjuna did not start out as Dronāchārya's favourite but earned his guru's grace through his devotion and perseverance. It was this dedication and single-minded focus that helped him master all the intricacies of music and dance in less than five years in Indra's palace during the time of vanvās. This art of the Gandharvas that he learnt from Chitrasena helped him disguise himself as Brihannalā, a eunuch, in the year of the agyātvās. As Brihannalā, he taught dance and music to the women in King Virāta's palace.

Arjuna's fervour to learn got him a friend and mentor like Krishna. For the Kurukshetra war, Arjuna could have asked for Krishna's army, the formidable Nārāyani Sena. Instead, he chose Krishna, not as a warrior but as a sārthi,[15] to guide him in the war. Krishna's guidance and Arjuna's humility to abide by it helped him steer through some serious moral dilemmas during the war.

Karna

Karna wasn't born to Adhiratha and Rādhā. Karna was born out of an innocent misadventure of Kunti's when she was still young and unmarried. Scared of her family, Kunti put the newborn baby in a basket and let it float away in the river Ashva that flowed across the kingdom of Kunti. The basket floated away from river Ashva to Charmanvati into Yamunā and then into Gangā. In the city of Champā[16] of Anga desh, Adhiratha and his wife Rādhā found this basket by the bank of Gangā.[17] Rādhā was ecstatic on seeing the baby inside the basket. The couple had been yearning for a child for long. They eagerly adopted this kid and raised him as their own son. As the baby had a golden armour and earrings, they named him Vasushena.[18]

Karna grew up to be a talented and brave young boy. When he was old enough, Adhiratha sent him to Hastināpur to get trained under Guru Dronāchārya along with his friend Dhritarāshtra's sons. It was in Dronāchārya's āshram that Karna first met Duryodhana as well as Arjuna. Karna, like Arjuna, developed expertise in archery. Like Arjuna, he too was agile and swift. For Karna, Arjuna was always a rival and a competitor he had to defeat. Out of jealousy, Karna would insult and mock Arjuna at every opportunity.[19]

One day, he approached Guru Dronāchārya and said, 'Sir, I wish to learn how to use the Brahmāstra to be able to fight with Arjuna.' Dronāchārya was aware of the ill will Karna had for Arjuna and did not consider him responsible enough to handle a weapon as deadly as the Brahmāstra. He, therefore, declined Karna's request.[20]

But Karna's mind was made up. By hook or crook, he wished to learn the forbidden weapon. Thus, taking on the identity of a Brāhmin boy from the family of Bhrigu,[21] Karna approached Parashurāma and sought him out as his teacher.[22] Parashurāma was impressed with Karna's manners and accepted the latter as his student, imparting to him all relevant skills related to weapons and warfare.

One day, when Parashurāma was resting with his head on Karna's lap, a scorpion bit Karna. Not willing to disturb the guru, Karna sat through the immense pain. On waking up, Parashurāma saw blood oozing out from Karna's thigh and understood the reason. He was livid. 'A Brāhmin boy cannot have had so much tolerance to pain!' exclaimed Parashurāma. 'You must be a Kshatriya. Tell me the truth! Who are you?'

Karna confessed, 'Sir, I belong to the Suta community. I lied because I was eager to learn the Brahmāstra. Please be considerate towards me. A guru is akin to a father. Hence, I said I belong to a family of the Bhrigu lineage, as you do.' Nevertheless, Parashurāma was angry. 'This knowledge gained through falsehood will not come to you when faced with death or a warrior as good as you are,' he said, adding, 'until then, you will become a warrior without a parallel by my grace. Now please leave. A liar has no place here.'[23]

Karna returned happy and even more proud of his superior skills. He believed he had found a foolproof way to defeat Arjuna when the time would come, once and for all.

ॐ ψ ॐ

7

The Nishāda Prince

Having heard of Dronāchārya's reputation as a teacher, Hiranyadhanu, the king of the Nishādas came to see Drona. He requested Drona to accept his son Ekalavya as a student. But Dronāchārya, with consideration to his existing students, refused.[1] Ekalavya touched his feet and went away.

In a forest not too far from where the Kaurava princes were studying, Ekalavya made Dronāchārya's idol, established it as his guru and immersed himself in the practice of archery.

One day, the princes went on a hunting expedition to a nearby forest taking along a dog. While loitering around, the dog saw Ekalavya and started barking. Ekalavya shot a slew of seven arrows in the dog's mouth to stop it from barking. The dog returned to the princes with its mouth wide open but stuffed with arrows. The princes were astonished and looked around to see who was the person responsible for their pet's condition. They saw Ekalavya and asked for his introduction. He obliged, introducing himself as Nishādarāja Hiranyadhanu's son and Dronāchārya's student.

On returning to the āshram, the boys informed Dronāchārya of this encounter with Ekalavya and got busy with their tasks. Arjuna could not get Ekalavya out of his mind. He respectfully asked Dronāchārya, 'Guruji, the other day you had affectionately hugged me and said that none of your students would be better than I am in archery. How is this student of yours, the son of Nishādarāja, more skilled than I am?' Drona gave it some thought and approached Ekalavya the next day, taking Arjuna along.

Ekalavya was delighted upon seeing Dronāchārya. He offered his reverence to Drona as a student should to his guru. Dronāchārya smiled and said, 'If you say you are my student then you should offer me gurudakshinā.'[2] Ekalavya was overjoyed. He replied, 'There is nothing that I wouldn't give you. Please command me. What can I offer?' Drona said, 'Give me the thumb of your right hand.' Without a moment's hesitation, Ekalavya chopped off his thumb and handed it to Dronāchārya.

Eventually, Ekalavya learnt to shoot arrows using just his fingers but the loss of a thumb impacted his shooting speed.[3]

Nonetheless, he became a formidable warrior. After Hiranyadhanu, Ekalavya became the king of the Nishāda kingdom. In that capacity, he was present in Yudhishthira's assembly during the Rājasuya Yajna. He was a key ally of Jarāsandha, the powerful king of Magadha. Ekalavya was killed by Krishna[4] himself when the former had led an attack on Dwārkā following Jarāsandha's death.

Who Are the Nishādas?

Per the Mahābhārata,[5] the Nishāda is a mixed jāti of offsprings of a Shudra man and a Kshatriya woman. In some other texts,[6] Nishādas are the progeny of a Brāhmin man and a Shudra woman. Their traditional occupations included fishing, hunting and making weapons. They were also considered to be very good warriors. Various Nishāda kingdoms participated in the Mahābhārata war from both sides. Ekalavya's father was a king of one such Nishāda kingdom.

Satyavati, the mother of Krishna Dwaipāyana Vyāsa and grandmother of Dhritarāshtra and Pāndu, was a Nishāda. She, and a twin brother, were born to King Uparichara Vasu of Chedi and a fisherwoman[7] of the Nishāda community. The king gave Satyavati to Dāshrāja, a Nishāda headman, and adopted the son. This adopted son went on to found the Matsya kingdom. Virāta, Abhimanyu's father-in-law, was his descendant. Satyavati grew up in the Nishāda community and eventually married Shāntanu of Hastināpur. Shri Rāma's very close friend was a Nishāda king named Guha.

ॐ ψ ॐ

8

The Marriage That Tied

The palace of lac in Vāranāvata was burnt down. Thanks to the alertness and help of Vidura, the Pāndavas and Kunti had safely escaped. But their lives were not yet completely secure. Duryodhana and his coterie of Shakuni, Karna and Duhshāsana couldn't be trusted. The blind king was so blinded by his attachment to his son that he would have done nothing to protect the Pāndavas had Duryodhana attempted another assault. Vidura advised the brothers and Kunti to go into hiding for a while. The time was not yet apt for Hastināpur to know about the Pāndavas being alive, Vidura reckoned.

Taking Vidura's pertinent advice, the Pāndavas hid themselves in the forests beyond Vāranāvata. In Kāmyakavana, Bheema met Hidimbā, sister of a man-eating rākshasa Hidimb. Hidimbā was attracted to Bheema and desired him as her husband. The union occurred with Kunti's blessings. The couple gave birth to a son, Ghatotkacha, who was to play a very important role in the lives of the Pāndavas.

One day, Krishna Dwaipāyana Vyāsa, who was aware of their safe escape, came to meet the Pāndavas in the forest. He took them to Ekachakra Nagar and put them up in a home of a Brāhmin. Disguised as Brāhmins, Kunti and her sons spent a few days there. It was in Ekachakra that Bheema killed Bakāsura, another man-eating demon, who had terrorised the town. The people of Ekachakra Nagar were overjoyed. But the Pāndavas were fearful of being identified. They believed it would be prudent to move out of the town at the earliest opportunity. As they made plans to leave, they learnt about the upcoming swayamvara[1] of the daughter of Drupada, the king of Pānchāla, from a Brāhmin who had come visiting.

'The daughter of Drupada is like none other. Her beauty is unparalleled in this world. Her eyes are like petals of a full-bloomed lotus. She exudes the fragrance of a blue lotus that can be taken in from a mile away. Her complexion is dusky and lustrous as the agni she came out of. Looking at her, one thinks she is a personification of Devi Durga herself. Devatas, Danavas, Gandharvas are yearning to make her their wife. Her name is Krishnā,' the Brāhmin had said.

Realising how captivated her sons already were at the description of Krishnā, Kunti proposed to go to Kāmpilya, the capital of Pānchāla, for the swayamvara. The Pāndavas readily agreed. On reaching Kāmpilya, the Pāndavas and Kunti, still disguised as Brāhmins, found shelter in a potter's home. The city had been ornately decked up to welcome the princes coming from all over Bhāratavarsha for Draupadi's swayamvara.

The day of the swayamvara arrived. Along with other Brāhmins, the Pāndavas too went to the venue and stood among the audience. The who's who of the elite families from across Bhāratavarsha had gathered there hoping to make Draupadi their wife. The Kaurava princes and Karna were also among the august gathering. Vāsudeva Krishna and Balarāma had come too. They, however, had come as guests and were not among the participating princes.

Drupada had long wished to make Arjuna his son-in-law. He had heard news about their death in the lac palace of Vāranāvata. But he hadn't quite believed it. Nevertheless, Drupada had designed a challenge for the swayamvara, which few other than Arjuna would have been able to fulfil. He had a machine suspended in the air with a target in it. The suitors had to first string the bow provided and then with that bow shoot five arrows right through a hole in the machine piercing the target. The bow was extremely sturdy and made specially for the swayamvara. One after another, the suitors came forward to take on the challenge. But none including Duryodhana, Karna,[2] Shālva, Shalya and Ashwatthāmā could even manage to tie the string to the bow.

When all the suitors had failed, Arjuna, in his Brāhmin avatār, walked towards the podium where the target was set. A thousand eyes followed him. 'How will this young Brāhmin do what even warriors like Karna[3] and Shalya couldn't?' murmured some in the audience. To everyone's bewilderment, in an instant, Arjuna strung the bow; in the next, he shot the target straight through. The hall arose in an uproar at his feat. 'A young Brāhmin who lives on alms has won the hand of the Princess of Pānchāla,' they exclaimed in awe. The princes assembled couldn't control their wrath at this young Brāhmin's insolence. They attacked Arjuna to stop him from taking Draupadi away. Bheema jumped in to support his brother. Together, the two defeated the warriors gathered there and walked out with Draupadi as Drupada, Dhrishtadyumna and the audience watched incredulously. Draupadi, however, was calm. She walked out with the young Brāhmin men without any resistance, of her own accord. To avoid being recognised, Yudhishthira, Nakula and Sahadeva had already left the place when the fight broke out. Kunti was busy with work in the potter's house when Arjuna and Bheema came with Draupadi. In order to surprise Kunti, they said, 'Mother, look at the bhikshā[4] we've got today.' 'Share it among the five of you,' she replied out of habit, without turning around to look at the 'bhikshā'. Seeing Draupadi, she immediately repented her words. But they had already been uttered.

There was one other complication—who among the brothers was most eligible to marry Draupadi? While Arjuna had won the swayamvara, Yudhishthira was the eldest. Per the norms of the day, the elder brother should be the first one to be married. The case of Hidimbā was different. Her union with Bheema was not a formal wedding, even though she was acknowledged as his wife and Ghatotkacha as his son. The final decision regarding Draupadi was deferred to Yudhishthira himself.

Beyond the technicalities and norms, there was another snag. All the five Pāndavas were smitten[5] by this woman of immaculate beauty. They couldn't take their eyes and minds off her. They stared at Pānchāli enraptured. She looked back at them. The brothers felt a shiver of excitement run down their spine. It was as if their whole being was shaken. Yudhishthira saw the state of his brothers and read their minds. He was a man of great wisdom and foresight. He realised Draupadi could either bind them or break them apart. The only way to ensure the brothers don't fall apart was by making Draupadi their common wife. Yudhishthira thought for some time and stated his decision, 'Draupadi will be a wife to us all.' The Pāndava brothers pondered over it but said nothing. Neither did Draupadi.

Kunti, like a gracious mother-in-law, took Draupadi under her wing and started telling her more about the Pāndavas, their preferences and personalities. She involved her in chores and made her feel at home. Draupadi happily complied. By then, she was aware that her husbands were no ordinary Brāhmins but the Pāndavas themselves. She pleasantly settled in the potter's hut.

When Dhrishtadyumna and Drupada got to know about the Pāndavas, their joy knew no bounds. But the arrangement of Draupadi marrying the five brothers was not to their liking. It was against the norms of the day. A husband having more than one wife was known but how could a woman have more than one husband? They expressed their concern and disapproval to Yudhishthira, Kunti and Krishna Dwaipāyana Vyāsa. Yudhishthira gave precedents of the past to show how the practice of polyandry, while uncommon, was neither non-existent and nor against any moral code. Vyāsa, who had a sense of the happenings of the future, intervened and convinced

Drupada of the appropriateness of the proposed arrangement. Drupada eventually acquiesced. And Draupadi became the common wife of the Pāndavas.

When Duryodhana, Karna and Shakuni heard that the Brāhmins who won Draupadi were none other than the Pāndavas, they were furious. Their scheming minds set to work again. 'If only something can be done to create differences between the sons of Kunti and Mādri, or if Krishnā can be provoked to give up the husbands, there is a chance the Pāndavas can be weakened and defeated,' suggested Duryodhana.

Karna disagreed. 'It is next to impossible to create a rift amongst the Pāndavas. Their unity has received a boost by way of their indulgence in a common wife, a wife as exquisite as Draupadi. The brothers happily agreed to this arrangement of a common wife. Trying to provoke Draupadi will be even more futile. She joyfully accepted the Pāndavas even when they were disguised as poor Brāhmins subsisting on alms. Now, having known the truth of their identity, she will certainly not give up on them,' he weighed in. With a wife like Draupadi and a father-in-law like the powerful king of Pānchāla, the Pāndavas had become stronger than ever before. Karna understood this well.

Draupadi became the bond that held the brothers together for life. The Pāndavas married other women too, but none could take the place of Draupadi in their hearts. She stood by them through thick and thin. Kunti doted on her. Through her devotion and her actions, Draupadi exhibited time and again that the reverence and the love she got was well deserved. Not just in beauty but also in strength of character, responsibility and courage, she was unmatched. Her personality shines through in various incidents narrated in the Mahābhārata.

The Queen of Indraprastha

One day, when the Pāndavas with Draupadi were serving the time in vanvās, Krishna came to pay a visit along with his wife Satyabhāmā. While the men got busy with their discussions, Satyabhāmā and Draupadi caught up with each other. They hadn't seen each other in a while. Draupadi was keen to know about the well-being of her sons who were growing up in Dwārkā as well as Kāmpilya. Satyabhāmā comforted her saying all the boys were well taken care of and were growing up to be great warriors.

Over the course of the conversation, Satyabhāmā asked Draupadi a rather teasing but intimate question. 'What have you done to rule the hearts of the five Pāndavas like you do?[6] They are ever ready to do your bidding. Their love for you manifests even in the way they look at you. Please share your secret with me! Is it some medicine or a herb or is it some vashikaran[7] practice that I can use to ensure Krishna always listens to me and stays interested in me like the Pāndavas are in you?'

Draupadi responded with poise. 'There is no magic recipe, Satyā,' she said. 'And neither do any vashikaran practices that claim to bring the husbands in control of the wife ever work. Instead, such attempts, if known to the husband, are more likely to destroy the marriage. Do not even think about these things. Let me rather tell you how I behave with them and treat them.' Draupadi goes on to explain her life as the queen and wife of the Pāndavas.

'My foremost concern is the well-being of my husbands and I do everything in my capacity to ensure their comfort, convenience and joy. As for my husbands, so with their other wives as well as my mother-in-law, I do not let ego come in the way of my behaviour with anyone and look after everyone without bias. I am always truthful and humble in my speech.

'I wake up early every morning and keep ready all the ingredients my husbands need for their yajna and other nitya karmas[8]. I keep the house in order and ensure everyone, including our helpers, are well fed. I eat only after everybody else has eaten. I maintain a reserve of food for emergencies. I attend to my mother-in-law, taking care of all her needs. I strive to live up to the norms and traditions of the family.

'When we lived in Indraprastha, every day 8,000 Brāhmins, 88,000 graduates and 10,000 ascetics were fed, given due charities and entertained. To take care of these and the other guests, over 1,00,000 women helpers were employed. I ensured that the helpers were well trained and all guests were well taken care of. I knew every helper personally by name and was always fully aware of not only who did what work and what was yet to be done but also whether they had eaten or not. Apart from these, there were other helpers and cowherds whom I managed.

'When Yudhishthira travelled as the king of Indraprastha, a large number of horses and elephants would accompany him. I would keep a count of the animals and preside over important arrangements of the travel. I would also keep a detailed account of all the earnings and expenditures of the Pāndavas. No one had the transparency of the accounts and the treasury as I did. This way, I shouldered the entire responsibility of palace and household with complete dedication.

'O Satyabhāmā, hard work and devotion are the mantras that have kept the Pāndavas interested in me,' concluded Draupadi, giving Satyabhāmā a peep into her life as the queen of Indraprastha and wife of the Pāndavas.

While describing the grandeur of Yudhishthira's Rājasuya Yajna, Vaishampāyana corroborates Draupadi's words by telling Janamejaya how Draupadi looked after the needs of every single guest, including the differently abled ones, and ate only after everyone was fed.[9]

Yudhishthira had once said of Draupadi—'She is the kind of spouse a man desires for a fruitful and rewarding life.'[10]

The Humiliation

The game of dice should not have happened. Vidura was vehemently opposed to it. He even warned Yudhishthira. Per the norms of the day, a warrior was expected to not back out if challenged for a duel or a game of dice. Yudhishthira was aware that the invitation for the game from Duryodhana was a trap. He made his discomfort known even in the game room.[11] Shakuni did not make much of the eldest Pāndava's hesitation. He knew Yudhishthira well. When challenged, even if unwilling, Yudhishthira would play, because that was expected of a warrior king. The game happened. Shakuni, by his sleight of hand, won all stakes one after the other. Yudhishthira staked his wealth, his kingdom, his brothers and himself, hoping at least one stake would salvage him. He lost it all.

The assembly looked on. Vidura objected and requested the blind king to stop the game. But Dhritarāshtra was too elated at Duryodhana's win to pay any heed to his objections. He let the travesty of the game continue. Yudhishthira gave up. He had nothing more to stake. But as cunning as Shakuni was, he provoked Yudhishthira further. 'You still have a chance at winning. You still have Draupadi to stake.' Yudhishthira was desperate. He staked the daughter of Drupada; he staked the woman he called his wife, his queen. Shakuni threw the dice. Yudhishthira lost again. Yudhishthira had lost Draupadi, his wife of unparalleled beauty and unrivalled virtues. Vidura objected. 'Yudhishthira had already staked himself and lost. Hence, he has no right to stake Draupadi,'[12] he said. He even warned Duryodhana of dire consequences, but to no avail.

What followed was one of the darkest episodes in the history of the Bhāratas. A menstruating lady was dragged by her hair and pulled into the hall of Hastināpur. An attempt was made at disrobing her. This lady was the queen of Indraprastha, the daughter-in-law of Hastināpur, the daughter of Pānchāla. The august assembly of the mightiest warriors looked on, her five powerful husbands looked on, as her own brother-in-law Duhshāsana, prodded on by Karna, put his hand on her garment. Karna even called her a prostitute.

Everyone was shocked—some closed their eyes, some looked down but no one said a thing. Vidura and Vikarṇa were the only two who opposed. When no pleadings seem to work and no sense seemed to prevail, Draupadi gave herself up to divine powers, taking the name of Hari.[13] Her shraddhā had its effect. As the garment got pulled, other similar ones kept appearing to keep Draupadi covered. Duhshāsana collapsed on the floor exhausted but couldn't pull away the garment off Draupadi's body. Everybody in the assembly witnessed this extraordinary happening that day. It could only have been divine intervention that saved Draupadi in that forsaken moment.[14]

Duhshāsana's disgraceful act angered Bheema to no end. Addressing the assembly, he screamed, 'Hear me today, O Masters of the Earth! Never before has something like this been spoken nor will it be spoken in the future. When the time arrives, I will rip apart the chest of this Duhshāsana and drink his blood. May I be doomed if I do not fulfil this vow.'

A Question of Legality

When Yudhishthira staked and lost Draupadi, Duryodhana, calling her a slave, asked one of his helpers to fetch Draupadi and bring her to the hall. The messenger conveyed the message to Draupadi and informed her of what had transpired during the game. Draupadi was no ordinary woman. She was erudite, wise and gutsy. 'Ask the king of Indraprastha, "Did he first lose himself or me?" I will come only after I know the answer,' she replied, appalled. But the messenger returned without an answer and Draupadi refused to go again. In between this, Yudhishthira stealthily sent another messenger whom Draupadi knew, to request her to come to the court weeping, in her menstruating state. 'That might get the courtiers to castigate Duryodhana,' he had said.[15]

Agitated by Draupadi's incompliance, Duryodhana sent Duhshāsana to drag her forcibly to the court. Helpless and angry, standing in a single piece of garment before the entire assembly, Draupadi looked askance at her husbands. If a glance could burn, hers would have set the Pāndavas on fire. She then asked the elders and warriors, 'Respected courtiers, please answer this question of mine. Do you consider me won over by Duryodhana?' No one spoke a word. Draupadi looked at Bhishma expectantly. 'The nature of dharma is very subtle. One cannot stake what is not his. But usually, a wife is considered subordinate to her husband. Yudhishthira is himself a keeper of dharma and has said that he has lost himself first. Given all these factors, I am unable to answer,' Bhishma said helplessly.[16]

Draupadi didn't yield. 'Yudhishthira is not an experienced player. He doesn't know this game well. Whereas, the opponents are experts in the game and deceit. Knowing this, how was this game even allowed? Why was Yudhishthira enticed into gambling?

Yudhishthira is naive about these things. He was duped into playing the game and then into staking himself as well as me. Taking all this into consideration, please do give my original question careful thought,'[17] she pleaded.

Bheema couldn't take it anymore. 'I am so angry right now that I can burn these hands of yours that staked Draupadi!' he screamed at Yudhishthira. Arjuna pulled him back, 'This is what Duryodhana wants. He wants to sow seeds of doubt amongst us brothers. Do not fall for it. Yudhishthira had no option but to play because that is the norm for us warriors,'[18] he said, trying to calm Bheema down.

Vidura had already shared his view about Yudhishthira having no legal right to stake Draupadi. Another voice supporting Vidura's view came from Vikarna, Duryodhana's brother. 'Draupadi has posed a valid question before us. If not resolved honestly, great misfortune will befall us. Even if none of you say anything, I will certainly share what I believe. The scriptures talk about four vices of a king—alcoholism, hunting, gambling and lust. A decision made when a person is deluded by one of these vices is not honourable. Yudhishthira staked Draupadi having lost his mind in gambling. In addition, he is not Draupadi's only husband; the other four brothers have equal claim on her. Above all, he lost himself before staking Draupadi. Moreover, Yudhishthira was provoked into staking Draupadi by Shakuni. With a view of all these factors, I do not consider Draupadi as won over by Duryodhana.'[19]

Vikarna was rudely dismissed by Karna; rather, he instigated the disrobing of Draupadi. When

Duhshāsana attempted what should never have been done and failed, Vidura once again asked the courtiers to ponder on Draupadi's query. She deserved an answer. More importantly, it was the duty of the court to deliver justice, he stressed.

Encouraged by the silence of the court, Karna instructed Duhshāsana, 'Take this slave woman home.'[20] Duhshāsana once again began dragging her. Suddenly, Draupadi remembered something. 'O Heavens, this cruel man has harassed me so much that I forgot my manners. I haven't yet offered my obeisance to my elders. Please accept by pranām,' she lamented, shivering with sorrow and embarrassment. 'Not even wind has touched me till date, and here Duhshāsana dares to drag me. I am the daughter-in-law of the Kurus and hence daughter-like. The way I have been treated here is unbecoming of the mighty kings sitting here. A righteous lady like me doesn't deserve this shameful treatment. I will not be able to tolerate this for too long. I urge you to answer my query—do you think I have been won over or not?' she asked.[21]

Bhishma bemoaned, 'Because of the subtle nature of dharma, I am not able to answer your question clearly. But what I do know is that the destruction of the Kuru clan is near. Your conduct in this treacherous moment is certainly befitting of you. Even in this grief, you did not deviate from dharma. I believe none of us can answer this question with certainty. Yudhishthira is best suited to answer it himself.'[22]

'Why don't you ask this question to your husbands? I leave the answer to Bheema, Arjuna, Nakula and

Sahadeva. If they state outright that Yudhishthira had no moral right to stake you and prove Yudhishthira wrong, I will let you go,' Duryodhana[23] mockingly said.

This was a smart move. Everybody turned to the Pāndavas to see how they responded. Eventually, Arjuna spoke up, 'Yudhishthira, being our elder brother, had the right to stake us. But after he staked himself and lost any claim on his own self, how can he have a claim over anyone else? The court needs to think over this.'

Suddenly, the assembly was distracted by the loud howling of a jackal. As if in response to that, other jackals also started howling. A huge commotion was created. Vidura and Gāndhāri were quick to recognise the bad omens and pleaded with Dhritarāshtra to intervene.

Draupadi Saves the Day for the Pāndavas

Shaken by Bheema's pledge and appearance of bad omens, Dhritarāshtra finally stood up and rebuked Duryodhana for his shameless action. To Draupadi, he said, 'You are a paragon of virtue and the best amongst my daughters-in-law. I grant you a wish. Ask me for anything and it will be done.'

Draupadi, even amidst the sheer display of ignominy and in spite of being immensely hurt and humiliated, exhibited her dignity and class. She responded, 'If you wish to give me something, liberate Yudhishthira from the servitude of Duryodhana.' Dhritarāshtra agreed and told her to ask for one more wish. This time, Draupadi sought the liberation of the other Pāndavas along with their weapons. 'So be it,' said Dhritarāshtra and then added, 'It is my desire to grant you one more wish.' This time Draupadi exclaimed, 'Greed destroys virtue. I have no desire, nor the right to ask for a third wish. Now that my husbands are free, they will fulfil my wishes by their own potential.'

The entire gathering was in awe of Drauapdi's response. Impressed, Karna commented, 'I have seen many beautiful women before but none has done what Draupadi did today. The Pāndavas were drowning in turbulent waters and this wife of theirs, like a steady boat, came by and safely steered them to shore.'

Duryodhana and his coterie, however, were still not deterred from their scheming. Another game of dice was arranged. The loser was to live the next twelve years in a forest and spend the thirteenth year in disguise. As expected, Shakuni won and the Pāndavas were banished to the forests. Draupadi could have gone back to her father's palace with her sons. But she chose to stand by her husbands and accompanied them to the forest.

The Days in the Forest

Draupadi was a princess who had lived in luxury in Drupada's palace. She lived in grandeur as a queen and wife of the Pāndavas. A forest life was not for her but she chose to be where her husbands were. In the forest, Draupadi assumed the responsibility of feeding rishis and guests who came to visit them. She remained a gracious host even in her forest hut. Neither did she ever complain about spending her initial few days with the Pāndavas in a potter's humble hut, nor did she complain about the hardships of forest life now. She opened her heart and vented out her pain only once when Krishna came to visit.

But Draupadi did not let herself forget the humiliation she faced in that assembly of Hastināpur. She did not let her husbands forget about the insult either. Her husbands had to avenge the affront—that much she was clear about. Hence, she wasn't averse to speaking her mind and reminding the Pāndavas of their goal when she had to. Draupadi's arguments were well thought out and aligned with dharma. She displayed her wisdom and learning in various conversations with the Pāndavas while dwelling in the forest.

Once, while explaining the roles of anger and forgiveness for a warrior, she said, 'A warrior who doesn't manifest his anger when the time demands is disregarded and one who doesn't forgive when the situation demands is not liked. Both anger and forgiveness matter and have to be employed with discretion as per the situation.'[24] Yudhishthira had his reasons to argue otherwise. He propounded the virtues of forgiveness and also told Draupadi to not question the ways of dharma. 'I am not doubting the ways of dharma at all. It pains me to see you brothers go through hardship that you do not deserve. I have only expressed my thoughts and I will continue to do so. You must listen to me graciously,' Draupadi asserted.[25]

She further explained the importance of enterprise for the successful achievement of a task and the attitude with which a task must be approached. 'It behoves every person to act per his nature and seek the fulfilment of his goals. Without enterprise, nothing can be achieved. Manu has said, "Every person must work. A man who does nothing is certainly defeated." Though enterprise alone doesn't determine the outcome. That depends on two additional factors—fate and the grace of the almighty. Hence, a man should strive to do his duty but not become dejected if the outcome is not per his choice. What matters is the effort that was put in. Therefore, irrespective of the result, one must work towards achieving a noble goal.'[26] She said this to motivate the brothers to not become content with forest life and focus on their ultimate objective. The Pāndavas had built Indraprastha with a lot of effort; the land was a part of their inheritance but the prosperous kingdom was what they had toiled to establish with their sweat and blood. They were noble-hearted and bore no ill will towards anyone. Hence, giving up their kingdom just because someone deceptively stole it was not an option agreeable to Draupadi.

Twice during the thirteen years of vanvās, attempts were made to violate her dignity. Once, when the Pāndavas had gone hunting, Jayadratha happened to pass by their āshram in the forest. Jayadratha was Dushālā's husband, Dhritarāshtra's son-in-law and the brother-in-law of the Kauravas and the Pāndavas. He saw Draupadi standing by the entrance of the hut and was beguiled. He was so taken in by her beauty that the sanctity of their relationship was lost on him. He tried to abduct her forcibly. Draupadi resisted fiercely but he was too strong for her. The purohit[27] of the Pāndavas, Rishi Dhaumya, tried to stop him in vain. Jayadratha captured him too and sped away.

The Pāndavas didn't take too long to return to the hut. The helpers told them about the abduction. The brothers went the way Jayadratha and his army had gone. A scuffle followed, after which Draupadi and Rishi Dhaumya were rescued and brought back. Jayadratha escaped but was pursued and caught by Bheema and Arjuna. Bheema trimmed his head bald, leaving five ponies and made him say, 'I am the slave of Yudhishthira.' Subsequently, thinking about Dushālā, Yudhishthira suggested they let him go. Draupadi agreed, 'Now that you have already ridiculed him by making him bald leaving these five tufts, and he has also accepted that he is Yudhishthira's slave, let him go,'[28] she said.

The other incident happened in Matsya desh during their year of agyātvās. Draupadi had found work in the royal palace as Sairāndhri, a handmaiden of Sudeshnā, the queen of Matsya. Initially, Sudeshnā hesitated. The queen was awestruck by Sairāndhri's beauty. 'The king will certainly fall for her if he sees her,' Sudeshnā thought. Only when Sairāndhri told her that she was a wife of five Gandharva husbands and they guarded her all the time, was Sudeshnā convinced. Sairāndhri also casually mentioned that she had worked as the handmaiden of Draupadi and Satyabhāmā before. That was a clincher.[29]

Sudeshnā had a powerful brother called Keechak, who was also the commander of her husband, King Virāta's forces. He saw Draupadi by chance while he was visiting his sister, and was struck by her beauty. He tried to charm Draupadi with his wealth and strength. Draupadi fended off his advances but he wouldn't refrain. Once, when he tried to force himself on her, she ran to the court of Virāta to seek protection. The haughty Keechak kicked her before the assembly and King Virāta looked the other way. Draupadi realised Virāta was too dependent on Keechak to give her justice. Nevertheless, she decided Keechak had to die for his misbehaviour. She sought Bheema's help. One morning, Keechak was found dead, his body gorily mangled. Everyone believed one of Sairāndhri's Gandharva husbands had punished Keechak.[30] No one messed with her after that. Whatever be the situation, Draupadi always held her head high.

Of War and Peace

The thirteen years of exile had ended. The Pāndavas' endeavour to get Indraprastha back had begun. They had not forgotten the insult heaped on them by Duryodhana and his coterie. But in the interest of their clan and to avoid bloodshed, Yudhishthira favoured getting his kingdom back by negotiations rather than by weapons. He was willing to settle for only five villages in lieu of Indraprastha if that could keep the war at bay. That, too, wasn't acceptable to Duryodhana. Even then, Yudhishthira wanted to give peace one more chance, so he requested Krishna to go to Hastināpur as their emissary.

Draupadi was not in favour of this prolonged pacifist stance. What upset her more was Bheema's stand, who, too, was inclined towards a peaceful settlement for the sake of keeping the family together.[31] She firmly believed Duryodhana, Karna and Duhshāsana and all those who favoured them deserved to pay for their misdeeds with their lives. As always, she let her views be known.

In Upaplavya, where Pāndavas and their allies had gathered to discuss negotiations with the Kauravas, addressing Krishna, she said rather sadly but firmly, 'Please do not negotiate any settlement unless Duryodhana agrees to give us the kingdom back. I am confident the Pāndavas, with their powerful allies, are very capable of facing Duryodhana's forces. True warriors should not refrain from executing those who commit punishable offences driven by greed. It is wrong to kill the undeserving; likewise, it is wrong to not punish the deserving. Nor should you forget how a woman like me, the wife of the Pāndavas, the mother of their sons, the daughter of Pānchāla, was humiliated in that court of Hastināpur. I am also the daughter-in-law of Dhritarāshtra and Bhishma and yet I was insulted before their eyes. Damned be the bow of Arjuna and the strength of Bheema if Duryodhana is allowed to live this way!' added Draupadi, unable to control the flow of emotions.

Holding forth her long black curly hair, she walked up to Krishna. 'When you talk about a peace treaty with the Kauravas, do recall the hand of Duhshāsana that dragged me pulling my hair. If Bheema and Arjuna are going to seek peace like cowards, then so be it. I am certain my old father and brother as well as my valiant sons, including Abhimanyu, will fight for my dignity. These talks of peace are burning my heart!' she agonised.

Krishna consoled her, 'Those who have disparaged you and made you cry, their wives and family will cry after them—that, I assure you. Yudhishthira, Bheema, Arjuna, Nakula, Sahadeva and I will do only that which you desire. Worry not and trust me. Your husbands will take back their kingdom soon.'[32]

The war happened. Her husbands, sons and brothers fought unafraid of the consequences, exactly as Draupadi would have wanted them to. Her father died on the battlefield, her foster sons, Abhimanyu, Irāvan and Ghatotkacha, laid down their lives, as did the sons of her brother. Draupadi took it in her stride. A warrior's wife had to be strong. But when she heard about the slaughter of her five sons by Ashwatthāmā, Draupadi was completely devastated and was unable to stop herself from showing her anguish. More than the death of her sons, it was the manner in which Ashwatthāmā has killed them that shook her.

Her children were great warriors like their fathers. They had survived the war but had fallen victim to Ashwatthāmā's deceit. He had attacked the Pāndava camp in the night when the warriors were fast asleep.

Such a cowardly act deserved the severest punishment. Draupadi demanded that her husbands punish Ashwatthāmā, the vile son of their guru, and get her the gem embedded in his forehead. She threatened to kill herself if Drona's son was let go with impunity for his treacherous act.

Bheema was already agitated. Draupadi's grief triggered his anger further. He left to look for Ashwatthāmā and the others followed. Ashwatthāmā was punished by Krishna. The gem he was born with was cut out from his forehead, leaving in its place an ever-festering wound. Bheema handed the gem to Draupadi. He recalled her words in Upaplavya. She had demanded justice, even if it meant a war to punish Duryodhana and his sympathisers. He said, 'We have claimed back what was ours and avenged the humiliation. We let Ashwatthāmā live because he is our guru's son but he has been reduced to merely a body. Remember those brave words of yours and grieve no more.'

She saw the gem and instantly calmed down. 'I was lamenting the death of my sons and seeking a fair retribution. As he was your guru's son, so was he for me. I did not want his death. This gem has given me the closure I sought. May Yudhishthira wear the gem on his crown,' she said, collecting herself.[33]

Post the war, when Yudhishthira was a shattered man and wanted to renounce the kingdom, Draupadi reminded him of his Rāja Dharma, his responsibility towards his kingdom, its citizens and his brothers.[34]

As the queen of Hāstinapur, she once again assumed all the responsibilities expected of her, including looking after her in-laws, the widowed wives of the Kauravas and the day-to-day administration of the palace and household. Such was her grace and wisdom.

Draupadi was not the only wife of the Pāndavas but she was the only one who was with them from the day of her swayamvara to the day of her death. Thirty-six years after war, when Yudhishthira renounced his throne and the Pāndavas ventured to the forest to spend their last days, the only wife they took along was Draupadi. Arjuna had remarked to Vyāsa after Krishna's death, 'Krishna, Draupadi and us five brothers are different bodies with one heart.'[35]

Myths about Draupadi

Myth: Draupadi mocked Duryodhana calling him the 'blind son of a blind man'.

Fact: The festivities of the Rājasuya Yajna had ended, Duryodhana stayed back in Indraprastha to explore the city and the palace, which was designed by Maya Dānava. Apart from being an architect par excellence, Maya was adept in creating illusionary structures. While exploring the palace, due to an illusionary image, he didn't see the pond of water and fell in.

Per some much-popularised stories in the media, it is said that seeing Duryodhana fall, Draupadi laughed and called him the 'blind son of a blind father'. This story is used to justify the subsequent humiliation of Draupadi and the war is attributed to her slight.

But there is no mention of any such insult by Draupadi in any of the accepted manuscripts or translations. Gita Press says, 'the Pāndava brothers and other helpers around laughed at the fall'. But no there is no mention of anyone saying anything to mock Duryodhana. When Duryodhana goes back to Hastināpur and narrates the incident, he includes Draupadi among those who laughed but doesn't say anything about him being called 'andhe ka putra andha—Blind son of a blind father'.

Myth: Draupadi asked for Duhshāsana's blood to wash her hair to avenge her humiliation.

Fact: Bheema had declared he would rip apart Duhshāsana's chest and drink his blood to avenge the latter's insult of Draupadi. Per his vow, Bheema did just that in Kurukshetra. However, there is no mention of Draupadi washing her hair from Duhshāsana's blood in the Mahābhārata texts. This story is a fictionalised account from a Sanskrit play *Venisamhāra* by Bhatta Narayan.

Myth: Draupadi was in love with Karna/Krishna.

Fact: There is absolutely nothing in the Mahābhārata that supports these claims. None of the known Sanskrit manuscripts and translations based on them, including the Gita Press, KMG, Dakshinātya recensions or BORI CE, have any verse implying the claim. This myth comes from 'reimagined', 'retold', 'creatively adapted' works based on the epic.

Draupadi looked up to Krishna as a friend and a guide. She shared her worries and pains with him. So did Arjuna. There was no romantic angle between Draupadi and Krishna. With respect to Karna, there is not one hint of Draupadi showing any interest in him.

From the incidents of Draupadi's swayamvara, the game of dice, Jayadratha's advances and Keechak's wooing, it is evident that Draupadi must have been a very attractive and sought-after woman. But nothing she did lends any credence to the myth of her being attracted to Karna or anyone else except the Pāndavas. Instead, in the Mahaprasthāna Parva 2.6, responding to Bheema's question regarding the fall of Draupadi on their final journey to heaven, Yudhishthira says, 'Though she was married to all of us, she loved Arjuna more.'

ॐ ψ ॐ

9

Sāvitri

That day in the Kaurava assembly, after the Pāndavas had lost it all in the game of dice, Draupadi salvaged their fractured dignity with her resoluteness, despite being subjected to inconceivable wretchedness herself. She had been nothing less than a saviour. Yudhishthira hadn't said much that day but he had never forgotten this unparalleled deed of hers.

One day, while the Pāndavas were living out their exile in the forest, Rishi Mārkandeya paid them a visit. During the conversation, Yudhishthira poured his heart out to the sage. Among other things, he said, 'I am not as anguished about losing my kingdom nor do the trials being faced by me or my brothers bother me as much as I feel woeful about what Krishnā is going through. She pulled us out of the distress that the evil Duryodhana and his friends had pushed us into during the game of dice. Even here in the jungle, people like Jayadratha have tormented her by trying to abduct her. Despite all this, she has been unflinching in her dedication towards us. Has there ever been any other lady in history who has been so steadfast in her commitment to her family and husbands like this daughter of Drupada?'[1]

Rishi Mārkandeya then told him the story of Sāvitri.

There lived a noble king named Ashwapati in Madra desh. The king had no child of his own even after years of marriage. Hence, with the hope to beget a child, he and his wife undertook rigorous austerities to appease Goddess Sāvitri. After eighteen years, a daughter was born to the couple. They named the girl Sāvitri, expressing their gratitude to the devi. The girl grew up to become a divinely beautiful young lady. She was wise and well versed in scriptures. Her aura was such that few princes had the courage to seek her hand in marriage.

When proposals were not forthcoming, Ashwapati asked Sāvitri to find a suitable match herself. 'Go find yourself a husband, a man equal in virtue to you. I will get you married to the boy you like,' he said. Off went Sāvitri, with some old ministers of her father, to search for a worthy partner. She travelled through various cities and towns, doing pilgrimages, meeting sages and looking for a prospective husband. While passing through a forest, she met a smart young man named Satyavān. Sāvitri was besotted in one meeting.

Satyavān was a prince of Shālva desh. When he was still a child, his father Dyumatsena was ousted from his kingdom by an act of aggression perpetrated by a neighbouring king. Since then, Dyumatsena and his wife, along with their baby boy, started living in the forest. Satyavān grew up in the forest. He was brave and humble, well mannered and well educated. Sāvitri had made up her mind to marry no one else but Satyavān. She returned to her kingdom and told her father as much.

But there was a problem. Devarshi Nārada, who was visiting the kingdom of Ashwapati, did not approve of the wedding. 'Is Satyavān not virtuous?' asked Ashwapati. 'Satyavān is as bright as the sun, as wise as the teacher of the devas, Brihaspati, as courageous as Indra and as firm and composed as the earth. He is generous, truthful, soft-spoken, restrained and very handsome,' replied Nārada, confounding both Sāvitri and her father. 'Then what is the problem?' they asked.

'Satyavān has a very short life. He has only a year left to live,' replied Nārada. Ashwapati, as would be expected of a father, did not wish to marry his only daughter to a person who was destined to die so soon. He asked Sāvitri to find another boy. Sāvitri, however, was adamant. 'I will marry Satyavān and no one else,' she asserted. Ashwapati gave in. He approached Dyumatsena to discuss the marriage of their children.

Dyumatsena hesitated at Ashwapati's proposal. 'Your daughter has grown up in the luxuries of the palace. We live here in the forest, in a humble āshram devoid of all comforts. If she marries into our family, she will have to live an austere life like ours. Do you think your daughter deserves this hardship?' he asked. Ashwapati responded affirmatively. 'Happiness and sorrow are ephemeral. Sāvitri and I have thought through all this and we believe you and your family are worthy of ours. Hence, we have approached you out of a genuine desire to have Satyavān marry my daughter.' Dyumatsena and his wife happily gave their approval for the wedding.

The marriage happened. Sāvitri went to live in the āshram with Satyavān and his family. She adjusted to the forest life very soon and very well. She was a good wife and a great daughter-in-law, taking good care of her parents-in-law. Satyavān, in turn, was a loving and affectionate husband. Sāvitri was blissful but also acutely aware that her bliss was going to be short-lived. She kept a mental note of the days that passed and those that remained. Even then, she did not let her anxiety show, nor did she tell anyone about it.

When there were only four days left in Satyavān's life, Sāvitri undertook a three-day fast. In addition to not eating, she had decided to stand all day and night for those three days. Her parents-in-law were surprised and worried. They tried to dissuade her but Sāvitri comforted them. 'I am doing this to fulfil my mental resolve. I will be perfectly fine,' she said. She desisted from telling them about what the resolve was, not wanting to worry them further.

The fourth day arrived. Satyavān got up to leave for the forest to get some wood and fruits for the āshram. Sāvitri requested him to take her along. 'The road is uneven and you haven't even eaten a morsel since the last three days. It is not a good idea to take this trip. I will be back soon,' he reassured her, but Sāvitri insisted, 'I do not wish to be away from you today. I haven't left the āshram in months. I'll be fine. Take me along.'

Satyavān relented and off they went. As they walked through the lush green forest, Satyavān was in a very happy mood. He pointed out the flowers, birds and fruits on the way. Sāvitri was torn inside. She loved the way his face lit up when he was happy and excited. She attempted to reflect his joyousness as she kept praying for his life in her heart.

After collecting the fruits and wood, Satyavān sat down for a bit. His head had begun to spin and he was profusely sweating. Sāvitri had a lump in her throat. The moment she so wanted to avoid was staring in her face. But she kept calm. She took Satyavān's head in her lap so that he could lie down and rest. His body had become cold. She could sense his energy drop. And then he was breathing no more.

Just then, a dark man with blazing red eyes and a bright aura appeared out of nowhere. Sāvitri softly put her husband's head on the ground and stood up to greet the stranger. 'You seem to me like a deity because your body is not like ours. Please tell me who you are and why are you here?' she asked. The stranger introduced himself, 'I am Yama, the lord of death. Mortals can't see me. You are able to see me because you are a virtuous and pious lady. Satyavān has reached the end of his prescribed life and I have come to take him away. You better get back now and do the final rites for your husband.'

He then pulled out a thumb-like flame of light from Satyavān's body and headed away towards the west. Sāvitri followed him. 'How can I leave my husband? It behoves me to go where he goes,' she said. Having walked a little further, she struck a conversation with Yama. 'Wise men have said that walking seven steps alongside a stranger establishes a bond of friendship between them. With the consideration of that friendship established between us, I wish to tell you something.'

'Go ahead, say what you want,' said Yama, intrigued.

Sāvitri began expounding on the concept of dharma and the importance of controlling one's mind and senses to lead a fruitful life. Yama was pleased with her wisdom as well as her speech. 'You are a wise woman. I wish to offer you a boon. Ask me for anything except your husband's life,' he said. 'Sir, if you so wish, please let my father-in-law get back his kingdom and his health,' she asked. 'It will be as you say. Now get back to your āshram,' said Yama and walked away. Sāvitri, however, continued to walk behind him.

Then she began talking about the importance of satsang—association with the wise and the learned to improve one's own life. Impressed with Sāvitri's knowledge, Yama offered her one more boon. She could ask for anything except her husband's life. This time, she requested Yama to bless her father with brave and capable sons who could carry forward his lineage and expand his kingdom. Yama agreed and again asked her to return. But she was not the kind to give up.

Sāvitri continued her conversation. This time she explained the qualities of sages and saints. 'People trust sages more than even their own selves. That is because sages are affectionate towards one and all. Affection inspires trust.' Yama was charmed, 'You surely are an astute woman. Rarely do I come across people with such maturity.' Saying so, he offered her one more boon. 'Anything except your husband's life,' he said. Sāvitri was not just wise, she was also very smart. 'May Satyavān and I have a hundred children, valiant and virtuous, who will carry the reputation of our family forward,' she asked.

'So be it, you shall have a hundred children. Now please go back. You have already come a long way,' said Yama without a moment's thought hoping she would go away. 'How can I return without Satyavān?' she asked. 'Your boon can come true only if I can live with Satyavān as his wife. To keep your word, Sir, I request you grant my husband life. Without him, I am as good as dead,' Sāvitri pleaded.

Yama laughed aloud. He had been outwitted by this damsel. 'You have won me over with your wisdom, speech and sincerity. I will do as you wish. Satyavān will regain his life. Together, you shall have a hundred children and live a healthy and happy life.'[2] Yama blessed her and went away.

Sāvitri bowed to the lord of death and rushed back to the place where Satyavān's body lay. Soon, he sat upright, as if he had just woken up from a deep slumber. He looked at his wife lovingly. 'It seems like I slept for too long.' Sāvitri smiled and the couple headed back to the āshram.

In due course, all the boons given by Yama began to materialise. She had kids of her own. Her father-in-law got back his kingdom through public discontent against the king who had ousted him. And her parents had the kind of children who could carry their prestigious name ahead.

'Thus, Sāvitri, by her devotion, wisdom and resoluteness not only resurrected her husband but also became the benefactor of her father and father-in-law,' said Mārkandeya to Yudhishthira.

ॐ ψ ॐ

10

A Friendship of Doom

Both were very strong and very brave. Both were capable and ambitious. One wanted to be the only inheritor of the mighty Hastināpur kingdom, the other wanted to be recognised as the greatest warrior on earth. One believed his blind father was unjustly not given the kingdom that belonged to him being the eldest son. The other believed he wasn't getting his due recognition only because everyone was biased towards Arjuna. Had the two not met, the course of history would have been different. But Duryodhana and Karna did meet. The resentment against the same enemy tied them together into an everlasting bond of interdependence. The war at Kurukshetra was a culmination of their ambition. Duryodhana believed a warrior like Karna by his side made him invincible. For Karna, victory mattered not as much as defeating Arjuna.

While introducing the Mahābhārata to Rishi Shaunak and his students in Naimishāranya, Ugrashravā Sauti says, 'Duryodhana was a huge tree of rage. Karna was the trunk of this tree, Shakuni its branches and Duhshāsana its fruit. Dhritarāshtra was the root of this tree.'[1]

The Making of the Bond

Karna and Duryodhana met in the āshram of Dronāchārya as students. Their jealousy of the Pāndavas brought them close. Karna wanted to learn the Brahmāstra from Dronāchārya to be able to fight with Arjuna. Drona refused his request. He did not consider Karna to be capable of responsibly handling such a deadly weapon. Moreover, he was aware of Karna's ill will towards Arjuna. Karna went away to Parashurāma, lied about being a Brāhmin and implored the latter to become his guru. Unaware of the falsehood, Parashurāma agreed. Karna was a dedicated student. He pleased Parashurāma with his hard work and skills. In return, Parashurāma gave Karna the knowledge of the Brahmāstra. When Parashurāma got to know of the lie, he warned Karna that the weapon acquired through falsehood would be of no use when faced with death or a warrior as good as he was. Nevertheless, Karna was happy. He was now well equipped to face Arjuna, he thought.

By the time Karna finished his training with Parashurāma, the Kauravas and the Pāndavas too had finished their training. A ceremony was held to celebrate the completion of education of the princes and allow the citizens to witness their skills. After Arjuna had left the audience mesmerised with his display of awe-inspiring weapons, Karna walked into the pavilion, uninvited and unexpected. Looking at Arjuna, he declared, 'I will display even more extraordinary acts than what you have shown, Pārtha[2]. You watch them and be amazed.' He sought Drona's permission, who, having recognised his student, allowed him to take the stage. Karna proceeded to exhibit his skills leaving the audience agape.

Duryodhana was elated to see Karna, and even more to see him challenge Arjuna. He welcomed him with open arms and said, 'It is my good fortune that you've come. I offer you myself and this kingdom. Live as you please and enjoy the luxuries with me.' Karna was also happy to see Duryodhana and was touched by his generous welcome.

'I trust your word. But all I seek is your friendship and a duel with Arjuna.' The Pāndavas were furious. Karna's challenge to Arjuna was uncalled for and unprovoked. Karna had gate-crashed a function meant to mark the completion of the training of the princes of Hastināpur. Nonetheless, not the one to back out, Arjuna accepted the challenge.

However, the function was to felicitate the princes and watch them demonstrate their skills. It was not a battleground. Kripāchārya, the royal priest of Hastināpur, handled the situation smartly. 'Only a prince can challenge a prince to a duel or a Kshatriya to another Kshatriya to ensure the fight is on equal grounds,' he said and then gave Arjuna's introduction. 'Now introduce yourself,' said Kripa to Karna. Karna stood there unable to speak. He was from a community of Sutas, a mixed community of Brāhmins and Kshatriyas. More importantly, he was not a prince.

Angered by Karna's unjustified aggression towards Arjuna, Bheema taunted, 'Why is a Suta challenging my warrior brother? Let him rather pick up the reins of a chariot.' Duryodhana hit back, 'A warrior's identity is his valour, not his birth. And if he needs to be a prince to challenge Arjuna, so be it. I pronounce him the king of Anga desh.'

Anga desh was the janapada of Karna's father Adhiratha. It was under allegiance to Hastināpur. He crowned Karna there and then. No one objected to the coronation—not then, not later. In all this discussion and verbal feud, the sun went down. The day ended and the duel was averted much to the relief of the elders.

Arjuna's superior warfare skills had been a source of constant worry for Duryodhana. With the arrival of Karna, Duryodhana was relieved;[3] he had found a warrior who could match Arjuna. Karna, on his end, felt indebted to Duryodhana. Standing with him would give Karna a chance to fight Arjuna and show the world he was the greatest warrior. Thus was laid the foundation of a lifelong partnership.

After being crowned the king of Anga desh, Karna became a regular in the Hastināpur court. He became an inseparable part of Duryodhana's close coterie of advisors, along with Shakuni and Duhshāsana. As a loyal friend, Karna stood by Duryodhana, irrespective of the merit of his decision. Rather, he ensured Duryodhana never compromised on his enmity with the Pāndavas. Whenever the Kaurava elders tried to reason with Duryodhana to patch up with the Pāndavas for his own interests and for the benefit of the kingdom, Karna would dismiss those concerns, bragging about his own skills. While he did not always approve of Shakuni's diplomatic manoeuvres, he was a willing accomplice. His preference, however, was to fight the Pāndavas head-on.

Indraprastha and the Game of Dice

The Pāndavas had survived the Vāranāvata fire. They were alive and deserved their share in inheritance. The Hastināpur assembly had gathered to decide the future course of action. Bhishma proposed the division of the kingdom so that both Duryodhana and Yudhishthira had a fair share of their ancestral kingdom. After the division, the fight over accession to the Hastināpur throne would end peacefully, he had hoped. Dronāchārya and Vidura supported the proposal, saying this was in line with tradition and in the interest of both sides. But Karna dissented. 'Even though you have always respected them and sought their advice, these ministers of yours are advising you to do that which is against your interest. What can be more shocking than this?! How will those with wicked intentions give you any beneficial suggestions?' he taunted Bhishma and Drona as he addressed Dhritarāshtra.[4] Not only did Karna oppose the proposal, but he also raised doubts over Bhishma and Drona's sincerity, commitment and intent towards Dhritarāshtra.

The decision of division was taken anyway. Duryodhana kept Hastināpur and the Pāndavas were given Khāndavaprastha, a barren land, which, through sheer effort, they transformed into a prosperous city of Indraprastha. In a very short time, Yudhishthira conducted the Rājasuya Yajna and became a sovereign king of Bhāratavarsha with the help of his brothers. The progress and grandeur of the Pāndavas was unbearable for Duryodhana. A game of dice was thus planned to trap them.

The occasion turned into an abhorrent display of malice where even the dignity of the daughter-in-law of Hastināpur was not spared. Shakuni provoked Yudhishthira to stake Draupadi. Yudhishthira did and lost; he had already staked his brothers and himself before and lost. Duryodhana ordered Duhshāsana to drag Draupadi into the assembly.[5] Duhshāsana pulled Draupadi by her hair and dragged his menstruating sister-in-law into the assembly full of men. Every single person in the audience was appalled but said nothing. Vikarna, Duryodhana's younger brother, rose in protest against such unjust and shameful treatment of Draupadi. Karna silenced him, calling him a destroyer of the Kauravas.[6]

Shakuni, Duryodhana and Duhshāsana had already crossed the line of decency by their words and actions. But Karna surpassed them all. He called Draupadi a bandhaki, a prostitute. He justified Draupadi being pulled by her hair and brought into the hall in just one piece of garment. 'A woman is prescribed only one husband. But Draupadi has five. That makes her no less than a prostitute. I see no problem for a woman like that to be brought into the hall with one garment or even no garment at all,' he mocked.

Turning to Duhshāsana, he said provocatively, 'Vikarna is young and stupid; hence he pretends to talk like a wise man. Disregard him and proceed to disrobe Draupadi, as well as the Pāndavas.[7] Duhshāsana began pulling Draupadi's garment, but all his efforts were in vain. He collapsed, embarrassed. Karna, however, was not done yet. He rebuked Draupadi for questioning the legality of being staked by Yudhishthira. 'A wife is always subservient to the husband. Your husbands have become slaves of Duryodhana and so have you. From today, the Kauravas are your masters. Serve them as a slave should. Or, if you so wish, find yourself a new husband,' he ridiculed.[8] Duryodhana, unable to hide his pleasure, laughed aloud and flashed his left thigh to Draupadi, inviting her to sit on it.[9]

Bheema had already pledged to rip apart Duhshāsana's chest for laying his hands on Draupadi. Seeing Duryodhana's lewd gesture, he roared even louder. 'If I do not break that thigh of yours in the war, may I never get the heavens.'[10] Every cell of Bheema's body was burning with anger. He could have punished Duryodhana right there but was held back by Yudhishthira's restraint.

Dhritarāshtra intervened and annulled that game, only to invite Yudhishthira to play another round, as Duryodhana desired. Yudhishthira had no option but to respect his uncle's invitation. He lost again and accepted the thirteen years of vanvās as per the condition set out for losing the second game of dice. The brothers and Draupadi followed Yudhishthira. Before leaving, Arjuna, like Bheema, took the vow to kill Karna and Sahadeva pledged to kill Shakuni if a war was mandated after their vanvās.

The Pāndavas left for the forest but Duryodhana was still not happy. A thought worried him incessantly—'What if Vidura, Bhishma and the others convince Dhritarāshtra to call the Pāndavas back sooner?' Shakuni's idea was to keep a track of the blindspots of the Pāndavas and exploit those for Duryodhana's advantage. Karna suggested they go and kill the Pāndavas in the forest itself and solve the problem forever.[11] Duryodhana agreed. But Vyāsa Muni intervened and stopped Duryodhana from attempting another misadventure.

The Cattle Inspection (Ghosh Yatra)

After having spent five years on an expedition to accumulate celestial weapons, Arjuna had returned with the Pashupatāstra and other weapons. The other brothers had embarked on a pilgrimage when Arjuna was away. In the meanwhile, Duryodhana had established his sway over other kingdoms in Bhāratavarsha as he had no fear from the Pāndavas. He was revelling in his power and luxury. One day, he learnt that the Pāndavas had camped in the forest of Dwaita near Hastināpur. 'Is there a more joyous experience than seeing your rivals in tatters? Imagine the happiness we would get seeing Arjuna clothed in the bark of a tree and animal skin? Let's go visit them. Let them look at our riches and lament at their misery,' suggested Karna and Shakuni.

Under the pretext of inspecting the cattle wealth of Hastināpur, off went an entourage of Duryodhana, including Karna, Shakuni, the other Kauravas with their large retinue of women and servants, to the forest where the Pāndavas were residing. They chose a campsite near the humble āshram that the Pāndavas had set up. Their aim was to show off their wealth and prosperity to the Pāndavas, but destiny had other plans. While trying to pitch their luxurious tents, Duryodhana and his army had a run-in with the Gandharvas who were also in the forest at that time. The clash quickly degenerated into a full-fledged battle. Karna and the other Kauravas put up a brave fight but the Gandharvas were way more powerful and elusive. At one point, Karna was so overpowered and injured that he ran away from the battlefield to save his life.

Duryodhana was badly injured too. He continued to fight but was captured by the Gandharvas, along with the other Kauravas and the women. The few soldiers who managed to escape rushed to Yudhishthira for help. Yudhishthira, as was expected of him, asked his brothers to rescue the cousins. The brothers, after some resistance, complied. Another terrible battle followed, this time between the four Pāndavas and the entire Gandharva army. The brothers prevailed and rescued the Kauravas. Yudhishthira assured them of a safe return to Hastināpur.

Karna joined the Kaurava crew on their way back to Hastināpur. Assuming the Gandharvas had been defeated by Duryodhana and his warriors, Karna congratulated Duryodhana and explained his running away. 'I was severely injured and in a lot of pain,'[12] he said. Duryodhana was so consumed by distress that Karna's running away meant little to him.

He told him the truth of their rescue by Bheema, Arjuna, Nakula and Sahadeva. The Pāndavas' feat was a clear testimony to their competence and their large-heartedness. By rescuing Duryodhana and his entourage, the Pāndavas had humiliated him. It was an embarrassment he did not wish to live with. He decided to fast unto death.[13]

For once, Shakuni gave him sane advice. 'The Pāndavas have treated you well. You shouldn't grieve over that. Rather, you should return their gesture in kind. Return to them their kingdom. Show your large-heartedness and be happy,' opined Shakuni.[14] His words aggravated Duryodhana's grief.

Karna consoled him, 'The Pāndavas have done you no favour. You are their king after all. It behooves the citizens to do what is right for their king. They have only done what is expected of your subjects.' To encourage Duryodhana, Karna added, 'In spite of losing everything, the Pāndavas haven't killed themselves; why should you?' These words didn't assuage Duryodhana's pain. Karna sensed what Duryodhana wished to hear, 'If Arjuna has scared you so much that you wish to die, then let me assure you that I will kill Arjuna. I vow to make the Pāndavas subservient to you after the thirteenth year of their vanvās,' he professed. Duryodhana relented and returned to Hastināpur.[15]

Indra's Request for Charity

Karna was born with the kavacha, a golden armour, and kundala, a pair of golden earrings. It was said that the kavacha would protect Karna's body from death in a war. He had been defeated in battles before but killing him was not going to be easy, not for Arjuna or anyone else. This had been a cause of worry for Indra, Arjuna's biological father. He thought of a plan to rid Karna of this congenital advantage.

Karna was a devout worshipper of the sun. It was his morning ritual to chant the Vedic mantras to the sun and give charities to seekers who came his way after the worship. He was under a self-imposed oath that he would never deny anything asked of him, if a seeker asked for it after his morning ritual, more so if the seeker was a Brāhmin. One such morning, Indra, in the guise of a Brāhmin, approached Karna and sought his kavacha and kundala. Karna was expecting Indra. He had been warned about Indra by his biological father, Surya. He had instructed his son against giving away the divine armour. But Karna did not want to break his vow. Surya then came up with another suggestion. 'When Indra asks you for your kavacha and kundala, seek a gift in return, a gift of his powerful Indrāstra.'[16]

On Indra's request, Karna agreed to give him his kavacha and kundala and asked for the Indrāstra in return. Indra agreed and gave Karna the weapon he desired. The weapon was foolproof but came with a clause. It could be used only once to kill only one warrior. 'So be it,' said Karna and gave away his kavacha and kundala.[17] His goal in life was to kill Arjuna. With this weapon of Indra's, he was now equipped to take down Arjuna—or so he thought.

Adhiratha and Rādhā had named their boy Vasushena as he was born with golden armour and earrings.[18] He came to be known as Karna because he readily cut off his kavacha and kundala, notwithstanding the excruciating pain.[19]

The Battle of Virāta

According to the condition of the game of dice, the Pāndavas had to spend the thirteenth year of the vanvās in hiding. If exposed, they would have to accept vanvās for another thirteen years. The Pāndavas zeroed in on Matsya desh to spend their year of hiding. Yudhishthira, as Kanka, became a courtier and confidant of Virāta, the king of Matsya. Bheema took up the role of the royal head chef, as Vallabha. Nakula, as Granthika, took charge of the horses and Sahadeva, as Tantipāla, began tending the king's cattle. Arjuna, as the eunuch Brihannalā, assumed the role of a dance and music teacher for the women in the palace. Draupadi, as Sairāndhri, became the handmaiden of Sudeshnā, the queen of Virāta, taking care of the queen's hair and dressing.

The year passed peacefully until Keechak saw Draupadi in Sudeshnā's palace one day. He was instantly infatuated by her beauty. He attempted to beguile her into accepting him as her lover. Draupadi rejected his overtures. She pleaded with him to stay away as she was married to five Gandharva men. Keechak didn't budge. When his entreaties turned into force, she complained in the court of Virāta. But the king, whose military prowess depended on Keechak, did nothing. As always, Bheema came to

Draupadi's rescue and killed Keechak. The people of Matsya believed Keechak was killed by one of Sairāndhri's Gandharva husbands.

In Hastināpur, Duryodhana had activated his spy network to track the Pāndavas. However, the year was almost ending and the efforts were yet to yield any result. Just when Duryodhana was wondering how to get to the Pāndavas, news of the death of the powerful commander of Matsya desh arrived. Keechak was so adept and strong that killing him was no trivial task. Only three warriors were considered capable enough of killing him—Bheema, Balarāma and Shalya.[20] Duryodhana pondered over the news. He had a strong inkling that the killer must have been Bheema. He needed to locate their hideout before the year ended. The question was how?

Coincidently, Susharmā, the king of the Trigarta,[21] approached Duryodhana with a proposal to attack Matsya desh. Keechak had been a source of constant harassment for the people of Trigarta. With him gone, King Virāta would be easy to subjugate, Susharmā had envisaged. The plan appealed to Duryodhana. Under the pretext of helping Trigarta to settle scores with Matsya and taking away its large cattle wealth, Duryodhana enlisted the support of Bhishma, Drona and others to wage a war against Matsya. The plan was to mount a dual attack, one led by Susharmā from the south-east on the seventh day of the waning moon, and on the next day by the Kauravas from the opposite side.

When Yudhishthira heard about the attack on Matsya, he convinced Virāta to take along Vallabha,

Tantipāla, Granthika and himself for its defence. 'These boys are capable warriors also trusted by the Pāndavas,' he said. Virāta agreed. The battle occurred and Susharmā's army was routed. He was himself captured by Bheema and was let go by Virāta on Kanka's advice. While Virāta and the four Pāndavas were busy with Susharmā, the Kaurava army had attacked Matsya from the opposite side as planned. In the absence of the king, the news of the attack was delivered to Uttar, Virāta's son.

Uttar was a young prince who had never faced a battle before. Nonetheless, in the charm of his youth, he believed he could easily take on the Kaurava army. Sairāndhri recommended that he take Brihannalā along. 'Even Arjuna would trust Brihannalā as his sārthi,' she convinced him. Uttar with Arjuna dressed as Brihannalā as his charioteer reached the battlefield where the Kaurava army was pitched.

Seeing the huge Kaurava army adorned by indomitable warriors such as Bhishma, Drona, Kripa, Duryodhana, Karna and Ashwatthāmā among others, Uttar was scared out of his wits. He jumped off his chariot and began to run away. Arjuna took charge. Revealing his real self to Uttar, Arjuna asked him to become the charioteer while he fought the Kauravas. By then, Arjuna was certain that their agyātvās year was over.[22]

The Kauravas were initially surprised to see a eunuch on Uttar's chariot. Soon enough, though, they guessed the man was none other than the tall and handsome Arjuna. Their expectation of victory had begun to diminish. Sensing strange omens around,

Dronāchārya expressed his concern, 'This eunuch is indeed Arjuna, the student of Indra himself, who has even humbled the mighty Shiva with his skill in warfare. I don't see any warrior here who can successfully face him.' Duryodhana was rather pleased. He believed he had achieved his goal of exposing the Pāndavas before the year of their hiding was up. Now they would have no choice but spend another thirteen years in the forest. However, he still needed to bring Arjuna out in the open. Hence, he asks the Kaurava elders to fight as promised to Susharmā, irrespective of who the eunuch was.

Karna, however, took Drona's words personally. 'You always praise Arjuna, but truly he isn't even a sixteenth as skilful as Duryodhana or myself,' he charged. Addressing Duryodhana, he said, 'The āchārya has always been biased towards the Pāndavas. That is why he talks about omens now. By declaring the eunuch as Arjuna, he is trying to scare our soldiers. Teachers like him are only good for teaching and telling stories. They are prone to timidity in a real war. You better place him at the back of the army and fight.'

Continuing to vent his bitterness, Karna added, 'If the Kaurava elders are scared and don't wish to fight, so be it. Even if that person is Arjuna, I alone will stop him from moving ahead with my excellent arrows. Arjuna may be a great warrior, but I am no less. I will kill him today in this war and fulfil the pledge I had made to Duryodhana. I will pounce upon him like a vulture pounces on a snake. Using all the weapons I have learnt from Parashurāma, I will destroy Arjuna with his chariot, horses and flag.

Others who do not wish to fight may just watch our combat.'[23]

Karna's boastful outburst angered Kripāchārya. 'Karna, when it comes to war, you have always been cruel and reckless. You rarely think about potential consequences. A war has to be fought carefully, considering the propriety of time and place. A reckless decision usually ends up in a defeat.' He then recounted all of Arjuna's war-time escapades, where he had defeated huge enemy forces and the mightiest of warriors single-handedly. Kripāchārya reminded Karna how Arjuna had spent the time of vanvās furthering his knowledge of weapons and had become stronger than ever before by the grace of Shiva and Indra who had bestowed upon him the best of weapons. 'What have you achieved Karna, to match the feats of the other Pāndavas, let alone Arjuna? Don't you boast about fighting Arjuna alone! If we wish to succeed, we must stand united and decide a strategy to face Arjuna,' countered Kripāchārya.

Ashwatthāmā was even more furious. Karna had insulted his father despite no provocation. 'Until now, we haven't taken the cattle away or even crossed the boundaries of Matsya. What are you bragging about, Karna?' Ashwatthāmā admonished. 'Wise men do not boast of their achievements even after they have proven their merit. What kind of warrior is content taking over someone's else's kingdom by cheating and not real war?' Addressing both Duryodhana and Karna, he said, 'Tell me one war where you have defeated any Pāndava? All you have done is snatched their property by deceit. Do you not remember the forewarning given by Vidura? When you had humiliated Draupadi and the Pāndavas deceitfully in the game of dice, Vidura had explicitly said that Arjuna will never forgive you for the slight. He will destroy you when the time comes. Do you think defeating the Pāndavas in a war is as easy as cheating them in a rigged game of dice? If you do believe you can defeat Arjuna by yourself, please go ahead and do it. We came here to fight King Virāta, not Arjuna, so I am not being party to this fight,' declared Ashwatthāmā.

Bhishma, until then, was a mute spectator to this discussion, which had gone awry. He stepped in to calm things down, bringing in a measured perspective. 'One should not disregard one's teachers. Drona and Kripa are right about taking a decision to fight only when the time and place are appropriate. Though, I believe, Karna said whatever he did only to boost the morale of the army. Ashwatthāmā, do forgive him. This is not the time for us to fight amongst ourselves but together think about how to deal with our opponents. I request Kripāchārya and Dronāchārya also to forgive whatever has been said.' Duryodhana agreed with Bhishma and apologised to Dronāchārya on Karna's behalf.

Bhishma clarified that the agyātvās of the Pāndavas had ended over five months ago.[24] Therefore, even if the eunuch was Arjuna, it wouldn't amount to exposing the Pāndavas. Nonetheless, having challenged Matsya, they did not have the choice of backing off and would have to go through with the initial battle plan. He advised Duryodhana to take the cattle beyond the boundaries of Matsya while the rest of them fought Arjuna. Duryodhana did as told and tried to escape.

Arjuna noticed Duryodhana attempting to escape with the cattle. He instructed Uttar to head towards Duryodhana ignoring the other warriors. He was not going to allow Duryodhana to take away the cattle wealth of Matsya. Having successfully halted Duryodhana, Arjuna turned his arrows towards the other Kauravas warriors. One by one, he vanquished Bhishma, Drona, Karna, Kripa, Ashwatthāmā, Duhshāsana and others, not once but multiple times over.

The fight went on for the entire day. Single-handedly, Arjuna decimated the entire army of the Kauravas. He fought them one on one and he even fought them together. But Arjuna was determined not to kill any of his relatives. Thus, when warriors had retreated injured, he released a Murcchitāstra, a weapon that diffused into the air and made the opponents temporarily unconscious. Leaving them to regain their consciousness, Arjuna retrieved the cattle and headed back to city, assuming his Brihannalā avatār.

No bravado of Karna, neither pride of Duryodhana saved the Kauravas from defeat at the hands of Arjuna in that battle of Virāta.[25]

The Attempt at Peace

The Pāndavas had successfully completed the twelve years of vanvās and one year of agyātvās. Now it was for Duryodhana to honour his word and give Indraprastha back to them. The Pāndavas did not want a war. Had war been their intention, they could have challenged Duryodhana much before. They were in no obligation to live through the thirteen years of hardship, nor were they afraid of a war. But they could foresee the destruction a war would unleash. Even Bheema, who otherwise provoked Yudhishthira to get back his kingdom by resorting to physical strength as warriors should, was willing to give negotiations a chance instead of going for an outright war.[26]

After consultations with well-wishers and friends, the Pāndavas sent a messenger on their behalf to Hastināpur with the request to give them their due. Most of the Kaurava ministers were in favour of patching up with the Pāndavas and returning their kingdom. Bhishma made the same recommendation to Dhritarāshtra. But he had barely finished speaking when Karna jumped in angrily. He opposed the Pāndavas' claim to the kingdom outright, 'Had Yudhishthira completed his vanvās as expected of them having lost the game, and then had asked for their share, Duryodhana would have given the earth. But here, the Pāndavas are trying to threaten Duryodhana, taking refuge in the strength of the Pānchālas and the Matsyas. Duryodhana will never give in to such threats. If the Pāndavas want their inherited kingdom, they should spend another thirteen years in the forest first.'

Towing Duryodhana's line, Karna implied that the Pāndavas had been exposed before the end of the thirteenth year and hence had lost again; this, despite

Bhishma having already explained how the Pāndavas had technically completed their year in hiding months before the battle of Virāta. Bhishma responded to Karna, calling out his farce and reminding him of his humiliating defeat at the hands of Arjuna in that battle.[27]

The to and fro of messengers continued in vain. Duryodhana was beyond any persuasion. Blinded by pride and greed, he heeded not a word of his elders. Karna further stoked Duryodhana's false sense of confidence by bragging about his valour and his acquisition of the Brahmāstra from Parashurāma. 'Though I lied to get the Brahmāstra, Parashurāma did not curse me, only warned that I will not remember its technique at the time of my death. I have that weapon and my death is not near yet. Let Bhishma, Drona and all other warriors stay here; I will go and kill Arjuna myself,'[28] Karna declared again. Once again, Bhishma had to show him his place by describing the feats of Krishna and Arjuna.

As a final effort at peace, Krishna himself went as a messenger to Hastināpur. He warned Dhritarāshtra about the dire consequences of a war. He conveyed to the assembly that the Pāndavas were ready to settle for just five villages if it averted the war. But Duryodhana was adamant. 'The Pāndavas lost the game of dice and went to vanvās, as was agreed. What have I done to deserve the blame for it? If you think threatening me with the consequences of a war will make me relent, then that is not going to happen. I have some of the best and invincible warriors such as Bhishma, Drona and Karna on my side. Giving Indraprastha to Yudhishthira was a mistake to begin with. But I was ignorant and young at the time. That is why I let them have a part of the kingdom that belonged to me through my father. Now I understand better. So as long as I am alive I will not give the Pāndavas even a needle's tip worth of land,' he proclaimed.[29]

Krishna responded with facts, telling Duryodhana exactly why he deserves the blame. 'Your envy couldn't tolerate the success and prosperity of the Pāndavas. They had done you no wrong. The idea of the game of dice was a trap you laid for the forthright Pāndavas. Is there anyone more depraved than you who would have thought of dragging his sister-in-law and humiliating her in an assembly full of men?' Krishna reminded him of his other deeds as well, including the plot of Vāranāvata.[30] Rather than imbibing the message of Krishna, Duryodhana, Karna and others stormed out of the hall, enraged.

Krishna advised Dhritarāshtra to use power as the final resort and check Duryodhana's misadventures. 'Imprison this son of yours and his friends. Save your family from destruction.'[31] That was not to be. Instead, Duryodhana went a step ahead and conspired with his gang of Karna, Duhshāsana and Shakuni to arrest Krishna while he was in Hastināpur. 'Without Krishna, the Pāndavas will be extremely disheartened. Defeating them would then be easy,' was their thinking.

Sātyaki got to know about this devious plan and he cautioned Krishna about what awaited him in the Hastināpur assembly. Krishna went to the court nevertheless. As planned, while Krishna was putting forth a case for peace, Duryodhana ordered his men to capture him. Krishna warded them off and manifested his virāta rupa[32]. The resplendent vision dazzled one and all. None except Bhishma, Drona and Sanjay could stand that blaze. Duryodhana and Karna were shaken and could do nothing except see Krishna walk away in anger.[33]

The Disclosure

The Pāndavas and their advisors could foresee the terrible destruction of Bhāratavarsha that the war would bring in its wake. Duryodhana's coterie, on the other hand, did not wish to look beyond their ambition. Krishna knew Duryodhana's eagerness for war rested on the encouragement and support of Karna. There was one thing Karna needed to know before the war cry was formally sounded. Krishna hoped the new piece of information might make Karna reconsider his position. He invited the latter for a personal chat before heading back to Upaplavya.

'Karna, you were born to Kunti before her marriage. Scriptures say such a son belongs to the husband who the mother eventually marries. By that, you are the eldest son of Kunti, the eldest Pāndava. Come along with me so that the Pāndavas would know you are their eldest brother. Once they know, they, along with their sons and relatives, will all fall at your feet. As the first-born, you will be made the king of Indraprastha,' said Krishna enticing Karna.[34]

Karna was not shocked. He knew he was Kunti's son given up at birth. His biological father, Surya, had already told him the truth. Yet, he was not prepared to leave Duryodhana. 'I was raised with love by Adhiratha and Rādhā. They consider me their son. I have grown up in that Suta family. I am married to women from the Suta community and have children with them. I am attached to them. At no price do I wish to give up those relations to form new ones,' said Karna. 'Moreover, it is due to Duryodhana that I have enjoyed the luxuries of a kingly life. He has challenged the Pāndavas today because he has faith in my abilities. I cannot break his trust for any relation or luxury,' Karna reaffirmed, refusing Krishna's request to join the Pāndavas.[35] Instead, he asked Krishna to not let the Pāndavas know about him being their elder brother. Karna was aware that the Pāndavas wouldn't fight if they were to know the truth.

Karna confessed to Krishna that he had been having bad dreams lately. He also mentioned having observed the omens visible in the sky and surrounding nature. The placement of the nakshatras and their movements all seemed to indicate Duryodhana's defeat and Yudhishthira's victory. But Karna ascribed the war to the will of destiny that could no longer be averted. He was firm about his loyalty to and support for Duryodhana.[36]

The Mother Meets Her Son

Krishna's efforts at peace had failed. Vidura was dejected. There was no stopping the battle now. Whichever side emerged victorious, destruction was a given. Vidura lamented the inevitable fall of the Kuru lineage to Kunti. Kunti wanted her sons to get their kingdom back honourably but she was also aware that Vidura was right about the impending annihilation of the Kurus. There was one more thorn in her heart. On the Kaurava side, none hated the Pāndavas as much as Duryodhana and Karna. And no one posed a credible threat to her sons as Karna did. Perhaps, it was time for her to face her past.

One morning, Kunti went to see Karna by the bank of the river Gangā. Karna had just finished his chant and his ritual. He turned around and saw Kunti. Respectfully, he bowed and said, 'Accept the obeisance of this son of Rādhā, venerable lady. Tell me, what can I do for you?' Kunti choked. 'You are not the son of Rādhā. You are the son of Kunti. You are my son.' She explained to Karna her utter helplessness that made her give up her just-born baby.

Kunti urged Karna to reconsider his decision of fighting against his brothers. 'If you and Arjuna get together as brothers, imagine what a formidable team you would make. Nothing in the world would be unattainable to you both.'[37] Karna was indignant. 'You have been unfair to me throughout. You gave me up when I should have been nurtured by you as a Kshatriya. But I lost that opportunity and was brought up in the Suta community. Never before have you bothered to express your motherly love towards me. Now that the war is imminent, you ask me to join the Pāndavas and desert the sons of Dhritarāshtra who gave me the respect and comforts that I sought. I will surely fight with your sons in the interest of Kauravas—that is for certain.'

But Karna did not send Kunti away empty-handed. He offered his word that whatever be the outcome of the battle between him and Arjuna, she will always be the mother of five sons. Karna promised that he will either kill Arjuna or get killed by him but he would not harm any other Pāndava.[38]

Karna first gave away his kavacha and kundala to Indra and now made this promise to Kunti, knowingly weakening himself and Duryodhana.

Ego Tussles and Imprudence

Karna was undoubtedly a warrior to reckon with. He had impressed the indomitable Jarāsandha with his archery and wrestling in combat.[39] Due to Karna's support, Duryodhana was able to win the princess of Kalinga as his wife, defeating an assembly full of warriors.[40] To help Duryodhana conduct the Vaishnava Yajna, he defeated the kingdoms of Kāmbhojas, Videhas, Ambāsthas, some Kirātas and other Himālayan kingdoms and got them to swear their allegiance to Hastināpur.

His record against Arjuna and Bheema, however, was underwhelming. At Draupadi's swayamvara, then again in the battle of Virāta, Karna had taken a beating at the hands of Arjuna. Likewise, in the battle against Gandharvas, Karna ran away to save his life while the four Pāndavas defeated them and freed Duryodhana and the other Kauravas. He had suffered defeat at the hands of Bheema in Anga desh before Yudhishthira's Rājasuya Yajna when he refused to profess allegiance to Indraprastha.[41] Before the war began, Duryodhana asked Bhishma to make an assessment of the warriors on the two sides. In the classification that Bhishma made, he put Karna in the lower order, calling him neither an atirathi[42] or a rathi. 'This beloved friend of yours, who has become your close adviser and always instigates you to quarrel with the Pāndavas, is boastful, haughty and rude. He was endowed with kavacha and kundala, which would have protected him in a war. But he stupidly gave them away. Moreover, he carries the curse of Parashurāma. Karna is significantly weakened by these rash acts,' stated Bhishma, clarifying that the assessment was not about Karna's skills as a warrior but for his attitude and disposition which hindered the outcome of his enterprise despite his superior weaponry skills.

Drona had known Karna since his student days. He had also witnessed Karna's conduct in the Hastināpur court as well as in the battle of Virāta. Agreeing with Bhishma's assessment of Karna, Drona added, 'He shows a lot of pride before every war but when the time comes, he turns away. He is passionate but reckless.'[43]

Karna went ballistic on hearing these words from Bhishma and Drona. He accused Bhishma of favouring the Pāndavas and working against the interest of the Kauravas. He alleged that Bhishma was trying to create discontent in the Kaurava side by slighting a warrior like himself. As if validating the comments made by Bhishma and Drona, Karna continued his acerbic outpouring. 'What does Bhishma know about the competence of warriors?

I can single-handedly stop the Pāndavas from moving ahead. My arrows are so potent that merely on seeing them, the Pāndavas and Pānchālas will run away in ten directions like oxen run on seeing a lion. Once on the field, I will destroy the Pāndavas in no time. But being the commander of the Kauravas, Bhishma will get credit for my valour. I will not allow that. Hence, I will not fight till Bhishma is the commander of the Kaurava army. As soon as he falls, I will join the battle,' Karna declared.[44]

The day the war was to commence, Duryodhana asked his key warriors, 'In how many days can you individually destroy the army of our opponents?' Bhishma said he would be able to crush the Pāndava army in a month. Drona said he too could accomplish the feat in a month. Kripāchārya estimated two months and Ashwatthāmā ten days. Karna boasted he could destroy the Pāndava forces in just five days.[45] The grandstanding notwithstanding, Karna was not even on the battlefield the day the war began. He stayed put in his camp for the first ten days of the war because Bhishma was the commander.

All this while, Karna had opposed tooth and nail any attempt at peace with the Pāndavas. He desperately wanted the war to happen. A full-fledged war would be his only opportunity to prove his superiority over Arjuna and repay the debt of Duryodhana's friendship. Yet, his claims of doing only that which would be in Duryodhana's interest rang empty when the choice was between his ego and his friend's victory.

Bhishma fell on the tenth day of the war. Karna was set to enter the fray. That night, he went to see Bhishma. The old Kuru lay on a bed of Arjuna's arrows with his eyes closed.[46] Karna was overwhelmed seeing one of the greatest warriors of all times in that state. Karna bowed and heralded his arrival by saying, 'Sir, I am Rādheya, the one you always despised.' The old man opened his eyes and looked at Karna with a lot of affection. 'You are not Rādheya, but Kaunteya,' said Bhishma, adding, 'I am aware of the story of your birth. I never despised you. I used harsh words hoping to dissuade you from stoking Duryodhana's rage. You kept instigating Duryodhana against the Pāndavas for no reason. You bore ill will for the Pāndavas out of jealousy.'

Then, as one last attempt to stop the war, Bhishma, praising Karna's valour and generosity, asked him to make peace with the Pāndavas. They were his brothers from the same mother after all. But Karna refused. 'My life is indebted to Duryodhana. There is no way to stop the war now. I am aware that the Pāndavas and Krishna are invincible. But I wish to fight with them and I am sure I will defeat them.' Bhishma knew it was too late to even wish for the enmity to end. 'I tried really hard to establish peace but I failed. Now if fight you must, fight leaving your ego at bay, fight as it would befit a Kshatriya and aim for the heavens,' so saying, Bhishma bid Karna a final farewell.

Dronāchārya succeeded Bhishma as the commander of the Kaurava army on the eleventh day. The Kaurava army was ecstatic with the entry of Karna. Their hopes of winning the war were rekindled. The battle got deadlier. The ground rules laid out by Bhishma were repeatedly broken. The armies continued to fight even after the sunset.

The killing of Abhimanyu, Arjuna's sixteen-year-old son, on the thirteenth day was the nadir of the Kauravas. Abhimanyu fought valiantly but couldn't survive the simultaneous attack of six mighty warriors. Karna was among them, as was Dronāchārya. That such mighty warriors could not contain or match the mettle of a boy as young as Abhimanyu was a testament to the courage of the Pāndavas and their sons.

The killing of Jayadratha at the hands of Arjuna on the fourteenth day was another humiliation for the Kauravas. In spite of the fence of the most outstanding warriors protecting the king of Sindhu desh, Arjuna killed Jayadratha and avenged Abhimanyu's death. No one, including Drona, Kripa, Karna, Ashwatthāmā or Duryodhana, could stop Arjuna from fulfilling his vow of killing Jayadratha that day. Aided by Bheema and Sātyaki, Arjuna broke the indestructible army formation made by Drona and demolished any obstruction that came his way to dispatch Jayadratha on his final journey of life.

Duryodhana was flustered. The realisation that there was no warrior in Arjuna's league—not Karna, not Ashwatthāmā, not even Drona or Kripāchārya—dawned upon him. That even Karna stood completely helpless before Arjuna upset him even more.[47] He blamed Dronāchārya for going easy on Arjuna. Drona asked him why the other indomitable warriors couldn't stop Arjuna if that were the case.

Karna surmised it was fate that sided with the Pāndavas every time.[48] That Arjuna was better in warfare and mental strength did not occur to him, or maybe it did but he did not wish to acknowledge the thought.

Jayadratha's death had lifted the spirits of the Pāndava side. They attacked the Kaurava army with even more vigour. Duryodhana was perturbed seeing his men fall like a pack of cards. Karna again went on a boastful rant to cheer up his friend. 'Be assured, I will soon kill Arjuna and the Pānchālas. Just like Kārtiyeka killed Tārakāsura and made Indra victorious, I will ensure your victory. Until I am alive, you don't have to worry at all.'

Kripāchārya, having heard this kind of bragging from Karna multiple times before, smirked. 'Karna, you say these big words in front of Duryodhana, but how is it that we have never witnessed the fruits of your action? Did you not run away in the battle with Gandharvas when the entire army was still fighting? Did you and your brothers not face defeat at the hands of Arjuna in the battle of Virāta? Arjuna had thrashed our entire army all by himself then. How many times have you been defeated by the Pāndavas till now? Do not roar like an empty cloud. Focus on the war. Warriors prove their courage by way of their performance in the battlefield. Arjuna has impressed Shiva himself through his performance; you only speak of yours.'[49]

In his defence, Karna explained he was only making his resolve known. 'I have resolved to kill the Pāndavas and am making my determination known. Destiny helps those who make a firm resolve to begin with.

There is nothing wrong in self-praise. It only helps to motivate oneself. Why do my words bother you?'[50] Kripāchārya reminded him that it was important to make a fair assessment of the opponents and not underestimate them. He went on to list some more exploits of Arjuna and Krishna to show that they were opponents to be reckoned with.

Kripa's words angered Karna. He laughed aloud and retorted, 'Sure, the Pāndavas are indeed brave. But forget not, I have Indra's shakti—the Indrāstra. Once I use it on Arjuna and kill him, the rest of the Pāndavas would be easily defeated.' Unable to control his rage, Karna started abusing Kripāchārya, calling him just a weak old Brāhmin, biased towards the Pāndavas, and threatened to chop off his tongue if he said anything more to displease him. 'The Pāndavas have managed to kill great Kaurava warriors due to sheer luck and no other reason. For Duryodhana's sake, I will fight to the best of my ability those you consider very powerful. Victory, however, is dependant on destiny,' he reiterated.[51]

Incensed at the insult heaped on his uncle, Ashwatthāmā charged at Karna with a sword intending to sever his neck. 'My uncle was only telling you the truth about Arjuna. There was no need for you to belittle him like that! Your empty boast of your courage is only out of spite for Arjuna. Where was this valour when Arjuna killed Jayadratha right before your eyes?' Kripāchārya held Ashwatthāmā back. But Karna called Ashwatthāmā a stupid and fallen Brāhmin, challenging him to a duel. Duryodhana had to intervene to calm things down.[52]

Karna's self-assurance of being capable of killing Arjuna was driven by his possession of the Indrāstra. On the night of the fourteenth day of the war, however, Krishna's intelligent war strategy forced Karna to use the weapon on Ghatotkacha. 'Why hadn't Karna used the weapon on Arjuna till then? Should he not have done that in the beginning?' asked Dhritarāshtra to Sanjay. Sanjay had no answer. 'Every night after the war, the Kaurava warriors would get together and instigate Karna to use the weapon on Arjuna or Krishna. That would pretty much end the war. But it never came to pass when on the field. For some inexplicable reason, or probably it was some fated intervention that deluded Karna's mind from using the weapon,' replied Sanjay.[53]

Every warrior had his better and worse days during the course of a war. Bheema defeated Karna in multiple duels and was defeated by Karna once. Arjuna too defeated Karna at least three[54] times when they faced each other before the final duel on the seventeenth day. Karna defeated Nakula, Sahadeva and Yudhishthira in the seven days that he was on the battlefield but did not kill them due to his commitment to Kunti. Likewise, Bheema and Sātyaki had come close to killing Karna a handful of times. But they did not because Arjuna had pledged that Karna would die by his hand.[55]

On the battlefield, there was a certain level of respect which the warriors extended to each other in their speech even if the opponent lost a duel. Even Duryodhana did not insult the opponents. Once when he came face to face with Sātyaki, Duryodhana and Sātyaki exchanged some banter from their student days. The otherwise quick-to-react Bheema, too, had maintained the decorum of his speech. But not Karna. Bheema had forced Karna to retreat several times. But the one time Karna managed to throw Bheema off his chariot and make him weaponless, he went on to heap electives on Bheema, calling him a glutton, cowardly and impotent.[56] Bheema and Arjuna were furious at this behaviour of his. Arjuna even called out Karna's brashness and vowed to kill his son Vrishasena to avenge the death of Abhimanyu.[57]

Karna was a fierce warrior, no doubt, but he had a major flaw—that of imprudence in speech and incessant bragging. His lack of restraint with words had enraged the Kaurava elders multiple times, both on the battlefield and off it. On every such occasion, Duryodhana had to intervene to calm the nerves down.

The Final Face-Off

After Dronāchārya was killed by Dhrishtadyumna on the fifteenth day, Duryodhana anointed Karna the commander of the Kaurava forces. The Pāndavas had an upper hand on the sixteenth day. Karna assured Duryodhana he would destroy Arjuna the next day. He was going to use his celestial bow, Vijay, gifted by Parashurāma himself.[58] Karna believed he was better than Arjuna at all aspects of warfare except one. He didn't have a sārthi as good as Krishna. But he knew the person who could be as good as Krishna, Shalya.

Shalya was Nakula and Sahadeva's maternal uncle. He was on his way to join Yudhishthira in the war. En route, beautiful camps equipped with food and entertainment were pitched especially for him. Shalya accepted the hospitality assuming it was Yudhishthira's. In reality, it was Duryodhana's ploy to get Shalya to fight on the Kaurava side. Shalya was indebted to him for the hospitality he had enjoyed and could not deny Duryodhana's request. While Shalya fought on Duryodhana's side and fought well, his emotions were with the Pāndavas. Bhishma had warned Duryodhana even before the war had begun that Shalya would not kill his nephews in Kurukshetra.

When Duryodhana requested Shalya to be Karna's sārthi, Shalya initially refused. Duryodhana persuaded him by praising his unparalleled skills both in warfare and chariot steering. Eventually, Shalya agreed.[59] As he steered Karna's chariot towards the battlefield, Karna began boasting about how he was going to cause the devastation of the Pāndavas and secure Duryodhana's victory with his sharp arrows. Shalya was a little taken aback. 'How do you disregard the Pāndavas like this? When you see them in action, you will certainly not speak this way,' reprimanded Shalya. 'Instead of showing bravado, strategise and fight Arjuna within the army formation,' he added. But Karna continued his self-praise and accused Shalya of discouraging him. Their conversation quickly deteriorated into insults and name-calling. To infuriate Karna, Shalya kept praising Arjuna. Karna reciprocated by slandering the people of Madra, the home state of Shalya. Karna called the people of Madra desh untrustworthy, wicked, deceitful, drunkard, fallen and much more. He even called their women depraved. Once again Duryodhana had to step in to stop the bickering of the two great warriors.[60]

That day, Karna fought with all his might. He massacred many warriors of the Pāndavas army. He defeated Yudhishthira, Nakula and Sahadeva individually but stopped short of killing them.[61] Bheema had always been a formidable match for Karna. That day as well, the two locked horns multiple times before Bheema went on to kill Duhshāsana and fulfil his oath.[62]

Later in the day, Karna finally came face to face with Arjuna. The two brothers knew this was their one last encounter. Both had been baying for each other's blood. Both were prepared to kill or to die. They attacked each other, exhibiting their best moves. It was a battle without a parallel in terms of dexterity, agility and weapons used. Their sharp arrows had pierced into each other's bodies and were spilling their blood. But their spirit was undaunted. At one point, when Karna seemed to dominate the duel, the Kaurava army began rejoicing.

Krishna and Bheema began cheering and encouraging Arjuna, reminding him of his past exploits. Energised, Arjuna was back in the game, showcasing his breathtaking archery. Karna then shot a deadly weapon called Sarpāstra. Shalya warned Karna that he had not positioned the weapon well and was likely to miss the target. Karna took it as an offence to his skill and shot from his chosen angle anyway. As Shalya had estimated, the arrow missed Arjuna's neck and zoomed past toppling off his crown. Krishna's fine manoeuvring of the chariot also played a role in saving Arjuna from the deadly weapon.[63]

Arjuna hit back with all his prowess. Every part of Karna's body was pierced by his arrows. Just then, the wheel of Karna's chariot sank into the ground. Ignoring that, Karna tried to invoke the Brahmāstra, given by his guru Parashurāma. But he just could not remember the mantra to summon it. Karna realised then that the death knell had been sounded for him and became agitated. 'Though we strive to protect dharma, dharma doesn't always protect us,' he moaned. His body was in excruciating pain inflicted by Arjuna's arrows. His grip on the bow slackened.

Karna hadn't given up yet. He fought back with vengeance and cut the string of Arjuna's bow eleven times. However, even before Karna could fire the next shot, Arjuna would string the bow back, every single time. The swiftness of Arjuna's action marvelled all those watching. Karna too was displaying exemplary skill and valour. He destroyed all the powerful arrows that Arjuna had shot at him. Pulling out the dreadful Raudrāstra[64], Arjuna took his ferocious attack several notches higher. On seeing the weapon, Karna jumped off his chariot to pull out the wheel that had sunk in. 'Hold off your arrows Arjuna, until I pull out the wheel stuck in the ground. Don't be a coward and follow the rules of a righteous attack. Follow your dharma,' urged Karna.

Hearing the high talk of dharma from Karna, Krishna was livid. 'It is indeed fortunate that you are reminded of dharma now. People always blame their destiny when faced with calamity. Never do they remember their misdeeds. Did you not think of dharma when a menstruating Draupadi was pulled by her hair in front of the Hastināpur assembly? Where was your dharma when Yudhishthira was cheated in the game of dice and had his kingdom usurped? Was it dharma when, even after thirteen years of vanvās, you all refused to give him back his kingdom? You were aware of the conspiracy of the lac palace where Duryodhana attempted to set the Pāndavas on fire; where was your dharma then? Where was your dharma when you mocked the helpless Draupadi being humiliated by Duhshāsana in the assembly full of people? Do you remember how you were staring at Draupadi in that hall and how you asked her to choose another husband, stating the Pāndavas were now fallen? Did you not think about dharma when conspiring with Shakuni? Did you all not compel Yudhishthira to play the game of dice again? Where was this talk of dharma when you, along with many other warriors, together killed a young boy like Abhimanyu? If at those occasions you weren't bothered about dharma, why are you drying your tongue exhorting on dharma now?'

Karna could say nothing. He picked up his bow once again to fight Arjuna. Turning to Arjuna, Krishna said, 'Kill Karna with your powerful celestial weapons.' Krishna's words had the expected effect on Arjuna. The painful memories of thc past floated before his eyes, burning every cell of his body. Arjuna pulled out a powerful arrow, the Anjalikā, infused it with powerful mantras and shot it at Karna with all his resolve. The arrow hit where it was meant to and severed Karna's neck.[65]

The Pāndava army was euphoric. There was no winning for the Kauravas now.

The Duel of the Maces

After Karna's death, Duryodhana was shattered. Kripāchārya once again tried to convince Duryodhana to negotiate peace with the Pāndavas. Duryodhana was aware that he was not going to win but how could he beg for forgiveness from the Pāndavas? So many kings and warriors had laid down their lives for Duryodhana. It would only be right to fight for the sake of those dead friends and well-wishers, he deliberated. So the fight continued.

Shalya was killed soon after, so was Shakuni. Duryodhana was left with only Kripārcharya, Ashwatthāmā and Kritavarmā. On the morning of the eighteenth day, Duryodhana did not appear on the field. He chose to rest in a pool of water. But the Pāndavas found him and challenged him to fight. Duryodhana was given a choice to pick his opponent for a duel. Duryodhana's pride was still unbowed. 'I will fight each one of you one after the other,' he boasted. Yudhishthira agreed and added, 'If you manage to defeat even one of us, I will give up my claim to the kingdom in your favour.' Duryodhana came out of the pool holding his mace. 'Come fight with me one by one. Do not forget that it is not right for multiple warriors to fight one opponent,' he said.

'How did this thought not occur to you when all of you got together to kill Abhimanyu?' mocked Yudhishthira. 'Pick one of us to fight with you,' he challenged.[66]

'None of you can match me in a mace fight, so you decide who wants to go first!' roared Duryodhana. Bheema jumped in with his mace. This duel was long overdue. Bheema was powerful but Duryodhana had thirteen years of rigorous practice with him. Duryodhana was waiting for this day. He had worked hard on his body and his mace when the Pāndavas were spending their time in the forest. A terrible combat ensued between the two. Bheema was giving his best, so was Duryodhana. Krishna realised that Bheema wouldn't win if the usual rules of the game were followed. He reminded Arjuna of the Bheema's oath during the disgraceful game of dice. 'I will break this thigh of yours on which you have told Draupadi to sit,' Bheema had thundered then. It was time to remind Bheema of his oath. At Krishna's prodding, Arjuna signalled to Bheema, pointing to his thigh. The latter understood. At the opportune time, as Duryodhana tried to jump, Bheema dealt a death blow on his thigh. Duryodhana collapsed on the ground unable to move. He was fatally injured.[67]

Balarāma, Krishna's elder brother, however, was furious at Bheema for breaking the rule of mace fighting. 'This is foul play! You cannot strike your opponent below the waist!' he screamed and dashed towards Bheema with his plough. Krishna held him back. 'The just and clear-hearted Pāndavas are our friends. Are you not aware that they have been repeatedly deceived by Duryodhana and his friends for no fault of theirs? Moreover, Bheema was oath-bound. In the assembly of Hastināpur, he had pledged to break the thigh of Duryodhana for his indecent gesturing at Draupadi. It was Duryodhana who instigated Karna to attack Abhimanyu from behind and cut his bow. After that, he, along with the other warriors, killed Abhimanyu even though the young boy had fallen on the ground and was weaponless. How was that fair? Bheema's oath was known to all, including Duryodhana, for the last thirteen years. Duryodhana should have remembered that before jumping so high.'[68]

Seeing Duryodhana fall, the warriors in the Pāndava army started showering heaps of praises on Bheema and sharp insults on Duryodhana. Krishna didn't approve of this. He stopped them saying, 'Bheema has already left him to die. Do not kill him again with your words. He was already dead when he made vicious, scheming people his ministers and followed their advice instead of that of men like Bhishma, Kripa, Drona, Vidura and Sanjay. He is neither anyone's friend nor foe. He is just a terrible human being. Do not waste any more words on slighting him. Let's leave him alone.'

Duryodhana cringed at Krishna's words. 'O, you son of Kamsa's slave![69] Are you not ashamed that I have been unethically defeated today? Do you not hate yourself for killing so many warriors deceitfully in the war? Bhishma was killed by positioning Shikhandi at the forefront. Dronāchārya was killed by misleading him with the news about the death of Ashwatthāmā, the elephant. Do you think I do not know this? Wasn't it your idea to push Ghatotkacha in the battle with Karna so that Karna had no choice but to use the Indrāstra which he had saved to kill Arjuna? Even Karna was killed through deceit. If you hadn't resorted to these unfair means, the Pāndavas would have never won. You are the greatest sinner Krishna!' cried Duryodhana.[70]

'You were on the pathway of sin Duryodhana. All the warriors you talk about have been killed because of *your* crimes. You wanted to usurp what rightfully belonged to the Pāndavas. You attempted to kill them many times. Even as young boys, you poisoned Bheema's food. With your aides, you hatched a plan to burn the brothers alive along with their mother in Vāranāvata. You deserved to be killed the day you ordered Draupadi to be dragged with her hair to that assembly of Hastināpur. You snatched Yudhishthira's kingdom through foul play. You killed Abhimanyu unfairly, breaking all rules of war. Now you talk of the faults in *our* deeds? Do remember, these have been brought upon you due to your misdeeds. Falling prey to extreme greed and rage, you did what should never have been done. Now you have to suffer the fruits of your actions,' Krishna replied.[71]

Krishna's words meant little to Duryodhana. Instead, he started boasting about the life of prosperity he had lived. 'I couldn't have asked for a better death. Such a death is suitable for a brave warrior like me,' Duryodhana blurted.[72] He died that evening, bereft of all his near and dear ones.

Duryodhana's frustration with the Pāndavas was understandable to an extent. He was jealous of the progress and prosperity of his cousins. What was Karna's reason for such extreme bitterness? Was it his obsession to be recognised as the greatest warrior in Bhāratavarsha? Or was it jealousy at the love and respect Arjuna attracted wherever he went? Or was this his way of proving his loyalty to Duryodhana at any given opportunity?

Karna did stand with Duryodhana in every act of his. He said exactly what pleased Duryodhana; nay, he went a step ahead and insulted Bhishma, Dronāchārya, Kripāchārya, Vikarna and all others when their words were not to Duryodhana's liking. Right or wrong, virtuous or vicious, the issue of ethics mattered little to Karna. If it made Duryodhana happy, Karna would say it and do it. He had the chance to patch up with the Pāndavas and avert the war. Instead, he chose to fight on the side of Duryodhana and accepted defeat and death.

Karna's loyalty to Duryodhana was unfailing—or was it? His humiliation of Draupadi that created a permanent rift between the cousins, his escape from the battlefield of the Gandharvas when Duryodhana was still fighting it out, his giving away of kavacha and kundala to Indra to ensure the reputation of his generosity was not sullied, his promise to Kunti about not killing any other Pāndava in the Kurukshetra war, his staying out of the Kurukshetra war for the first ten days due to an ego tussle with Bhishma, his constant bragging in front of the Kaurava elders at every given opportunity only to be reprimanded by them and his incessant stoking of Duryodhana's rage to make Kurukshetra happen against the wishes of everyone else—none of these actions were in Duryodhana's interest.

What was this relationship between the two? Was it friendship? Would Duryodhana have continued to patronise Karna had Karna taken a moral stand against Duryodhana's insistence on taking away the kingdom of the Pāndavas at any cost? Could Duryodhana and Karna remain friends had Karna advised against the war which Duryodhana imposed upon Bhāratavarsha, just to satisfy his jealousy? But then, Karna wanted the war as much as Duryodhana, maybe even more. He knew, as he had mentioned to Krishna, about the likely defeat of the Kauravas. He wanted the war nevertheless. The war, he had believed, would be his ladder to greatness—one last opportunity to prove he was better than Arjuna.

Duryodhana and Karna both wanted the war and to that end, they were in alignment. Both fought valiantly and perished. With them perished a generation of warriors of Bhāratavarsha.

Both aggravated the inherent tamas[73] in each other.

ॐ ψ ॐ

11

Kurukshetra Encounters: Bheema and Arjuna versus Duryodhana and Karna

The amount of destruction that Bheema unleashed in Kurukshetra was second only to Bhishma, who killed at least 10,000 soldiers every day. All the hundred Kaurava brothers were killed by Bheema. Even in duel clashes, Bheema was a force to reckon with, not just in mace but also in archery.

Over the eighteen days of the war, Duryodhana and Bheema, as well as Karna and Bheema, faced off many times. Arjuna was more occupied with Bhishma, the Trigartas, Bhagadatta and such other allies of the Kauravas. He did face-off with Karna and Duryodhana a handful of times though, as seen in the table.

Table 11.1: Encounters at Kurukshetra

	Bheema			Arjuna		
Face-offs	Wins	Losses	Inconclusive	Wins	Losses	Inconclusive
Duryodhana[1]	6	0	2	1	0	0
Karna[2]	6	1	3	4	0	0

Win/Loss: When a warrior either kills or leaves an opponent without weapons and chariot in a way that the opponent cannot hit back or causes an opponent retreat from combat, it indicates a win for the former and loss for the latter.

Inconclusive: If opponents are reinforced with support from other warriors so that a win/loss situation doesn't arise, and if the opponents eventually move on to fight others, it is an inconclusive duel.

Karna initially fought mildly with Bheema but seeing the latter's powerful comebacks, Karna upped his attack. Of the ten times they collided, nine were on the fourteenth day, when Arjuna was engaged in 'Mission Jayadratha'. Both Bheema and Karna had the opportunity to kill each other that day, but both remembered the vows. Karna has promised Kunti to not kill any Pāndavas except Arjuna. Bheema remembered Arjuna's oath to kill Karna.

Apart from Arjuna and Bheema, Karna was defeated in the face-offs by Sātyaki once,[3] while two of their duels remained inconclusive[4]; and once by Abhimanyu.[5] Karna defeated the other Pāndavas—Nakula, Sahadeva and Yudhishthira—the couple of times he faced off with them over his seven days in Kurukshetra.

Arjuna was the only warrior in Kurukshetra who did not lose a single face-off. On the fourteenth day, he walked away from Dronāchārya because he did not wish to waste time fighting him. It was not a retreat or a defeat. Bhishma was another warrior who was practically undefeated until Arjuna felled him with the support of Shikhandi.

ॐ ψ ॐ

12

A Warrior Mother

Kunti immediately recognised Karna when he entered the pavilion. Her sons, along with Gāndhāri's, were demonstrating the expertise that they had developed under Dronāchārya's tutelage that day. The golden kavacha and kundala shone on him. Kunti knew them instantly. She had seen them when she had set afloat the baby boy in a basket. Karna walked in, as proud and confident as a lion. All eyes were on him. Quite unexpectedly, he challenged Arjuna to a duel. The bitterness in his voice was evident. Her heart skipped a beat. Her eldest son was challenging his youngest brother, both unaware of their relationship.

Karna had come back into the radius of Kunti's life. To her distress, he already seemed to hate the Pāndavas and had joined hands with Duryodhana. Shocked at the turn of events, Kunti fainted. Vidura asked the handmaidens to sprinkle some sandalwood water on her. By then, the sun had set and the duel was averted. The secret of Karna's birth was still safe with her and she chose to keep it that way.

Kunti was born as the eldest daughter of Yādava chieftain Shurasena. She was named Prithā. Like Karna, Kunti also grew up away from her parents. Though, unlike Karna, she was not unaware of who her real parents were. She was given away by her parents in the care of her father's friend, Kuntibhoja, who had no kids of his own then. Karna, on the other hand, was a baby when Adhiratha found him in a basket and he learnt only much later about the truth of his biological parents.

Growing up in Kuntibhoja's household, Prithā was a very disciplined, soft-spoken and responsible girl. She was well mannered and well behaved with one and all.[1] Once, a rishi named Durvāsā visited Kuntibhoja and expressed a desire to spend a few days in the king's palace. Durvāsā was known to be a very demanding and exacting rishi who had a reputation of being offended easily. Kuntibhoja assigned Kunti to his service. Kunti served Durvāsā with all her heart and patience. Once in a while, to test her, Rishi Durvāsā would throw tantrums and make difficult requests. Kunti kept her calm and fulfilled all the demands to the best of her abilities. Impressed with her dedication, and as if inspired by destiny, Durvāsā blessed her with a mantra, one that would allow her to call upon any deity and beget a child from him. The boon was to play a big role in Kunti's future, about which she had little clue then.

'Is it really possible to call any deity using the mantra?' wondered Kunti. She was just a young girl then. Curiosity got the better of her and she called upon Surya deva. Much to her astonishment, he came intending to bless her with a son. Scared to wits, Kunti asked for forgiveness and requested him to go away. What would she tell her parents, who had put so much trust in her? How could she have a child? She wasn't even married! Surya deva, however, was bound by the power of the mantra and couldn't return without fulfilling the deed for which he was called. Kunti relented and, as anticipated, was soon holding a baby in her womb. Kunti made excuses to stay within her room so that no one could see her carrying the baby. Only one of her old handmaidens knew. She arranged for the delivery of the baby. Kunti was torn. Soon, she had a beautiful son with a natural kavacha and kundala that gave him a divine aura. But the reputation of her father, who was also the king of Kunti desh, was paramount. She wished to do nothing that could bring her parents shame.

Kunti wrapped the baby, put him in a basket and let it float away, praying Surya deva would take care of his child. The basket was retrieved in the city of Champa of Anga desh by Adhiratha and his wife Rādhā of the Suta community. They adopted the baby as their own child, christening him Vasushena. Kunti confirmed through her spies that the child was safe and growing up in Adhiratha's household.[2]

The knowledge of being a foster daughter and hence the need to be beyond reproach might have weighed heavily on young Kunti's mind. Only once did she let this weight show. When lamenting to Krishna about her fate and that of her children having to live in vanvās, she said, 'I do not blame Duryodhana for my sorrows. If someone can be blamed for this, then it surely is my father, who gave me away when still a child to his friend, as if I were a thing for charity. Like my father, my in-laws have also treated me with disregard.'[3]

When Kunti was of marriageable age, her foster father arranged a grand swayamvara for her. Princes from all over had come to participate in the ceremony. Among the distinguished gathering, she chose the handsome and gallant king of Hastināpur, Pāndu.[4] Kunti became the queen of Hastināpur. Pāndu took a second wife Mādri soon after and left on a conquest of Bhāratavarsha.

Once when the three of them were vacationing in a forest, Pāndu unknowingly killed Rishi Kindama and his wife while they were making love. He had mistaken them for a pair of deer. The couple died but not before cursing Pāndu: 'You too will meet your death when, possessed by lust, you will make love to your wife!' moaned the rishi in pain. 'It was a mistake,' urged Pāndu, horrified by what had happened. The rishi replied, 'You have sinned not because you shot us instead of a real pair or deer. You have sinned because you shot at a couple making love. Even if it were two animals in the act of mating, you should have waited for them to finish[5]. Your behaviour has been indiscreet.'

Dejected, Pāndu took a vow of celibacy and decided to spend the rest of his life in the forest. Kunti and Mādri followed him in his penance and relocated to the forest to lead an austere life. Pāndu desired to have children who could carry forward his lineage but the rishi's curse made it impossible. He suggested to Kunti that she participate in niyoga and beget children. Kunti remembered Durvāsā Muni's boon and informed Pāndu of the same. Pāndu was elated. He requested Kunti to call upon thc lord of dharma, Yama. From that union, Yudhishthira was born. Then, Pāndu wanted a son unparalleled in strength, and he urged Kunti to call Vayu deva; and Bheema was born. A year later, through Indra, Kunti gave birth to Arjuna. Mādri beseeched Pāndu to request Kunti to share the mantra so that she could become a mother too. Kunti agreed. Mādri called upon the twins, Ashwini Kumars[6] and got a pair of twins through them, Nakula and Sahadeva.

The initial years of the Pāndavas were spent in Tapovan in the midst of nature and devoid of palatial luxuries. One day, Pāndu and Mādri were taking a walk in the forest. Suddenly, enchanted by the nature around and enraptured with Mādri's beauty, Pāndu was overcome with lust. Mādri was shocked and resisted but Pāndu was deluded, and he forgot all about the rishi's curse. The moment he got close to Mādri with the intent of making love, the curse had its effect. Pāndu died. Unable to carry the guilt of being the reason for her husband's death, Mādri jumped into her husband's pyre, leaving her young sons in the care of Kunti.

In the forest, Kunti had striven all those years to ensure Pāndu's safety and now here she was, left alone to take care of five young boys. As advised by rishis and elders in the forest, Kunti came to Hastināpur, the city of her husband and the rightful home of the Pāndavas. They were welcomed in Hastināpur by all. None of the elders had foreseen the impact of their arrival on Duryodhana. The eldest Kaurava was not happy sharing the limelight with the Pāndavas. His jealousy made him do things to harm them.

Especially after the attempt to poison Bheema, Kunti was worried but chose to stay quiet on Vidura's advice.

Soon after, the boys were sent to get trained under Kripāchārya and then Dronāchārya. Life had not been easy for Kunti all these years, but she was happy to see her sons grow up into smart and brave young men. The day she saw Karna in Hastināpur was also the day she was seeing her other sons after many years.

The citizens of Hastināpur loved Yudhishthira. Bhishma, Vidura and other elders too considered him worthy of the throne. Dhritarāshtra was left with little choice but to make Yudhishthira the crown prince, which he did grudgingly. Yudhishthira's popularity was making Duryodhana very uncomfortable. He convinced Dhritarāshtra to send the Pāndavas and Kunti to Vāranāvata, where he had already made arrangements to kill the brothers in a fire. Vidura's foresight saved them. But Vidura also requested them to stay hidden for a few days as their safety was not yet guaranteed. And thus after a few years in the palace, the Pāndavas and Kunti were back in the forest, this time hiding their identity.

One day, the Pāndavas and Kunti came to Ekachakra Nagar and found shelter in a Brahmin's home. A demon named Bakāsura had been a source of terrible worry for the villagers. When Kunti heard that one person from her host's family was going to be offered as food to the demon, she stepped in. With warriors like her sons around, how could she let such a calamity befall the host? Kunti comforted her hosts and asked Bheema to go as Bakāsura's food. Yudhishthira, however, wasn't happy. How could Kunti, as a mother, knowingly offer her son at the altar of a demon to save someone else's son? Bheema was their strongest support in those days and the only one who gave sleepless nights to Duryodhana.

Kunti was firm. Even in her pain, Kunti hadn't forgotten that she was a daughter, wife and mother of warriors. As a Kshatriya woman, she had to safeguard her hosts at any cost and she did. 'We have stayed happily in this house of our host for so many days. Their shelter has allowed us to live safely and comfortably while concealing our identities. I see this as the only appropriate way to express our gratitude to them. If someone does us a favour, we must return that with more than what we have received. That is respectable human behaviour. As Kshatriyas, it behooves us to support all those in need,' she explained.[7] Bheema went and challenged Bakāsura. As Kunti had expected, Bheema was more than a match for him. He killed the demon and freed the village from his menace.

Subsequently, the Pāndavas left Ekachakra, married Draupadi and came out of hiding. They were given a part of the Hastināpur kingdom to set up their reign. Through sheer hard work, the Pāndavas established the city of Indraprastha and conducted the glorious Rājasuya Yajna. It seemed like the hardships were a thing of the past.

However, the luxury of Indraprastha did not last long. Duryodhana, with Shakuni, Karna and Duhshāsana, plotted to deceitfully cheat the Pāndavas of their kingdom and riches. The game of dice followed and then it was thirteen years of forest life once again. This time, Kunti couldn't go. Yudhishthira and the brothers did not want their mother to suffer another decade of hardship; she had aged by this time. But to register her protest at the ill treatment of her sons and daughter-in-law, she chose to not live in the Hastināpur palace. Instead, she spent those thirteen years staying in Vidura's home.

When Vaishampāyana narrated the game of dice incident, Janamejaya was bewildered, 'The decision of agreeing to play dice was Yudhishthira's. The other brothers went through the ordeal for no fault of theirs. Why did they continue to stand by Yudhishthira?'[8] Draupadi had been one of the factors that united the brothers. But the foundation of the bond was laid by Kunti's upbringing. Kunti loved Mādri's sons as her own and for them, she was the only mother. Among the five, she was most concerned about Sahadeva. She had even told Draupadi to specially take care of him when the Pāndavas were leaving Hastināpur to spend thirteen years in vanvās.[9]

Thirteen years passed but peace was still elusive. Duryodhana, prodded by Karna, wanted war with the Pāndavas. Krishna had come to Hastināpur to explore the possibility of a peaceful settlement but his efforts had also failed. War was imminent. Before heading back to the Pāndava camp, Krishna came to meet Kunti and see if she had any message for her sons.

Indeed, Kunti had a very strong message to send. Her sons had never strayed from the path of dharma. They had even taken the deceit by the cousins in their stride and had served the time in the forest. The schemings of Duryodhana notwithstanding, Kunti had never encouraged the Pāndavas to seek revenge. But this refusal to return their own kingdom to them was not something she could tolerate anymore.

Kunti began her message addressing Yudhishthira. She reminded him of his duties as a warrior and a king. 'You have been striving for peace thus far. But that is only one aspect of dharma. It is akin to a person chanting the Vedas without really understanding the meaning of the mantras. In this effort, your responsibilities as a king towards your citizens have suffered.[10] Look at how your father and grandfather established their Rāja Dharma.[11] One who only shows mercy all the time cannot be a just administrator,'[12] she exhorted. 'Seeking alms for a living or engaging in farming is not appropriate for you. You are a warrior and your duty as an administrator is protecting your people from adversities. But your kingdom has been wrested from you by your enemies. Therefore, it is only befitting of you to take it back either by diplomacy or by strength and restore it to its past glory. Live by your Rāja Dharma and fight. Don't sully the name of your ancestors and brothers by your cowardice,'[13] urged Kunti.

Kunti then narrated to Krishna the story of Vidulā and her son Sanjay. She asked Krishna to convey the same to Yudhishthira. Once upon a time, there lived a courageous, righteous, foresighted and noble

Kshatriya woman by the name Vidulā. Well versed in various scriptures, she was revered by kings of the day. One day, Vidulā found her son lying down in his room in an extremely pitiable state. He was defeated by the king of Sindhu desh in the war and had given up. Seeing him in that miserable state, Vidulā was livid. 'You were conceived in my womb but to me, you bring no joy. Instead, you are the one who pleases his rivals. I doubt whether you are indeed born of me and your father. From where has a coward like yourself appeared in our family? You have no rage. You are not worthy of being counted amongst warriors. You are a man only in name,' she screamed.

'Are you going to live like this miserably all your life? Get up son, shun your fear and get ready to fight and claim your right. Do not disregard your own self giving in to meekness. Cleanse your mind of petty emotions and resolve to strive and be brave. Do not sleep like this, defeated by your enemies doing nothing. Devoid of honourable living, you are making your enemies rejoice and pushing your loved ones in sorrow,' Vidulā chided.[14]

Continuing her reprimand, she said, 'Even if there is a chance you may lose your life, you must not give up the fight. Either holler aloud like an eagle unafraid to announce its presence or quietly slink like a rat to look for the chinks in your opponents' armour. But do not lie down like a dead man struck by lightning. Stand up right now and reclaim your honour with valour. Better to live short but shine like a brilliant flame than cling to your life burning like a stick, flameless and smoke-filled. A short but heroic life is more desirable.'[15]

'It is possible that one does not achieve the result he hoped for. Wise men do not grieve over failures. They continue to strive to the best of their abilities as long as they live. Dear Son, live keeping your dharma in mind. Do what you must, even if that means death in the battlefield. Death is certain for all beings anyway. You have lost your wealth and reputation. You have given up on your scripture-ordained actions. What is the point of such a wretched life? Without any notable human pursuit and strength of character, a person leaves no legacy. Such a man is a worthless addition to the population on earth. A person who does not make a name for himself either by way of generosity, penance, truthfulness, knowledge or wealth creation is as good as human excreta, nothing more. Let no lady ever give birth to a son bereft of passion, zeal, strength and valour. Therefore, my boy, invoke your self-respect and your inherent strength. Decide your end goal and endeavour to uplift this fallen lineage of ours,' instigated Vidulā.[16]

The son, still pitiable, retorted, 'If I am not alive, what happiness will you get even if the entire earth were yours? What would the ornaments and wealth do for you, if I am not here? With my death, what will you achieve with all the luxuries and comforts?'[17]

Vidulā was not the one to give in to such emotional reactions. 'A Kshatriya who is so attached to his life that he refrains from performing to his true potential for his people is akin to a thief. It is unfortunate that like a person on a deathbed who does not respond to any medication, no sensible words seem to appeal to your heart,'[18] she replied firmly.

Hoping to shake her son's ennui, Vidulā continued, 'If only you weren't so attached to your life, you would have defeated the enemy. A respectable warrior has only two options, die fighting and achieve heaven or enjoy the luxuries of earth by winning over his opponents. Let me not see my brave son so distraught and meek. You are endowed with good looks, youth, knowledge and nobility. If a valiant man like yourself gets scared when an opportunity arises, that is as good as being dead.'[19]

'Your father was a giver. He never said no to anyone who came seeking. It will be unbearable for me if now we have to seek obligations from others and not be the ones giving shelter. May such people living in poverty and pity, only concerned about "what will I eat for lunch today" be born to our opponents. Do not follow the lead of those who are dependent on others for their living. Be like that fruit-giving tree which nourishes people who seek shelter beneath it. Only those who live a worthy life built on the basis of their own endeavour and fortitude achieve fame in this world and the next.'[20]

Then, giving some practical advice on the path ahead, Vidulā said, 'The citizens of Sindhu desh are not happy with their king at all but because of your weakness they have been left in a state of bewilderment, unsure of their next steps. They are waiting for some calamity to strike the king to get rid of him. If you show intent and prowess, the citizens and other kings will rally behind you. Make the right alliances and wait in hiding till the time is right to strike. No king is immortal. The right time will present itself if you keep a lookout and stay prepared. Conquer the opponents and become worthy of your name. Sanjay means "the one who is triumphant"[21]. When you were a child, a Brāhmin had told me that you will face a great challenge but come out victorious. Hence, I am certain you will indeed succeed. But you must fight without worrying about whether you will gain or lose. Fight because it is your duty,' she encouraged.

Sanjay was shaken at his mother's words. 'Is your heart made of iron? How are you so compassionless? You are pushing me into this war as if I am someone else's son and you someone else's mother. It is baffling that you talk to me so harshly,' he uttered. Vidulā was unmoved. She explained, 'I am inciting you to fight because it is your duty. A great opportunity has come your way to exhibit your heroism. If you let this pass and do not behave as is expected of you, great ignominy will come to you. Given the situation, if I say nothing to you, my affection for you will be as worthless as a donkey's love. Only when you behave like a responsible man will you become dear to me.'[22]

Sanjay was now getting riled up. 'It is not right for you to express such thoughts towards me. I am your son, Mother! You, especially, must treat me with affection,' he whined. Vidulā smirked, 'I am happy you have started to at least think in terms of right and wrong behaviour. Just like you are urging me to behave like a mother should, I am also urging you to behave as a warrior should. When you return victorious, having defeated all the warriors of Sindhu desh, I will welcome you with open arms.'[23]

Sanjay, though, was unconvinced. 'I have no wealth nor an army to help me fight the war. How am I going to win in these circumstances? That is why I have given up the desire to reclaim my kingdom. Do you see any means by which I could win? Suggest a solution and I will ensure it gets done.'

Vidulā emphasised on having the right attitude to action. She said, 'Without initiating an action, our desire will certainly not materialise. It is likely that the outcome may not always be as we desire. But that can be known only after the action is done. That is why, results notwithstanding, wise men continue to engage in their work. Success and failures are anyway ephemeral. Hence, believing firmly that success will come, one must engage in work. You too must now get ready to act.

'First of all, find the right allies. Reach out to people who are either upset with the king of Sindhu desh, those who were slighted by the king before and are seeking revenge, those who have been defeated by the king in the past and those who can be bought by money. Involve them in your mission. Give them due respect and pay them upfront. That way, they will acquiesce and make you their leader. Show your opponent that you are ready to fight without any attachment to your life. If the opponent is much stronger, unleash your spy network and create factions in his army. Come what may, do not be afraid. If fear does grip you, do not ever show it. Nothing kills an army's morale like a frightened commander.'

Vidulā told Sanjay she only wished to ensure he fought with passion and resolve. She assured him that she had savings that could be used for war preparations. Sanjay was enthused. 'With a mother like you, I cannot be a weakling. Hearing your words makes me happy. I am ready to strive to get my right,' he said confidently.

This story of Vidulā was specifically for Yudhishthira. Kunti then addressed a message to Arjuna and Bheema. 'Tell them, Krishna, the occasion for which a Kshatriya woman gives birth to a child has now arrived. Come what may, great men do not lose their passion and hope.'[24] To Nakula and Sahadeva she exhorted, 'Achieve prosperity in the way that befits warriors—through your might and dharma.' Finally, Kunti reminded the Pāndavas of Draupadi's humiliation in Hastināpur. 'Draupadi was insulted in front of your eyes. What kind of warriors can forget the words that were hurled at her in that assembly?[25] I am not so unhappy about the loss of the kingdom nor do I grieve the vanvās as much. But what was done and said to Draupadi by Duryodhana, that has inflicted immense sorrow on me. Tell Arjuna that he must do what Draupadi desires,'[26] said Kunti as she bid farewell to Krishna.

When Kunti had seen Karna in the pavilion challenging Arjuna the day the princes had returned from their gurukul, she was shocked but remained a silent onlooker. Now that Duryodhana had chosen not to budge and a war had become a real possibility, Kunti thought it was time to disclose the truth to Karna, hoping it could still avert the war. She approached Karna and urged him to consider getting together with the Pāndavas as their eldest brother. This was her first and the only real encounter with Karna. But it came too late. Karna had chosen his path and his side. He promised to not kill any other Pāndava except Arjuna in the war, and, like he told Krishna, he asked Kunti to not let the Pāndavas know about this secret, lest they decide to not fight.

Karna was killed by Arjuna on the seventeenth day. The Pāndavas were still unaware of Karna's truth. The war ended with the killing of Duryodhana and the massacre of Draupadi's brothers and sons. Dhritarāshtra with Gāndhāri, Kunti and other women of the royal household came to pay their homage to the dead warriors. The survivors conducted shrāddha and jala dāna rituals for the dead, seeking favourable gati for their departed souls. Only then did Kunti speak up, unable to contain her maternal instinct any longer. 'For that warrior who was amongst the greatest, the one who exuded brilliance like the Surya deva himself, the one who led the army of Duryodhana valiantly, for that Karna, who was your eldest brother, you should offer jala dāna,' she said. The Pāndavas were aghast. 'How can that be? How could you possibly hide such a thing from us? Was Karna really our brother? Have we killed our own brother, being unaware of this truth?' A barrage of questions followed her disclosure. 'Even the killing of my sons hasn't caused me so much pain as this secret you hid from us,' bemoaned Yudhishthira. 'Had I known about this, I would have never undertaken this war.

Only because I was unaware, I committed the sin of getting my brother killed. I proclaim that no woman will be able to keep a secret from today,'[27] he condemned.

Kunti was mourning her son's death too, but she was a warrior mother, after all. Softly but firmly, she tried to console Yudhishthira. 'Do not grieve like this. Karna knew he was your eldest brother. Both I and his father, Surya deva, had told him the truth. We tried to convince him to let go of the acrimony and make up with you. But our efforts were in vain. Karna continued with his bitter ways and sought revenge with you all as if driven by fate. I had to give up on him.'[28]

Yudhishthira took over the reign of Hastināpur. Slowly, the wounds of the battle had begun to heal. Yudhishthira and his brothers had successfully conducted the celebrated Ashwamedha Yajna and had become the sovereign rulers of Bhāratavarsha. Fifteen years had passed since the war. Though Bheema wouldn't let go of an opportunity to make a snide remark, Yudhishthira, Draupadi, Arjuna, Nakula, Sahadeva and all their other wives took a lot of care of Dhritarāshtra and Gāndhāri through these years. The guilt of being a force behind Duryodhana and causing the destruction of his children, however, never left Dhritarāshtra. One day, he decided that Gāndhāri and he would spend whatever was remaining of their lives in the forest doing penance. Yudhishthira grudgingly let them go.

But when the old couple was leaving, Kunti held Gāndhāri's hand and prepared to leave as well. Turning to Yudhishthira, she said, 'Dear Son, never be harsh on Sahadeva. He has always been fully devoted to you. Always strive to keep my daughter-in-law Draupadi and your other brothers happy. And always let Karna be in your thoughts. Whatever charity you do, do it in his name as well. He died because of my indiscretion. I should have informed you all of his existence. I didn't and became a reason for his death. My heart must surely be made of iron that it hasn't broken into a hundred pieces, not seeing Karna here today,' she choked.[29] Kunti had always put up a brave face, but in her heart, she had never given up on her first-born, nor had the guilt of not disclosing his identity to the other Pāndavas left her.

The Pāndavas were shocked. Their mother had lived through hardships and sorrow all her life. Only after the war was there some semblance of peace and comfort in her life. And she wished to give that up in favour of further hardship! The Pāndavas and Draupadi pleaded to Kunti to not go. Bheema couldn't control his emotions. 'Why did you instigate us to fight this war if you wished to throw it all and go away like this? Why did you get us boys to Hastināpur at all if you preferred staying in the forest? Please don't go, Mother!' implored Bheema earnestly.[30]

Kunti was overwhelmed. Tears filled up in her eyes and rolled down her cheeks. But her mind was made up. She had decided to accompany Dhritarāshtra and Gāndhāri to the forest and continue serving them as a daughter-in-law[31] should. Kunti looked affectionately at her sons and said, 'Yes indeed. I motivated you to fight the war and take back your kingdom. I wanted you to be independent and self-sufficient and not at anyone's mercy. Whatever happened on the day of the game of dice, the utter humiliation of the daughter-in-law of the Kurus, was not aligned to dharma. It was an omen that augured the end of the Kuru clan. Hence, to see the continuation of Pāndu's lineage and the restoration of your honour, I provoked you to fight. It was not for my comfort and luxuries. I do not seek these palatial comforts. I want to devote my remaining years to penance and service of my elders.' Kunti's gave one last message to Yudhishthira before she walked away.

'धर्मे ते धीयतां बुद्धिर मनस ते महद अस्तु च'

(May your intellect be fixed in Dharma and may your mind be great [generous]).[32]

Kunti, along with Sanjay, became the crutch and eyes of Gāndhāri and Dhritarāshtra in the forest. Some years later, the Pāndavas got the news of the death of Dhritarāshtra, Gāndhāri and Kunti. The three had willingly given themselves up in a forest fire.[33]

Till the very end, Kunti served the blind couple with complete devotion. Her entire life was an epitome of service and endurance.

ॐ ψ ॐ

13

A Friendship That Groomed

The wedding of Arjuna's son Abhimanyu with Uttarā was quite a significant event for the Pāndavas. It marked the successful completion of their thirteen years of vanvās and got them a powerful ally in King Virāta of Matsya desh. Uttarā was the daughter of Virāta. The wedding brought all the Pānchālas and Yādavas to Upaplavya, a city in Matsya desh.

After the wedding festivities concluded, the allies of the Pāndavas gathered to discuss the way ahead. Hastināpur had not initiated any dialogues even though Dhritarāshtra was aware that the thirteen years of exile were over. Yudhishthira desired a peaceful resolution but not at the cost of injustice, to which the allies agreed. Krishna asked the guests to think of a way that would be favourable for both Yudhishthira and Duryodhana.[1]

An emissary was sent to Hastināpur to request Dhritarāshtra and Duryodhana to return Indraprastha to the Pāndavas. In response, Dhritarāshtra sent Sanjay to Upaplavya. He spoke nothing about returning Indraprastha or inviting them to Hastināpur. Instead, his message to them was to maintain the status quo and not gear up to fight. Killing their own brethren in the war was not the righteous thing to do, Dhritarāshtra preached through his message.[2]

Sanjay returned to Hastināpur with the message of the Pāndavas. The trip had left him sombre. What he had seen in Upaplavya had fully convinced him that victory would kiss the feet of the Pāndavas. In the Hastināpur assembly, Sanjay recounted all that he saw, heard and discussed in Upaplavya. The Pāndavas and their allies had minced no words. Krishna had said, 'The Pāndavas are ready for war and peace.' Arjuna had reiterated Krishna words.

The Pāndavas were more than prepared for war if one was forced on them. However, in the interest of all, they sought a peaceful solution. They wanted their kingdom back and were even willing to forgive the past misdeeds of Duryodhana. Arjuna, while conveying his message, had given a brief illustration of the feats and capabilities of all the major warriors on their side.

The plain-spoken language of the messages from Upaplavya had sufficiently demoralised Dhritarāshtra. But when Sanjay narrated the scene inside Arjuna's palace, there was not an iota of doubt left in the blind king's mind about what awaited the Kauravas in the battlefield. Sanjay went on, as if reliving those moments in Arjuna and Krishna's company.

'I was led to Arjuna's private quarters, a room not even accessible to Nakula and Abhimanyu. Arjuna, Krishna, Draupadi and Satyabhāmā were already there. Arjuna and Krishna were dressed in rich garments and adorned beautiful ornaments. Their bodies were smeared with fragrant sandalwood. The two friends were comfortable and joyous in each other's company, drinking sweet wine. They were seated on grand, gem-studded seats of gold. Krishna and Arjuna were completely relaxed. Krishna's feet were in Arjuna's lap and Arjuna's feet were in Draupadi and Satyabhāmā's laps. Arjuna offered me a golden footstool to sit on but I chose to sit on the floor instead. From my position, I could see Arjuna's feet. His feet have marked rising lines, indicating very auspicious omens,' Sanjay had observed.[3]

'The splendid aura of both these youthful, dusky, broad-shouldered and muscular men, seated together, frightened me. By then, I was certain that Duryodhana's brain has been deluded by the braggings of Karna and the assumed support of Bhishma and Drona. He is not able to see the prowess of these two men. Seeing them together is like witnessing Indra and Vishnu descend on earth. There remains no doubt in my mind that if these two are so eager to serve Yudhishthira, Yudhishthira's resolve will be fulfilled.'

The Bonding

Krishna and Arjuna were first cousins. They were born about six months apart. Krishna was born in a prison in Mathura and shipped out stealthily by his father to Gokul to protect the baby's life. Arjuna was born in the lap of the Himālayas. When Arjuna and the Pāndavas were being nurtured with love and care by their parents, though in a forest, Krishna had killed Kamsa and liberated his parents and grandfather from prison. When the Pāndavas were getting trained by Dronāchārya, Krishna and the Yādavas were busy warding off Jarāsandha's attacks. Subsequently, the Yādavas, under the leadership of young Krishna, shifted their base to Dwārkā. The first time they met as adults was at the swayamvara of Draupadi. When Arjuna, disguised as a young Brāhmin, walked towards the centre of the pavilion, Krishna had instantly recognised him. 'The Pāndavas are alive,' he said, smiling happily at his elder brother Balarāma.

Since meeting the Pāndavas in the potter's hut that day after Draupadi's swayamvara, Krishna became their friend, mentor and ally. With Arjuna, in particular, he shared a special connection. He was the one who suggested to Arjuna that he elope with his sister Subhadrā. The marriage not only tied Arjuna and Krishna in a much stronger bond but also brought the Yādavas and the Pāndavas closer as formal allies. The marriage fructified in the form of Abhimanyu, the child warrior who brought formidable Kaurava warriors to their knees in the Kurukshetra war. Arjuna and Krishna together satisfied Agni deva by letting him feast on Khāndavavana by keeping Indra at bay. From Agni, Arjuna received his Gāndiva, the inexhaustible quiver of arrows and his special chariot. To Krishna, Agni gave the Sudarshan Chakra.[4]

At the time of the Rājasuya Yajna that Yudhishthira conducted after he established himself at Indraprastha, Krishna played a key role by helping the Pāndavas strategise and defeat Jarāsandha, the powerful king of Magadha. This helped clear the way for Yudhishthira's yajna. The importance of Krishna in the lives of the Pāndavas was underscored by Bhishma endorsing Krishna's name for being the guest of honour at the Rājasuya ceremony. The Pāndavas seconded the proposal and accorded Krishna the ritual reverence by washing his feet.

Krishna returned from the Rājasuya and got busy with a war in Dwārkā. Back in Hastināpur, the game of dice was played and the Pāndavas, with Draupadi, were banished to thirteen years of vanvās. After Dwārkā was secured, Krishna came to visit the Pāndavas in the forest. 'If I were around, I would have never allowed such a game of dice,' he regretted. Before heading back to Dwārkā, Krishna reassured his support to the Pāndavas if Duryodhana refused to hand back their kingdom at the end of the vanvās.

The Defence of Dwārkā

Shishupāla's transgressions at Yudhishthira's Rājasuya Yajna had caused Krishna to kill him. Enraged, Shālva, a close friend of Shishupāla attacked Dwārkā to avenge his friend's death. When the game of dice was played, Krishna was busy warding off Shālva's attack. Krishna got to know of the deception and exile of the Pāndavas only after the war with Shālva ended. He came to see the Pāndavas in Dwaitavana soon after.

Yudhishthira expressed curiosity about the war and the defence preparations of Dwārkā. Krishna explained the measures taken to keep his city secure.

The city of Dwārkā was adorned with flags, tall archways, towers and palaces. Situated by the sea, the topography itself secured Dwārkā. Nevertheless, the Yādavas made adequate preparations to buttress the city. The fortifications[5] put in place by them are as follows:

1. At every nook and corner of the city were stationed groups of soldiers—on foot, horse, elephant and chariot—well equipped with all kinds of arms and ammunition, boulders and other equipment necessary for the defence of the city. All the warriors were assigned various positions across the city to keep vigil.
2. Tunnels were dug at appropriate locations in the city for shelter as well as movement.
3. Iron nails and rods were installed along the road to impede the march of the enemy army if one did enter.
4. Mile-wide trenches surrounding the main fort were made dry. Sharp rods and spears were installed at the bottom of the trenches.
5. All routes towards the city, including bridges from the mainland, were broken. Boat services were stopped.
6. Large drums of foodgrains and drinking water were stored in the towers to secure food supply for the citizens and soldiers.
7. A city-wide ban on intoxicants and alcohol was implemented.
8. All actors, dancers and performers were asked to leave the city immediately.[6]
9. During the time of the war, no one was allowed to enter or leave the city without proper identification and the royal seal.
10. Strict guidelines were followed to induct soldiers in the Yādava army. Only those with proven merit and capability were selected. No special favours were granted to anyone.
11. All the soldiers were paid their salaries and bonuses and were given additional benefits well in advance to keep them loyal and in good spirits.

Shālva was a powerful enemy. It was a gruelling battle but the Yādavas eventually won and Shālva was killed by Krishna.

Arjuna's Request to Krishna

At the end of the Pāndavas' vanvās, it was becoming increasingly clear that Duryodhana, goaded by Karna, wanted a war, nothing less. Both sides began seeking alliances with other kingdoms to fortify their side for the impending war. Krishna returned to Dwārkā after kicking off the initial rounds of negotiations between the Kauravas and the Pāndavas. To formally seek the support of the Yādavas, both Duryodhana and Arjuna headed to Dwārkā. Duryodhana reached Krishna's quarters before Arjuna. But Krishna was asleep. So Duryodhana waited by the side of his bed close to Krishna's head. Arjuna came in, saw Duryodhana and quietly waited by the foot of the bed.

Krishna woke up to see Arjuna sitting before him. Then he noticed Duryodhana. Krishna knew the motivations of their visit. He proposed two options; his huge Nārāyani army on one side and himself alone on the other. 'Neither will I fight nor pick up any weapon in the war. Now choose the option you like,' he said. As Arjuna was younger to Duryodhana and Krishna had seen him first, he asked Arjuna to pick his choice. Arjuna chose Krishna. Duryodhana got the army sans Krishna.

Duryodhana was delighted. One akshauhini army over one man was quite a steal, he thought and left for Hastināpur, content.

After Duryodhana left, Krishna asked Arjuna the reason for choosing him instead of the army. Arjuna replied, 'I trust I do have the potential to fight my enemies myself but Krishna, your eminence is unmatched in this world. Wherever you go, glory follows. I too am a seeker of glory. Thus, I urge you to choose me. I have had a long-standing desire to hand the reins of my life and chariot to you. Please become my sārthi in this war and fulfil my desire,' requested Arjuna.[7] Krishna agreed.

(Picture: Patung Arjuna Wijaya, Jakarta, photographed by the author)

The Sermon on the Battlefield

The dreaded day had arrived. The armies of the cousins stood facing each other. The Pāndava fleet was smaller in size. Their hope was hinged on the might of their warriors, most of all on Bheema and Arjuna. For his part, Arjuna had been waiting for this day. He had spent a significant part of the thirteen-year vanvās doing penance and collecting celestial weapons for a probable war. After all modes of a peaceful resolution were exhausted, a war for justice had become inevitable. Yudhishthira was very upset. 'How do we expect to win by killing our own elders and teachers? They are not worthy of being killed,' moaned Yudhishthira. Arjuna consoled him, 'Had it been an unrighteous act, Krishna, Vidura and our mother Kunti would have deterred us from the war. They have encouraged us to take this path as it is the right thing to do. We shouldn't be abandoning the war now.'[8]

The morning before the armies proceeded to the battlefield, Yudhishthira was informed of the conversation in the Kaurava camp about the prowess of their warriors. Concerned, he called his brothers and other key allies to share what he had heard about the might of the Kaurava army. Arjuna reminded Yudhishthira of his previous exploits and possession of the Pashupatāstra, which none of the warriors on the Kaurava side had. He clarified, though, that it would be used only as the last recourse as such deadly weapons were not meant for use on human beings under normal circumstances. Arjuna listed out the mighty warriors who were there to support the Pāndavas to assuage Yudhishthira's concerns. 'And what to say about your prominence? When filled with rage, you can destroy the enemy with a mere glance,' Arjuna said encouragingly.[9]

Yet, as he saw Bhishma, Dronāchārya, Kripāchārya and his cousins standing across him on the battlefield ready to fight and die, Arjuna himself was rattled. 'What is the point of a victory that will be covered in the blood of the same people for whom I wish to win. And win what? Just the luxuries of a kingdom? I would rather die than fight this war that entails me to kill my people. I will not fight this war,'[10] declared a dejected Arjuna, collapsing in his chariot. In that moment of bewilderment, Arjuna forgot the injustice done to them and Draupadi. He forgot that the entire Pāndava forces' hopes of victory hinged solely on his bow. He forgot that only a few months back, he had single-handedly defeated the Kauravas in the battle of Virāta.

Krishna smirked. Appealing to Arjuna's warrior spirit, he said, 'From where has this unworthy sorrow befallen you? Don't give in to cowardice. Get up and fight.'

Arjuna was too perturbed to make much of being called a coward. But he did realise that he was not thinking clearly. Very humbly, he sought Krishna's guidance, 'My mind is completely bewildered. I can't decide what is the right thing for me to do. I, therefore, come to you as a disciple. Please guide me.' For the one considered the greatest warrior in Bhāratavarsha, to accept that he was confused and needs help was quite a humble gesture—and a sincere one.

Krishna, as a friend and a mentor, reminded Arjuna of his swa-dharma.[11] He explained to Arjuna why he needs to act and how. Krishna assured him that he will stand by Arjuna at all times but also made it clear that he can only be a guide. The eventual decision and action will have to be Arjuna's to own. At the end of his discourse,[12] Krishna said, 'I have told you everything that you need to know. Now mull over it and do what you deem right. (यथेच्छसि तथा कुरु[13]).'

Sense prevailed. Arjuna geared up to fight. The war commenced.

Arjuna's Dilly-Dallying

Dhrishtadyumna was selected as the commander of the Pāndava forces while Bhishma led the Kaurava side. 'I will kill all warriors I fight with on the battlefield except the Pāndavas. Nor will I kill a woman or anyone who was a woman before. You may have heard that Shikhandi was born a woman and later became a man. Hence, I will not kill him either,' Bhishma had informed Duryodhana. But he had also promised to subjugate the Pāndava forces to the best of his abilities.[14] Every day, Bhishma had targeted to kill ten thousand foot soldiers and a thousand rathis—warriors fighting from chariots.[15]

With the blowing of the conches and the beating of the drums, the two armies charged at each other. Bhishma launched a full-blown attack on the Pāndava army. His vigour was unparalleled. Whatever came in his way was destroyed. It seemed as if the god of death himself had descended on the earth. The first day ended with heavy losses for the Pāndava side. Back in the camp, Yudhishthira was very upset. If Bhishma was allowed to continue this rout, the Pāndava forces were sure to be destroyed soon, he worried. He was also not happy with Arjuna's restraint towards Bhishma. 'Arjuna seems disinterested in the battle.

Only Bheema is fighting like how a warrior must. But he alone cannot contain Bhishma. What am I to do? We are sure to lose this battle if Bhishma is not stopped,' complained Yudhishthira.[16] Krishna and other warriors comforted him and discussed the war strategy for the next day.

As the war progressed, bodies of soldiers, as well as of the horses and elephants, kept piling up. The bodies were badly mutilated. Some had their heads severed, some their limbs. One day, the Kauravas would have an upper hand and the next day, the Pāndavas would overpower them. Arjuna was able to contain Bhishma's attack but he was still shy of launching an offensive to kill him. The war had reached an impasse. Arjuna wouldn't kill Bhishma. Other warriors were not capable of killing him. For his part, Bhishma wouldn't kill the Pāndavas or their sons, nor would Drona. Karna was sitting out. The armies, however, kept dwindling. Duryodhana was frustrated, as was Yudhishthira.

The ninth day dawned. The Bhishma juggernaut was unstoppable. Unable to bear Bhishma's rage, the Pāndava army ran helter-skelter. Arjuna continued to stay passive against Bhishma and wouldn't retaliate with his true vigour. Krishna tried to coax him by reminding him of his past exploits and vows. Arjuna was still unable to shake off his hesitation. 'How do I kill him who is worthy of my reverence, Krishna?' Arjuna argued, 'But I will do what you say.' Krishna steered the chariot towards Bhishma.

Both Arjuna and Bhishma were ace archers. They were both agile and adept. But both fell short of a real attack on one another. Seeing Arjuna continue to remain lenient on Bhishma, Krishna was furious. He jumped out of the chariot swooshing his whip. His eyes were blazing red as he dashed towards Bhishma's chariot, determined to kill the old Kuru. Arjuna was jolted out of his apathy. He jumped off the chariot, ran behind Krishna and held his feet. He reminded Krishna of his vow to not pick up a weapon nor fight in the war. 'Do not break your vow. I promise to fight with all my might and kill Bhishma,' Arjuna begged. Krishna relented.[17]

Restraining Bhishma was not a trivial task. As long as he held the bow in his hand, Bhishma was invincible. He could be defeated only if he was somehow made to drop his bow. On the night of the ninth day of the war, the Pāndavas and Krishna approached Bhishma. They wanted to know the strategy to defeat him. Bhishma smiled and replied, 'If a woman, any unworthy man, anyone with the name of a woman, anyone who is the only son of his father or anyone who has inauspicious marks on his flag comes before me to fight, I will drop my weapons. You must be aware that Shikhandi on your side was a born a woman before he became a man. His flag has inauspicious marks. If he or anyone else fulfilling the conditions that I have stated comes before me, I will not fight him. Then Arjuna can easily take me down.'[18]

The Pāndavas returned to their camp to plan Bhishma's defeat. Arjuna observed, 'I have seen Bhishma retreat every time he comes across Shikhandi. Shikhandi might indeed be his nemesis. Let us keep him ahead of us tomorrow and fight.'

The next morning when the fight began, the Pāndavas encouraged Shikhandi to challenge Bhishma. Shikhandi, surrounded by Arjuna, Bheema, Sātyaki and other warriors, accosted Bhishma for a duel, shooting three arrows at him. Bhishma laughed and refused to fight back. Arjuna kept Shikhandi's morale high by goading him to take Bhishma down. 'I will take care of all those who come to protect Bhishma. You continue your attack. I am here to protect you,' assured Arjuna.[19] Shikhandi kept shooting arrows but Bhishma did not retaliate. Shikhandi's arrows were too soft to hurt him in any significant way. Like a raging forest fire, Bhishma upped his attack on the Pāndava forces, side-stepping Shikhandi.

Arjuna once again prompted Shikhandi to attack Bhishma. This time, he asked Shikhandi to go ahead and stand facing Bhishma, while he would take charge of the attack. Hearing Arjuna's instruction, the Kaurava warriors made their way towards Bhishma to protect him. The Pāndavas' warriors took positions to stop the Kauravas from reaching the old son of Shāntanu. A horrific combat followed. With Shikhandi in the forefront, Arjuna shot a barrage of sharp arrows at Bhishma. The arrows pierced Bhishma's armour and punctured his chest in multiple places. Bhishma hit back with other powerful weapons, trying to avoid Shikhandi. Arjuna destroyed them midway. Bhishma's body was completely mangled with Arjuna's arrows. To Duhshāsana who had come for his protection, Bhishma smiled and said, 'These arrows have struck me like lightning. The pain is unbearable. These can't belong to Shikhandi. These can only be Arjuna's arrows that are savouring my blood.'[20] The arrows kept coming till there was not an inch on Bhishma's body left unpierced. He stumbled. The arrows jutting out of his body stopped him from touching the ground. It was as if he lay on a bed of arrows. The grand old man of the Kauravas had fallen. Arjuna had fulfilled the promise made to Krishna.

The Chakra Vyuha

With the fall of Bhishma, the Pāndava camp got a much-needed boost. While the loss was quite significant, Karna entering the war had reinvigorated the Kaurava army too. Duryodhana appointed Dronāchārya as the commander of the Kaurava forces and requested him to capture Yudhishthira alive. 'If Yudhishthira is killed, the Pāndavas and their allies would seek revenge. But if captured alive, Yudhishthira could be cajoled into playing dice again. That way, the Pāndavas could be packed off to the jungle for another thirteen years,' Duryodhana reasoned. Dronāchārya agreed, 'Consider Yudhishthira captured if you manage to keep Arjuna far away from him. Even Indra cannot defeat a raging Arjuna in a war.'[21]

A horrific battle played out on the eleventh day of the war, Drona's first day as the commander. However, Yudhishthira was not captured because the Kaurava warriors couldn't keep Arjuna at bay. On the twelfth morning, as was strategised in the Kaurava camp, Susharmā, the king of Trigarta, with his brothers and his army of Samshaptaka[22] warriors dared Arjuna to a battle. They had sworn to keep Arjuna engaged in combat away from Yudhishthira. Arjuna had a self-assumed rule of never backing off when dared. Unaware of Drona's strategy, he took Susharmā's bait. Appointing Satyajeet, the Pānchāla prince, to protect Yudhishthira, Arjuna headed southwards where Susharmā and his forces were waiting. A bloodbath followed in which many brave warriors of Trigarta army were killed.

When Arjuna was fighting the Samshaptakas, Drona and Bhagadatta, the king of Prāgjyotisha, rampaged through the Pāndava army. Satyajeet fought till his last breath but got his head severed by Drona. On the other side, Bheema was struggling to contain the advances of Bhagadatta. Meanwhile, Arjuna had caused the Samshaptakas to retreat. He returned and joined Bheema's defence against Bhagadatta, who released the deadly Vaishnavāstra[23] on Arjuna. But Krishna's astute manoeuvring of the chariot saved him. Krishna took the blow of the weapon on himself; he was endowed with the power to withstand the shakti of the weapon.

Another day ended without Yudhishthira being captured. Duryodhana was indignant and accused Drona of being a foe in the garb of a friend. Drona was hurt. He reiterated that defeating Arjuna was impossible. Arjuna had to be led far enough to ensure he didn't come back before the day ended. Susharmā again volunteered to face Arjuna. Simultaneously, Drona decided to organise the army in a Chakra Vyuha[24] to trap Yudhishthira. Drona was aware that none except Arjuna could successfully penetrate the formation and get out of it alive. What he didn't know was that Abhimanyu, Arjuna's young son, knew how to enter the formation but not how to get out.

As planned, when Susharmā led Arjuna much further away, Drona unveiled the Chakra Vyuha. Yudhishthira entrusted the task of entering the vyuha to Abhimanyu. He assured the young warrior that once he made way inside, others would follow. However, once Abhimanyu entered the vyuha, Jayadratha held back the rest of the Pāndava warriors single-handedly. Abhimanyu got trapped in the formation. Nonetheless, he fought like Kārtikeya[25] himself. No Kaurava warrior could match him in a duel. Eventually, the teenager was killed unethically by a simultaneous attack of six warriors, including Drona and Karna, even though he was weaponless and on the ground.

Arjuna was devastated when he heard about the ruthless killing of Abhimanyu. Krishna too was in pain. Abhimanyu was his nephew and had grown up in his care. Even then, Krishna was the only one who could hold Arjuna together in that moment. Everybody else was at loss of words to console Arjuna.

Yudhishthira was even more repentant. He had assured Abhimanyu that they would all protect him. He had failed Abhimanyu. Yudhishthira explained the details of the encounter to Arjuna, stating his helplessness and that of the others in moving past Jayadratha. 'How could Jayadratha hold back such indomitable Pāndava warriors?' enquired Arjuna. He was told of the boon granted to Jayadratha by Shiva that could be used once. The boon made him invincible for a day. Jayadratha had used the boon on that day. Incensed, Arjuna vowed to kill Jayadratha. 'If I don't kill Jayadratha tomorrow, I will jump into the fire and accept death!' he roared.[26]

The Killing of Jayadratha

Arjuna's vow of killing Jayadratha or giving up his own life was reckless. Krishna was not pleased. He rightfully chided Arjuna for this thoughtless declaration. 'The vow you took today without consulting either your brothers or me was a very brash act. You have forewarned your opponents. Now they will be well prepared to protect Jayadratha and you will become a laughing stock,' Krishna scolded. His spies had brought the news of the strategy the Kauravas were planning to employ the next day.[27] Drona had planned three-layered fortification to guard Jayadratha. Six warriors, namely, Karna, Bhurishravā, Ashwatthāmā, Vrishasena, Kripāchārya and Shalya were assigned to protect Jayadratha in the innermost formation. Drona was going to protect the mouth of the outermost ellipsis. To get to Jayadratha, Arjuna would have to break the layers and then defeat each of the six warriors.

While Arjuna expressed confidence that with Krishna's help he would be able to overpower the opponents, Krishna was worried. Arjuna would need divine power to break through the protective ring Drona would create around Jayadratha. All Kaurava resources would be employed only to save him. There couldn't be a better outcome for the Kauravas than seeing Arjuna invite his own death by jumping into a bonfire. With him gone, it would be game over for the Pāndavas.

Krishna made Arjuna meditate on Shiva that evening and seek protection. But he was still ill at ease. At midnight, Krishna called for his own sārthi Daruk and asked him to keep the chariot and the weapons ready. Krishna was willing to risk the violation of his pledge and take up weapons to fight the Kauravas if such a need were to arise, to save Arjuna.[28] *Justice had to prevail, even if it demanded the sacrifice of personal reputation.* Nevertheless, the need to break the vow did not arise.

Dawn broke over Kurukshetra. Arjuna entrusted Sātyaki with Yudhishthira's security and proceeded for his mission with the blessings of the elders. The Kaurava warriors were determined to stop Arjuna. Arjuna, too, was invigorated by his own pledge and Shiva's grace. Abhimanyu's death was already burning him from within. Blowing his conch, Arjuna announced his entry and intention loud and clear. Within minutes he had vanquished the opposing armies of Durmarshana and Duhshāsana.

Dronāchārya tried to impede Arjuna's march towards Jayadratha. 'You cannot reach Jayadratha till you defeat me,' Drona laughed as he shot a few arrows injuring both Arjuna and Krishna. Arjuna retaliated. But defeating Drona was not Arjuna's target that day. 'We have a great task to accomplish today and not enough time. Let's leave Dronāchārya and move on,' Krishna suggested. Arjuna concurred. After a few shots, he bowed to Drona, took his auspicious blessings and moved on. 'Where are you going Arjuna? You have never walked away like this without defeating your enemy,' smirked Drona. 'You are not my enemy. You are my guru and I am your student, as beloved to you as your son. Nobody can defeat you in the war,' Arjuna replied with utmost reverence as Krishna pulled away.[29]

Like a raging forest fire, Arjuna started slaughtering Kaurava warriors one after the other. Yudhāmanyu and Uttamaujas were protecting his rear. Flustered and anxious, Duryodhana hastily approached Dronāchārya to stop Arjuna. Once again, he started accusing Drona of going soft on the Pāndavas and reminded him where his loyalties lay. This time Drona stated matter-of-factly, 'Arjuna is an unmatched warrior and Krishna, the most able sārthi. Don't you see my arrows, which would have otherwise flummoxed most others, are not even able to keep up with the speed of Arjuna's chariot? Moreover, I can't leave my position. With Arjuna gone, I have a chance to trap Yudhishthira. You are an able warrior yourself. Don't be afraid. Go and stop Arjuna before he reaches Jayadratha. You have able fighters to support you.' Drona gave Duryodhana an impenetrable armour to shield him from Arjuna's incisive arrows.[30]

The sun had begun to move westwards. Arjuna realised his horses were exhausted and injured. He requested Krishna to feed the horses and remove the arrows stuck in their bodies. Krishna loosened the reins and stopped. Seeing Arjuna stranded, the Kaurava army attacked him. But Arjuna was more than a match for all of them. He fought with them standing on the ground. Once the horses were fed, Arjuna and Krishna mounted the chariot and embarked towards Jayadratha, smashing any opposition in the way.

Duryodhana tried his best to halt Arjuna's blitzkrieg but in vain. Drona's armour could not protect Duryodhana from being routed by Arjuna's exceptional archery. Every uncovered part of his body, including his palms and the flesh under the nails, was pierced by Arjuna's arrows. Duryodhana was forced to retreat. Jayadratha was now in Arjuna's line of sight but still a long shot as he was surrounded by six mighty warriors.

As Arjuna came close, the six of them, along with Jayadratha, attacked him all at once. But Arjuna was not Abhimanyu. Not only were his skills unparalleled he also had a treasure of battle experience with him. In the meanwhile, Bheema and Sātyaki came to bolster Arjuna's attack. Bheema duelled with Karna and Sātyaki with Bhurishravā. Finding a gap, Arjuna launched a frontal attack on Jayadratha. Duryodhana requested Karna to intervene and ward off Arjuna's attack. Karna attempted to check Arjuna's assault and fought valiantly. So did the other warriors, including Ashwatthāmā. But Arjuna's focus and determination were impregnable. The Kaurava warriors drowned in the deluge of Arjuna's unassailable arrows.

Jayadratha was within reach but still kept secure by other Kaurava warriors. Just then, it seemed as if the sun had suddenly disappeared.[31] Light had faded. Jayadratha and the Kaurava forces were euphoric. They assumed that the sun had set. The warriors dropped their guard. Jayadratha was perplexed. Again and again, he looked around in the sky to check if the sun had really set. 'Look, the king of Sindhu desh has lost his vigil. He is looking for the sun instead of focusing on you. This is your chance. Kill him and fulfil your pledge,' advised Krishna. On cue, Arjuna started demolishing Jayadratha's protective guard. Karna, Kripa, Ashwatthāmā, Vrishasena, Duryodhana, Shalya were left aghast at the aggression and precision of Arjuna's attack. Other soldiers assigned to protect Jayadratha, unable to take the sheer force of Arjuna's volleys, ran away to save their lives.

Jayadratha was now fully exposed. Krishna instructed again, 'Take Jayadratha down immediately. The sun is about to set any time now. And be cautioned. Do not let his head fall on the ground. Strike him in such a way that the head falls in his father's lap.'[32] Jayadratha had a boon from his father Vriddhakshatra that whoever causes his severed head to fall on the ground will himself explode.

Heeding Krishna's advice, Arjuna employed a mantra-infused missile and severed Jayadratha's neck with such momentum that the arrow seemed to fly away with the severed head, like a hawk flying away with its prey. He then speedily shot successive arrows to keep the head in flight and led it towards Vriddhakshatra, who was meditating in the forest outside Kurukshetra. The severed head fell in Vriddhakshatra's lap. Taken aback, Vriddhakshatra reflexively stood up, dropping the head on the ground. He exploded as per his boon to Jayadratha.[33] It was one of the most extraordinary feats performed during the war.

Arjuna had avenged his son's death.

The Squandering of the Indrāstra

Arjuna was one of the greatest warriors in Kurukshetra. He had proven that many times. Yet, since Karna had entered the battlefield, Krishna was concerned. Karna had given his kavacha and kundala to Indra and obtained Indra's lethal shakti, the Indrāstra also called Vaijayanti. As long as Karna was in possession of it, Arjuna was not safe. Krishna had tried to keep Arjuna away from Karna as much as possible. And the three times they did fight, of which twice was on the day of Jayadratha's killing, Karna had not used it, in spite of having taken a beating. A final face-off between the two was imminent. Krishna was waiting for an opportune moment that would compel Karna to employ that 'one-time-use' shakti *on someone else*. The opportunity presented itself sooner than imagined.

On the fourteenth day, the war continued even after the death of Jayadratha late into the evening. The embarrassment of not being able to save Jayadratha had added to the ferocity of Kaurava warriors. Drona and Karna were especially embarrassed and wanted to make up for the defeat to Duryodhana. Karna went on a rampage, crushing the Pānchāla soldiers en masse.

Yudhishthira was worried. He pleaded with Arjuna to do something about Karna. Krishna, however, did not think it was appropriate for Arjuna to challenge him just yet. In the heat of the moment, Karna would use the Indrāstra if Arjuna was to come in his way. Krishna suggested Ghatotkacha be tasked with checking Karna's aggression on the field. Ghatotkacha was as strong as Bheema and well versed in a variety of powerful weapons. More importantly, his strength increased manifold after sunset. 'Be the ship and save the Pāndava army from drowning,' exhorted Krishna to Ghatotkacha.[34]

Ghatotkacha did not disappoint. He devastated the Kaurava army and overpowered Karna with his demonic prowess. The Kauravas were so disquieted by the carnage that they entreated Karna to use the Indra's weapon that he had acquired on Ghatotkacha. Karna was left with little choice. He hurled the weapon he had so carefully saved for Arjuna at Ghatotkacha. True to its claim, the shakti pierced his chest and tore it apart. Ghatotkacha was slain. Kauravas rejoiced. Bheema grieved the death of his eldest son. So did Yudhishthira and the other Pāndavas. Krishna was relieved. The only real danger to Arjuna's life was now averted.

It was midnight but the fight continued. Exhausted, dazed and almost blinded by sleep, the soldiers carried on with their duties out of a sense of commitment and responsibility. But the fatigue was interfering with their thinking and responses. Some were not even aware who they were fighting with and ended up hitting soldiers on their own side. Arjuna noticed that the soldiers as well as the animals on both sides were completely worn out. He called out aloud, 'Everyone is extremely tired. Darkness and dust have engulfed the field. If you think it is feasible, let us halt the battle for a while. You all can catch some sleep right here on the field. Let the animals rest too. We can resume our fight afresh when the moon appears.'[35]

Both the Pāndava and Kaurava troops readily agreed. They commended this thoughtful gesture of the youngest son of Kunti. 'Arjuna is not only intelligent and courageous but also has a lot of compassion for one and all,' they praised. The troops slept where they were, along with their opponents and weapons.[36] The soldiers were up and about as soon as the moon peeped. Fight resumed, and the sun came soon after. It was the fifteenth day of the war.

When Arjuna Almost Killed Yudhishthira

Dronāchārya fell on the fifteenth day. Karna became the Kaurava commander. The sixteenth day was relatively lacklustre. In their camp that night, Karna pledged to kill Arjuna. He requested Duryodhana to convince Shalya to become his charioteer. Shalya agreed. Karna was in his finest form on the seventeenth morning, egged on by his determination. The altercation with Shalya wasn't helpful but that didn't dampen his spirits. This was going to be a day of reckoning.

Arjuna and Krishna also knew that the day heralded the final battle between Arjuna and Karna. As his sārthi, Krishna prepared Arjuna for the imminent face-off. He explained to Arjuna the strengths, weaknesses as well as major exploits of Karna and Duryodhana in the war.[37] It was important to ensure Arjuna knew the opponent for what he was and did not over or underestimate him.

Karna entered the field and began looking out for Arjuna. He promised rewards to whoever gave him his location. Armed with his imposing Vijay bow, he thrashed everyone who came his way. Only Bheema could resist his strike and make him retreat. Earlier in the day, Karna had severely injured Yudhishthira in a duel. Shalya's discouragement and his word to Kunti stopped him short of killing Yudhishthira. Humiliated and in extreme pain from the wounds Karna had inflicted, Yudhishthira retired to his camp to get some anointment and rest. His absence, however, got Arjuna and Bheema worried. Bheema asked Arjuna to go check on Yudhishthira while he took the Kaurava army head-on. Off went Arjuna along with Krishna to seek out Yudhishthira.

Seeing Arjuna come to the camp while the battle was still going on, Yudhishthira assumed Karna was killed. 'Arjuna has eliminated Karna and has come to give me the good news,' he thought. Yudhishthira was elated and excitedly congratulated Arjuna, who denied killing Karna. 'I was fighting the Samshaptakas and Ashwatthāmā. Having exterminated many warriors among them, I came to see if you were alright. But now I will go back and kill Karna,' he pledged.[38]

Arjuna's response greatly irritated Yudhishthira. The excruciating pain was making it difficult for him to think clearly. 'It doesn't behoove someone like you to leave your soldiers to die at the hands of Karna like this! Because you couldn't defeat Karna, you came running here, leaving Bheema to deal with the Kauravas. What kind of a brother are you? If you were so scared of Karna, why did you assure us that you will kill him? We agreed to this war trusting you. Arjuna, you have failed us,' Yudhishthira snapped. 'Duryodhana had claimed you are no match for Karna. I foolishly did not trust him then. If you do not have the resolve to fight Karna, give your Gāndiva to Krishna or some other king. Let them fight. Shame on your Gāndiva and shame on your valour. If Abhimanyu and Ghatotkacha were alive, they would have certainly killed our enemies already,' he angrily ranted.[39]

Yudhishthira's words riled up Arjuna. Seething with anger, he pulled out his sword. Krishna immediately intervened. 'What are doing, Pārtha? You had come to check on Yudhishthira's well-being. Shouldn't you be happy to see that he is fine? What do you intend to do with this sword?' he asked. 'I have sworn to sever the head of anyone who tells me to hand this Gāndiva to someone else. Yudhishthira said these words, right here in front of you,' he growled, breathing heavily. 'I am bound by my pledge. I have to stay true to my pledge, as is expected of a warrior. For the sake of truth I will have to kill my elder brother,'[40] Arjuna said in a fit of rage. The implication of his own words hit him only after he had said them.

'Anyone who has any understanding of the truth wouldn't do what you intend to do here. Not only are you forgetting your duty, but you are also being stupid,' Krishna scoffed. 'One who attempts to do that which cannot be done, or does that which he may be capable of doing but shouldn't be done, is a stupid man. Even more of an imbecile is the one who lacks discretion of what is right and what is not, but he thinks he knows it all. Though ignorant of the nuances of truth, you speak of upholding truth as if you are an expert. Like a naive kid, you took some oath in the past out of sheer foolishness. And now to justify that idiocy you have risen to kill your brother? Do you not understand that by killing Yudhishthira, you would be committing unjustified violence? He is your elder brother, not your enemy and has done you no wrong. Right now, he is in pain due to his injuries. He is not even armed. Therefore, even by ethics of warfare, he does not deserve to be killed,' Krishna said, attempting to restore some sense into Arjuna.[41]

By way of anecdotes and stories, Krishna explained to Arjuna the nuances of dharma and truth.[42] He made Arjuna see the context-sensitive nature of truth and the need for discretion in all decision-making and actions. 'No doubt, truth is paramount. But understanding the nature of truth in practice, as lived by noblemen, is a difficult endeavour. An apparent lie that saves an innocent life is more virtuous than an apparent truth that harms those who deserve to be protected. One should know what matters and when,' Krishna emphasised.[43]

Story of Rishi Kaushika and the Nuance of Dharma and Truth

In a forest, there lived a rishi by the name of Kaushika. He was very learned in scriptures and lived an austere life. Kaushika was sworn to speak the truth. He had never spoken a lie in his life and was determined not to speak one, ever. That was his key to heaven, so he believed.

One day, a few men from a nearby village entered the forest trying to escape a bunch of dacoits. Kaushika saw them hide amongst some bushes and trees. The dacoits came looking for those men. They saw Kaushika and asked him the whereabouts of those villagers.

Kaushika was aware of the evil intention of the dacoits. But one lie would destroy his penance of speaking the truth all these years. He decided in favour of speaking the truth. Truth is supreme, he rationalised, and pointed the dacoits to the hiding place of the villagers. As intended, the dacoits looted and killed the villagers.

A few years passed and Kaushika reached the end of his life. He was certain he would be welcomed in heaven. He had stayed true to the virtue of truth all his life. But that was not to be. Kaushika was dispatched to hell to repent for a great sin he had committed. By his indiscreet insistence on speaking only the apparent truth, he had become responsible for the death of innocent villagers. His lie could have saved them.

Truth is dharma and dharma is truth. But what is dharma?

'Because it upholds and protects, it is called dharma. Dharma sustains society. Hence, only that action which protects and upholds is said to be aligned with dharma,' said Krishna.[44]

धारणात् धर्म इत्याहुः धर्मों धारयति प्रजाः ।
यः स्यात् धारणसंयुक्तः स धर्म इति निश्चयः ।।

dhāraṇāt dharma ityāhuḥ dharmoṃ dhārayati prajāḥ ।
yaḥ syāt dhāraṇasaṃyuktaḥ sa dharma iti
nishchayah ॥

Arjuna realised the absurdity of insisting on the fulfilment of his oath. But an oath is an oath, after all. Arjuna needed a way to get out of the predicament without completely violating his oath. Krishna reminded him of the edict of the *Atharva Veda*. It says, 'Insulting a person who is worthy of our reverence is as good as killing him.'

Krishna advised, 'You have always addressed Yudhishthira as bhavān out of respect. Now call him tvam. Such disrespect would amount to killing him. Do that and seek his forgiveness.'[45]

The Pronouns for Respect and Insult

In Sanskrit, bhavān (भवान्) for men and bhavati (भवती) for women are terms used to respectfully address all elders as well as reverential people. Tvam (त्वम्) is used to address friends and those younger to us. Both bhavān/bhavati and Tvam mean 'you'. The Hindi equivalent of bhavan and tvam are 'aap' (आप) and 'tu' (तू). To this day, addressing elders as 'tu' is considered rude and irreverent in most parts of India.

Arjuna relented. As suggested by Krishna, he began his outburst at Yudhishthira, 'You have no right to say anything to me. You are hiding here having escaped from the battlefield. You have always been protected by your well-wishers. Hence, you cannot criticise me. Yes, Bheema has the right to criticise me as he is out there showing his grit against the rivals. Even Sātyaki, Sahadeva, Dhrishtadyumna have earned the right to chastise me due to their performance in the war. Not you. You are a ruthless man. Here I am trying to do everything to make you happy and all you do is taunt me. Your kingship does not make me happy because you are infatuated with the game of dice. We all have suffered enough due to your gambling addiction. Now don't whip me with your harsh words.'[46]

Having said all this, Arjuna was filled with remorse. Never had he spoken like this to his elder brother. He pulled out his sword again, this time to kill himself. Krishna smiled lovingly and said comfortingly, 'You are so upset at having used harsh words against your brother. Imagine what you would have done if you had killed Yudhishthira out of sheer stupidity. Also, remember—the sin one incurs from killing oneself is even worse than that incurred by killing one's brother. Instead, praise yourself and boast about your qualities. Self-praise is akin to committing suicide,' Krishna explained.[47]

Arjuna again turned to Yudhishthira and started blowing his own trumpet. He glorified his exploits, achievements and skills. Saying thus, he was overwhelmed. Arjuna joined his hands, bowed to Yudhishthira and apologised. Reiterating his resolve to kill Karna, Arjuna touched Yudhishthira's feet, took his blessings and headed back to the battlefield.[48]

Finally, the ultimate encounter happened. Guided by Krishna, Arjuna killed Karna. Yudhishthira survived and so did Arjuna on the seventeenth day of the dharma yuddha. The next day Duryodhana was killed by Bheema. The war ended, taking with it three generations of warriors. The outcome did not shock many, not even Dhritarāshtra. He was sad but not shocked. Sanjay had predicted the outcome in favour of the Pāndavas even before the war began. He had sensed it in Upaplavya.

Krishna did not fight in the war, as he had pledged. His Nārāyani army was one among Duryodhana's eleven akshauhinis. The Pāndavas had only seven. Numbers were not on the side of the Pāndavas but a friend like Krishna was. Though he did not pick up any weapons, he mentored the Pāndavas and helped them strategise. Most of all, he served as the guiding light that steered Arjuna towards victory.

Krishna didn't flatter Arjuna with irrelevant praise. He did not use euphemisms to show Arjuna his faults. He was harsh when he needed to be. He praised the opponents when they did something commendable and had noteworthy strengths. He said what had to be said to keep Arjuna focused on his dharma. Krishna did not think twice about rebuking Arjuna when his behaviour left much to be desired. He was as affectionate as a mother when Arjuna needed comforting but he was also a friend who was not averse to giving matter-of-fact feedback. He was the one whose wisdom could be relied upon when Arjuna was faced with ethical dilemmas.

Arjuna did not throw ego tantrums when rebuked or when given feedback. He did not become suspicious of Krishna's intent when Krishna praised Karna or other warriors. Nor did he start boasting of his prowess when another warrior was commended. Arjuna was not shy to ask for guidance. He questioned when he was not convinced. Once convinced, he was humble enough to listen and mend his ways. He knew the value of having a friend like Krishna and cherished what they shared.

Arjuna and Krishna's relationship was mutually nurturing. It was based on mutual affection, not on common hatred for the enemy. It was a relationship where each cared for the holistic well-being of the other. Krishna was not interested in pampering Arjuna's ego and neither did Arjuna expect that. The truth mattered to both. Righteousness mattered to both. Dharma mattered to both. Dharma was the cornerstone of their friendship.

That is why Sanjay had remarked, 'Where there are Krishna and Arjuna, victory, prosperity and justice will surely follow.'

यत्र योगेश्वरः कृष्णो यत्र पार्थो धनुर्धरः।
तत्र श्रीर्विजयो भूतिर्ध्रुवा नीतिर्मतिर्मम।।[49]

yatra yogeśhvaraḥ kṛiṣhṇo yatra pārtho
dhanur-dharaḥ
tatra śhrīr vijayo bhūtir dhruvā nītir matir mama

ॐ ψ ॐ

14

The Ten Names of Arjuna

Before the beginning of the battle of Virāta against the huge Kaurava army, Arjuna disclosed his real identity to Uttar, the prince of Matsya desh. Uttar, however, was disbelieving. 'How can the greatest warrior of Bhāratavarsha be dressed like a eunuch! Brihannalā, the eunuch teaching music and dance to the women of the palace, was being audacious,' he thought to himself. Uttar decided to test Brihannalā. He said, 'If you claim to be Arjuna, then recount the ten names by which Arjuna is known and explain their meanings.'[1]

Arjuna begins to recite his names and also enumerates their meanings—'Arjuna, Phalguna, Jishnu, Kiriti, Shwetavāhana, Bibhatsu, Vijay, Krishna, Savyasāchi and Dhananjaya.'

अर्जुनः फाल्गुनो जिष्णु किरीटी श्वेतवाहनः ।
बीभत्सु विजयः कृष्णः सव्यसाची धनञ्जयः ॥

Arjuna: Due to his rare splendour and virtuous deeds, he got the name Arjuna, which means white, pure and radiant.

Phalguna: As he was born on a Himālayan peak in the Uttar Phalguni nakshatra, he is called Phalguna.

Jishnu: Being the son of Indra and difficult to be conquered, he came to be known as Jishnu (vanquishing) in the world of men and gods.

Kiriti: While fighting the dānavas, Indra placed a crown as radiant as the sun on Arjuna's head, making him known as Kiriti (kirita: crown).

Shwetavāhana: When he fought on the battlefield, his chariot was yoked with white horses covered in golden armour. Because he rode a chariot pulled by white horses, he got called Shwetavāhana (shweta: white, vāhana: vehicle).

Bibhatsu: Never did he indulge in any loathsome or cruel action, not even on the battlefield. Thus, he came to be known as Bibhatsu (bibhatsa: loathsome, cruel).

Vijay: Having never returned from a battlefield without defeating the enemy, he was called Vijay (vijay: victorious).

Krishna: Krishna was the name given by his father Pāndu, out of love for this son with a resplendent dark complexion and a heart that attracted (krishna: dark, one that attracts).

Savyasāchi: With equal ease and dexterity, he could use both his left and right hand to shoot arrows from his Gāndiva. This skill made him known as Savyasāchi among humans and gods.

Dhananjaya: Having won over various janapadas, he acquired a lot of treasure from them. He lived surrounded by wealth, hence the name Dhananjaya (dhana: wealth, jaya: the one who has won).

(Picture: Arjuna, the warrior, Bali, photographed by the author)

ॐ ψ ॐ

15

Dharma Meets Strength

'Call upon Yama, the lord of dharma, to beget our first child. May our eldest child be forever engaged in dharma.[1] May he be regarded as the most virtuous even among the virtuous Kurus,' said Pāndu. Kunti meditated on the lord of dharma who appeared before her. Through his union with Kunti, Yudhishthira was born. Kunti's eldest son had all the qualities his father had desired for him—virtue, sense of justice, wisdom, compassion, maturity, a sense of responsibility, humility and patience.

'For warriors, strength is paramount. May you now call upon Vayu deva to get a son who will be unmatched in strength and physical prowess,' requested Pāndu. Kunti complied and Vayu deva manifested before her. Through him, Kunti gave birth to Bheema. Once, when he was just a few days old and was sleeping in Kunti's lap, the roar of a tiger shook the forest. Frightened, Kunti reflexively jumped up. The baby fell off her lap and hit the ground. Kunti froze. To her surprise, the stone on which he fell had broken into pieces but the child was hale and hearty. It is said Bheema had the collective strength of ten thousand elephants.

Next, Pāndu wanted a son who was valiant and enterprising as the king of the devas, Indra, himself.

Kunti called upon Indra and Arjuna was born through their union.

After Pāndu's death, Yudhishthira assumed the responsibility of his younger siblings and became a source of strength for Kunti. Within a short time of their arrival in their father's city, Yudhishthira, by his maturity, demeanour and compassion, endeared himself to the populace of Hastināpur, much to Duryodhana's chagrin.

After the Kaurava and Pāndava princes finished their training with Dronāchārya and returned to Hastināpur, Dhritarāshtra was faced with a critical task. He had to declare his successor to the throne. Yudhishthira's administrative acumen had become evident to the courtiers and the citizens by then. Dhritarāshtra gave in to public pressure and declared Yudhishthira the crown prince of Hastināpur. Subsequently, Duryodhana plotted to kill the Pāndavas and the disaster of Vāranāvata happened. The Pāndavas once again had to live in the forest, hidden. Bheema's presence kept them safe in the jungle from the mighty, man-eating rākshasas and wild animals. Only after the marriage with Draupadi did they come out of hiding and got their share of the kingdom.

The decision of the five brothers to marry Draupadi was Yudhishthira's. It was a very brave move, considering that it was not a norm for a lady to have multiple husbands. But it was a very pragmatic call.

Draupadi's charm was such that every brother desired her. Yudhishthira had read that in their eyes. A wrong decision had the potential to fracture the unity of the brothers. Draupadi didn't resist it either.

'Draupadi will be the queen of all of us. Our mother has approved of the alliance and my intuition does not fail me. Hence, I believe this is the right thing for us to do,' Yudhishthira stated. To convince Drupada about the scriptural legality of such a polyandric arrangement, he quoted examples from the scriptures: a Brāhmin lady named Jatilā married seven rishi brothers, and Vakshi, the daughter of Rishi Kandu, married ten brothers, named the Prachetas. Such a marriage was not condemned by the scriptures.[2]

Veda Vyāsa endorsed Yudhishthira's decision, allaying Drupada's fears. And thus Draupadi became the common wife of the Pāndavas.

The Rājasuya Yajna

Dhritarāshtra divided the kingdom and gave the Pāndavas the barren wasteland of Khāndavaprastha. There, with their own sweat and blood, and Krishna's guidance, the Pāndavas established the city of Indraprastha and Yudhishthira became its king. The citizens were happy with his reign. Like his father, Yudhishthira was an able administrator, noble and just. The days in Indraprastha were among the best that the Pāndavas had so far experienced. Abhimanyu as well as the five sons of Draupadi were born in Indraprastha. The beautiful palace of illusion—the

Māyā Sabhā—was constructed for them by an architect called Maya.

Yudhishthira desired to solemnise the Rājasuya Yajna. Only a king who had vanquished all other kings of Bhāratavarsha, either by force or friendship, was entitled to solemnise this ritual. He deliberated with his ministers and brothers about the feasibility of undertaking the yajna. Everyone agreed that the Pāndavas were strong enough to bring the other kingdoms under their subjugation and conduct the Rājasuya Yajna. Yudhishthira, however, wanted an unbiased view. He knew that would come only from Krishna.

Krishna reaffirmed the eligibility of Yudhishthira for the yajna but highlighted the obstacles that could derail the task. 'The yajna wouldn't be possible unless Jarāsandha, the strong and cunning king of Magadha, is reined in,' Krishna said. He very categorically mentioned that many other powerful kings of Bhāratavarsha revered Jarāsandha and would stand by him if a direct war were to happen. A war, therefore, was not the solution to tackle him. Jarāsandha had to be coaxed into a duel. To accomplish the task, Bheema, Arjuna and Krishna went to Magadha disguised as bachelor[3] Brāhmins and challenged Jarāsandha to fight with one of them.

Jarāsandha picked Bheema as Krishna had hoped. An unprecedented hand-to-hand combat took place between the two giants. Bheema prevailed and killed Jarāsandha. With Jarāsandha gone, the road to the Rājasuya Yajna was clear. The Pāndava brothers then embarked on the Digvijay Yatra[4] to establish their authority on all other kings of Bhāratavarsha and brought them under the sovereignty of Indraprastha. Subsequently, the Rājasuya Yajna was solemnised and Yudhishthira became the chakravarti[5] king, like his father Pāndu.

Yudhishthira was ambitious but he wasn't rash with decision-making. He involved all his ministers in the process and specifically reached out to Krishna to understand the challenges likely to be faced while undertaking a task. This consensual style of decision-making was evident in Upaplavya as well, where the Pāndavas and their allies had gathered to decide the strategy of getting Indraprastha back. Throughout the negotiations with the Kauravas, taking the final decision regarding the war and subsequently, while selecting the commander of the Pāndava army, Yudhishthira sought the opinion of everyone involved. All views and ideas were deliberated upon jointly before a decision was taken. Yudhishthira's style was one of the reasons why the Pāndavas warriors did not have any mutual ego clashes that were common on the Kaurava side.[6]

The Game of Deception

Compelled by Duryodhana, Dhritarāshtra sent Vidura to invite Yudhishthira to Hastināpur to play the game of dice. Vidura was against such a game. He was aware a game like this would spell trouble for the Kauravas and the Pāndavas. 'Why do you look as if something is bothering you? Is the king doing fine?' asked Yudhishthira on meeting Vidura, who then stated the reason for his arrival. 'The king has constructed an assembly as ornate as yours in Hastināpur. He invites you to see the palace and play a game of dice with your cousins.'

Yudhishthira was visibly surprised. 'A game of dice is more often a cause of a larger dispute. A wise man would not agree to indulge in it. But if you think it is appropriate then we will do as you say.'

Vidura replied grudgingly, 'I am aware. Gambling causes conflicts. I tried to warn the king. But he insisted I come to invite you. Shakuni, who is an expert in the game and master of sleight, will be there along with other players. So do as you deem right.'

Yudhishthira was worried. 'This is a dangerous proposition. But seems like such is destined. I will obey the order of the king of Hastināpur. As a son, that is what I am expected to do though I do not wish to play the game. Had the king himself not sent the invitation, I would have never agreed to play with Shakuni. But if invited, I can't refuse. That is my vow. I will come to Hastināpur,' he said.[7]

The Pāndavas entered the exquisite game hall. Shakuni glibly invited Yudhishthira to begin the game. Yudhishthira was ill at ease. He stated clearly that gambling is not a praiseworthy task and certainly not meant for noblemen. Shakuni ignored his misgivings and instigated him to play, well aware that Yudhishthira was a man of his word. He was not going to back out when challenged. As planned, the game of deception began. It was supposed to be a game between Duryodhana and Yudhishthira but Duryodhana craftily announced that Shakuni will throw the dice on his behalf. 'It is not appropriate for someone to play on behalf of someone else,' Yudhishthira objected but to no avail.[8] The game happened. Everything was lost. Draupadi was humiliated. And the Pāndavas were banished to thirteen years of exile.

The other four Pāndavas looked on enraged and embarrassed as Yudhishthira staked them. They looked on even more helplessly when he staked himself and Draupadi. But when Draupadi was openly humiliated in the court, Bheema could no longer keep quiet. He did not shy away from expressing his displeasure at Yudhishthira. He called him out for staking Draupadi. 'Even dishonourable gamblers wedded to unchaste women do not stake their wives like you have. Even they have more sympathy for their wives. You staked all our wealth and us as well. I did not mind that. You do have right over us. But by staking Draupadi, you crossed the line. Just because she married us doesn't mean she deserves to be tormented like this. For this plight of hers, I hold you solely responsible. Sahadeva, get me fire. I will burn these hands of Yudhishthira that put Draupadi at stake!' Bheema hollered. Arjuna tried to cool him down. Yudhishthira had accepted to play only in accordance with the norms of the day and Shakuni was trying to intentionally provoke discord among them, he explained.

Yudhishthira did not fight the outcome. He accepted the exile. The brothers followed him, so did Draupadi. They had enjoyed the luxuries of Indraprastha together. They would stay with their elder brother in misery too.

The Days in the Forest

Before departing, the younger Pāndavas pledged to kill Shakuni, Duryodhana, Karna and Duhshāsana. Yudhishthira stayed calm. He was respectful towards Dhritarāshtra, knowing fully well that the blind king was complicit in their plight. He was going to spend the time in exile in contemplation and atonement, in the company of sages.

The brothers and Draupadi adapted quickly to forest life. They were accompanied by some of their helpers, handmaidens and priests. They spent their time hunting, gathering food, practising archery, engaging in spiritual discussions with men of learning and playing host to all those who came visiting. Forest-dwelling ascetics and rishis would visit often, so would their relatives and friends, including Krishna and the Pānchālas.

The Pāndavas would stay in one forest location for a few months and then move on to another and set up their camp. The idea behind shifting locations was the preservation of ecological balance in the area. In the initial years, once when Vyāsa had visited the Pāndavas in their forest dwelling, he had advised Yudhishthira to move to Dwaitavana from Kāmyakavana. 'Your prolonged stay here full of hustle and bustle disturbs the lives of other forest-dwelling austere rishis who have made this place their home. Moreover, the need for food for your cohorts and visitors has depleted the flora and fauna of this place.'[9]

Their life had become busy once again but the disgrace meted out by Duryodhana continued to fester in the hearts of the Pāndavas. Draupadi and Bheema were more vocal about their emotions than the others. Draupadi would often remind Yudhishthira to not lose sight of their eventual goal and never forget the injustice done to them by the Kauravas.

Bheema was more incisive and aggressive in his expression. 'Indra himself couldn't have harmed our kingdom, which was protected by Arjuna's Gāndiva. But we lost it all due to your lack of caution. We all have accepted this suffering because of our affection for you,' he would sometimes say. Ever so often, he would incite Yudhishthira to cut short the forest stay and wage a war against the Kauravas immediately. 'It is better for us to die in battle than resort to this kind of disinterest. In special cases, thirteen months are representative of thirteen years. Thus, considering our exile complete, we must challenge Duryodhana immediately and take back our kingdom, as is befitting for warriors like us.'[10]

One other worry troubled Bheema. 'How would we get through the thirteenth year of disguise?' he wondered. 'How will we, who are so easily identifiable in any crowd, conceal ourselves in a way that no one would recognise? I am sure Duryodhana would have spread his spies far and wide to ascertain our identities. Even then, if we do complete the year of disguise successfully, I fear Duryodhana might again entice you to another game of dice and you will accept it like you did when invited to play the second game in spite of the humiliation of the first one. And once again, we would be banished to years of suffering,'[11] he would conjecture while trying to persuade Yudhishthira to launch an offensive on the Kauravas at the earliest.

Bheema's words would pinch but Yudhishthira took them in his stride. He regretted his indiscretion in those moments and accepted the criticism gracefully. 'The way you pierce my heart with your words is not inappropriate. I cannot condemn you for the use of those words because, undoubtedly, it is my fault that such a calamity has befallen all of you. I was unaware of the deceitful moves of Shakuni and got tricked. Even then, on seeing how Shakuni's dice were turning according to his wishes, I should have become cautious. But the shock of losing every round and the hope to salvage it got me deluded and I couldn't stop. Intense desire kills a man's fortitude. That happened to me and hence I do not find fault in your words,' Yudhishthira said.

Recalling the incidents of the day, he reminded, 'I willingly agreed to the condition laid out by Duryodhana in the second round of dice. You were there when he was spelling that out. Why did you not stop me then and there while I was agreeing to it? You raised your objection but only after I had accepted the condition of exile and the invitation to play. Nonetheless, what hurts me is the torture Draupadi was subjected to and we did nothing to help her. It was like we willingly drank a vial of poison. The pain of that helplessness haunts me to this day. But now that I have given my word to live through the thirteen years of vanvās, I cannot renege on that and call for a war.'[12]

There was another reason, a practical challenge, due to which Yudhishthira was willing to wait it out for thirteen years. 'We cannot make a decision about war recklessly. It will lead to more loss and pain. To be able to succeed, we need to deliberate, strategise, make a clear plan of action and then execute it to the best of our abilities. A task thus undertaken is more likely to be favoured by destiny too. Intoxicated in your pride, you are becoming restless for a war. But let me tell you the opposition we will be faced with: Bhurishravā, Bhishma, Drona, Ashwatthāmā, Karna, Duryodhana himself and his brothers. These are all exceptional warriors and are well versed in the use of celestial weapons. Bhishma and Drona empathise with us but they are in the service of Dhritarāshtra. If a war were to happen, they would fight for Duryodhana. Moreover, the kings we had subjugated during Rājasuya Yajna would ally with Duryodhana against us. Duryodhana has been keeping his armies in good humour, paying timely wages and luring them with rewards. Defeating them is not going to be easy unless we are well prepared,'[13] Yudhishthira explained his stance.

Soon after, on Yudhishthira's advice, Arjuna left to get trained in exquisite celestial weapons not accessible to ordinary warriors to start preparing for a future war. 'Duryodhana's side is adorned by Bhishma, Drona, Karna, Ashwatthāmā and other such warriors. Our success depends on you. Hence, I suggest you go to the north and strive to secure the knowledge of celestial weapons,'[14] Yudhishthira said. In the five years that Arjuna was away, the other Pāndavas and Draupadi undertook pilgrimages, met various rishis and had some interesting adventures.

Yudhishthira's Dream

After returning from their pilgrimage, the Pāndavas had once again camped in Dwaitavana and resumed their āshram life. One night, Yudhishthira had a dream. The animals of the jungle had come to see him. They were sorrowful and sobbing loudly. 'Who are you? Please tell me whatever you wish to,' asked Yudhishthira with folded hands.

'We are the animals of this forest. Due to your hunting, only a handful of us are alive now. Please do not destroy us completely. Leave this forest and go to another location so that we can multiply and replenish our species,' the animals urged.

'So will it be,' promised Yudhishthira in his dream.

The next morning, on waking up, the eldest Pāndava was reminded of his dream. He was overcome with compassion. He recounted the dream to his brothers and said, 'I believe, the animals are right. We have lived here for over a year-and-a-half. It's time we move.'[15] They did.

Bheema's Exploits during the Vanvās

Three days into their vanvās, the Pāndavas were attacked by a rākshasa named Kimir. He had specially come to kill Bheema to avenge his brother Bakāsura's death, whom Bheema had killed in Ekachakra Nagar. Kimir was huge and extremely powerful. He challenged Bheema. Bheema was already raging due to the Duryodhana's deceit. Now Draupadi was also looking at him with admiration in her eyes.

This further encouraged him. Kimir and Bheema fought with the might of two huge boulders. Eventually, Bheema crushed the rākshasa dead.[16]

Later on, when Arjuna was away on an expedition to get the celestial weapons, the other four Pāndavas with Draupadi undertook a long trip to various places of pilgrimage. During one such trip in the Gandhamādan[17] mountains, a beautiful lotus, whose fragrance pervaded the air around, caught Draupadi's attention. She was charmed by the sweet fragrance of the lotus and desired for a bunch of those divine flowers. She lovingly requested Bheema, 'If I am dear to you please get me those flowers. I wish to take them back to our āshram in the forest.' How could Bheema refuse! He picked up his gold-studded weapons and left, determined to please Draupadi.

The route to the lotus pond was beautiful but daunting due to the steep slopes and huge boulders along the way. The affection in Draupadi's eyes kept Bheema going zestfully. Soon, he reached the pond covered with fragrant lotuses. But before he could take the flowers, a rākshasa named Krodhavasha with his army of other similar-looking rākshasas stopped him. 'This pond is not meant for humans such as yourself. If you wish to take the flowers, get permission from our master Kuber.' Bheema replied firmly, 'I do not see your master around. But even if I did, I do not see any need to get his permission as this is a natural pond. It is not in your master's home. All living beings have as much right to this natural pond as your master.' Saying so, he attempted to enter the pond.

To prevent him from entering, the rākshasas attacked Bheema. Kunti's second son born of Vayu deva was more than a match for them. Few rākshasas survived the wrath of his mace. Having defeated them, Bheema swam in the pond delightfully and then plucked the flowers for Draupadi.[18] To fulfil another such request made by her, of being able to see the peaks of the mountains near Rishi Arshtishen's āshram, Bheema killed a rākshasa named Manimān and made the area safe for Draupadi and other rishis to wander.[19]

Towards the end of the pilgrimage, the Pāndavas resided in Badrikā āshram waiting for Arjuna to return. Another rākshasa by the name Jatāsura came to stay with them disguised as a rishi. He desired Draupadi. Once, when Bheema was away on some errand, Jatāsura assumed his original humongous avatār and kidnapped the three brothers along with Draupadi. Somehow, Sahadeva managed to get himself and his weapon freed from Jatāsura's grip and ran to call for Bheema. When he came, a gory fight took place, at the end of which the daunting Jatāsura was reduced to being a lump of flesh without life.[20]

After Arjuna returned, other instances caused the Pāndavas to pick up their weapons and fight. The Pāndavas, on Yudhishthira's insistence, fought the Gandharvas to liberate Duryodhana and his friends. Then, they had to fight Jayadratha, their brother-in-law, to rescue Draupadi. Whatever be the situation, Bheema stood strong to keep the Pāndavas and Draupadi safe.

Yudhishthira's Wisdom Saves the Brothers

After Arjuna's return from the expedition, the Pāndavas spent another year in the Himālayas before returning to Dwaitavana. En route to the forest, they stopped in the Kirāta desh, the kingdom of Subāhu. One day, during their stay here, Bheema went hunting in the nearby forest. Chasing some huge snakes, he reached deep inside the jungle, when a huge yellow snake caught hold of him. Bheema had the strength of ten thousand elephants but he was helpless against the grip of the mighty snake. After struggling for some time, Bheema gave up. 'Even the mightiest of lions can't prevail over me the way you have! You cannot be an ordinary snake. Who are you?' asked Bheema, astonished.

'I am Nahusha, one of your ancestors. I was cursed before to take birth as a snake and hence here I am. I have been starving for many days because I am under oath to accept only that as food which falls into my grip at this time of the day on its own. However, I have been given a boon too. If someone answers all my questions satisfactorily, then I will be liberated from this snake avatār,' the snake replied.

Meanwhile, as Bheema had not returned from the forest, the Pāndavas got worried. Yudhishthira ventured to look for him and reached the spot where Nahusha had held Bheema. He offered himself as food to Nahusha. The snake refused, repeating his pledge. 'But if you answer all my questions properly, then I will let your brother go,' Nahusha said. Yudhishthira agreed.

'Who should we know as a Brāhmin?'

'One who is truthful, charitable, forgiving, well mannered, compassionate, austere and merciful is to be considered a Brāhmin.'

'But these qualities can be seen in a Shudra as well. How then do we decide?'

'If a Shudra has these qualities and a Brāhmin doesn't, then a Shudra is not a Shudra and a Brāhmin is not a Brāhmin. One who has these qualities is to be considered a Brāhmin and one who lacks these virtues is to be considered a Shudra.'

'So if only actions determine whether one is a Brāhmin or not, being born in a Brāhmin family would mean nothing?'

'I believe determining a person's varna[21] at birth is very difficult because a lot of intermingling of varnas and races has happened. Therefore, the wise consider only action as the indicator of varna.'

Nahusha was happy and satisfied with Yudhishthira's answers. 'You know all that is worth knowing. How can I eat your brother now? I am letting him go.'[22]

Towards the end of the twelfth year, the Pāndavas came back to Dwaitavana, this time living only on a diet of fruits. One day, a priest came running to seek their help. A wild animal had taken away his wood and churning stick. Without those, the priest couldn't do his ritual yajna. The brothers immediately took off to find the animal and retrieve the wood and churning stick. But their efforts were in vain.

They reached deep within the forest looking for the animal. Finding none, they rested for a bit hoping to get some water.

Yudhishthira sent Nakula to fetch some water for them. Nakula approached a lake nearby and was about to plunge in to drink some water when a voice stopped him from doing so. 'O Son of Mādri, I have a claim over this lake. To drink water from here, you will have to first answer my questions.' Nakula looked around but didn't see anyone. The thirst was making him desperate. He shrugged off the warning and drank the water. In an instant, he fell unconscious.

'What is taking Nakula so long?' wondered Yudhishthira and sent Sahadeva to look for Nakula and get water. Sahadeva met the same fate, as did Arjuna and Bheema. Eventually, Yudhishthira himself went looking. He was shocked to see his brothers lying unconscious on the ground. 'How can this be possible? My brothers are invincible. Moreover, there seem to be no marks of injury on their bodies. This seems like the work of some demonic power,' Yudhishthira thought as he tried to make sense of this strange happening. His eyes fell on the water and he got up to parch his thirst.

The voice roared again, 'Do not dare to drink this water before answering my questions! Your brothers did, hence I killed them!' Yudhishthira stopped in his tracks. 'You must be someone really distinguished because no ordinary being can do this to my brothers. I am curious to know you as well as I am a little bewildered. Please do reveal yourself.'

'I am Yaksha. I rule over this lake. Answer my questions if you wish to drink this water.'

'I do not wish to take away that which is yours. I will certainly attempt to answer your question to the best of my ability.'

Yaksha began his volley of questions. Yudhishthira politely answered. Yaksha was pleased and convinced that Yudhishthira was indeed a man of wisdom.

'You have answered my questions. I grant you the life of one of your brothers. Who would you like to be brought back to life?' Yaksha asked. Without a moment's hesitation, Yudhishthira requested for Nakula to be resurrected. Yaksha was surprised. 'I am aware that Bheema is dearest to you and to win the war you most definitely need Arjuna. Then why do you pick Nakula who is, after all, your stepbrother?'

'Dharma[23] destroys those who destroy it and protects those who protect it. Hence, I will never rescind dharma. My father had two wives, Kunti and Mādri. They are both my mothers and I regard them equally. It is only fair that both of them have at least one of their sons alive,' Yudhishthira replied.

Yaksha was extremely happy to see Yudhishthira not lose sight of dharma even in the face of sorrow. He resurrected all the Pāndavas and revealed his real identity. 'I am your biological father, Yama, the lord of dharma. I am happy to see you steadfast in your virtues,' said Yama. He granted the Pāndavas a boon that they would remain unidentified in their disguise in the thirteenth year of exile and left.[24]

Yaksha Prashna

Some of the questions asked by Yaksha and answers given by Yudhishthira are:

'What kind of a person who breathes has intelligence and is also well known, but is really as good as dead?'

'The one who does not serve the devas,[25] guests, ancestors, family members and his ātmā is as good as dead even if alive.'

'Who is the friend of a traveller? Who is the friend of a householder? Who is the friend of the unwell and who is the friend of the one who is about to die?'

'Co-travellers are friends of a traveller. A wife is the friend of a householder. A doctor is a friend of the unwell and charity is the friend of the one who is about to die.'

'What is the footing of dharma? What does fame stand on? What is the basis of heaven? What is happiness based on?'

'Enterprise[26] is the footing of dharma. Charity brings fame. Truth is the basis of heaven and virtuous character brings happiness.'

'Who is the best amongst the wealthy? What is the best among wealth? What is worth gaining? Who is the happiest amongst all?'

'Amongst the wealthy, those who are enterprising are the best. Knowledge of the Vedas is the best wealth. Good health is worth gaining. A content person is the happiest.'

'When is a person considered to be dead? When is a country considered to be dead?'

'A man in extreme poverty is as good as dead. A country in anarchy is considered to be dead.'

'Giving up what makes a person agreeable? Renouncing what does a person not grieve? Giving up what makes a person prosperous? Giving up what makes a person happy?'

'Giving up pride endears a person. Renouncing anger, he does not grieve. Giving up unwanted desires makes a person prosperous. Giving up greed makes a person happy.'

'What is real knowledge? What is equanimity? What is compassion? What is forthrightness?'

'The knowledge of the essence of God is real knowledge. Equanimity is tranquility of mind. Desiring well-being of all is compassion. Even-mindedness towards all is forthrightness.'

'Who is the biggest enemy of man? What disease has no cure? Who is a noble man? And who isn't?'

'Anger is a man's biggest enemy. Greed has no cure. One who desires the well-being of all is a noble man. One who has no mercy or compassion is not.'

'What is ignorance? What is pride? What is lethargy? What is grief?'

'Not knowing one's dharma is ignorance. Self-conceit is pride. Not doing one's duty is lethargy. Ignorance of true knowledge is grief.'

'When is a person be considered a Brāhmin—by birth, action, education or listening to scriptures?'

'Not by birth, not by education, not by listening to scriptures does one become a Brāhmin. Only by action can a person be considered a Brāhmin.'

'What does a person who has a sweet speech gain? What does a person who acts with discretion gain? What is the gain for him who has many friends? What does a man who is engrossed in his duty gain?'

'A person with sweet speech endears all. A person who acts with discretion increases his chances of success. A person with many friends lives with joy. A man engrossed in his duty achieves bliss[27] in this world and next.'

'Who is truly happy? What is most astonishing? What is the right path? What information is worth having?'

'One who is not indebted to anyone, not away in a foreign land and eats food in the fifth or sixth part of the day[28] cooked in his own house even if with scanty vegetables is truly happy. Every day in the world umpteen creatures die, but those who are alive desire to live forever. What can be more astonishing than this? Wise men have differing opinions; logic can also lead to multiple conclusions and the scriptures sometimes have contradictory indications. Hence, the right path is that which was taken by noble people. The only information worth having is this—time is cooking us all in the pan of this delusional world, with a ladle of months and seasons on the fire of the sun fuelled by night and day.'

Yaksha was very pleased. 'You have responded to my questions well. Now answer this last set—Define Purusha[29]—the one who is truly known to exist? Who is Sarvadhani—one who has all kinds of wealth?'

'As long as a man's virtuous actions are known in the world, he is known to truly exist. One who is free of dualities and maintains his equanimity in all situations—happiness and sorrow, pleasure and pain—truly has all kinds of wealth.'

Satisfied with the answers Yaksha, revealed his real self to Yudhishthira and brought the brothers to life.

The Year in Disguise

Twelve years in the forest had gone by. The coming year had to be spent in disguise. The Pāndavas bade farewell to their priests and helpers requesting them to take shelter in kingdoms of allies. Before leaving, their royal priest, Dhaumya, gave them some practical advice on how to live like common citizens to avoid standing out in the crowd:[30]

1. Serving a king living in his palace is not easy. During this one year of disguise bother not about your pride and ego. Whatever comes your way, humbly tolerate.
2. Do not trust a king completely. Do not start behaving as if the king likes you even if he does. Do not use his seat, chariot, bed or any other item.
3. Seek relevant permissions with relevant authorities before you proceed with a task. Keep the king informed about whatever you undertake.
4. Do not give unsolicited advice to the king about his responsibilities. But do praise the king as opportune.
5. Do not become too friendly with the queens, those who regularly interact with the queens or those who the king doesn't approve of. Maintain your distance.
6. Always remember the royal etiquettes and do that which is in the best interest of the king.

The Pāndavas took his suggestions and deliberated on the place where they could live in disguise. Arjuna suggested a few names from which Yudhishthira selected Matsya desh. King Virāta of Matsya was very powerful, old, generous and had been fond of the Pāndavas when they were still in Indraprastha.

'But what will you do in Matsya desh? You are soft-spoken, just and generous. How will you manage to live like a commoner in Virāta's kingdom?' asked Arjuna to Yudhishthira. 'I will dress like a Brāhmin, take the name Kanka and become a courtier in Virāta's assembly. I will display my skill in playing dice and keep the king and other courtiers entertained,' Yudhishthira said smiling. He asked the brothers and Draupadi to choose their disguise. Bheema decided to take up the role of a royal cook, as Vallabha. Nakula proposed to become Granthika and take charge of the king's horse stables. Sahadeva said he would assume the name Tantipāla and tend the king's cattle. Arjuna declared he would present himself as a eunuch and take the name Brihannalā. He would use the music and dance skills he learnt in Indra's palace to teach dance to the women in the palace. Draupadi said she would assume the role of Sairāndhri and seek to work as the handmaiden of Sudeshnā, the queen of Virāta, taking care of the queen's hair and dressing.

Walking through the rugged terrain and crossing mountains, forests and rivers, the Pāndavas reached Matsya. First, they had to find a place to hide their weapons. Arjuna suggested storing away their weapons on a huge shami tree near an isolated cemetery, atop a hillock surrounded by forests, en route to the city of Virāta. The brothers agreed. Having hidden their weapons among the lush branches of the tree, they hung an orphaned dead body lying around in the cemetery on one of its branches. The rotting smell of the body would keep people from coming near the tree, they presumed. Some cowherds saw the body hanging on the tree when the Pāndavas were leaving. 'It is a custom followed in our family,' said the Pāndavas in explanation and walked away.[31]

They arrived in Matsya desh. The brothers got the jobs they wanted and settled in. For Draupadi, however, it wasn't that simple. Seeing her roaming in the city near the palace, Sudeshnā and the women in the palace were bewildered. 'Why is a woman of such immaculate beauty roaming around like this in the city?' they wondered. Sudeshnā called for Draupadi to be brought to the palace and asked her the reason. Draupadi said she was looking for a job in the palace as a handmaiden. 'I refuse to believe you are a handmaiden. And I am worried about keeping you in the palace too. If the king sees you, he is sure to be infatuated by your beauty. He will leave me for you. By keeping you in my palace I will bring upon my ruin,' said Sudeshnā, concerned.

Draupadi replied firmly, 'No king or any other man can have me. I am wedded to five young Gandharva men. They are extremely strong and always watch out for me. I am no walkover either. My husbands stay pleased with those employers who do not give me stale food and do not make me wash their feet. And if any man tries to harm my modesty, they will certainly kill him that very night. You need not worry.' Her fears thus assuaged, Sudeshnā employed Draupadi in her service.

One day, a renowned wrestler named Jimuta came to the city to challenge the wrestlers of Matsya. All those who accepted his challenge were defeated and killed in the wrestling pavilion by Jimuta. When no other wrestler had the heart to come forward, Virāta called for his cook Vallabha. Bheema hesitated as he was worried about being recognised. But refusing the king was not an option. He came, fought and, in a nail-biting wrestling match, defeated and killed Jimuta.[32] Everyone was all praises for Vallabha but luckily no one questioned his identity. Not then.

Most of the year passed by in relative peace. Then one day, Keechak, Sudeshnā's brother and commander of Virāta's army, set his eyes on Draupadi. Enraged to see a handmaiden not entertain his advances, Keechak tried to force himself on her. Draupadi ran to the court of Virāta to seek help. Keechak ran behind her and kicked her. Draupadi fell in front of all the courtiers. Virāta looked the other way. Yudhishthira and Bheema were there too. Bheema was so furious that he could have killed Keechak there and then, but Yudhishthira stopped him. They had to live through this only for a few more days.

Draupadi lamented aloud about Keechak's attempt to defile her. She wondered why her husbands were not coming to her rescue. The courtiers, on hearing her story, were all praises for her gumption but no one had the courage to speak against Keechak. Yudhishthira was also very angry at Keechak. Hiding his anger, however, he asked Draupadi to leave and not disturb the king, but not without hinting to her his wish. 'Do not create a scene here in the court. This is not the right time. Your Gandharva husbands will fulfil your wishes. Anyone who has wronged you will be punished by them. Leave now,'[33] he said, trying to sound dismissive. 'Let that person who put his hand on me be killed,' said Draupadi and walked away.

That night, Draupadi approached Bheema discreetly. She wanted Keechak dead, nothing less. And she was aware that Bheema was the only one who would fulfil her wish. Bheema was seething with anger at Keechak anyway. They made a plan. Draupadi was to behave as if she was ready to entertain Keechak and invited him to an unmanned Nrityashālā the room used for dance and music, the next night. Draupadi played along. Keechak was overjoyed. He thought his power had brought Draupadi to her knees. The next night, he came hoping to satiate his lust for Draupadi. But a shock awaited him. Not Draupadi, but Bheema was waiting for him.

A gruesome duel ensued. Keechak was powerful but Bheema even more so. In a few hours, Bheema had completely overpowered him. Keechak roared frightfully like a broken trumpet struggling to get out of Bheema's steadfast grip. He was fast losing consciousness. Bheema began to whirl the powerful Keechak on the ground. When he was almost motionless, the son of Kunti grasped his throat and squeezed it tight. Pouncing hard on the waist of Keechak, whose limbs had already cracked and eyeballs had popped out, Bheema slayed him as one would slay a beast. Keechak's body was reduced to a lifeless ball of flesh.

Draupadi was delighted. Excitedly, she called the guards of the palace to go and witness the gruesome end of him who attempted to violate her sanctity. 'Come and behold how the mighty Keechak has been slain by one of my Gandharva husbands for lusting after another's wife,' she smirked. People of Matsya believed Draupadi's claims about her husbands and dared not bother her after that incident.[34]

Keechak's death made Duryodhana suspicious enough to plot with Susharmā, the king of Trigarta, and attack Virāta. Their plot failed. Both Susharmā and the Kaurava army were defeated, the latter by Arjuna alone.

The restraint shown by Yudhishthira in Virāta's court the day that Draupadi had come to seek punishment for Keechak was not a one-off incident. When Yudhishthira was verbally and physically assaulted by King Virāta on one occasion, he displayed the same restraint and did not even let his brothers know, lest they react and endanger their disguise. The incident happened when the news of the defeat of the Kaurava army at the hands of Uttar and Brihannalā reached King Virāta's palace.

Virāta pride knew no bounds. He attributed the success to his son Uttar's valour and couldn't stop talking about it. While playing a game of dice with Kanka, Virāta praised his son again. Very naturally, Kanka, replied, 'With a mighty warrior like Brihannalā by his side, how could Prince Uttar not win. Brihannalā is unmatched in prowess and valour.' This was not the first time Kanka had praised Brihannalā. Virāta was furious. 'How dare you compare my son to a eunuch! Have you no discretion about what to say and what should never be uttered? I have cautioned you before as well to not sing high praises of Brihannalā and insult me. You can't seem to shut up!' Saying so, Virāta hit Yudhishthira's face with the dice he was holding. The dice hit Yudhishthira's nose hard, causing blood to ooze out.

Yudhishthira immediately put his hands under the nose to stop the blood from falling on the ground. Draupadi was standing nearby and saw the event play out. She rushed to Yudhishthira with a bowl to collect the blood. She knew what would happen if the other Pāndavas would see Yudhishthira hurt. Just then, a messenger came in to inform the arrival of Uttar and Brihannalā. Yudhisthira discreetly told the messenger to not let Brihannalā come into the room at that time. 'If he sees my injury and blood, he will not leave anyone alive.'[35] Draupadi, too, didn't utter a word to anyone, not then. It was now just matter of a few days before the Pāndavas would reveal their identity.

Though the year of disguise had ended before the war of Virāta, the Pāndavas came out of hiding a few days later. It was now time to claim their kingdom back.

The Blessings

Talks of peace had fallen flat. Yudhishthira was ready to settle for just five villages instead of Indraprastha. War would mean destruction of the clan, he knew. But

Duryodhana declared he would not even give them a needle's tip worth of land. All modes of diplomacy had failed.

The armies had assembled in the battlefield of Kurukshetra and stood facing each other. The war conches had been blown. The armies were waiting for the signal to attack. Instead, Yudhishthira removed his armour, left his weapons on the chariot and walked towards the Kaurava army. The brothers were baffled. They too got off their chariots and followed the eldest son of Pāndu, so did other warriors along with Krishna.

'What has come upon you? Why are you heading towards the enemies without your weapons and on foot?' the brothers asked. Yudhishthira did not speak. He kept walking. 'I believe he is going to take the blessings of Bhishma, Drona and other elders. There is an ancient belief that if one goes into a battle without seeking permission of the elders, he is sure to lose,' conjectured Krishna. He was right. Yudhishthira stopped before Bhishma's chariot.

With folded hands, he bowed to his grandfather, 'I have come to ask your permission to fight with you. Please endow your blessings on me.'

Bhishma smiled. 'Had you not come, I would have cursed you to lose. Now I am pleased. Go fight with all your might. May success be yours,' Bhishma blessed, adding, 'And let me know if there is anything else you desire. I am indebted to Dhritarāshtra. I serve at the pleasure of the king of Hastināpur and thus I am beholden to fight on the side of Duryodhana. Therefore, except for fighting on your side, you can ask me for anything. I will happily grant your wish.'

'I need your wise counsel, nothing more. You are invincible. I do not see any warrior today who can defeat you. Please suggest a way by which we can defeat you,' Yudhishthira asked politely.

Bhishma laughed and replied, 'You are right. Nobody can kill me in the war. But the time is not yet ripe for my death. Come back again with this question at another time. I will tell you then.' Yudhishthira bowed again and walked towards Dronāchārya. He sought Drona's permission and blessing. Drona offered to grant a wish as well. Yudhishthira asked Drona the way to overpower him. 'As long as I hold weapons in my hand, none of you can kill me. Strive to get me to drop my weapons and sit down in the field. If I hear some extremely unpleasant news, I will give up my weapons.' The Pāndavas took the blessings of all their elders and came back to their chariots. The war formally commenced.[36]

Bhishma led the Kaurava army for the first ten days. Every day, he was depleting the Pāndava army by thousands of soldiers and warriors. The only way to get him out of the way was to ask him the way to defeat him, as Yudhishthira had on the first day. On the ninth night, he again approached his grandfather to seek an answer to that question. This time, Bhishma told them the answer. He fell on the tenth day, unable to withstand Arjuna's arrows coming from behind Shikhandi.

The Fall of Dronāchārya

Dronāchārya took on the Kaurava mantle after Bhishma. With his arrival, the war became deadlier.

The rules of engagement were flouted. The Pāndavas lost their dear sons, Abhimanyu and Ghatotkacha among others.

The death of Abhimanyu and Ghatotkacha had greatly agitated Yudhishthira. He held Dronāchārya and Karna squarely responsible for their deaths. He wanted them dead and sooner. Yudhishthira summoned Dhrishtadyumna before the war commenced on the fifteenth day. He reminded Dhrishtadyumna of the motive of his birth, 'Move ahead and destroy Dronāchārya. You have taken birth to be his nemesis. Fear not.'

Duryodhana once again called Dronāchārya a traitor for failing to protect Jayadratha. Once again, hurt by Duryodhana's taunts, Drona had pledged his loyalty to Duryodhana. On the fifteenth day, Drona entered the battlefield determined to crush the Pāndava army. That morning, umpteen Pāndava warriors fell prey to Drona's arrows, including Drupada, Draupadi's father and the king of Pānchāla, and Virāta, Uttarā's father and the king of Matsya.

Krishna knew that defeating Dronāchārya while he still held weapons in his hand was a hopeless task, as Drona had also told Yudhishthira on the first day. There was only one way to make Drona drop his weapons. 'If only he is convinced that Ashwatthāmā is dead, he would give up fighting. Someone should tell him that Ashwatthāmā is dead,' said Krishna. Yudhishthira, though hesitant, agreed with Krishna's suggestion. Bheema didn't waste a second. He rotated his mace and threw it on an elephant named Ashwatthāmā in his troop and killed him. Then, within Drona's hearing range, Bheema screamed, 'Ashwatthāmā is dead.'[37]

Drona was shocked but he was also suspicious of the veracity of the news. He knew about the capability of his son. It wasn't easy to defeat let alone simply kill Ashwatthāmā. Drona ignored and continued his offensive. In his eagerness to prove allegiance to Duryodhana, Drona did the unthinkable. He drew out his Brahmāstra, one of the most potent weapons of those times. Such weapons were not meant for use on human beings. Fortunately, before Drona could hurl the Brahmāstra, the voice of the rishis[38] desisted him from committing one more sin. The immoral killing of Abhimanyu was already a blot on his virtue. Drona withdrew the Brahmāstra but continued the rampage of the Pāndava troops.

The words of Bheema, however, were still disturbing him. He decided to confirm with Yudhishthira, who he believed would tell him the truth. Krishna had forewarned Yudhishthira of the consequences of sticking to his truth indiscreetly, 'The way Dronāchārya is fighting, if allowed to continue for even half a day more, your army will be exterminated. Sometimes, a lie that saves lives is more important than a truth that kills.' Bheema agreed with Krishna and cajoled Yudhishthira to confirm Ashwatthāmā's death. Ashwatthāmā the elephant was indeed dead.

Yudhishthira was in a dilemma about the right mode of action. Nevertheless, when asked by Drona, Yudhishthira replied affirmatively, 'Ashwatthāmā is dead.' Then in a very low voice, he uttered, 'नरो वा कुंजरो वा' ('It could be a man or an elephant.')[39]

Dronāchārya heard only the first half of Yudhishthira's utterance. Utterly dejected at what he thought was the loss of his son and exhausted from the incessant fighting of the past fourteen days and a half, Drona couldn't immediately respond to Dhrishtadyumna's attack as he otherwise would. But he quickly got himself together and launched an offensive at Dhrishtadyumna. Twice, Dhrishtadyumna had to be saved, once by Sātyaki and later by Bheema.

Drona was still in no mood to drop his weapons. This time, Bheema moved closer to Drona and said softly with a hint of derisiveness, 'The son for whose well-being you have been fighting is lying dead. Why are you still interested in actions that don't suit your calibre. You are a peace-loving teacher. So much bloodshed doesn't befit you.'[40] The words had their desired effect. Dronāchārya dropped his weapons and sat down in samadhi at the back of his chariot. Taking advantage of this very moment, Dhrishtadyumna, Draupadi's twin brother, the prince of Pānchāla, killed Dronāchārya.

The war continued for three more days after Dronāchārya's death. Karna, Duhshāsana, Shakuni, Shalya and Duryodhana himself fell soon after. The Pāndavas lost their sons and relatives too. Every warrior had a huge role to play in the victory of the Pāndavas. But three warriors stood out—Bheema, Arjuna and Sātyaki.

Arjuna had misgivings about killing his relatives. Nevertheless, he destroyed armies and armies of the

Kauravas. He killed some of the most daunting warriors on the Kaurava side like Bhagadatta of Prāgjyotisha, Susharmā of Trigarta, apart from Jayadratha and Karna. But when it came to his teacher and grandfather, his will to win fell short.

Bheema had no such misgivings. He had shown that he was in the war to win. Relationships were not his concern once the war began. All the hundred Kaurava brothers were killed by him. On the fourteenth day, as Arjuna got closer to Jayadratha, on Yudhishthira's advice, Bheema went to back him up. Drona tried to obstruct his way. Bheema did not shy away from retaliating. He broke his teacher's chariot eight times before moving on.

Bheema was passionate and aggressive. The patience of Yudhishthira or the emotional effusiveness and humility of Arjuna were not for him. Even as a child, he was mischievous and often played pranks on kids his age or younger. But Bheema was also the gentle giant. He was kind and committed to his mother, brothers and Draupadi. He was always there for his family, keeping them safe from dangers and hardships as best as he could. That is also why Yudhishthira had objected to Kunti's decision to let Bheema face Bakāsura in Ekachakra Nagar.

Bheema was straightforward and spoke his mind, sometimes without consideration of any discretion. Even after the war, he couldn't keep himself from throwing taunts at Dhritarāshtra now and then. In rage and pride, he was more like Duryodhana. But one of the most important qualities that set the two apart was Bheema's deference to his elder brother's wisdom. Duryodhana was a law unto himself. His haughtiness was only aggravated by the indulgence of his father, uncle and Karna. For Bheema, however, whatever be his view, he would eventually trust his brother's judgement and act accordingly. Yudhishthira and to some extent Draupadi were the pivots of his life. Yudhishthira, on his end, had special affection for Bheema. He knew he could depend on Bheema fully, in war and in life.

Yudhishthira did not have the aggression of Bheema nor the effusiveness of Arjuna. At times, he came across as devoid of emotion. Though that would be misreading him. His repentance at his helplessness during Draupadi's humiliation, his sorrow seeing his brothers unconscious at the lake, his hesitation for a war, his grief when informed about Karna being their brother, his breakdown after the war witnessing the destruction—these incidents give a glimpse of the emotional side of Yudhishthira.

One of the major strengths of Yudhishthira was that he did not let emotions and impulses come in way of the larger goal. He was pragmatic when the situation so demanded. He knew a war was a real possibility post their years in exile. Hence, he encouraged Arjuna to prepare for that eventuality and collect celestial weapons. During the year of disguise, his goal was to ensure not being identified. He, therefore, chose not to impulsively react when Draupadi was humiliated in the court of Virāta and not even when he was physically hurt by the dice thrown at him by King Virāta. But he also assured Draupadi that she would get due justice and made no attempts to stop Bheema from punishing Keechak when the time was right. During the war, his goal was to win. That is why he reached out to Bhishma, lied to Drona and also chastised Arjuna when he sensed that his younger brother was not fighting with his heart. His pragmatism was evident even during the marriage of the Pāndavas to Draupadi. As an elder brother, he had the right to marry Draupadi himself. But that would have disrupted the unity of the brothers. He did what he thought was the right thing to do then, even if it meant going against established norms.

The only blot on his conduct was the indiscriminate staking during the game of dice. Per the norms of the day, Yudhishthira couldn't refuse the invitation to play and back out from staking as long as he had any wealth left. But couldn't he have put his foot down when Shakuni instigated him to stake Draupadi? Or did he believe the courtiers would be more sympathetic if Draupadi was with them and that could save them from ignominy? Or had the desperation at the loss in the game got the better of his discretion and patience? He did tell Bheema during the stay in the forest that the shock of losing and hope of salvaging the situation deluded him. Or was it that he was letting destiny take its course, as he had told Vidura when the invitation to the game was extended? He did send Draupadi a message through his trusted man to come to the assembly and express her pain.[41] Had Draupadi not come to the court that day, Dhritarāshtra may have never intervened. One can only guess how history would have panned out in that situation.

Yudhishthira was patient and had an immense sense of justice, of dharma. His discussions with Nahusha and Yaksha, his request to resurrect Nakula, his determination to live through the years in exile—as it was a condition he had agreed to—are a testimony to that. For the sake of peace, he agreed to play the game of dice and accepted exile, knowing well that he was being duped. He agreed to save Duryodhana and his ilk from the Gandharvas. He was also willing to forgive and cede his kingdom to Duryodhana for just five villages in return. However, peace cannot come at the price of tolerating outright injustice forever. Justice and dharma had to prevail eventually. Hence, when Duryodhana refused even the five villages, Yudhishthira was not willing to cede anymore. By taking the final resort of war, only after doing all he could to establish peace, Yudhishthira ensured the Pāndavas would stay on the right side of history and dharma.

Dharma cannot exist in a vacuum. To sustain, it needs to be rooted in enterprise, strength, compassion and ingenuity. Pāndu knew this well, wise man that he was. He ensured his eldest son Yudhishthira, the son of Dharma, was backed by the strength of Vayu and ingenuity of Indra. Compassion and enterprise, they all had.

ॐ ψ ॐ

16

Name Games

A name mix-up of Ashwatthāmā, the elephant with Ashwatthāmā, the warrior, led to the death of Drona. There are a couple of other instances in the Mahābhārata where a 'name' either saved or killed a person.

Āstik, the Saviour of the Nāgas

While Janamejaya's Sarpa Satra was ostensibly to avenge the death of his father and teach the reckless serpents a lesson, there was a backstory that led to the unfolding of these events. The snakes were living with a curse pronounced by their mother Kadru. Once, in a fit of fury over her wish not being obeyed, Kadru proclaimed her disobeying sons would be wiped out from the face of the earth.

Even the gods in heaven were shocked at the cruelty of this punishment lashed out by a mother on to her children. Brahmā deva explained, 'Everything happens for a reason. Many serpents had become vile and dangerous for the beings in the world. This curse will serve as an antidote to their nuisance.' Vāsuki, the gentle king of the snake world, was extremely worried about this eventual destruction of the race. He sought Brahmā's intervention. Comforting Vāsuki, the latter said, 'Do not worry. Your sister's son will be the saviour of your race. When the appropriate time comes, marry your sister to the rishi named Jaratkāru.'

Jaratkāru was a great rishi. He had spent several years doing rigorous tapasyā. The householder's life meant little to him but just to ensure his ancestors were not disappointed, he resolved to get married and have a child who could carry forward the ancestral lineage. However, he decided he would marry only and only if

1. the girl had the same name as his,
2. the girl was offered to him and he didn't have to go find her and
3. the responsibility of taking care of the girl was not to be his.

Rishi Jaratkāru moved from forest to forest in vain, hoping a girl would come his way. But a girl who met all his conditions was not easy to come by, until the day he reached the forest where Nāgrāja Vāsuki lived with his sister. As fate had already planned, Vāsuki's sister was also named Jaratkāru.

Janamejaya wondered what Jaratkāru meant. Vaishampāyana explained, 'The one whose body has become thin by way of rigorous austerities is a Jaratkāru. Both the rishi and Vāsuki's sister had acquired the name due to the impact of the austerities.'

Rishi Jaratkāru, on entering the forest where Vāsuki dwelled, muttered, 'I seek a girl for marriage, one who is my namesake and doesn't need me to support her.' One of the Nāgas heard this muttering and ran to inform Vāsuki. On hearing about Rishi Jaratkāru's arrival, Vāsuki was elated. He took along his sister and offered her to him as his wife. The rishi was still not very certain, because the girl had to be his namesake—a challenging condition. Vāsuki convinced him that his sister was indeed Jaratkāru and also that the responsibility of looking after the sister would be his own.

Through the union of the rishi and Vāsuki's sister, a bright boy was born. This boy was Āstik. Blessed with wisdom, Astik learned the shāstras quite early in life and grew up to be a wise young man. By getting Janamejaya to stop the yajna midway, Āstik became the saviour of his mother's family and saved the snakes from annihilation.

All thanks to Jaratkāru finding Jaratkāru!

Chitrangad

After Shāntanu's death due to old age, Chitrangad, the eldest son of Satyavati was crowned the king of Hastināpur. Chitrangad was brave and strong but also a brat. The power of the crown had made him reckless. He had become rude and looked down upon other kings and even learned men.

It so happened that the king of the Gandharvas was also named Chitrangad. At some point, due to his haughtiness, the Kaurava Chitrangad had managed to enrage the Gandharva Chitrangad. To avenge the humiliation, Gandharva approached the Kuru prince. He said,

'त्वं वै सदृशनामासि युद्धं देहि नृपात्मज। नाम
वाऽन्यत्प्रगृह्णीष्व यदि युद्धं न दास्यसि।।'
(Ādi Parva 108.9)

'O Prince, you have the same name as me, so either fight with me or change your name. I can't let him go who is undeserving of my name.'

Proud of his ancestry of mighty warriors, the Kaurava Chitrangad was not the one to bow out, nor did he have the discriminatory intelligence to think through the wisdom of accepting the challenge. He immediately agreed. The Gandharva proved to be the mightier warrior of the two and killed the Kaurav Chitrangad.

Had Chitrangad lived and remained the king, the Mahābhārata as we know could have been entirely different.

ॐ ψ ॐ

17

The Blindfolds

Dhritarāshtra, Pāndu and Vidura had finished their education and training. It was time to get them married. Bhishma had heard many good things about the daughter of the king of Gāndhār, Subal. Gāndhāri was a virtuous young lady, well versed in economics and administration[1]. An ardent devotee of Shiva, she had received a boon from Him to beget a hundred sons. Bhishma thought she could be a worthy spouse to Dhritarāshtra.

Bhishma visited Subal with the proposal for Gāndhāri's marriage to Dhritarāshtra. On being told about the lack of eyesight of the prince, Subal hesitated. But then, the Kuru kingdom of Hastināpur protected by Bhishma was mighty, renowned and prosperous. Hence, giving the proposal some serious thought, Subal agreed to marry his daughter to Dhritarāshtra.

When Gāndhāri learnt about the blind prince and that her parents were in favour of the marriage, she did not object. Instead, she took a silken cloth, made many folds and tied that sash around her own eyes. This was Gāndhāri's way of indicating her acceptance of her husband and her future life. 'I will never see any flaw in my husband,' she vowed. The marriage was solemnised. Gāndhāri was received by Bhishma and the Kaurava family with a lot of respect. On her part, Gāndhāri, with her devotion and affectionate conduct, quickly won over the hearts of her husband's family.[2] Veda Vyāsa was so impressed by Gāndhāri's service that he conferred upon her the boon of begetting hundred sons, once again.

Gāndhāri's joy knew no bounds on the day she realised she was pregnant. Dhritarāshtra had harboured a desire of having a son before Pāndu would. He hoped his son would be the eldest of all the Kuru children of that generation. Gāndhāri had wished that too. But that was not to be. Although her delivery was overdue the labour was not starting. Then came the news of the birth of Yudhishthira to Kunti and Pāndu. Frustrated, she hit her stomach hard to get the baby out. To everyone's surprise, what came out was a lump of flesh. Gāndhāri thought she had a miscarriage and was about to throw away the lump but Vyāsa stopped her.

'Soak the lump in cold water now. Get me a hundred pots filled with ghee and make arrangements to store these pots in a dark and cool place, where they cannot be easily accessed,' Vyāsa instructed. Gāndhāri and her maids did as they were told. When the lump was properly soaked in water, one of the maids was asked to separate the ball of mass into hundred thumb-sized smaller lumps. Gāndhāri had an intense desire to have one daughter along with the hundred sons as per the boon. Vyāsa had read her mind long before.

After the maid made hundred equal-sized lumps, one additional lump remained. Vyāsa asked for one more pot of ghee. He then put the lumps in the pots, covered their mouths and asked them to be hidden in the appropriate location. 'Let them be hidden for the length of your pregnancy. Only then open the lids of the pots,' he said and went away.

At the stipulated time, Vyāsa came back. He got the pots opened one by one and took the babies out. The first one to be taken out was Duryodhana. As soon as he was brought out, he started crying loudly. His cry sounded like the braying of a donkey. As if responding to his cry, donkeys, jackals, crows and other such creatures started croaking loudly, creating a hideous commotion. A sudden thunderstorm struck the city. These omens were inauspicious. Dhritarāshtra was too elated to bother about omens. 'This eldest son of mine is second only to Yudhishthira in our family. Will he become the king of Hastināpur?' he excitedly asked Vidura and Bhishma.

Vidura hadn't missed the omens. 'The indications that have emerged at this boy's birth do not augur well for the family. He seems to be a harbinger of destruction. It might be a better idea to give up this kid and save the larger family,' he warned. 'You will still have ninety-nine other sons. Wise sages have said, "If need arises, for the sake of the family, one should sacrifice the son. For the sake of the town, a family should be sacrificed and for the sake of the country, the town should be sacrificed",' Vidura added.[3]

Dhritarāshtra was already enamoured by his eldest son and did not heed Vidura's advice; not this time nor in the future. His love and ambition for his son only increased as the boy grew up. A father who was naturally blind had further been blinded by ambition and a mother who had made a conscious choice to not see—neither of them could see the man their eldest son was growing up to be. When they did see, it was already very late.

Duryodhana hated his cousins from the moment they came to Hastināpur. His hatred got a boost due to the indulgence of his father and maternal uncle Shakuni. He even tried killing Bheema by poisoning his food. Dhritarāshtra and Gāndhāri were either so out of touch with their son that they didn't know of his deeds or if they did, they looked the other way. Vidura and Kunti too decided to keep quiet about Duryodhana's machinations. And the eldest son of Dhritarāshtra continued to act with impunity.

The boys grew up and finished their training with Dronāchārya. Considering Yudhishthira's wisdom and virtues, the elders advised Dhritarāshtra to declare him as the crown prince of Hastināpur. Dhritarāshtra agreed. He wasn't happy but could not find a valid reason to refuse. Duryodhana was not pleased but kept quiet. The Pāndavas were becoming increasingly popular with the citizens of Hastināpur. The people couldn't stop talking about Yudhishthira's sense of justice, Bheema's strength, Arjuna's humility and their conquests of the kingdoms around.[4]

Dhritarāshtra did not hate the sons of his younger brother. Nevertheless, the ambition to see Duryodhana become the king of Hastināpur was strongly etched in his heart. The popularity of the Pāndavas was giving him no peace. He was aware that the Pāndavas outdid his sons in virtue and valour. To seek a solution, he consulted a sage named Kanik, an expert in diplomacy. Kanik, by way of a fable, encouraged the king to act with tact and eliminate a stronger enemy without overt aggression.[5] The idea seemed to suit Dhritarāshtra.

The Cunning Jackal

Dhritarāshtra wanted to know how to use diplomacy to deal with stronger opponents. Kanik told him a story of five friends—a jackal, a lion, a mouse, a mongoose and a wolf. One day, the friends were trying to hunt a deer but the deer was very agile and couldn't be caught. The friends deliberated and came up with a strategy. As per the plan, the mouse nibbled the feet of the deer when it was asleep. The deer woke up with wounded feet. It couldn't run anymore and wobbled as he moved. Taking advantage of that, the lion easily hunted it down.

When the friends gathered to relish the meat, the jackal stopped them. 'Why don't you go and freshen up? I will guard the meat,' he said. The others liked the suggestion and went to the lake nearby to bathe. The lion was the first one to return. Seeing the jackal sad and worried, he enquired what the matter was. The jackal replied with anguish evident in his voice, 'How do I not be upset? Do you know what the mouse said about you? He said, "Damned be the power of the lion. He considers himself the king of animals but couldn't even kill the deer by himself. Now he is going to relish the deer which was in reality killed by me." The mouse claimed credit for the meat with so much pride that I wish not to eat the meat of any animal that was hunted with the help of a tiny little mouse!'

The lion's ego was hurt. 'Huh, yes, you are right. I too do not wish to eat this meat. I will hunt alone and prove to the mouse that I don't need his help!' roared the lion and walked away.

Next came the mouse. He too asked the jackal the reason for his sad face. The jackal replied, 'I have to warn you, dear friend. The mongoose has refused to eat this meat. He says the lion's bite has made it poisonous. Instead, the mongoose plans to kill you for his food.' The mouse was frightened and disappeared into some hole to save his life.

Then came the wolf. To him, the jackal said, 'I don't know what happened between the two of you but the lion is upset with you. He has gone to get his wife so that together they can pounce and feast on you.' The wolf was taken aback. He did not wish to take any chances and ran away as fast as he could.

The pattern followed when the mongoose returned. Only this time, the jackal had changed his expression. He looked menacingly at the mongoose and threatened, 'I have just defeated the lion, the mouse and wolf with the strength of my brawn. If you wish to eat this meat, you will first have to fight and defeat me.' The mongoose chickened out. 'If the lion and the wolf couldn't defeat you, who am I to even attempt to challenge you?' saying so, he ran away.

The jackal had a hearty laugh and relished the meat all by himself.

'O King, this is how a smart administrator should deal with his enemies. Scare the meek, bow to the powerful, entice the greedy with money and challenge the weak,' explained Kanik.

Duryodhana had already begun plotting to get the Pāndavas out of his way with the help of his uncle Shakuni, brother Duhshāsana and new-found friend Karna. Stating his concern regarding the growing popularity of the Pāndavas, he asked Dhritarāshtra to get them out of sight and mind of the subjects by sending them away to a faraway town of Vāranāvata under some pretext. Dhritarāshtra liked the idea.

What Duryodhana had not told his father was the plot of killing the Pāndavas once they reached Vāranāvata. He had engaged a person named Purochana to construct an inflammable palace for the Pāndavas. Once Purochana had won the brothers over with his sweet talk, he was to set the palace on fire and burn them alive.

Dhritarāshtra instructed Yudhishthira to visit Vāranāvata along with his brothers. The Pāndavas, unaware of the schemings, happily obeyed and left for Vāranāvata with their mother. Vidura learnt of this devious plan from his spies. When the Pāndavas were leaving, he forewarned Yudhishthira of the imminent danger that awaited them. He said it in a language of Mlecchas[6], which few others apart from him and Yudhishthira knew.

In Vāranāvata, Purochana acted his role per the script. The Pāndavas played along. At an opportune time, before Purochana could realise what was happening, they set the palace on fire and escaped. People believed the Pāndavas were burnt dead along with Purochana in the palace. The news of their death reached Hastināpur. Everyone mourned the death of their favourite princes. Dhritarāshtra expressed his despair in public and quickly declared Duryodhana the crown prince of Hastināpur.

The Pāndavas came out of hiding only after securing Draupadi as their wife and the powerful Pānchālas as their in-laws. Vidura gave the news of the Pāndavas' escape and subsequent marriage to Dhritarāshtra. The king displayed his delight and praised the virtues of Yudhishthira, more out of compulsion than genuine joy. He expressed his displeasure to Duryodhana later and confessed he had to put up a happy face before Vidura. He also asked Duryodhana and Karna to figure out a way to deal with the Pāndavas in the changed circumstances in consultation with the ministers of Hastināpur.[7]

Bhishma stated his position clearly. 'I do not discriminate between the sons of Dhritarāshtra and Pāndu. Duryodhana believes Hastināpur is his inheritance, so do the Pāndavas and rightly so. It will only be fair that both Duryodhana and Yudhishthira get a fair share of their inheritance by dividing the kingdom,' he proposed.[8] All other ministers agreed. They asked Dhritarāshtra to divide the kingdom and give half of it to the Pāndavas. The blind king could not contest the unanimous suggestion and gave Khāndavaprastha to Yudhishthira.

Peace prevailed for a few years until Yudhishthira successfully conducted the Rājasuya Yajna. The prosperous Khāndavaprastha, which was now named Indraprastha, bedazzled the Kauravas. Duryodhana was green with envy. He vented out his frustration to Dhritarāshtra and pestered him to invite the Pāndavas for a rigged game of dice. Dhritarāshtra had misgivings about such a game. He wanted to avoid any confrontation with the Pāndavas, who were now powerful and had very strong allies. But he had to yield to his son's obstinacy.[9] Vidura tried to dissuade the king from becoming the cause of a larger family clash. 'If destiny has planned such, so will it be,' shrugged Dhritarāshtra.[10]

The game happened. Shakuni won strike after strike for Duryodhana. Vidura kept raising his objections. But Dhritarāshtra couldn't hide his pleasure at his son's winning streak. Only when Draupadi shamed the assembly and Gāndhāri requested his intervention, Dhritarāshtra stopped the ridicule. Though within a few hours, coerced by Duryodhana, he changed his mind. 'If you let the Pāndavas go away to Indraprastha now, they will surely attack us. Instead, if we take away their wealth and use it to buy support from other kings, we will become much stronger to face the Pāndavas,'[11] Duryodhana had argued.

Gāndhāri shuddered at the thought of the direction in which her sons were headed. She shared her misgivings with Dhritarāshtra. 'Do not yield to Duryodhana's whims. Vidura had warned us during his birth that he will lead the family to destruction if not given up. Be aware that you do not become the cause of the devastation of the Kuru lineage by toeing the line of Duryodhana. You should have punished him for his transgressions before but you condoned them. Even now, it is not too late. Rein him in. If not, give him up and save our family from the impending carnage,' she implored. Dhritarāshtra brushed off her concern. 'I cannot dissuade Duryodhana from acting per his wishes. If that means destruction of our clan, so be it,'[12] he said, summoning the Pāndavas to another round of the game, losing which they would have to accept thirteen years of exile.

As expected, the Pāndavas lost and left for the forest but not before pledging to kill the sons of Dhritarāshtra in the war that would happen after thirteen years.

The Birds That Spewed Gold

The way the game of dice was unravelling, it was clear to one and all that Duryodhana and his friends intended to usurp all that the Pāndavas had. As Dhritarāshtra himself was encouraging the deceit, all the guests and courtiers watched in silence. Only Vidura and later Vikarna voiced their concern. Vidura pleaded with Dhritarāshtra to consider the potential consequences and stop the game. To underscore his point, he narrated a parable.[13]

In a forest lived a pair of birds that spewed gold every time they chattered. The king heard about these extraordinary birds and asked a hunter to capture them. When the birds were resting in their nest, the hunter caught them and presented them to the king. The king observed that the birds indeed spewed gold when they chattered. Overcome with greed, he thought, 'There must be a lot of gold in their stomach. I can get all that gold in one stroke by killing these birds.' He ordered his servant to cut open the stomach of the birds and take all the gold out. The birds were killed but no gold was found.

'The king, blinded by his greed and desirous of a quick gain, lost both the birds and the gold that they would have produced in the future. Likewise, do not get swayed by the greed to acquire the wealth of the Pāndavas by treachery. Or like the king who killed the birds, you too will have to repent in the future. Instead, nurture the Pāndavas with your love and benefit for the rest of your life,' Vidura had advised.

Thirteen years ended, and with that, the exile of the Pāndavas. Duryodhana had made it clear that he had no intention of returning Indraprastha to the Pāndavas. He knew Dhritarāshtra would not take any decision against his wishes. He was aware that if Dhritarāshtra ordered a war, all the Hastināpur warriors, including Bhishma, Drona and Kripa, would fight on his side, whatever be their misgivings. Karna was already willing to die for him. In the meanwhile, Duryodhana had managed to forge alliances with many other kings of Bhāratavarsha.

To avoid the war, Dhritarāshtra sent Sanjay to Yudhishthira to request him to do the 'right thing' by not initiating a war against his own brethren but offered nothing in return. The preaching was not acceptable to the Pāndavas who had kept their word of thirteen years of exile in spite of knowing it was a rigged game. As the war seemed more and more real, Dhritarāshtra got worried. He never had any illusions about his son's prowess nor had he ever underestimated the capabilities of the Pāndavas, especially when backed by allies such as the Yādavas and the Pānchālas. He had a premonition of how a battle with them would end—certainly not in Duryodhana's favour.

This time, Dhritarāshtra made a genuine effort to convince Duryodhana to give up his obsession of warring with the Pāndavas. So did everyone else in the Hastināpur assembly. Even Krishna had appealed to the king to step in and stop Duryodhana from plunging the country into ruin. All efforts were futile. As a final measure, Vidura urged Dhritarāshtra to imprison Duryodhana and save the family. Dhritarāshtra did not pay heed to that but he did ask Gāndhāri to make her son see some sense.

Gāndhāri was more direct in her reproach. To Dhritarāshtra she said, 'You are as much to be blamed for the situation we are faced with today. Your overindulgence in your son has brought us here. You relinquished your power and discretion to your cruel son and his crooked advisors. Should you not have punished Duryodhana when he was going astray and creating fault lines in the family?'

To Duryodhana, she exhorted the virtue of listening to the wisdom of his elders and not get deluded by greed and anger. 'Greatness is achieved only by practising self-control. Emotional reactions and unchecked desires only lead to a person's downfall. Control yourself before you aim to control your enemies.

Live a prosperous life taking care of your part of the kingdom and let the Pāndavas have their share. Your elders have as much affection for you as they have for the Pāndavas. Listen to their counsel. Do remember, the only reason they will fight on your side is because of their loyalty to the Hastināpur throne, not because they believe in you. They will never be able to look at the Pāndavas as their enemies.'[14]

The wise advice and counsels fell on Duryodhana's deaf ears. It was too late to make him see sense. He had rarely heard no for an answer, definitely not from his parents. His jealousy of the Pāndavas and desire to harm them should have been disciplined when he was still young. Dhritarāshtra was blinded by his love for his son. But what had Gāndhāri done? Was Duryodhana not her son too? The blindfolds of the parents were probably too thick to see the course of the future.

The Kurukshetra war happened. Destiny prevailed. All the sons of Dhritarāshtra and Gāndhāri were killed. The blind king was shaking with grief. 'Who must be as unfortunate as I am today, losing every single person I cared for? I don't remember committing any such grave a sin in this birth that deserved such a terrible punishment. Surely, I am being punished for something done in my previous birth,' he moaned.

Sanjay reminded him. 'All the elders of Hastināpur had expressed to you their concern over the arrogance and highhandedness of Duryodhana. You ignored their pleas. Duryodhana wanted the kingdom and wealth for himself by hook or by crook. In his greed, he did not listen to any word of caution. He surrounded himself with equally bigoted ministers like Duhshāsana, Karna and Shakuni. You did not chastise your son when you should have. Rather, out of your greed, you encouraged Duryodhana. Now you mourn like a person who cries about getting burnt after setting a cloth on fire and wrapping it around his body himself.'[15] Vidura was a little more compassionate in his speech and comforted the king, explaining the helplessness of man before destiny.

To perform the final rites of the fallen heroes, Dhritarāshtra, Gāndhāri, Kunti and the wives of the warriors headed to Kurukshetra. The Pāndavas came to see them. Everyone was grieving. The loss of sons, husbands and fathers was real and irreversible. Dhritarāshtra was most angry at Bheema. This middle son of Kunti had been responsible for the death of every single son of his, including his favourite Duryodhana. When Bheema approached Dhritarāshtra and bowed to him, the blind king called him closer to embrace. Krishna had sensed his anger. He pulled Bheema back and placed an iron statue before Dhritarāshtra. The force of the king's embrace was such that the statue crumbled and the king's mouth started bleeding. He thought he had killed Bheema and began to wail. Sanjay held the king. 'Bheema is fine but what you did wasn't right,' he said dispassionately.[16]

Krishna came down on him even more harshly. 'You are wise and knowledgeable, O King. You had the chance to make a decision about this war. You did. Now why should you be so angry? You had been warned about the disastrous consequences by one and all. Just look at you; your behaviour has never been just. You let yourself be subservient to Duryodhana. It was Duryodhana who got Draupadi dragged to your court and humiliated her. Bheema had pledged right then to kill him. Bheema only fulfilled his pledge in this war. Do give a thought to the cruel acts of Duryodhana who harassed and exiled the Pāndavas for no fault of theirs before you hold them guilty.'

Dhritarāshtra had calmed down by then. 'The love for my son and his loss had agitated my mind. I am glad you saved Bheema. The Pāndavas are the only ones I have now to live for,' he said, embarrassed and tearful.[17]

The complete annihilation of her sons had unsettled Gāndhāri. When Yudhishthira and the brothers went to see her, she got up to curse them. Veda Vyāsa had read her expressions and mind. He stopped her, 'Do not say what you've gotten up to say, Gāndhāri. Before, when Duryodhana came seeking your blessing for his victory, you refused to indulge him stating, यतो धर्मः ततो जयः (Victory will be on the side of justice). In this great battle, your words have come true. Victory has been on the side of justice. You have always tread the path of dharma. Now why do you wish to go astray? Forgive the Pāndavas.'

Gāndhāri stepped back, holding herself steady and replied, 'I do not wish ill for the Pāndavas. But what do I do? The death of my sons has devastated me! I know this disaster has been caused by my eldest son and my own brother. I have nothing against any of the Pāndavas. There is just one thing that I am not happy about—the way Bheema killed Duryodhana!'[18]

Bheema politely explained his action, reminding Gāndhāri of the incident in the game of dice, his pledge and the need to kill Duryodhana to secure the kingdom for Yudhishthira. Gāndhāri couldn't fault the reason. She then spoke about the gory act of Bheema of drinking the blood of Duhshāsana. That act was not befitting of a warrior, she claimed.

Bheema again explained that he was bound by his oath taken in the assembly of Hastināpur. 'But I did not drink his blood. Not even a drop of blood went beyond my teeth. I only touched the blood to my mouth to fulfil my pledge,' he clarified, adding, 'That said, you were aware of the cruel ways of Duryodhana towards us. You did not stop him then. Why do you blame us now?'

Gāndhāri understood all the explanations mentally, but her emotions were still not in her control. She was a mother, after all, who had lost a hundred sons in eighteen days. Addressing Bheema, she again deplored, 'You are an invincible warrior, Bheema. You killed a hundred sons of mine. Why did you not let even one of my sons live? Dhritarāshtra and I are old. For our sake, you should have let go of at least one of my sons. I wouldn't have been so broken today if you'd let one of them live.' Thus saying, she again became livid and screamed out for Yudhishthira. The heat of her anger could be felt from a distance. Even through the blindfolds, her gaze blackened Yudhishthira's toenails.

Nobody said anything. In a few moments, Gāndhāri's fury had settled.[19] She then wished to see the bodies of the warriors lying on the field. The Pāndavas and Krishna accompanied her. Her daughters-in-law were already on the field trying to locate the bodies of their husbands and sons. Some were wailing uncontrollably, some were lamenting aloud, while some others were fainting from shock and grief. She could smell the rotting flesh. She could hear the sounds of jackals, crows and vultures aiming to bite into the flesh of the corpses. She even tripped over some severed limbs and trunks a few times. She touched the mangled and mutilated bodies of her sons, feeling their injuries and their blood that had dried. She heard the loud mourning of her daughter Dushālā who was struggling to find the head of her husband Jayadratha.

Turning to Krishna, Gāndhāri wept, 'Krishna, I am certain, it is only because of you that the Pāndavas survived this war. How else could anyone stay safe having faced the mighty warriors like Drona, Karna, Bhishma and Ashwatthāmā? The day you left Hastināpur unable to convince Duryodhana for a treaty, Vidura had warned us of the devastation.'

Her heart was overcome with fury and grief. 'Krishna, you were right here. You saw the cousins destroying each other. How did you allow it to happen? You are very powerful. You wielded a special kind of reverence among both the Pāndavas and the Kauravas. If you had really desired, the war wouldn't have happened. But you let the war happen. I can only deduce from this act of yours that you wanted our clan to get destroyed. You've committed a crime, no less. Now face the consequence of it.'

Then, in a fit of desperation, she cursed Krishna, 'Because you ignored this massacre of the cousins of our family, you will have to see the massacre of your own family. Thirty-six years from now, your brothers, sons and cousins will kill each other in front of your eyes and seeing them all perish, you will roam around the forest, meeting an obscure death. The women of your clan will cry over the bodies of their husbands just like my daughters-in-law are lamenting today!'[20]

Krishna let Gāndhāri pour her heart out. A mild smile danced on his face. 'So it will be as you say. You have only stated what the future holds. No doubt the Yādavas will be destroyed. They have become too powerful for their good. That said, do look at your actions too. Your evil-minded son was cunning, envious and extremely conceited. He was cruel and a personification of malice. He disobeyed everything the elders told him. You did little to curb these vices of his. Instead, he was only encouraged. Do you think what you did was fair? How then do you hold me responsible for the inevitable outcome?' he said plainly but calmly.

When Gāndhāri calmed down, Krishna was more affectionate. 'A warrior lady like you gives birth to sons to fight valiantly in the battle and lay down their lives fighting, without succumbing to fear. Your sons have died a heroic death,' he consoled[21] the helpless mother.

Gāndhāri's grief subsided with time—the loss was permanent, so were her blindfolds.

18

The Ideal of Fetters and Freedom

Bhishma

'Do not kill this baby of mine. You have drowned seven of our babies already. What kind of a mother are you? What a grave sin has been committed by you!' screamed Shāntanu, trying to save his newborn child.

Shāntanu was the king of Hastināpur. He was the son of Pratipa, born in the distinguished lineage of Kuru and Bharata. One day, he met a beautiful woman named Gangā by the banks of the river Gangā. They fell in love. Shāntanu proposed marriage to Gangā. She agreed but with a condition, 'I will marry you if you promise to never question me for any decision or action of mine. The day you do, I will leave.' Shāntanu readily agreed.

Their life was blissful, right up until the day that the queen delivered their baby boy. As soon as the child was born, she took the baby to the bank of the river and drowned him. This happened every time a child was born to her. One by one, Gangā had drowned seven of her sons. Shāntanu's heart sank every single time but he couldn't muster the courage to stop Gangā for the fear of losing her.

Eventually, the couple had an eighth child, also a son. This time, Shāntanu had reached the end of his tolerance. He was not going to let Gangā kill his child. He stopped her. She smiled and said, 'Now that you have stopped me, I will not drown this child of yours. However, it does seem like my time with you is over. You have broken your word. So I will leave now and take this baby along. At an appropriate time, I will return to you this prince of Hastināpur.' Saying so, she walked away with the baby, who was named Devavrata.

Gangā raised the baby well till he became a smart young boy. He learnt the Vedas, became an ace archer and acquired expertise in warfare, diplomacy, administration and economics. He learnt warfare under the guidance of the great Parashurāma. After Devavrata had finished his education, Gangā brought him back to Hastināpur and left him in the care of his father Shāntanu, who was delighted to see his son. Devavrata resembled him in looks as well as in virtue. The citizens of Hastināpur adored him instantaneously. Shāntanu nominated him as the crown prince of his kingdom.

One evening, a few years later, Shāntanu went hunting in a forest near the river Yamunā. The whiff of an intense but alluring fragrance caught his attention. He looked around to find its source. To his surprise, he saw a divinely beautiful lady who appeared to belong to the local fishing community. The fragrance seemed to emanate from her body. He was immediately struck by her beauty. He approached the girl to know more about her. 'I am Satyavati, the daughter of Dāshrāja, the headman of the Nishāda community here. I row the boat to ride the travellers across the river,' she said.

Desirous of marrying this Nishāda girl, Shāntanu approached her father. 'I wish to marry your daughter,' he said. The father replied, 'I would happily give you my daughter if you commit to make her son the heir to your throne, not otherwise.' The king was taken aback. He refused to comply and returned to Hastināpur. His yearning for Satyavati, however, refused to die down.

Devavrata was worried seeing his father lost in thought and disinterested in the affairs of the kingdom. He asked his father the cause of his worry. 'You are the only son I have. God forbid something happens to you, what will happen to our lineage? This is my worry,' replied the king. Devavrata was not convinced with that answer. He took one of his father's trusted ministers into confidence to know the real reason. The minister told him about the daughter of Dāshrāja who had enticed the king's heart.

Devavrata went to see Dāshrāja and requested the hand of his daughter for his father. The headman of the Nishādas repeated his condition. Devavrata promised to give up his claim on the throne in favour of Satyavati's son. But Dāshrāja's concern was not allayed. 'I have complete trust in your words. But what if your children lay their claim on the throne in the future?'

'Hear me then. Such a pledge has not been taken before. I have given up my claim to the throne already. Now I vow to remain celibate all my life. May the gates of heavens be open to me despite not procreating,'

Devavrata declared. Since then, Devavrata came to be known as Bhishma due to the severity of the pledge he lived by his entire life. Dāshrāja sent Satyavati with Bhishma for Shāntanu. The king was beyond himself at his son's conduct. He gave Bhishma the boon of 'swacchanda maranam'—the power to choose the time his death.[1]

Satyavati and Shāntanu got married. They had two sons—Chitrangad and Vichitravirya. Shāntanu died soon after. Tragically, Chitrangad was killed by a Gandharva of the same name. Vichitravirya, who was still very young, was crowned the king of Hastināpur. The administration and security of the kingdom was completely under Bhishma.

When Vichitravirya was old enough, Bhishma took away the daughters of the king of Kāshi—Ambā, Ambikā and Ambālikā—from their swayamvara, as wives for his stepbrother. King Shālva challenged Bhishma to defeat him before taking the princesses away. Bhishma defeated Shālva and rode away. Of the three princesses, Ambikā and Ambālikā did not object to the marriage. They were happy to become the queens of Hastināpur.

Ambā was not happy. She was in love with Shālva. They both had mutually decided that she would choose Shālva in the swayamvara. She had even informed her father about her choice. On reaching Hastināpur, Ambā told Bhishma of her inclination towards Shālva. Consulting the scriptures for the right move to make in such circumstances, Bhishma respectfully had her sent to Shālva.

Shālva, however, was seething from his defeat at the hands of Bhishma. 'I cannot accept what I lost to Bhishma. I am scared of another fight with him,' he said, rejecting Ambā, breaking her heart. She blamed Shālva for rejecting her, she blamed herself for not jumping out of Bhishma's chariot and climbing on Shālva's when the two faced off. But eventually, she held Bhishma responsible for her plight. Had he not come to Kāshi and taken her away, she would not have been in this situation. She wanted revenge but could not think of a way to achieve that.[2]

The other option Ambā thought of was living a life of an ascetic doing tapasyā. Thinking about her options, she headed to the forest and sought shelter in an āshram of rishis. There she met her maternal grandfather Rajarshi Hotravāhana and another rishi by the name of Akrutvrana. She narrated to them her sorrow and sought help. Akrutvrana asked, 'There are two people who have hurt you, Shālva and Bhishma. If you wish, Rishi Parashurāma can instruct Shālva to marry you or he can challenge and defeat Bhishma in a duel. Bhishma is Parashurāma's student. What is your wish?'

Ambā politely replied, 'When Bhishma took me away, he did not know about my love for Shālva. Hence, I seek your guidance about what is the appropriate thing for me to do.' Akrutvrana gave it some thought and concluded that Bhishma was the primary cause of Ambā's sorrow. Had he not gone to Kāshi and abducted the princesses, Shālva would have happily married Ambā. 'Seeking revenge from

Bhishma is the better option for you,' the rishi told Ambā.[3] Ambā, too, desired the same. She wished to see Bhishma defeated in a war.

Coincidentally, Parashurāma came to the āshram the next day. He heard Ambā's story, who had just one wish—to see Bhishma defeated in a war. Only Parashurāma had the potential to do that. He yielded to her wishes. He called for Bhishma and asked him to accept Ambā or fight with him. 'This girl has been left in the lurch because you crossed your limits and abducted her. It is only fair that you accept her and let her fulfil her role as wife,' Parashurāma ordered.[4] Bhishma refused to accept Ambā for his brother because she had herself confessed her love for Shālva. He chose to fight Parashurāma.

An unprecedented fight took place between the teacher and the student. Even more unprecedented was the outcome—Parashurāma could not defeat Bhishma. The student had become as good as his teacher.

Ambā was distressed. She retired to the forest and plunged herself in severe tapasyā. She wanted revenge. If no one else could defeat Bhishma, she desired to acquire the power to do so herself, if not in this birth then in next. Engaged in penance, she gave up her body and was born as a woman who remembered her past birth. Once again, she immersed herself in tapasyā. She wished to be born as a man to be able to challenge and defeat Bhishma in the war. She wanted to become the reason for his death.

Shiva gave her the boon she desired. Ambā entered the fire and was born to Drupada and his wife as

Shikhandi. People said Shikhandi was born a woman but by Yaksha Sthunākarna's blessings, she became a man.

Shikhandini

Drupada and his chief queen, who were both desirous of begetting a son, undertook austerities with that objective in mind. They were given a boon by Lord Shiva that they would have a child who will be born a girl but become a man later on in life. Few months later, a beautiful girl was born to the queen, who declared that she had a baby boy. She was named Shikhandini by the mother but was known to all as Shikhandi. Drupada, fully aware of the charade, went along with it. The baby was brought up like a boy and was given the education befitting a prince. When Shikhandini was old enough, Drupada got her married to the daughter of the king of Dashārna, Hiranyavarmā. However, the boon of Shiva hadn't yet materialised.

The newly wedded wife of Shikhandini didn't take too long to realise that her husband was not a man but a woman. She was terrified and informed her father of the betrayal. Furious, Hiranyavarmā began gathering forces to attack Pānchāla for the deceit and humiliation. Drupada and his wife were extremely worried. To buy time, Drupada reached out to Hiranyavarmā and called him to verify for himself that Shikhandi was a man, hoping against hope that by some miracle, Shiva's words would come true.

Shikhandini was extremely sorrowful upon seeing her parents upset. 'How would Drupada prove that she was a man when in reality she wasn't! Drupada and Pānchala were sure to get destroyed,' Shikhandini thought and blamed herself for being the cause of their pain. To avoid the ordeal, she left the palace to give up her life. She found her way into a forest, started doing penance and gave up food, hoping to die. A Yaksha named Sthunākarna, who claimed lordship over the forest, spotted Shikhandini and was moved by her plight. He granted her a boon, 'I will assume your femininity and impart you my masculinity for a few days. Once your work is accomplished and the danger on your father is warded off, you must come back and return my masculinity.' Shikhandini happily agreed. The sex change happened and she returned to the palace as Shikhandi.

Hiranyavarmā sent a few women to verify Shikhandi's manliness. Women were satisfied with what they found. Their report satisfied Hiranyavarmā too and he gave up the plan to attack Pānchāla. Her task accomplished, Shikhandini returned to the forest per her promise to the Yaksha. However, another event had played out in the forest while she was away in her palace. Kuber, the lord of the Yakshas, had come visiting. He was shocked to see Sthunākarna as a woman. On learning the entire story, he was even more enraged. 'By giving away your masculinity and assuming feminity, you have done an unjustified act. For this stupidity of yours, I curse you to continue being a woman in this life,' Kuber said.

And so it was that Shikhandini became Shikhandi for life—one man's curse had transformed into another's boon!

Bhishma narrates the entire story of Amba's birth as Shikhandi to Duryodhana when the latter was curious about the old Kuru's condition that he would not kill Shikhandi.

After just seven years of Vichitriyavirya's marriage, misfortune struck. He died at a young age of tuberculosis and was childless. Satyavati, though grieving the death of her second son, was mindful of her duty as the queen mother. Hastināpur needed a king and an heir. Who better than Bhishma could fit the role! For all practical administrative purposes of the kingdom, Bhishma was in charge already.

She called Bhishma for a chat. 'I trust you to forever take the most appropriate decision in favour of dharma, of that which is right. Your understanding of the right path is as profound as that of Brihaspati and Shukra, the divine teachers of the devas and asuras. Hence, I urge you to marry the two young widows of Vichitryavirya and beget children from them for Hastināpur. I also want you to formally take the throne of Hastināpur,' proposed Satyavati.[5]

Bhishma was not willing to break his vow of celibacy. 'What you propose mother is a solution accepted by the scriptures. However, I remember every word of the pledge I made during your wedding to my father. The sun may give up its radiance; fire its heat. But I cannot make false the promise I have once made—not for this kingdom, and not for the kingdom of the gods. For a warrior, especially, reneging on this pledge is not a respectworthy act,' he asserted.

'I am aware the truth matters to you more than anything else and that is how it should be. Our ancestors have pronounced the acceptability of exceptional decisions in exceptional circumstances. What we are faced with is definitely an exceptional and unforeseen situation. You must take that into consideration before making a final decision,' Satyavati insisted.

Bhishma's mind, however, was made up about not ascending to the throne or marrying. They agreed on the other viable alternative suggested by scriptures in such exceptional circumstances—niyoga. Satyavati summoned her eldest son, Krishna Dwaipāyana Vyāsa—a son born before her wedding through her union with Rishi Parāshar. He was raised by his father. The rishi imparted Krishna Dwaipāyana with all the knowledge and wisdom he had.

Vyāsa obeyed his mother's orders and spent a night each with Ambikā and Ambālikā when they were ovulating. Ambikā was scared seeing the unkempt Vyāsa, as he had come straight from a long penance, and closed her eyes. Ambālikā, equally frightened, paled considerably when she saw him, so much so that the colour of her skin faded. They conceived and gave birth to the blind Dhritarāshtra and anaemic Pāndu, respectively. Satyavati wanted one more child of the two queens. She called for Vyāsa again, hoping the queens would be better prepared. But the previous encounter had left an indelible mark on them. Hence, they sent one of their maids in the service of the rishi. The maid served Vyāsa with sincerity and affection. Through her, the wise Vidura was born.

Until the boys grew up and finished their education, Bhishma managed the affairs of the kingdom. At the appropriate time, Pāndu was crowned the king. Dhritarāshtra's blindness made him ineligible for the throne even though he was the elder of the two. Vidura became the prime minister of Hastināpur, owing to his expertise in administration, law and diplomacy, and his astute wisdom.

The Kauravas and the Pāndavas were born of Dhritarāshtra and Pāndu, respectively.

Time went by. Pāndu died. Dhritarāshtra became the king of Hastināpur. The Kauravas and the Pāndavas finished their education. It was time to appoint a successor to the Hastināpur throne. Yudhishthira, being the eldest of all, and also the most suited for the role, was appointed the crown prince. Duryodhana couldn't stand to lose what he assumed was his sole right. He began plotting to get the Pāndavas out of the way.

Bhishma was not aware of the Vāranāvata plot. He came to know of it only when the Pāndavas came out of hiding. Bhishma understood Duryodhana's desire. He proposed the division of the kingdom so that both Duryodhana and Yudhishthira got their share of their ancestral kingdom. And so the Pāndavas got Indraprastha and the Kauravas kept Hastināpur. Bhishma was fair to both sets of his grandchildren.

It was during the game of dice that Bhishma was faced with his first major ethical dilemma. He was aware that the game spelt trouble. He was aware that Shakuni was cunning and couldn't be trusted but he let the game happen. Dhritarāshtra had not sought his opinion and hence Bhishma did not offer any. He was witness to the dragging of Draupadi and her subsequent humiliation. He was squirming inside but watched on, a mute spectator.

Draupadi implored Bhishma to decide if Yudhishthira had the legal right to stake her after having lost himself. Bhishma avoided answering. When Draupadi kept prodding, he responded. 'The laws regarding this are very subtle. A person who has lost himself cannot stake what is not his. But a husband has been seen to still have a claim on his wife. Hence, my intellect fails me. I cannot decide what is right and wrong here. But I do foresee that consumed by greed, the Kauravas would soon invite their end,'[6] he said while requesting Yudhishthira himself to judge what is appropriate.

Bhishma was not technically wrong. It was a delicate point to adjudicate on. Does the relationship of a husband and a wife end if the husband has staked himself and lost? If not, does it become alright to stake one's wife? Isn't protecting one's wife one of the key responsibilities of the husband? Bhishma did indicate his unease when he told Draupadi that he foresaw the destruction of the Kauravas. But unlike Vidura and Vikarna, he stopped short of taking a stand against the ridicule playing out.

Does loyalty to the throne mean tolerating blatant injustice?

Bhishma tried his best to dissuade Duryodhana from waging a war against the Pāndavas. Duryodhana called him biased and Karna insulted him, but Bhishma did not give up. However, he stopped short of threatening to not fight on the side of the Kauravas. Despite Bhishma's pleadings against the war, Duryodhana knew well that if a war were to happen, the old Kuru would fight on his side. That surety gave him the confidence to persist with his war plans.

The war happened. Bhishma fought on Duryodhana's side and also led the army as his commander but not unconditionally. He stated to Duryodhana before the war began that he will not kill the Pāndavas and Shikhandi[7]. Neither did he convince Karna to stay on and fight when the latter decided to sit out of the war due to their war of words just before the battle.

Once on the battlefield, Bhishma fought like the god of death himself. At a minimum, he killed ten thousand soldiers and one thousand chariot warriors every day. Even then, during the ten days of the war, Bhishma tried to convince Duryodhana to reconcile with the Pāndavas. After his fall on the tenth day, he made one last attempt to convince Karna to stop the war, in vain.

Lying on the bed of arrows in Kurukshetra, Bhishma saw all his friends, his grandsons and even his great-grandsons perish. He saw his effort of years spent trying to protect the throne of Hastināpur reduced to ashes. But he was happy that the throne had gone to the most deserving.

Bhishma was an excellent administrator. After Shāntanu's death, till Pāndu was crowned the king, the governance of Hastināpur was managed by Bhishma. His acumen had made it a prosperous and safe kingdom. He was well versed in scriptures and diplomacy. He had decades of experience that few others could talk of. That is why, after the war ended, Krishna advised Yudhishthira to imbibe all he can from Bhishma's wisdom and experience. Yudhishthira humbly approached the grand old Kuru. Bhishma obliged and gave a profound discourse on the gross and subtle nuances of dharma and Rāja Dharma.

Discourse on the Death Bed

After the war ended, the Pāndavas were victorious but it had come at the cost of the lives of their cousins and uncles. Yudhishthira was distressed and did not dare to face Bhishma, who lay in Kurukshetra on the bed of arrows. Krishna informed Bhishma of Yudhishthira's reluctance and embarrassment.

Bhishma smiled. He asked Yudhishthira to come closer to him and said, 'When faced with a war, it is the duty of a warrior king to kill those who have taken the path of adharma, be it his father, brother, teacher or close relatives. You have done no wrong. Do not hesitate. Come sit next to me and ask whatever you wish to.'[8] Yudhishthira held his feet and asked about Rāja Dharma—the responsibilities and duties of a king—and Moksha Dharma—the way to achieve liberation and eternal peace.

Bhishma indulged him and shared all that he had learnt and gained through scriptures and experience. An entire range of topics related to governance were covered. A summary of the last discourse given by Bhishma to Yudhishthira on Rāja Dharma is given below:

While success depends on both effort and destiny, a king should be engaged in enterprise and activity all the time. Destiny by itself cannot achieve anything unless a serious effort is made. One shouldn't be disheartened if a task doesn't achieve its stated objective because destiny has a role to play. Nevertheless, a king should continue to work with genuine effort. Enterprise trumps destiny.

There is no substitute for truth. A king who wishes to invoke trust in his subjects must adhere to truth, no less. Be upright in all that you undertake. A virtuous, well mannered, generous king with his mind firmly under his control is sure to be successful.

However, a king who is always only upright and soft is not respected. People tend to transgress him. Even his subordinates take him for granted. Hence, he needs to use both softness and strictness as the situation demands. Neither should he disregard diplomacy when need be, especially when it comes to keeping his and the kingdom's strengths and weaknesses as well as discussions and deliberations confidential.

A king should give up every kind of addiction. Any kind of addiction has the potential to bring dishonour. His attitude towards his subjects should be like that of a pregnant lady. A pregnant woman gives up even the things she likes to ensure good health and safety of her yet-to-be-born child. Likewise, a king's focus should be his citizens. He should do all that it takes to ensure their welfare, giving up indulgence in his sensual pleasures.[9]

Learned men, priests and those engaged in teaching and studying of scriptures should be respected and given patronage to. These people propagate and uphold the knowledge of the Vedas.[10] If a crime is committed by them, it is better to exile them rather than imposing a penalty of death. However, if such men take up arms against the king and the kingdom or become destructive to society at large, then they too must be punished and destroyed like anyone else.[11]

Anyone who goes against the interest of the state and harms the seven limbs of governance with the intention to harm the state must be punished. These seven limbs are king, ministers, state, treasury, army, forts and friendly states and allies. The perpetrator, even if he is one's teacher or friend, should be punished.[12]

A king who wishes to remain in power should not destroy the wealth of his citizens. All dues owed to the citizens should be repaid timely. There is no greater sin for a king than not being able to protect and look after the welfare of his citizens. Thus, only a person who has achieved control over his senses, mind and anger, is decisively well versed in the knowledge of the scriptures, is always engaged in protecting dharma and generating resources and is capable of keeping his decisions to himself until the opportune time comes is worthy of becoming a king.[13]

While delegating responsibilities, it is important to give full accountability of a task to one individual. If multiple people are given the same task, it creates discord and impacts the work at hand.[14]

A king must also be cautious of his extended family members. Family is important and family members should be taken care of and respected. But it is also important to not trust anyone blindly, including family members. The closest person has the potential to do the most harm. A person/king, therefore, must be watchful of everyone—family members, friends and enemies—while having a friendly demeanour towards all.[15]

A king needs to appoint a group of ministers representing various communities of the society and involve them in the routine work of governance. However, there are four things which he should do himself—allocation of spies and getting updates from them, confidential discussions and decision-making, supervision of the treasury, and imparting justice and punishment.[16]

A king needs to adhere to righteousness always. But there could be exceptional circumstances which may require the king to act in other ways to protect himself and his kingdom. Even in those circumstances, however stark, there are certain acts which remain condemnable—killing the innocent who is not in a war with you, raping a woman, kidnapping a young girl, destroying someone's life and taking everything he has. Even in exceptional situations, some lines must be drawn.[17]

After a detailed discourse on every aspect of Rāja Dharma, Bhishma explained the virtues of bhakti, ādhyātma and moksha.

What if Bhishma had taken a moral stand and refused to fight? He was equally related to both the Kauravas and the Pāndavas. He was their grandfather, just like Veda Vyāsa. Dronāchārya's compulsion to fight for Dhritarāshtra can be understood. He was a paid employee. Bhishma considered himself as a paid employee too. But was he just that?

His vow tied him to celibacy and to never pose a challenge to the throne. But the war was an exceptional situation, Ambā's was an exceptional situation, Draupadi's was an exceptional situation. He could have broken free of his fetter of unquestioned loyalty to the throne. But he chose to remain fettered. To stay true to his pledge was the objective of his life. The fetter had become a pivot on which his life hinged. He was bound by another fetter too—one he did not choose but Ambā did. Becoming the cause of Bhishma's death was the pivot of Ambā's 'lives'.

Death set them free.

Vidura

He was the biological stepbrother of Dhritarāshtra and Pāndu. Born of Veda Vyāsa through a maid of Ambikā, Vidura received the same education and training as the two princes. He had a special acumen for diplomacy and law. When Pāndu was crowned the king, Vidura was made the prime minister of Hastināpur.

Just like Bhishma, Vidura was tied for life to Hastināpur by blood, both the kingdom and the throne. His role in the affairs of the kingdom became even more prominent after Pāndu's death when Dhritarāshtra became the king. Like Krishna was to the Pāndavas, Vidura was to Dhritarāshtra. He gave the most appropriate advice devoid of any self-interest, always, even if it meant expressing an opinion contrary to that of Dhritarāshtra's.

While seeking the king's interference to stop the game of dice, Vidura had mentioned, 'It's easy to find cunning men who will always say what we wish to hear. But it is rare to find one who says what is right for us even though it may not be to our liking. Thus, I will say only that which is good for you.'[18] He objected to the dragging and humiliation of Draupadi, pleading the courtiers to speak up. Despite Duryodhana's insults, he stood firm, forewarning Dhritarāshtra that the game will have disastrous consequences.

When the omens indicated doom at Duryodhana's birth, Vidura requested Dhritarāshtra to give up the boy in the interest of his family and kingdom. He reminded Dhritarāshtra of his advice at the time of Duryodhana's birth when the disdainful game of dice was being played. That Dhritarāshtra didn't listen was his prerogative. Vidura stayed true to his dharma by making himself heard.

After the Pāndavas had lived through thirteen years of exile, when Duryodhana refused to give back their kingdom provoking them for a war, Vidura was the only one—apart from Krishna—who advised Dhritarāshtra to arrest Duryodhana and negotiate with the Pāndavas for peace. He never gave his consent to the war. Neither he did leave Dhritarāshtra. He was always there, whenever the king wanted him by his side, giving the most appropriate advice.

Dhritarāshtra was not always patient with Vidura's plain-speaking. A few days after the Pāndavas were exiled, Dhritarāshtra called upon Vidura. He was worried about the repercussions of sending the Pāndavas into exile. 'What can we do to quell the anger of the citizens and regain their love?' he asked. Vidura proposed the most optimum solution. 'There is only one option. Do the right thing. Call the Pāndavas back, give them their kingdom and disregard Shakuni. If Duryodhana doesn't agree, restrain him. Let Duhshāsana seek forgiveness from Bheema and Draupadi. Else, if a war with the Pāndavas happens, the destruction of the Kauravas is certain,'[19] said Vidura, without mincing words.

This was not the answer Dhritarāshtra wanted to hear. 'Your proposal is favourable towards the Pāndavas. There is nothing in it for my sons. Now I am fully convinced that you are concerned only about the well-being of the Pāndavas, not ours. How can I give up my sons for their sake? Undoubtedly, Pāndavas are my sons too. But Duryodhana is born of my body. I was hoping to get an unbiased opinion from you. Instead, you are cunningly forwarding the case of the Pāndavas. I don't want to concern myself with you. Stay or feel free to leave and go wherever you wish!'[20] the king snapped and walked away.

Vidura left. He went to Kāmyakavana to live with the Pāndavas for a few days. Dhritarāshtra, however, could not bear the separation with Vidura for too long. As soon as his fury subsided, he realised his folly and sent Sanjay to get Vidura back. Dhritarāshtra and Vidura shared a unique bond. The king had immense trust in Vidura's wisdom, even though he was not always appreciative of his matter-of-fact speech.

While Dhritarāshtra wanted the throne and all luxuries for his sons, he was not keen on a war with the Pāndavas. Duryodhana's obstinacy had made the war inevitable. Sanjay's dispirited expression indicating doom for the Kauravas on his return from Upaplavya was hounding Dhritarāshtra. He couldn't sleep. There was only one man he wanted by his side at that time—Vidura. He called for Vidura, who came at once.

'I have been restless since Sanjay returned and blamed me for the situation we are in. I am unable to sleep. Hence, I wish to hear your views about the dharma that would be favourable to me. You are amongst the wisest men I know,' said Dhritarāshtra.

'There are four types of people who cannot sleep at night—one who has picked a fight with someone much more powerful, one who is consumed with lust, one who desires the wealth of others out of greed and a thief who works at night. Is your inability to sleep driven by one of these causes?'[21] asked Vidura and followed it up with a profound discourse on living with wisdom and compassion, working with enterprise and becoming an able administrator.

'Yudhishthira is better suited to be the king. He is better than your sons in every aspect. Call the Pāndavas back and return their kingdom. They look up to you like their own father. Treat them like your own sons and do what is right. Only the right action will give you peace and joy,'[22] Vidura concluded.

Vidura Niti

This is a summary of the discourse given by Vidura to Dhritarāshtra.

A wise man is he who knows clearly what is worth doing and what is worth giving up. Such a man is not perverted by anger, joy, pride, stubbornness and ego. A wise man does not boast prematurely of his achievements. People get to know of his work only after it is accomplished but never know what is in his mind. He does not let heat and cold, wealth or the lack of it, fear or joy interfere with the work he is set out to do. He knows his potential and takes up tasks accordingly without looking down upon any task, however small. A wise man deliberates upon and plans his task properly before starting. Once he begins the work, he stays disciplined, doesn't procrastinate and sees it to completion. He doesn't get overexcited when praised nor does he become agitated when criticised; he stays calm in every situation.[23]

One who is proud without any learning has luxurious needs despite his poverty and wants to acquire wealth without any hard work is a stupid man. So is he who disregards his duties but rushes to fulfil the responsibilities of others. Such a man desires those who disregard him, disregards those who care for him and picks up unnecessary fights with those much stronger than him. A stupid man unnecessarily doubts everyone and everything, wastes time in doing things which can be quickly completed and spreads himself thin. He tends to blame others for his faults and gets angry over others doing tasks even though he is incapable of doing those himself.[24]

There are two ways of wasting wealth acquired through genuine means—giving to the undeserving and not giving to the deserving.

Two types of people do not deserve to live—a rich man who doesn't do any charity work and a poor man who cannot bear physical inconvenience.[25]

Never get into any secret discussions or dealings with four types of people—those who are stupid, reckless, tend to procrastinate or needlessly flatter.

Four things give instant results—the will of the gods, the influence of the wise, the humility of the learned and the destruction of the unrighteous.[26]

A man who seeks prosperity and success should keep these six vices at bay—sleep, drowsiness, fear, anger, lethargy and procrastination.

Six virtues worth imbibing—truth, generosity, enterprise, absence of jealousy, forgiveness and fortitude.

Six things that bring comfort in life—wealth, good health, a good spouse who is favourably inclined and soft in speech, obedient children and professional acumen.

Six enemies that reside in the mind—lust, anger, greed, attachment, lethargy and jealousy.[27]

Six professionals that depend on these six kinds of people for their living—thieves on uncautious men, doctors on the diseased and unwell, prostitutes on lustful men, priests on the householders, kings and administrators on people in discord and the intellectuals on the ignorant.

Six situations make life joyful—being healthy, being able to earn as per one's capabilities and inclinations, being debt-free, engaging with decent people and not having to live in a foreign land.

Six kinds of men are always unhappy—those who are always jealous, hateful, angry, discontent, suspicious and those dependent on others for their livelihood.[28]

Seven vices worth giving up for a king/administrator—lustfulness towards women, gambling, hunting, alcohol, harsh speech, extreme punishments and wastage/improper usage of resources.

Ten states in which a man would not know what is right and what is not—intoxicated, inattentive, insane, exhausted, angry, very hungry, hasty, greedy, scared and overcome with lust.

The king who displays the following traits gains prosperity—one who invokes trust, punishes only after a crime is indisputably proven and knows when to punish, how much to punish and when to forgive.'[29]

The discourse went on all night. Vidura made it relatable and lucid using parables and anecdotes.

Vidura knew when to speak and when not to. He was aware of Duryodhana's plot to kill the Pāndavas in Vāranāvata. But he chose to remain quiet at the time. It was important to ensure the Pāndavas remained safe and the perpetrators weren't alarmed. He also knew when to speak harsh words and when being harsh was futile. Until the war became a reality, he tried to stop it in every way. But once the war was over, and Dhritarāshtra had lost all his sons, Vidura became much softer. The king was suffering and the suffering was going to stay with him for the rest of his life. To such a man, one could only offer words of consolation that might bring some peace.

'Death of the living is certain. The brave and the meek all eventually die. All those who have taken birth must die. There is no other way. Your sons were learned men who did not run away when faced with an opponent and died fighting on the battlefield. They had come from the unmanifest world to this manifest world and have now gone back into the unmanifest. Why should you then grieve for those courageous warriors?'[30] Vidura consoled the blind king. Then, as Krishna had exhorted Arjuna in Kurukshetra, Vidura expounded to Dhritarāshtra the phenomenon of the impermanence of the body, the cycle of life, the supremacy of karma and the importance of mental discipline.

After the Kurukshetra war, Yudhishthira became the king of Hastināpur, Bheema was appointed the crown prince and Vidura was asked to retain the prime ministership.[31] He was one man who could be trusted fully. Vidura served Hastināpur for another fifteen years before retiring to the forest with Dhritarāshtra, Gāndhāri, Kunti and Sanjay.

Once, when Yudhishthira, the other Pāndava brothers and the women of the palace had gone to meet Kunti, Dhritarāshtra and Gāndhāri in the forest, they were surprised to not find Vidura. They were told he had taken up severe tapasyā. He had given up food and even clothes. While they were talking, Yudhishthira spotted Vidura. The ex-prime minister of Hastināpur, his uncle, was naked and had been reduced to a structure of skin and bones. Yudhishthira ran out of the āshram to meet him. Vidura was so alarmed at seeing so many people in the āshram that he ran even faster, avoiding them all.

When they reached deep inside the forest, Vidura stopped and stood steady, his back against a tree. Yudhishthira caught up with him and got close enough to bow down to him. Vidura looked straight into his eyes, unblinking. Yudhishthira froze. He could feel Vidura's strength. He too kept looking into Vidura's eyes. Yudhishthira felt a burst of heat and energy in his body as if a divine power had entered within him. Vidura's body was still standing by the tree but there was no life in it. It is said that through yoga, Vidura had transferred his ātmashakti into Yudhishthira.[32]

Vidura had once said to Dhritarāshtra, 'It behooves a man to tell the truth to him whom he does not wish to see unsuccessful, irrespective of whether the man finds it pleasing or not. That is why I will only tell you that which is beneficial for you.'[33] Until the very end, Vidura lived up to this principle of his. His loyalty to Hastināpur and Dhritarāshtra was absolute, not unlike Bhishma. But Vidura was even more loyal to dharma.

No fetters can bind the man established in dharma. Such a man is a free man. Vidura was a free man. Yudhishthira was the son of dharma. Vidura, Vyāsa had said, was dharma himself.[34]

ॐ ψ ॐ

19

The Prodigious Sons

Irāvan

Draupadi being the wife of the five Pāndavas, it was important for the brothers to set certain rules of engagement. To ensure the brothers got privacy with her, a code of conduct was agreed upon. Per that, if any brother intruded when the other brother was in his private quarters with Draupadi, the intruding brother would have to go away and live in the forest for twelve years.[1] Once, during their early Indraprastha days, Arjuna entered the room when Draupadi was with Yudhishthira. He had gone to the chamber to get his weapons to help retrieve the stolen cattle of a Brāhmin. Even though it was an unintentional intrusion for a noble cause, his action had violated the code of conduct. Hence, on his own accord, Arjuna left Indraprastha to spend twelve years in the jungle and visit pilgrimage places in Bhāratavarsha.

In the initial part of his journey, Arjuna came to Haridwār. Having finished his daily vandanā[2] and fire rituals, he stepped in the holy waters of Gangā to bathe. It was here that Uloopi saw him. One look and she was mesmerised. Uloopi was a Nāga princess, the daughter of King Kouravya of the Nāgas. Overcome with desire, she approached Arjuna, introduced herself and took him to her majestic palace. She expressed her yearning to Arjuna honestly, 'I have been hopelessly infatuated ever since I have seen you. I have not felt like this for any other man. Please oblige me.'[3]

Arjuna was sworn to celibacy per the condition laid out. 'I would like to please you, O Lady, but I cannot breach the oath. Suggest a way by which I can fulfil your desire while staying true to the vow,' he asked her.[4] Uloopi responded thoughtfully, 'The condition of celibacy was laid down with respect to Draupadi. Hence, if you were to satisfy the desire of another woman, you do not falsify your oath. And even if it does breach the condition slightly, wise men have propounded that showing compassion to those who seek you is a greater virtue. If you disregard my plea, I will surely die of pain. To you, I have come as a seeker. Be compassionate and fulfil my desire,' she pleaded. Arjuna conceded. They spent the night together in the palace. Happy and content, Uloopi promised Arjuna that whenever in need, her people would help him. She then dropped Arjuna back to Haridwār and let him go.[5]

Of this union, Irāvan was born. He was brought up by his mother in the maternal home of Kouravya. Like his father, Irāvan grew up to be a handsome, strong, courageous and virtuous young man. He knew Arjuna was his father but had never met him in his growing-up years. When Irāvan learnt about the vanvās of the Pāndavas and Arjuna's visit to Indra's palace for celestial weapons, he decided to visit his father. On seeing Arjuna, he bowed down reverentially and introduced himself. Arjuna was overjoyed to see this son of his. Together, they spent a few days in Indra's palace getting to know about each other's lives. When it was time for Irāvan to leave, Arjuna apprised him of an impending war and asked him to support the Pāndavas when the time came. Irāvan took Arjuna's words as an order and complied.[6]

Irāvan participated wholeheartedly in the war along with his people. He was a unique horse warrior. His fleet of powerful horses of different breeds seemed to fly when they ran. Not one to back down when challenged, Irāvan defeated and destroyed many horse warriors and horse-riding armies in the war. Princes of Avanti, Vinda and Anuvinda were defeated by him but they survived the day.[7] His key victims were the six illustrious princes of Gāndhār, who were unmatched in their warfare skills and the strength of their armies. Fighting valiantly, Irāvan first routed their armies. Furious at this feat, the six haughty warriors attacked him all at once. Irāvan retaliated with vengeance but collapsed on the ground, not able to resist their collective force. The six men were pleased at the thought of capturing him alive. But as soon as they came close, Irāvan swooshed his sword using both his hands and cut their limbs.

Duryodhana was shocked seeing his maternal relatives being butchered so ruthlessly. He summoned the powerful rākshasa Alambusha to eliminate Irāvan. The young man fought gallantly but eventually succumbed to the illusory prowess of the rākshasa.[8] Irāvan was Arjuna's eldest son and the first among the Pāndavas' progeny to lay down his life in Kurukshetra, on the eighth day of the war.

Abhimanyu

Bhishma was unstoppable from day one of the war. Trampling the armies of Chedi, Kāshi and Pānchāla, his chariot seemed to dance along the battlefield, felling soldier and warriors of the opposing army. Witnessing the carnage of his side, Abhimanyu, the son of Arjuna and Subhadrā, charged at Bhishma and the warriors who were protecting him. One after the other his sharp arrows left even veterans such as Kritavarmā and Kripāchārya in disarray. The Kaurava elders couldn't help but marvel at the sixteen-year-old's agility, speed, knowledge of weapons and their flawless execution.[9]

Over the course of the first ten days of war, Abhimanyu had fought with and defeated warriors such as Ashwatthāmā, Kritavarmā, Kripāchārya, Duryodhana's son Lakshman, Bhurishravā, Chitrasena, Vikarna, Shalya, Ambashtha, Jayadratha and Brihadbal. Quite often, he fended off group attacks by Kaurava warriors. He fought like a lion's cub among elephants.[10] When Abhimanyu roamed around the battlefield trouncing the mightiest of opponents and strongest of armies, people wondered if there were two Arjunas fighting on the Pāndava side.[11]

On the ninth day of the war, disturbed by the devastation caused by Abhimanyu, Duryodhana once again called for Alambusha, entrusting him with the task of killing Abhimanyu.[12] Just a day before, Alambusha had killed the eldest Ārjuni,[13] Irāvan. But this time Abhimanyu was protected by the five sons of Draupadi. When Alambusha targeted Abhimanyu, the Draupedayas[14] together launched an assault on the rākshasa. Prativindhya propelled sharp iron-laced arrows at Alambusha. The arrows punctured his armour and pierced through his chest. Before the rākshasa could recover, the brothers shot another volley of pointed arrows, maiming every part of his huge body. Alambusha became unconscious for a moment but quickly got himself together. He now directed his attack on Prativindhya and his brothers. In one strike he killed their horses and destroyed their chariots.[15]

Alambusha was about to pounce on the Draupadeyas when Abhimanyu alerted them and launched an offensive on him. Though heavily injured by the rākshasa, Abhimanyu stood his ground and deftly destroyed the dreadful weapons thrown at him. Alambusha was frightened and flustered at the ineffectiveness of his weapons on Abhimanyu and retreated to avoid getting a fatal drubbing from the young warrior.[16]

Abhimanyu's birth was also an outcome of Arjuna's twelve-year pilgrimage necessitated by his unavoidable intrusion on Yudhishthira's private time with Draupadi. Towards the last leg of his forest stay, Arjuna visited Dwārkā to see Krishna. In Dwārkā, Arjuna was lovestruck seeing Subhadrā, Krishna and Balarāma's younger sister. Their marriage resulted in the birth of Abhimanyu, who was long-armed and broad-shouldered just like his father. In looks, he resembled Krishna. True to his name, Abhimanyu was unafraid and passionate.[17] Arjuna was his first teacher and he was an ardent and sincere student. When the Pāndavas lost the game of dice and spent thirteen years in the forest, Abhimanyu stayed in Dwārkā where his education and training continued under the loving care of the Yādavas.

'The best of the virtues of Krishna and the best of the qualities of the five Pāndavas are present in Abhimanyu. He has taken the splendour of Yudhishthira, character of Krishna, the daredevilry of Bheema, beauty, heroism and wisdom of Arjuna and the humility of Nakula and Sahadeva,' Sanjay had said to Dhritarāshtra while narrating the events of the thirteenth day of the war.[18]

Dronāchārya made a Chakra Vyuha on the thirteenth day of the war. Only Arjuna, Krishna and Krishna's son Pradyumna knew how to enter and exit such an army formation, he believed. That is why Susharmā and his brothers were tasked with challenging Arjuna early that morning and leading him far away. Pradyumna was not in Kurukshetra. Hence, Drona was sure he would capture Yudhishthira alive that day.

But he was only partly right. There was one warrior who knew how to enter the Chakra Vyuha, Abhimanyu. Arjuna had taught him how to enter. But he was yet to learn how to exit the formation if in danger. Yudhishthira asked Abhimanyu to lead the way and promised the other warriors would follow right behind him as he created an opening for them.

Abhimanyu marched ahead and started finding his way inside the vyuha. The others, however, were held back by Jayadratha who had been blessed with a boon that would make him invincible for a day, for everyone except Arjuna. Filled with passion and rage, Abhimanyu began decimating every impediment that came his way. Struck by his arrows, the Kaurava soldiers started falling rapidly. Duryodhana, Karna, Ashwatthāmā, Duhshāsana and the other warriors tried stopping the juggernaut named Abhimanyu but in vain. Many warriors were severely injured. Many fell unconscious. A lot more perished. Abhimanyu fell like a wheel of fire on the Kaurava armies, breaking the formation one layer at a time. The casualties of Abhimanyu's blitzkrieg included Duryodhana's son Lakshman, Karna's brothers and the king of Kosal, Brihadbal, among others.

Shakuni was so tormented by Abhimanyu's onslaught that he warned Duryodhana, 'If we continue fighting one on one, he will finish us all today. Before he does that, let's attack him in a group and kill him.'[19] Afflicted by Abhimanyu's arrows, Karna asked Drona to find a way to stop him, 'The force of his arrows is unbearable. I stand here only because running away is not an option for a warrior,' he said.[20]

Dronāchārya couldn't help but admire Abhimanyu's dexterity and fervour. 'Ah, look at the speed with which he shoots arrows! All one can see is the bend of his bow. There is not even a tiny chink in his combat armour, that is obvious. I see no difference in

Abhimanyu and Arjuna today,' Drona exclaimed in awe.[21] Turning to Karna, Drona advised, 'You won't be able to injure Abhimanyu by aiming for his chest. But if you focus properly, you might be able to break his bow. You can also break the reins of his chariot, his wheels and kill his horses. There is a chance to subjugate Abhimanyu only if he drops his weapons. Else even the gods will not be able to defeat him today. Do what you can.'[22]

Hearing these words of Dronāchārya, the Kauravas jumped into action. Simultaneously, they launched an offensive on the young boy. Karna cut his bow, Kritavarmā killed his horses and Kripāchārya broke his chariot. Abhimanyu fell off his chariot weaponless. In that state, six Kauravas warriors showered a volley of arrows on him all at once. Abhimanyu didn't budge. He took out his sword and shield and leapt in the air. Dronāchārya swiftly broke his sword and Karna shattered his shield. Abhimanyu's body was covered with arrows penetrating deep into his flesh. His clothes were completely drenched in his blood. Even in that pain and completely exposed, this son of Subhadrā kept the fight on. He picked up the wheel of his chariot and rushed towards Dronāchārya. The warriors on the chariot destroyed that wheel too. Abhimanyu then picked up his mace. With one stroke he killed Ashwatthāmā's horses, with another he smashed the chariot of Gāndhār prince Kalikeya and with one more stroke he destroyed the chariot and horses of Duhshāsana's son. Enraged, Daushāsani[23] pulled out his mace and attacked the already injured Abhimanyu. But he fought with the passion still alive in him. Fighting each other, they fell on the ground. But Daushāsani swiftly got up and dealt one lethal blow of the mace on Abhimanyu's head.

Abhimanyu collapsed, never to get up again. Nature was in shock. Abhimanyu's killing was one of the most dreadful and abhor-worthy events of Kurukshetra. All rules were broken, all ethics sidelined. Abhimanyu's death expedited the end of the Kauravas. Neither Krishna nor Arjuna would allow any of the culprits to forget this act.

Ghatotkacha

After escaping from Vāranāvata, the Pāndavas and Kunti spent time hiding in a forest, which also happened to be the home of a cannibal rākshasa[24] named Hidimb. Smelling the fragrance of humans in the forest, he sent his sister Hidimbā to hunt them down for a nice feast. Hidimbā came looking for the humans. Her eyes fell on the tall and broad-shouldered Bheema. She could feel the strength in his physique. His face glowed with youth. His muscles were chiselled. Hidimbi was besotted. 'Only he can be a worthy husband for me. I will not kill him for my brother's food,' she thought. She approached Bheema and warned him about Hidimb. Then, smiling coyly, Hidimbā expressed her desire for him. 'I have been struck by cupid since my eyes fell on you. I would not wish for any other husband but you,' she asserted.

Wondering why it was taking so long for Hidimbā to return, Hidimb went searching for her. Seeing

Hidimbā dressed up and talking to Bheema, he guessed she was trying to woo him. Furious at her defiance, he leapt to kill her. Bheema stopped him and the two clashed like two giant elephants. Hidimb was killed in the tussle that followed. The noise had woken up the other brothers and Kunti by then. Hidimbā informed Kunti about what had transpired while they were asleep. She then bowed to her and sought her permission to marry Bheema. Yudhishthira and Kunti acquiesced but with a condition: 'You spend the day with him as you like but in the night let him come back to us.'

Hidimbā and Bheema spent a few happy months together. From their union, a big and healthy son was born. He was born with a pot-like bald head, hence Hidimbā named him Ghatotkacha.[25] This son of Bheema's was the oldest upa-Pāndava.[26] Being born to a mother of the rākshasa tribe, he grew up much faster than other human babies. He was a good and obedient child. All the brothers and Kunti were very fond of him. Then, at some point, Hidimbā realised it was time to let Bheema go. He had a path ordained for him. Ghatotkacha sought the blessings of his father, uncles and grandmother and promised to be there for the Pāndavas whenever they needed him.

Pāndavas had secured Khāndavaprastha from Dhritarāshtra and transformed it into Indraprastha. Due to just and people-centric administration of Yudhishthira and the brothers, it had become a prosperous city. Then one day, Yudhishthira was inspired to conduct the Rājasuya Yajna that would make him the sovereign king of Bhāratavarsha. For that to happen, all other kings in the land had to be convinced or vanquished. The four brothers picked a direction and embarked on a journey to subjugate the kings and get the right to earn royalty from them.

Sahadeva went southwards. He won over all kingdoms of the South including Pandya, Dravida, Kerala, Āndhra and Kalinga just by sending his messengers. The one kingdom he was yet to reach out to was Lanka. But that entailed crossing the sea. Sahadeva called for Ghatotkacha and sent him as a messenger to Lanka.[27] Ghatotkacha immediately complied. He proceeded to the spot from where Shri Rāma had constructed the bridge to get to Lanka. He looked with bewilderment at the Rāma Setu, thinking about the feat of Shri Rāma and crossed over to Lanka.[28] On giving his introduction, he was welcomed warmly by the king of Lanka, who gave many precious gifts to Ghatotkacha for Yudhishthira.[29]

The Rājasuya Yajna happened but it turned out to be a bête noire for the Pāndavas. The game of dice incident happened soon after. The Pāndavas lost everything and were banished to thirteen years of vanvās. Life wasn't easy but with the guidance of sages, they used the time productively. In expectation of a war, Arjuna had gone to the palace of Indra to gather celestial weapons. The other Pāndavas had stayed back in the forest with Draupadi. On the advice of Sage Lomash, they embarked on a pilgrimage.

Having travelled through Uttarākhand and religious sites by the Gangā, the Pāndavas headed to the Gandhamādan mountain. It was a long, strenuous climb. At one point, Draupadi fainted out of exhaustion. She couldn't walk anymore. Once again, Ghatotkacha was summoned. He came along with his friends and carried Draupadi, the Pāndavas and other sages on their shoulders all the way to Badrikā āshram on Gandhamādan. Ghatotkacha and his friends were constant companions of the Pāndavas during these days of their vanvās.

The rākshasa tribes were considered especially fearsome in the war as they had illusionary powers which became even stronger after sunset. Both sides had rākshasa warriors fighting for them. Ghatotkacha, his son Anjanaparvā and his men were on the Pāndava sides. Alambusha, Alāyudha and their armies were on the Kaurava side. Ghatotkacha was out on the battlefield along with other sons of the Pāndavas from day one. In skill, prowess and heroism, he was no less than Bheema, sometimes even better.[30] Bheema had sounded the death knell for the Kaurava army. But twice, when Bheema was in trouble, Ghatotkacha came to his rescue.

On day four of the war, the mighty elephant warrior, Bhagadatta, the king of Prāgjyotisha, had caused Bheema to faint. Ghatotkacha and some other rākshasa warriors mounted elephants and rushed at Bhagadatta and his men. Elephants collided with elephants and men with men. The day was saved for the Kauravas and more so for Bhagadatta due to Bhishma's quick thinking. Convinced that it wasn't wise to face Ghatotkacha head-on at that time, he announced the closing of the war day as the sun was to set soon.[31]

Ghatotkacha continued to trample the Kaurava army over the days of the war until his death. The fourteenth day was especially significant—it was the day that Arjuna killed Jayadratha. The most legendary warrior that day, however, was Ghatotkacha. In a way, his heroics that day clinched the war decisively in favour of the Pāndavas. But for him, the victory would have been a distant goal.

Ghatotkacha's first major victim on the fourteenth day was the dreadful rākshasa Alambusha. After injuring the demon with multiple arrows, Ghatotkacha leapt onto Alambusha's chariot. The son of Bheema lifted Alambusha and spun him around for a few minutes before banging him hard on the ground. The rākshasa could not survive the blow and died.[32]

The other major casualty of his that day was another powerful rākshasa Alāyudha, who was the brother of Bakāsura, the demon whom Bheema had killed in the Ekachakra Nagar before their marriage to Draupadi. He was also a relative of Hidimb and Kimir, two other mighty rākshasas killed by Vrikodara.[33] Alāyudha was even more upset at Hidimbā's wedding with Bheema. He had entered the battle swearing to avenge the death of his mates by killing Bheema in Kurukshetra.

Duryodhana summoned Alāyudha to stop the Ghatotkacha from wreaking havoc on Karna and his men. When Alāyudha was about to attack Ghatotkacha, Bheema counter-attacked. The rākshasa was waiting for his chance to fight Bheema. He responded by catapulting a barrage of powerful weapons at Bheema, who resisted the assault but was struggling to retaliate in kind. Sensing his father was in danger, Ghatotkacha shifted his attention from Karna to Alāyudha.

Ghatotkacha and Alāyudha engaged in a deadly duel, fighting with maces, missiles, arrows and several other weapons. Both had recourse to illusory powers. Their weapons clashed, making thunderous noises and scaring away the best of the soldiers. When weapons didn't help, they wrestled, pulling each other's hair. Then, just like Alambusha, Ghatotkacha raised Alāyudha over his head and banged him down, dealing a lethal blow to the otherwise invincible warrior.[34]

Earlier that evening, Ghatotkacha had witnessed the death of his son Anjanaparvā at the hands of Ashwatthāmā.[35] But the most crucial event of the fourteenth day was yet to happen.

After Jayadratha's death, the Kauravas were in shock. They fought back vengefully. The war continued late in the night. Unable to bear the sight of Duryodhana's pain, Karna was determined to rout the Pāndava army. There was no stopping him. Arjuna could have stopped him but Krishna did not want their combat to happen yet. Karna was in possession of the lethal Vaijayanti astra,[36] the only one which Arjuna did not have a counter to. The only other capable person who could have faced Karṇa was Ghatotkacha. And being a rākshasa, he fought even better in the night.

Ghatotkacha took on the mantle and headed straight towards Karna in his giant eight-wheeled chariot drawn by a hundred horses. Tall and muscular, resembling a giant mountain, his appearance was enough to send shivers down the spine of ordinary humans. Duryodhana sent many warriors to stop Ghatotkacha from approaching Karna but Ghatotkacha was unstoppable. Slaying all those who came in his way, Ghatotkacha attacked Karna, who retaliated in equal measure. The two looked like mighty elephants colliding. A deadly combat ensued and continued way past midnight. Their armours were mangled and limbs completely mauled.

When nothing seemed to mellow down Ghatotkacha, Karna decided to use his celestial weapons. Ghatotkacha too roared and employed his illusory powers. His roar was so frightening that it caused elephants to urinate. The Kaurava forces ran helter-skelter to save their lives. Only Karna stood strong unperturbed. The ferociousness of their duel kept getting worse with no end in sight. At one point, Karna killed Ghatotkacha's sārthi as well as all his horses. Ghatotkacha disappeared and using his illusory prowess, began to trouble Karna creating illusions and dropping meteor-like rocks from the sky. With another weapon, he killed Karna's four horses.

By then, Karna had utilised most of his celestial weapons. The Kauravas were getting increasingly jittery. They implored Karna to use the shakti he had received from Indra, the Indrāstra, and neutralise the eldest son of Bheema, lest he annihilate the entire Kaurava army. 'Only if we live to see another day will we fight Arjuna and Bheema,' they urged. Already seething with anger due to the ineffectiveness of his celestial weapons on Ghatotkacha, Karna heard the cries of the Kauravas and shot the Vaijayanti astra at Ghatotkacha. The weapon was fatal, as Indra had promised. It ruptured Ghatotkacha's chest. Knowing he wasn't going to survive this assault, Ghatotkacha did something astonishing. He expanded his body using his capabilities one last time and let his body collapse on the Kaurava forces. Ghatotkacha died but even in his death, he destroyed one akshauhini army of Duryodhana.[37]

(Picture: Ghatotkacha–Karna Combat, Bali, photographed by the author)

Yudhishthira couldn't hold back his tears when he learnt about the death of Ghatotkacha. He couldn't even get himself to go back to the battlefield. Krishna consoled him and coaxed him to give up sorrow and get ready to fight. The war was far from over. Wiping his tears, Yudhishthira replied, 'A man who forgets the beneficence done on him is as sinful as a murderer. Ghatotkacha has forever been at our beck and call. When we were living in the forest, he helped us through the most difficult times. When Arjuna had gone to get the celestial weapons from Indra, Ghatotkacha voluntarily came and stayed with us. He carried Draupadi on his back to help her climb the Gandhamādan mountain during our pilgrimage. He was fully devoted to me. I too loved him like I love Sahadeva. We were all present right there and couldn't do anything to save Ghatotkacha from getting killed at the hands of Karna!'[38]

Yudhishthira then suddenly stood up and declared, 'If it is right for us to kill our enemies, those who deserve to die the most are Karna and Drona. They were the prime warriors who killed Abhimanyu. Not Jayadratha; he was only a minor player. Now Ghatotkacha is dead. Karna and Drona are the ones causing the most damage to my army. Even then, Arjuna chose to go after Jayadratha instead of Karna. But now I will kill Karna myself.' Saying so, he headed out to the field, only to be held back by Vyāsa Muni.[39] The sorrow of Ghatotkacha's death, however, still engulfed him.

Draupadeyas

The days spent in Indraprastha were the few years of happiness for the Pāndavas and Draupadi. It was during these years that Draupadi gave birth to five sons, one with each of her husbands.

Yudhishthira's son, the eldest of the Draupadeyas, was named Prativindhya, the one who would be steadfast as the Vindhya[40] mountains in warfare.[41]

Bheema's son was named Sutasoma, the one who was as splendid as the sun and moon, and the one who was born after Bheema had conducted a thousand Soma Yajnas.[42]

Arjuna's son was named Shrutakirti, as he was born after Arjuna had returned from his renowned and virtuous twelve-year pilgrimage across Bhāratavarsha.[43] Shrutakirti was the youngest son of Arjuna, the eldest being Irāvan followed by Babruvāhana and Abhimanyu.[44]

Nakula's son Shatānika was named after one of the illustrious ancestors of the Kuru lineage.[45]

Sahadeva's son was born in the Krittika Nakshatra of Agni devata, hence he was named Shrutakarma.[46]

The Draupadeyas spent a large part of their childhood in Kāmpilya and Dwārkā, in the care of their maternal relatives and Krishna. Satyabhāmā had reassured Draupadi of the well-being of her sons when she had come visiting their forest āshram. 'Your sons are happy and taken care of with love in Dwārkā. Subhadrā, Rukmini, Krishna and the Yādavas of Dwārkā shower their love on your sons. The five boys have finished their education and have become experts in warfare. Worry not,' she had comforted.

When Bhishma was assessing the warriors on the Pāndava side, he had called the five sons of Draupadi as 'mahārathis',[47] implying they were well-trained and capable warriors.

The Draupadeyas mainly fought as a team alongside Abhimanyu, protecting him and the other warriors when in danger. They were instrumental in backing up Abhimanyu on multiple occasions. They stopped the onslaught of Duryodhana on the sixth day.[48] They fought the unstoppable Ashwatthāmā on the seventeenth day of the war. They had their share of trophies in duels as well. Over the eighteen days, they fought against some of the most eminent Kaurava warriors. Against some, they won; against some others, they were pushed back. But at no point did the young boys flinch. Unrattled, they persisted on the battlefield until the very last day.

Some of their prominent combats include:

1. Prativindhya[49] fought against Shakuni, Alambusha, Ashwatthāmā, Duhshāsana, and Chitra. On the eleventh day, he duelled with Ashwatthāmā when stopped from attacking Dronāchārya. He killed Chitra on the sixteenth day of the war in a nail-biting combat. Every weapon, from bows and arrows to maces and spears were used in the duel. After killing Chitra, Prativindhya attacked his army. A large number of soldiers got killed. Others who were lucky fled away.
2. Sutasoma[50] battled Vikarna, Vivimshati and Shakuni. On the sixth day, he saved Shrutakarma from being killed by Durmukha, one of the brothers

of Duryodhana. Durmukha broke Shrutakarma's chariot but he continued fighting from the ground fearlessly. Sutasoma came by quickly and pulled his younger brother on to his chariot.

3. Apart from Durmukha, Shrutakarma[51] fought with Sudakshin, the king of Kāmbhoja. On the eleventh day, he faced off with Duryodhana's brother Chitrasena's son. Then on the fourteenth day of the war, Shrutakarma killed Shala, the son of Somadatta and brother of Bhurishravā. It was a joint effort by the five brothers. They individually combated Shala first and left him weaker before Shrutakarma finally severed his head. Shrutakirti killed Shala's horses, Shatānika killed his charioteer, Sutasoma cut his bow and Prativindhya his flag. On the sixteenth day, the son of Sahadeva killed the king of Abhiras, Chitrasena and destroyed his army. Shrutakirti backed him up in this feat. On the seventeenth day, the son of Devāvradha was killed by Shrutakarma.
4. Shatānika[52] fought Jayatsena, Chitrasena, Dushkarna and Shrutakarma—the brothers of Duryodhana, Ashwatthāmā and Vrishasena among others. He killed Bhutakarma on the eleventh day of the war when Bhutakarma tried to stop him from attacking Drona. Shatānika helped Dhrishtadyumna make the troop formation for the Pāndavas on the fourteenth day. On the seventeenth day, he killed a young prince of Kalinga.
5. Shrutakirti[53] faced off with Jayatsena on the sixth day. On the eleventh day, he had a one-on-one

with Duhshāsana's son while attempting to attack Dronāchārya. He was the youngest of the Draupadeyas and a great team player.

After Duryodhana fell, the conch was blown, suggesting the end of the war. Among the sons of the Pāndavas who had fought in Kurukshetra, only the Drauapadeyas had survived through the eighteen days. That night, per Krishna's suggestions, the Pāndavas rested in the Kaurava camp. The sons of Draupadi and the surviving warriors of Pānchāla—Dhrishtadyumna and Shikhandi among them—rested in their own camp. Many near and dear ones were lost to the war, but at least the consolation of not having to fight the next morning let them sleep in relative peace.

The Kauravas had lost. But three warriors, Ashwatthāmā, Kritavarmā and Kripāchārya, were still alive. For that matter, Duryodhana was on his deathbed but not yet dead. The sight of the eldest Kaurava, the ever-proud Duryodhana drenched in blood, lying in mud by a pool, waiting for death to alleviate his pain, was quite heart-wrenching. Ashwatthāmā was grief-stricken on seeing the plight of his friend. For all his vices, Duryodhana knew how to maintain friendships. He was generous and indulging for those he called his friends.

'I pledge to kill all the Pāndavas and Pānchālas today to avenge what they have done to you,' Ashwatthāmā fumed. His words came as a succour to the dying crown prince of Hastināpur. He nominated

Ashwatthāmā as the commander of the Kauravas.[54] Not that there were any Kauravas or allies left to lead but it was a formality, more like Duyodhana's gesture of gratitude. The three warriors couldn't go back to their camp. Instead, they chose to spend the night in the forest. Kripāchārya and Kritavarmā fell asleep on the ground by a tree.

Ashwatthāmā was wide awake wondering how he could avenge his friend's defeat. 'There is no way I can kill the Pāndavas in a battle now. But I am oath-bound. To stick to the usual rules of a war wouldn't be wise. That way, I will call upon my own end,' he thought. Just then, his eyes fell on a tree nearby. A fleet of crows was perched on one of its branches, asleep. Out of nowhere, an owl hovered by and attacked the unaware crows. Most of the crows were unable to fly due to the suddenness of the owl's strike and became the predator's easy victims. Ashwatthāmā jumped up. He knew how his revenge would look.[55]

Having decided his plan of action, Ashwatthāmā woke up his uncle Kripāchārya and Kritavarmā. Venting out his frustration over the devastation of Duryodhana and the Kaurava army, he laid out his plan for revenge. Kripāchārya attempted to dissuade him. 'Duryodhana got what he deserved. Driven by impulse and greed, he plunged himself and all others into this thoughtless and cruel act of war disregarding all sane advice. The pain we are faced with is also our own doing. We followed Duryodhana knowing fully well he was on the path of destruction. Let us rather go to Hastināpur and seek counsel of Dhritarāshtra, Gāndhāri and Vidura,' he said.

Ashwatthāmā was in no mood to listen. Anger had shrouded his discretion. 'I have decided to kill the Pāndavas and the Pānchālas tonight itself, as they sleep peacefully in their camp. The Pāndavas have resorted to deception during the war. That's how they killed my father Drona, Karna and even Duryodhana. I won't be doing anything wrong,' saying so, Ashwatthāmā rushed to his chariot. Kripa and Kritavarmā followed. Together they headed to the camp of the Pāndavas.[56]

The camp was quiet. The soldiers and caretakers too had fallen into a deep slumber, assuming the war was over. Ashwatthāmā stealthily entered the tents and started slaying whoever his sword could find. Like crows left aghast at the owl's attack, the warriors in the camp were horrorstruck. Even before they could realise what had hit them, their necks were severed by the swiftness of Ashwatthāmā's strike. He killed Dhrishtadyumna, Uttamaujas, Yudhāmanyu and their servants. The few who did manage to escape were slain by Kritavarmā and Kripāchārya who were waiting by the entrance.

Shikhandi and the sons of Draupadi woke up with a jolt due to the commotion caused. They came out of their camps and started showering arrows at Ashwatthāmā. As if fuelled by the lord of destruction himself, Ashwatthāmā couldn't be contained. One after the other the Drauapadeyas and Shikhandi were slain by the force of Ashwatthāmā's sword. In that one night, Ashwatthāmā exterminated more people than he had in the days of the war.[57] Having killed to his heart's satisfaction, he came out of the camp. The three of them rushed to the pool by which Duryodhana lay and boasted of Ashwatthāmā's exploit. Duryodhana was overjoyed. He passed away soon after.

As Sanjay narrated the gory destruction inflicted by Ashwatthāmā on the Pāndava camp, Dhritarāshtra was half-awed and half-surprised. 'If Ashwatthāmā wished my son's victory, why did he not do this before? Why did he wait for my son to die to destroy the opponents?' he asked.

'Ashwatthāmā greatly feared Arjuna, Krishna and Sātyaki. Had Arjuna been around, Ashwatthāmā would have never succeeded,' replied Sanjay.[58]

Ashwatthāmā didn't stop at that. He tried to use the Brahmāstra on the Pāndavas, failing which he directed the deadly weapon at Uttarā's womb to kill her unborn child. He did not succeed in that either. But for all the offences he committed, Ashwatthāmā did get his comeuppance, a retribution worse than death. He was cursed by Krishna to live for three thousand years, roaming on earth alone, diseased, with an ever-festering wound on his forehead, smelling of pus and blood.[59]

Shwet

Uttar and Shwet were young sons of King Virāta of Matsya desh. Uttarā, Abhimanyu's wife, was their sister. Uttar was the prince who had been Arjuna's sārthi during the battle of Virāta. Both these brothers had participated in the war on the side of the Pāndavas. Uttar fought valiantly but was killed by Shalya, the king of Madra, on the very first day of the war. Shwet saw Uttar die. Upset and enraged, he launched an aggressive attack on Shalya to avenge his brother's death. Shalya was completely cornered. Seeing him unable to move, Shwet was about to jump onto Shalya's chariot. But before Shwet could kill Shalya, seven warriors, including Jayadratha and Brihadbal, counter-attacked. It was a simultaneous attack but Shwet was feisty. In a flash of a second, he cut their bows with his arrows. The warriors pulled out other bows. Again, before they could realise, Shwet shot another blast of arrows and broke the bows in half. Shwet made them retreat and aimed for Shalya once again.

This time, armies led by Bhishma and Duryodhana launched an assault on Shwet and his fleet of soldiers. Unflustered, Shwet killed many young warrior princes that day. Many had their heads severed, others their limbs. So ferocious was Shwet's onslaught that the soldiers of Bhishma's army ran helter-skelter, leaving Bhishma alone. Observing that no one else was capable of restraining Shwet, Bhishma upped his assault. They fought like wild intoxicated elephants displaying their excellence in warfare. Bhishma was a veteran. But Shwet was unyielding. The Pāndava forces were in awe of Shwet. The young man was proving to be more than a match for the eldest Kaurava. At one point, seeing the flag of Bhishma's chariot cut, the Kauravas assumed Shwet had killed Bhishma.

Duryodhana sent warriors like Bāhlika, Kritavarmā and Shalya to protect Bhishma. Shwet stopped them in their way by directing an offensive of arrows and weapons at them. Bhishma's body was also mangled by his arrows. Shwet then threw a mace on Bhishma's chariot, crushing the horses as well as the body of the chariot. Bhishma quickly got onto another chariot and this time launched one final fatal attack on Shwet. Unable to withstand the blow of the grand old warrior's attack, the boy succumbed. In this glorious death, Shwet immortalised himself.[60]

Shankha, one more son of Virāta's, died on the sixth day of the war. He was killed by Dronāchārya when he came to the rescue of his father.[61]

The victory of Kurukshetra was not trivial. Its price was the life of a generation of warriors.

ॐ ψ ॐ

20

The Post-War Hastināpur Days

Yudhishthira Dejection

The war lasted for eighteen days. The Pāndavas had won but the victory had come at a huge cost. There was not a single warrior family left in Bhāratavarsha that had not lost a father, son, brother or husband. The five Pāndavas had survived but they had lost their grandfather, cousins, teachers, uncles, brothers-in-law as well as all their sons from Draupadi, Subhadrā, Uloopi and Hidimbā.

Consumed with extreme guilt of participating in this destruction, Yudhishthira, in a fit of distress, announced he didn't want the kingdom nor the riches. He would rather do prayashchit[1] by spending the rest of his life in vanvās. 'Had we taken shelter in Dwārkā and begged for a living, such calamity wouldn't have befallen us. For the sake of this kingdom, we killed all those who were dear to us. We killed the young sons of parents who were yet to fulfil their duties towards them and experience the joys of their life. We have certainly sinned. I cannot live here anymore. I need to repent for my sin. I will take your leave and go live an ascetic's life in the forest.'[2]

The other brothers tried to pull him out of his sorrow and urged him to reconsider his decision.

'Going away to the forest at this juncture is akin to running away from your responsibility towards the kingdom,' Bheema said.[3]

'One does not throw away the wealth that he has rightly gained; rather, it should be used for the welfare of the kingdom. You have this opportunity to sacrifice yourself and everything you have for your subjects by way of administration and by conducting grand ceremonial yajnas. As a king, that is the most virtuous path for you to take,' encouraged Arjuna.[4]

Nakula opined, 'It is foolish to think one is a noble by just giving up a householder's life and going to the forest. A noble man is he who uses his discretion to understand his duties towards his family and society and acts accordingly, keeping his own desires in check.'[5]

'True happiness lies in giving up attachment to things including our ego and doing what must be done,' added Sahadeva. Draupadi, Kunti, Krishna and Veda Vyāsa too urged Yudhishthira to reconsider his plans for renunciation and accept his kingly duties. Not only was his responsibility towards the citizens of Hastināpur but also towards all those kingdoms that had participated in the war from either side.

In addition to exhorting Yudhishthira to govern the kingdom like his ancestors did, Vyāsa gave very sound advice to establish peace in the region, 'Go visit all these kingdoms and crown whoever is their rightful heir, probably the son or the grandson. If a male heir doesn't exist, crown their daughters. Console their citizens and the womenfolk. Help them deal with their grief and establish peace in the country.'[6]

Vyāsa encouraged the eldest Pāndava to get over his grief and when the time was right, to solemnise the aspirational yajnas like Ashwamedha and Sarvamedha, just as his ancestors had done. 'Once you are disposed of all your duties and have repaid the debt to the society, to your ancestors and the gods, you may retire to the forest happily,' added Vyāsa.[7]

Yudhishthira eventually yielded and was crowned the king of Hastināpur. The idea of conducting the yajna appealed to him but that would require a full treasury. As the war had happened not too long ago, the coffers were empty. Veda Vyāsa directed the Pāndavas to a location in the Himālayas where immense treasure was hidden. If they managed to find and secure that wealth, the treasuries could be filled soon.[8]

A king named Maruta in the lineage of Ishwaku had conducted a yajna at that spot several years ago. After having given away a lot of wealth in donation, the king still had a lot more gold left. This he had stored in that location, getting a treasury made. Over the years, the location and the wealth were lost to his successors[9]. The Pāndavas went to that place in the Himālayas and excavated pots of gold, jewellery, precious stones and utensils made of gold. The amount of wealth they found was enough to undertake a grand fire ritual, the Ashwamedha Yajna.

Ashwamedha Yajna—the Initiation

Despite the tragedies of the war, the birth of Parikshita had sent a wave of joy throughout Hastināpur. The

Pāndavas had hit a jackpot in the Himālayas. Thus, Yudhishthira began to plan the organisation of the Ashwamedha Yajna as suggested by both Veda Vyāsa and Krishna. Only a king who had significant wealth for donation at his disposal and the subordination of the other kings of Bhāratavarsha could solemnise this ritual. Similar to the Rājasuya Yajna, getting the other kings to accept the host king's domination, by diplomacy or strength, was mandatory. Like Rājasuya, this yajna too entailed giving humongous amounts of charity in the form of food and wealth to all those who came seeking and were invited, including ordinary citizens and heads of other kingdoms who had accepted the host king's sovereignty. Rather, that was the idea, to assuage the miseries of war-struck citizens by at least ensuring they were materially taken care of.

There was one major difference between the two rituals. In the Ashwamedha Yajna, a horse of an excellent breed was let loose and allowed to roam around at his will for one whole year. The kingdoms that were transgressed by the horse had two options: Let the horse pass through indicating their acceptance of the host as the supreme king; or hold the horse, implying they were opposing the host's dominion. For the yajna to happen, the host king had to defeat or convince the opposing king and make them relent.

For Yudhishthira's yajna, a well-bred horse was selected and set free. Arjuna was appointed to follow the horse and ensure it came back at the end of the stipulated period. 'As far as possible, convince the kings through your words. Try not to have a full-fledged war with them,' Yudhishthira opined.[10] Arjuna embarked on the mission with a huge army. He would first attempt to persuade the kings peacefully and would fight them only if they did not budge. Even when compelled, he avoided killing the princes or the kings. Having put them in a weaponless, chariot-less state, Arjuna would let them go once they accepted Yudhishthira's command.

Dushālā's Plea

Although Arjuna did not wish for a war with any kingdom, the wounds of Kurukshetra were still being nursed by some. They were waiting for this opportunity to fight Arjuna. The kingdoms of Trigarta, Kirātas and Mlecchas attempted to stop the horse but got a drubbing from Arjuna. After Bhagadatta's death in Kurukshetra, his son Vajradatta became the king of Prāgjyotisha. He challenged Arjuna and a fight followed. Vajradatta lost but Arjuna did not kill him. Conveying the invitation for the yajna and getting Vajradatta's allegiance, Arjuna moved on. The horse then turned towards Sindhu desh.

Jayadratha, the brother-in-law who Arjuna had killed on the fourteenth day of Kurukshetra to avenge Abhimanyu's death, was the king of Sindhu desh. Subsequently, his son Surath was crowned king. Jayadratha was also the one who had tried to abduct Draupadi during their years in exile. After that incident, though the Pāndavas hadn't killed Jayadratha, they had significantly humiliated him. Since then, the Saindhavas[11] harboured special hatred towards the five brothers. Hence, when they learnt of the horse entering Sindhu territory, the warriors of Sindhu attacked Arjuna, who retaliated. He was more than a match for all Sindhu warriors put together.

Arjuna coaxed them to back off but the Saindhavas were ready to die. When many warriors on their side began to fall, Dushālā, Arjuna's cousin sister and Jayadratha's wife rushed onto the field with a toddler in her hand. She requested Arjuna to forgive the Saindhavas for the sake of the toddler and not kill any more warriors. Arjuna himself didn't want to kill anyone. Now the plea came from his cousin. He immediately stopped his attack and enquired about the child. Dushālā informed him that the boy was Surath's son and her grandson. She also told him that Surath had died just that day from the shock of the news of Arjuna's attack.[12]

Dushālā then requested her own people to drop their weapons and make peace with the Pāndavas. It was Dushālā's wisdom that saved the Saindhavas that day. Arjuna was happy to comply. He comforted Dushālā, invited her to the yajna and moved on to the next destination.

Following the horse around like this, Arjuna entered the kingdom of Manipur.[13]

The Son Who Defeated Arjuna

Many years ago, when Arjuna was on his twelve-year journey around Bhāratavarsha after having intruded on Yudhishthira and Draupadi's privacy, he had come to Manipur. Towards the south, crossing over Mahendragiri mountains, walking by the coastal route, he had reached this beautiful kingdom.[14] Roaming around in the city, he saw an astoundingly beautiful young lady. On enquiry, he learnt she was Chitrāngadā, the princess of Manipur and the daughter of King Chitravāhana. Arjuna approached the king and introduced himself. He requested the king for his daughter's hand. He wished to make Chitrāngadā his wife.

Chitravāhana accepted the alliance with a precondition. Per the tradition in their family, the son born to the daughter would live in his maternal home and eventually become the heir to the throne. Therefore, the child born of the union will have to be left back in Manipur along with the mother. Arjuna agreed. He and Chitrāngadā were married and had a son, Babruvāhana. After his birth, Arjuna resumed his journey.[15]

When Babruvāhana learnt of the arrival of his father in Manipur with the horse, he was elated. Along with his ministers, he went to welcome Arjuna, who wasn't pleased. 'Have you forgotten that you are a warrior? I have entered your territory with this horse. You must thwart my way ahead and fight with me. Instead, you are here to welcome me,' he chastised. Uloopi, Arjuna's other wife and Babruvāhana's stepmother, who had accompanied Arjuna, explained to Babruvāhana the purport of his father's harsh words. 'Your father comes from the best of the warrior families and wishes to see how capable you are. You must fight him. That will make him happy,' she advised.

Babruvāhana put on his armour, picked up his bow and quiver of arrows and got on his chariot. He ordered his men to capture the white Ashwamedhi[16] horse and challenged Arjuna. A vigorous combat ensued. The father and the son showered a volley of sharp arrows at each other. Babruvāhana propelled some of his best weapons and arrows, wounding his father badly. Deftly, he cut down the arrows that Arjuna shot at him. Seeing his son's manoeuvre, Arjuna was delighted. 'Blessings to you, O Son of Chitrāngadā! Your valour impresses me. Now see how I attack you. Be alert!' Saying so, Arjuna killed Babruvāhana's horses and crushed his chariot. Angered, Babruvāhana shot some extremely sharp poison-tipped arrows that pierced through Arjuna's armour and chest. Arjuna collapsed on the ground unconscious. Babruvāhana himself was terribly wounded. He too fell on the ground unconscious.[17]

Chitrāngadā was aghast when she saw her husband and son lying lifeless on the ground. 'You made the son and father fight! Now you bring Arjuna back to life, else I will kill myself!' she said accusingly to Uloopi. Soon enough, Babruvāhana regained consciousness. But Arjuna lay unconscious still. Extreme sorrow gripped Babruvāhana's heart. He thought he had killed his father. What could be a greater sin? Babruvāhana declared he couldn't live after having committed such a grave sin and would kill himself by fasting unto death. Uloopi comforted them. 'Your father is a virtuous man and an invincible warrior. Not even Indra can defeat him. I have a Sanjeevani gem which we Nāgas use to resurrect our wounded warriors. Take this and place it on your father's chest,' she said, handing the gem to Babruvāhana.

Arjuna woke up rubbing his eyes as if he was waking up from a deep sleep and wondered what everyone was doing standing around him. Babruvāhana bowed to him and asked Uloopi to narrate the story of his falling unconscious.[18] After spending a few happy days in Manipur, Arjuna proceeded on his mission inviting Chitrāngadā and Babruvāhana to visit Hastināpur.

This was the first time in his life that Arjuna had been defeated in a duel. The only other time he would be vanquished was a few years away.

Tracing the horse's route, travelling through areas of the south, then coming upwards along the coast to Saurashtra and Dwārkā, Arjuna reached Gāndhār. This was amongst his last few destinations before heading back to Hastināpur. One of Shakuni's sons was the king of Gāndhār at that time.

The people of Gāndhār had no love for the Pāndavas. The death of Shakuni along with many other Gāndhār warriors in Kurukshetra had angered them. They attacked Arjuna and the horse. Arjuna responded in kind. Again, a lady came to the rescue of the Gāndhāras. She was Shakuni's wife. She pleaded with the Gāndhār warriors to seek peace and asked Arjuna to forgive her people. Arjuna offered her reverence as he would to his maternal aunt. She was Duryodhana's aunt, after all. The Gāndhār warriors surrendered. Hoping to normalise relations with this once-upon-a-time enemy state, Arjuna invited Shakuni's son to Hastināpur for the yajna ceremony.[19]

Arjuna returned to Hastināpur having successfully protected the Ashwamedhi horse. Yudhishthira solemnised the fire ritual amidst guests from every corner of Bhāratavarsha. He distributed a huge amount of wealth among priests, citizens and participating guests from all over. The guests left happy and content, singing paeans to the generosity of Yudhishthira and the valour of the Pāndavas.

With Yudhishthira at the helm of Hastināpur empire, Krishna knew Bhāratavarsha was in strong and compassionate hands. Krishna had been pivotal in the success of Pāndavas and now it was for them to carve their path ahead. It was time for him to head back to where he belonged, to Dwārkā.

The years following the yajna were spent in rebuilding the kingdoms. The land of Bhāratavarsha, devastated by one of the bloodiest wars, would finally experience a period of relative peace. Kaliyuga[20] was still some years away.

ॐ ψ ॐ

21

The End of an Epoch

Daruk looked visibly shattered. He had just arrived from Dwārkā and wanted to see Arjuna at the earliest. Daruk was Krishna's trusted friend and charioteer. On seeing Arjuna, the otherwise composed Daruk broke down, 'A huge tragedy has struck the Yādavas. The Yādava warriors have killed each other. Sātyaki, Kritavarmā and the sons of Krishna are all dead. The ladies and children have been left in a lurch. Krishna has requested you to come immediately,' said Daruk, trying to control the tremor and the dejection in his voice.

Arjuna was shaken. 'How is that even possible?' he asked in disbelief. Daruk then told him in detail about the tragic accident which led to Yādavas killing Yādavas.[1]

Long ago, some very accomplished rishis had camped in Dwārkā. In a rather ill-destined moment, some young Yādavas, including Krishna's and Jāmbavati's son Sāmba, thought of playing a prank on them. They dressed up Sāmba in the guise of a pregnant woman and approached the sages. 'This lady is the wife of the great Yādava Babru. She craves for a son. O Noble

Sages, please do tell us if she would beget a son?' they joked. The rishis saw through the prank and were greatly enraged. 'You desire to be pregnant, so you will be. You will deliver an iron club tomorrow. And that club will be the end of the Yādavas,' the rishis cursed. The boys were frightened and went running to the Yādava chief Ugrasen and Krishna to tell them what had happened.

The next day, as the rishis had cursed, a big mass of iron was removed from Sāmba's stomach. Ugrasen had it crushed and thrown into the sea. Afraid of the rishis' curse, to ensure the Yādavas do not lose control of their senses and do nothing stupid, a complete ban on alcohol was imposed in Dwārkā. 'If a person is even seen in possession of alcohol, he will be executed,' announced the royal herald.

After that, a few years went by peacefully. The Yādavas as a clan had become powerful after the Kurukshetra war. The power had made them haughty and hedonistic. Personal boundaries were readily breached and morality in social life had taken a dip. As if wishing to teach them a lesson, nature began behaving erratically. Storms of sand began to rise out of season. Seasons and the timings of sunrise and sunset fell out of sync. The omens did not augur well for Dwārkā.

One day, when deep in thought, Krishna was reminded of Gāndhāri's words. Extremely rattled hearing the wails of her daughters-in-law over the death of her sons, she had addressed Krishna and said, 'Thirty-six years from now, you too will witness your brethren kill each other just like the Kauravas have destroyed themselves in Kurukshetra.' Krishna realised that the thirty-sixth year had arrived. The omens suggested Gāndhāri's curse—and that of the rishis'—might soon play out. Krishna was going to let time and fate take its course.

One day, the Yādavas decided to go on an excursion by the sea. Baskets of food and drink were carried along. Happily, they camped by the shore. Musicians and dancers took to the floor. The ban on alcohol was forgotten and pots of wine were brought out. Sātyaki, Kritavarmā, Krishna's sons and all other Yādava warriors began drinking in front of Krishna, who stood by, a silent spectator. The men began to get intoxicated with all the wine that they had imbibed. In that state of intoxication, Sātyaki suddenly got up and accused Kritavarmā of being a cruel warrior, who had killed the sons of Draupadi and the Pānchāla warriors in their sleep, in the middle of the night, completely unprovoked. Some Yādavas concurred with Sātyaki and began abusing Kritavarmā.

'Says he who killed the unarmed Bhurishravā. Was that not cruel?' Kritavarmā angrily retorted. The arguments became violent. In the heat of the moment, Sātyaki severed Kritavarmā's head. A scuffle followed among the Yādava warriors in which they all ended up killing one another. Only Krishna, Balarāma and Babru survived. While the Yādavas were fighting each other, Balarāma, who was also intoxicated, walked away into a nearby forest and sat under a tree, as if in meditation. Krishna asked Daruk to rush to Hastināpur and seek Arjuna's help. He asked Babru to take the womenfolk back to Dwārkā and inform his father Vasudeva about the unfortunate happening. But before Babru could leave, he was struck by an iron club thrown from somewhere.[2]

Krishna himself took the women back to Dwārkā and told Vasudeva about the destruction of the Yādava clan. 'Arjuna will be here soon. He will probably take all the survivors to Hastināpur. Everyone must leave before it is too late. From the way the ocean has been behaving, Dwārkā will drown soon. I have been a witness to the destruction of the Kauravas. Now I have seen my people kill themselves. I cannot bear to live in this city devoid of my brethren anymore. I will spend my days in the forest along with Balarāma,' said Krishna and walked away.

By the time Krishna reached Balarāma, he was no more. Krishna and Balarāma had been inseparable all their lives. Right from their childhood days spent in Gokul and the struggles in Mathura to the making and destruction of Dwārkā, they had been through everything together. Krishna was now alone and exhausted. It had been an eventful day. He lay down under another tree as if awaiting his death. Suddenly, a poisonous arrowhead of a hunter pierced through Krishna's foot. The hunter had shot Krishna, mistaking him for a wild animal.

The poison was strong. Krishna died instantly.[3] With his death, the age of Dwāpar had ended, the epoch of Kali had begun!

Arjuna got to Dwārkā as fast as he could. His arrival was greeted by the wailings of the women. It was not the Dwārkā he remembered. The city of his memories was grandiose and joyous. This city was haunted like a widow who had lost it all. Arjuna's throat choked, so did his eyes but he had a task at hand. Hence, gathering himself, he went to see Vasudeva, his uncle. Already old, he had become even more frail after the horrific turn of events. His eyes looked listless, like that of a man who had no will to live. Vasudeva had somehow managed to stay alive to give Krishna's message to Arjuna, who had no words to console him. He assured Vasudeva that he would take the survivors back to Hastināpur. 'Krishna, Draupadi and us five Pāndavas are different bodies with the same heart. We cannot imagine living without each other. Seems like our end is near too,' muttered Arjuna.[4]

Vasudeva passed away that night. Arjuna performed his last rites and that of the other Yādava warriors. He sent people to look for Krishna and Balarāma. Their bodies were found in the forest. Arjuna did the last rites for them as well. On the seventh day, he left for Hastināpur from Dwārkā with all the women, children and other survivors. The entourage had just about moved out of the city gate when, as Krishna had predicted, the ocean began roaring tumultuously. Its waves rushed up to encroach upon the lands of the magnificent city of the Yādavas. In no time, the city was completely engulfed by the waters, leaving no trace of its existence.

Crossing the mountains, forests and mighty rivers, Arjuna reached the Panchanada.[5] The entourage camped there for the night. Some dacoits of the Abhira community saw this retinue comprising women and children. This would be an easy group to rob and make a bounty, they thought and attacked their camp. Arjuna and the accompanying soldiers made an attempt to resist the attack. But something extremely peculiar happened. Arjuna, the greatest of the archers of his times, had difficulty stringing his Gāndiva. Then, to ward off the Abhiras who had attacked in large numbers, he decided to use his celestial weapons. However, he couldn't remember how to make them work. Arjuna started showering his arrow nevertheless, but in no time his quiver was empty. In front of his eyes, the dacoits took some women away and killed others who resisted.

It was a moment of extreme embarrassment and rude awakening for Arjuna. A man considered invincible had lost to some lowly dacoits. This was Arjuna's second defeat. The first one was at the hands of his son Babruvāhana. Though in that battle, Arjuna wasn't fighting to win. In this one, against the Abhiras, he had failed like never before. He had failed the Yādava women. He couldn't yet give up. Some women and kids had survived. Arjuna took them to Hastināpur and got them settled in appropriate places.[6]

The loss of Krishna had left an unfillable void in Arjuna's heart. The defeat at the hands of Abhiras had disturbed him even more. He realised his power and skill had significantly depleted. Restless and anxious, he went to see his great-grandfather Veda Vyāsa. Upon hearing his plight, Vyāsa smiled, 'You have done all that you needed to on earth. Now is the apt time to retire and prepare to leave this earthly abode,' he said.[7]

As it so happened, Yudhishthira had been thinking about retirement himself. He had observed omens which indicated it was time to depart. The brothers and Draupadi concurred. Yudhishthira began delegating his responsibilities. He crowned Abhimanyu and Uttarā's son Parikshita the king of Hastināpur. He appointed Krishna's grandson Vajra as the king of Indraprastha. He handed over the overall management of the kingdom to Yuyutsu and declared his intention to spend the last days in the Himālayas with his brothers and Draupadi.[8]

Fifty years ago, the Pāndavas and Draupadi had left Hastināpur, giving up all the luxuries of a royal life to spend thirteen years in the forest. They left again, leaving everything behind—this time, of their own volition and to never come back.

ॐ ψ ॐ

Part 3

Mahābhārata Trivia

22

The Legend of the Scripting of the Mahābhārata

> All wisdom pertaining to the four Purushārthas—Dharma, Artha, Kāma, Moksha—found here may be found elsewhere, but that which is not here is not to be found anywhere.[1]
>
> धर्मे चार्थे च कामे च मोक्षे च भरतर्षभ।
> यदिहास्ति तदन्यत्र यन्नेहास्ति न कुत्रचित्। (Ādi Parva 62.53)

Thus said Vaishampāyana when extolling the glory of the Mahābhārata to Janamejaya.

While the core of the Mahābhārata is the history of the Kauravas and the Pāndavas, interspersed throughout the kāvya[2] is the wisdom of the Vedas and Smritis. That was the intent of Vyāsa Muni, to preserve the history as well as the wisdom of Bhāratavarsha for generations to come. Ugrashravā explained this context of the Mahābhārata to Rishi Shaunak and his students in Naimishāranya. He also narrated to them what he had heard about the scripting of the Mahābhārata. This legend occurs in the very first chapter of the Ādi Parva.[3]

Krishna Dwaipāyana Vyāsa had mentally composed this tale of his grandchildren and their ancestors including all necessary details and stories that would make the kāvya enriching. The number of shlokas had crossed the hundred-thousandth mark. Preserving and spreading the kāvya would necessitate proper scripting and chronicling—a humongous task. Vyāsa Muni had to find a scribe of proven distinction. Once, pondering on this very question, Veda Vyāsa received an inspiration from Brahmā deva himself—to seek the support of Ganesha deva.

Who better than the lord of wisdom, the one who helps us sail through all the hurdles in life, the Vighnahartā, to undertake a task of such epic proportions! Vyāsa Muni approached Ganesha with this request.

'O Ganesha, become the writer of this itihāsa of Bhāratas as I narrate it. I have already developed it in my mind,' requested Vyāsa.

Ganesha agreed but laid down a condition. 'If you ensure my pen doesn't stop even for a bit, then I can become your writer.'

This condition implied that Vyāsa Muni had to recite the shlokas non-stop. Not one to be bogged down, Veda Vyāsa agreed. Nonetheless, he asked for a reciprocation.

'O Deva, have your way but do not write anything without understanding it.'

'Om,' said Ganesha and the Mahābhārata got written!

Sometimes, Vyāsa would compose a complex verse so that Ganesha would need some time to decipher and that would give Vyāsa some time to think. Vyāsa composed eight thousand and eight hundred (8,800) such verses.[4]

Where was the Mahābhārata Written?

Dakshinātya rendering of the Mahābhārata makes a note of where it was written.[5]

पुण्येहिमवतः पादे मेध्येगिरिगुहालये।
विशोध्य देहं धर्मात्मा दर्भसंस्तरमाश्रितः।।
शुचिः सनियमो व्यासः शान्तात्मातपसि स्थितः।
भारतस्येतिहासस्य धर्मेणान्वीक्ष्य तां गतिम्।।

At the foothills of Himālayas, in a mountain cave, Vyāsa Muni meditated and recounted the itihāsa of Bhāratvarsha.

This place has been traced to a small but extremely picturesque village, Mānā (माणा), situated a few kilometres beyond Badrināth, ensconced amongst the mighty Himālayas, along the Indo-Tibetan border. In Mānā, there are two caves—one known as Vyāsa Gufā and about a hundred metres below is another cave known as Ganesha Gufā. Even today, the two caves are popular among pilgrims and tourists alike.

Folklore also suggests that the Pāndavas and Draupadi had come to Mānā on the way to Swargaloka, having crowned Parikshita the king of Hastināpur.

(Picture: Vyāsa Gufā, Mānā, Uttarākhand, photographed by the author)

In How Many Days was the Mahābhārata Composed?

Vaishampāyana tells Janamejaya that it took Krishna Dwaipāyana Vyāsa three years of concerted effort to compose the Mahābhārata, the history of Janamejaya's ancestors.

त्रिभिर्वर्षैः सदोत्थायी कृष्णद्वैपायनो मुनिः।
महाभारतमाख्यानं कृतवानिदमद्तम्।। (Ādi Parva 62.52)

Various Names of the Mahābhārata

There is a popular theory about three forms of the Mahābhārata. Jaya being the original as narrated by Krishna Dwaipāyana of 8,800 shlokas, followed by Bhārata, which was narrated by Vaishampāyana of 24,000 shlokas and finally the one we know as Mahābhārata, narrated by Ugrashravā consisting of 100,000 shlokas. However, till date there have been no separate manuscripts of Jaya or Bhārata found that support the above theory.[6]

The number 8,800 is mentioned in the Mahābhārata text. But that is the count of the complex verses written by Vyāsa. The number 24,000 is also mentioned. It indicates the compilation of 24,000 shlokas excluding the Purānic stories, also composed by Vyāsa and taught to his son Shukadeva. This was known as Bhārata.[7]

The text further suggests that the Mahābhārata of 1,00,000 verses is also composed by Krishna Dwaipāyana Vyāsa himself. When asked by the rishis gathered at Rishi Shaunak's āshram in Naimishāranya about where he was coming from, Ugrashravā had replied, 'I am coming from the Sarpa Satra of King Janamejaya, having heard there the stories from the Mahābhārata recounted by Vaishampāyana composed by Krishna Dwaipāyana Vyāsa.'[8]

Then again in the sixty-second chapter of the Ādi Parva, before proceeding to narrate the story to Janamejaya, Vaishampāyana, while explaining to him the importance of the Mahābhārata, says, 'These 100,000 shlokas have been composed by Krishna Dwaipāyana Vyāsa, the son of Satyavati. This great story of the birth and lives of the progeny of Bharata is called the Mahābhārata.'[9]

In the same chapter, Ādi Parva 62, Vaishampāyana tells Janamejaya, 'This itihāsa by the name Jaya should be heard by all who desire for victory.' It seems to suggest that Jaya is another name for this history of Bhāratas—the Mahābhārata.

The above implies the context-setting shlokas added by Ugrashravā and Vaishampāyana are in addition to the 100,000 shlokas of Vyāsa. It is very likely that additions, modifications and deletions have happened to the shlokas over years. But the theory of the evolution of Jaya into Bhārata into Mahābhārata seems unlikely based on what the text tells us.

ॐ ψ ॐ

23

Vyuhas: Army Formations in the Mahābhārata

An arrangement of troops in a territorial battle including placement of foot soldiers and warriors on horseback, elephant back and riding chariots aligned with the strategy of the day— defensive or offensive— is called a Vyuha.

Every night, in Kurukshetra, both sides discussed the happenings of the day and planned the strategy for the next day, including the placement of the troops. The vyuhas[1] formed by them are tabulated in Table 23.1.

Table 23.1: Vyuha Formations by Both Armies Through Eighteen Days of War

Days	The Pāndavas	The Kauravas
1	Vajra Vyuha (Thunderbolt)	Sarvatomukhi Vyuha (Faces on all sides)
2	Krauncha Vyuha (Heron)	No name specified
3	Ardha Chandra Vyuha (Half-moon)	Garuda Vyuha (Eagle)
4	Ardha Chandra Vyuha (Half-moon)[2]	Vyal Vyuha[3] (Huge cloud-like formation)

Days	The Pāndavas	The Kauravas
5	Shyena Vyuha (Falcon)	Makara Vyuha (Crocodile)
6	Makara Vyuha (Crocodile)	Krauncha Vyuha (Heron)
7	Vajra Vyuha (Thunderbolt)	Mandala Vyuha (Multi-chambered)
8	Shringātaka[4] (Three-peaked)	Mahā Vyuha (Wave-like formation)—no name specified
9	Invincible Maha Vyuha—no name specified	Sarvatobhadra Vyuha (Safe from all sides)
10	No name specified (description of formation is similar for both sides, one led by Shikhandi, the other by Bhishma)	
11	Krauncha Vyuha (Heron)	Shakata Vyuha (Cart)
12	Mandala Ardha Vyuha (Half-circle)	Suparna Vyuha (Bird)
13	No name specified	Chakra Vyuha (Wheel)
14	Vyuha made by Dhrishtadyumna and Shatānika—no name specified	Chakra Shakata Vyuha (Elliptical)
15	None mentioned	Drona divided the army into two factions—no name specified
16	Ardha Chandra Vyuha (Half-moon)	Makara Vyuha (Crocodile)
17	No name specified	Karna made an array instructed by Brihaspati with many wings—no name specified
18	No name specified	Shalya divided troops in many factions—no name specified

Examples of Select Vyuhas

Sarvatomukhi Vyuha

Chariot warriors such as Bhishma, Kripa, Drona and Ashwatthāmā were in the lead in this vyuha. They formed the head of the formation. The elephant warriors made the body and the horse warriors flanked the formation on two sides. It was a position of offence.

Vajra Vyuha

The formation is in the shape of Indra's thunderbolt weapon. Arjuna made this formation on the first day of the war. It was led by Bheema. Behind him was a layer comprising warriors such as Nakula, Sahadeva, Abhimanyu and the Draupadeyas protected by Dhrishtadyumna. Following him was the army led by Shikhandi, which was protected by Arjuna. Arjuna was followed by Sātyaki, Uttamaujas and Yudhāmanyu. Yudhishthira was in the centre of the formation surrounded by warriors on elephants, followed by the armies of Virāta and Drupada. Before Bheema was a fortification of lakhs of soldiers on foot. It was a position of defence.

Krauncha Vyuha

A krauncha is a long-beaked bird, like a heron. On the second day when the Pāndavas made this formation, Arjuna was positioned at its beak. Drupada and his army stood at the head. Kuntibhoja and Dhrishtaketu with their armies made the eyes. Various other armies consisting of Dashārna, Kirātas among others made the neck of the bird. Bheema and Dhrishtadyumna were placed as the open wings of the krauncha. Behind them stood lakhs of other warriors. Surrounded by the Nishādas warriors and other soldiers, Yudhishthira stood at the back of the formation. This vyuha was countered by a very large layered formation led by Bhishma. Its name is not explicitly mentioned in texts.

On the sixth day, Bhishma too arranged his troops in the Kraunch Vyuha as against the Makara Vyuha of the Pāndavas. In that, Dronāchārya formed the beak and Ashwatthāmā and Kripāchārya, the eyes. Kritavarmā stood at the head, Duryodhana in the neck region and Bhagadatta occupied the chest area. The rest positioned themselves in the wings, abdomen and tail regions.

Garuda Vyuha

On the third day, Bhishma made the Garuda Vyuha where he was the beak. Drona and Kritavarmā with their armies made the eyes of the eagle. Ashwatthāmā and Kripa stood at its head position. Bhurishravā, Shalya, Bhagadatta and others formed the neck of the bird. Duryodhana was positioned at the back. The Kalinga warriors with some others made the right wing while Brihadbal of Kosal made the left wing.

Ardha Chandra Vyuha

In response to the Garuda Vyuha of the Kauravas, Arjuna and Dhrishtadyumna made the half-moon formation. Bheema led its right horn followed by armies of Drupada and Virāta. Towards the centre from the right stood Neela, the ruler of Anup desh and Bheema's close friend,[5] Dhrishtaketu and the warriors of Chedi, Kāshi and others. Arjuna led the left horn followed by Ghatotkacha and Kekaya princes. Towards the centre from the left stood Irāvan, Abhimanyu and the five sons of Draupadi. The centre of the half-moon was fortified by Shikhandi, Dhrishtadyumna and warriors of Pānchālas. Yudhishthira was also in the middle of the army protected by Dhrishtadyumna and the warriors on elephants.

Shyena Vyuha

This falcon-shaped vyuha was formed by the Pāndavas on the fifth day. Bheema was positioned at the mouth of the falcon. Shikhandi and Dhrishtadyumna made the eyes of the bird and Arjuna stood at its head. Drupada with his other sons formed the left wing and Kekaya princes formed the right wing. Abhimanyu and the Draupadeyas stood towards the back end, as did Yudhishthira, protected by Nakula and Sahadeva.

Makara Vyuha

On the fifth day, Bhishma made the crocodile-shaped vyuha. He stood at the mouth of the formation. The other warriors took their positions in the designated places. The Pāndavas made this formation on the sixth day. Arjuna and Drupada were at the head of the crocodile. Nakula and Sahadeva placed themselves at the eyes. Bheema stood the mouth. Abhimanyu, Ghatotkacha, the Draupadeyas, Sātyaki and Yudhishthira took positions in the neck region. Virāta and Dhrishtadyumna took the position around the stomach. The Kekaya princes stood on the left side of the crocodile while Dhrishtaketu and Chekitan stood on the right side. Kuntibhoja and Shatānika occupied the limbs. Shikhandi and Irāvan occupied the tail of the formation.

Mandala Vyuha

On the seventh day, Bhishma went for the impenetrable Mandala Vyuha, in which the troops were arranged in multiple similar smaller groups. Every elephant was followed by seven chariots. Each chariot was backed by seven horse warriors. Each horse warrior lead ten thousand archers and soldiers equipped with swords. The Pāndavas countered the Mandala with Vajra formation.

Mahā Vyuha

On the eighth day, Bhishma formed a Mahā Vyuha,[6] an array of troops spread wide and layered, giving an impression of the waves of a mighty ocean when it moved. Bhishma led it from the front along with warriors from Avanti, Mālwa and the southern provinces. Dronāchārya followed them with warriors from Pulinda and Parada. Following Drona was the powerful Bhagadatta with Kalinga and Pishācha warriors among others. Behind him came Brihadbal from Kosal, Ashwatthāmā and

Duryodhana in multiple layers. The remainder of the huge Kaurava army followed, surrounding Duryodhana from all sides.

Shringātaka Vyuha

To counter the Maha Vyuha, Dhrishtadyumna arranged the Pāndava forces in a three-peak formation on the eighth day. Bheema and Sātyaki were placed at the two side horns along with thousands of their soldiers. Arjuna took the middle-horn position. Yudhishthira stood in the middle behind Arjuna along with Nakula and Sahadeva. Abhimanyu, the five sons of Draupadi and Virāta along with others fortified the back end.

Sarvatobhadra Vyuha

Bhishma made a rectangular formation called 'safe from all sides' on the ninth day. In that, Bhishma, Kripa, Kritavarmā, Shaibya, Shakuni, Jayadratha along with the surviving Kaurava brothers except Duryodhana were stationed in the foremost part of the formation. Drona, Bhurishravā, Bhagadatta and Shalya guarded the right side. Ashwatthāmā, Somdatta, Vinda, Anuvinda guarded the left. Duryodhana, surrounded by the Trigartas, was in the middle of the formation. Alambusha and Shrutāyu were positioned at its rear end.

Shakata Vyuha

On the eleventh day of the war and his first day as the commander of the Kauravas, Dronāchārya positioned the troops in a cart-like formation. On the right side were Jayadratha, the king of Kalinga and Vikarna, flanked on the extreme right by Shakuni with some prominent horse warriors of Gāndhār. Kripa, Kritavarmā, Chitrasena, Vivimshati and Duhshāsana were positioned on the left, flanked on extreme left by warriors of Kāmbhoja, Sudakshin and others. Karna led the troops. Behind him stood Duryodhana, followed by warriors of Ambashtha, Trigarta, Sauvira, Shibi and others. On the same day, the Pāndavas again arranged themselves in the Krauncha Vyuha.

Suparna Vyuha

On the twelfth day, Drona made a bird-shaped vyuha. The structure is similar to the Garuda Vyuha mentioned above.

Mandala Ardha Vyuha

In response to Drona's Suparna Vyuha, Yudhishthira formed the Mandala Ardha Vyuha. This formation is similar to the Ardha Chandra Vyuha.

Chakra Vyuha

To trap Yudhishthira, Drona made the wheel-shaped Chakra Vyuha on the thirteenth day of the war. All princes and warriors were positioned in a way to indicate spokes of a giant wheel. Duryodhana's son Lakshman led the troops from the front. Duryodhana surrounded by Karna and Duhshāsana was in the middle of the circle. Dronāchārya and Jayadratha guarded the front end. Ashwatthāmā flanked one side of Jayadratha while the other was flanked by thirty Kaurava brothers, Shakuni and Bhurishravā. Abhimanyu penetrated through the formation but couldn't get out and was killed.

Chakra Shakata Vyuha

To protect Jayadratha from Arjuna, Drona arranged his troops in a wagon-wheel-like formation. Its length was twelve gavyuti (approximately 20–24 miles) and breadth, five gavyuti (approximately 8–10 miles). Within this ellipsis were other formations namely, the Padma (lotus-shaped) Vyuha, which was like a densely packed womb towards the rear end. In the middle of the Padma Vyuha, he made another formation, the Suchimukha, which means shaped like a needle's mouth. Kritavarmā was at the forefront of the Suchimukha, backed up by the king of Kāmbhoja, Jalasangh, Duryodhana and Karna. Over one lakh soldiers were positioned to guard the front end of the Chakra Shakata. On one of the sides of Suchimukha stood Jayadratha protected by a huge army. The mouth of the Chakra Shakata was guarded by Drona himself.

On the seventeenth day, Karna formed a great array with multiple wings. Then, after Karna's death, on the eighteenth day, Shalya divided the remaining army into multiple factions. The war strategy that day was to not fight any Pāndava warrior alone. The attack as well as defence was to be done in a group. No names have been given for these formations.

ॐ ψ ॐ

24

Antiquity of the Mahābhārata

When did the Mahābhārata happen? This has been a question of interest for a lot of researchers for several years. The research interest has been fuelled by the observations made in the Mahābhārata itself. Vyāsa has recorded the position of the stars, constellations and planets along with the movements in a lot of detail, especially from the time the war became a distinct possibility (in Udyoga Parva). The text has over 200 such astronomical observations.

The research in this area has received further impetus due to astronomical software programmes such as SkyGlobe, Voyager and Sky Gazer that can extrapolate the positions of stars and constellations with respect to earth stretching centuries into the past. While the dates of the war proposed by the researchers range from first millennium BCE to sixth millennium BCE, the latest researches with even more powerful software programmes have narrowed the time frame. The latest estimations of the date fall in either the third millennium BCE or sixth millennium BCE, purely based on astronomical observations.

One of the phenomenal observations in support of the date falling in sixth millennium BCE is that of the 'twin stars', Arundhati Vasishtha (Alcor-Mizar). Today, we see Arundhati trailing Vasishtha. In the Mahābhārata, while telling Dhritarāshtra about the omens suggesting a devastating war, Vyāsa observes:

अरुन्धती तयाप्येष वसिष्ठः पृष्ठतः कृतः ||
(Bhishma Parva 2.31)
रोहिणीं पीडयन्नेष स्थितो राजञ्शनैश्चरः |
व्यावृत्तं लक्ष्म सोमस्य भविष्यति महद्भयम् ||
(Bhishma Parva 2.33)

'Arundhati has left Vasishtha behind. Saturn is afflicting the Rohini Nakshatra and the mark on the moon has become invisible.'

Shri Nilesh Nilkanth Oak explains in his book, *When did the Mahābhārata War Happen? The Mystery of Arundhati*, that the phenomenon of Arundhati appearing ahead of Vasishtha had occurred between 6500 BCE to 4500 BCE. This period, therefore, gives the upper and lower limits of the date of the Kurukshetra war. By putting in other observations, Oak arrives at the year for the war as 5561 BCE.

Dates proposed by some other eminent researchers for the Mahābhārata war using astronomical observations are Shri P.V. Vartak 5561 BCE; Shri Kota Venkatachalam 3138 BCE; Shri Vedveer Arya 3162 BCE and Shri M.M. Pandit 3067 BCE.

While one consensual date is still being debated, the research does show that astronomically, the war happened at least 5,100 years ago, and by Shri Oak's estimates, over 7,600 years ago.

Disclaimer: The author does not claim any expertise in this topic of dating. Her understanding of the topic comes largely from following the work of Oak. In the book, When did the Mahābhārata War Happen? The Mystery of Arundhati, *he gives a detailed account of his tests and assumptions as well as a date-wise chronology of pre-war, war and post-war happenings.*

ॐ ψ ॐ

NOTES

INTRODUCTION: WHAT IS DHARMA?

1 Sri Aurobindo. *Essays on Gita* (Puducherry: Sri Aurobindo Ashram Publication Department, 1977), pp. 171–2.

CHAPTER 1 JANAMEJAYA'S REVENGE ON THE NĀGAS AND THE NARRATION OF THE MAHĀBHĀRATA

1 The land of the Bhāratas, the descendants of King Bharata. The land to the south of the Himālayas and north of the Ocean.
2 Shalya Parva 61.53
3 परिक्षीणे कुले यस्माज्जातोऽयमभिमन्युजः। परिक्षिदिति नामास्य भवत्वित्यब्रवीत्तदा।। (Ādi Parva 62.52)
4 The Nāgas or sarpas (i.e. snakes) mentioned in the Mahābhārata might have been people of a tribe with close association to snakes. The Mahābhārata has many instances of encounters and marriage associations with the Nāgas. Uloopi, one of Arjuna's wives, was a Nāga princess. The maternal grandfather of Kunti's father, Shurasena, was a Nāga named Āryaka implying Kunti's paternal grandmother was a Nāga too.
5 History
6 The lineage of Bharata.
7 Naimishāranya was a forest region to the south of Hastināpur. Today, this area lies 90 km north of Lucknow in the state of Uttar Pradesh. The forest doesn't exist anymore but there are temples here which strive to keep the memories of the ancient seers alive. This forest is also mentioned in the Rāmāyana and other Purānas.
8 Anushāsana Parva 48.10
9 Charioteer

CHAPTER 2 THE BHARATA VAMSHA FAMILY TREE

1 Within the Mahābhārata, there are discrepancies in listing of the exact generation-wise genealogy. But the prominent kings are the same, as is the order. The most important ones are listed here.
2 Article 1(1) of the Indian Constitution says, 'India, that is Bharat, shall be a Union of States.' Bharat (pronounced Bhārata) is the official name of this land till date and it comes from King Bharata.
3 Ādi Parva 195.32
4 Ādi Parva 1.94 and 170.12
5 Descendants of Kuru were the Kauravas. Thus, Bhishma, Dhritarāshtra, Pāndu and the Pāndavas are also Kauravas, not just Duryodhana and his brothers. The Pāndavas have been so called to differentiate them from their cousins.
6 The act of giving up the life of a householder and accepting the life of an ascetic devoid of luxury in search of true wisdom.
7 Per the directions given in Ādi Parva 214, the province of Manipur lies beyond Kalinga desh and the Mahendragiri mountains, by the coast. This could likely be in present-day Odisha or Andhra Pradesh.
8 *Shrimad Bhāgvata Purāna* 10.68

CHAPTER 3 THE GEOGRAPHICAL COVERAGE OF THE MAHĀBHĀRATA WAR

1 The Mahābhārata has umpteen instances of interactions among kingdoms from the east, west, north and south of the present-day Indian subcontinent. The territorial integrity of Bhāratavarsha was known then as it is now.
2 Udyoga Parva 19. The directions are with respect to Indraprastha, aligned with the directions of kingdoms the four Pāndava brothers went to before the Rājsuya Yajna. The list is not exhaustive. Other kingdoms, including Kāshi, Dashārna, Ambashtha, as well as various Nishāda and Kirāta kings, had sent their warriors as well.
3 Some tend to consider Prāgjyotisha to be in the east, around the present-day Assam region. However, the Prāgjyotisha of Bhagdatta as mentioned in the Mahābhārata is towards the north, what is the present-day Uttarakhand–Himachal

region. Before Yudhishthira's Rājasurya Yajna, Arjuna had gone to win over the kingdoms in the north of Indraprastha; Prāgjyotisha was one of those kingdoms.

4 Udyoga Parva 51.4–5
5 Udyoga Parva 55.31–33
6 Sabhā Parva 25–28
7 Arjun reaches Kimpurusha after crossing the Shweta Parvat, literally the white mountain, indicating the Himālayan range. Having won over Kimpurusha and Hātak, he reached Lake Mānsarovar, which is in present-day Tibet (Sabhā Parva 28.1–3).
8 Sabhā Parva 29–30
9 Sabhā Parva 32
10 Sabhā Parva 31

CHAPTER 4 SANJAY'S NARRATION OF THE KURUKSHETRA WAR

1 Bhishma Parva 3
2 Bhishma Parva 13
3 Shalya Parva 1.14
4 Karna Parva 2.1
5 Bhagavad Gitā 1.1: 'धर्मक्षेत्रेकुरुक्षेत्रेसमवेतायुयुत्सवः।मामकाः पाण्डवाश्चैवकिमकुर्वतसञ्जय।।' किमकुर्वत = किम् + अकुर्वत; अकुर्वत is the past tense of the verb 'to do'.
6 Shalya Pava 25
7 Shalya Parva 29
8 Shalya Parva 64; Saupatika Parva 9
9 An offering made to a guru or someone venerable.

CHAPTER 5 SHAKUNTALĀ'S GRIT

1 Ādi Parva 68
2 Hermitage
3 Paying a visit to seek the blessings of anyone or anything venerable.
4 One of the four Vedas, the holiest scriptures of Hindu dharma. The other three are *Rig Veda*, *Yajur Veda* and *Atharva Veda*.
5 Ādi Parva 71.16–17
6 Austerities; a ritual of self-discipline performed for the fulfilment of intended desires.

7 A Sanskrit word for bird.
8 Ādi Parva 72
9 Warrior class
10 Roughly translated as soul, conscience and/or self.
11 Ādi Parva 73.1–21
12 Ādi Parva 74.1–16
13 Ādi Parva 74.21–32
14 Ādi Parva 74.33–72
15 Ādi Parva 74.73–81
16 One amongst the most sacred mountains in Hindu and Buddhist legends.
17 Ādi Parva 82.108
18 Ādi Parva 82.109–114; Bharata is a Sanskrit word that comes from Bhartavya (भर्तव्य), which means the one who is nourished.

CHAPTER 6 THE FOUNDATIONAL YEARS

1 Rāja Shuka is mentioned in the Dakshinātya reading of the Mahābhārata as noted in the Gita Press edition in Ādi Parva 124. There are various manuscripts of the Mahābhārata of which some are more regarded than the others. But broadly, there are two recensions of the epic—the northern recension and the southern recension. The Gita Press Mahābhārata refers the northern recension, on which a commentary has been written by a Sanskrit scholar of 17th century, Neelkantha Chaturdhara. The southern recension is called Dakshinātya. While the overall storyline is aligned in both, there are some variations in the details. Rather, the southern recension has additional details and verses not present in its northern counterpart. The Gita Press Mahābhārata has picked relevant additional verses from Dakshinātya recension and added them to the text. These additional verses have been clearly marked for the knowledge of the readers.
2 Mace
3 Arjuna's age is mentioned in the Dakshinātya Mahābhārata as noted in the Gita Press version in Ādi Parva 125.
4 Ādi Parva 129.39
5 Ādi Parva 127.63–65

6 Ādi Parva 131.11; Vana Parva 302.9, 309.17
7 Ādi Parva 131.12
8 Ādi Parva 131.16–20
9 Ādi Parva 131.21–27
10 Ādi Parva 131.69–79 to 132.1–9
11 Ādi Parva 132.11–22
12 Ādi Parva 131.61–65
13 Karna had returned and was befriended by Duryodhana at the time of the demonstration of the skills event. Hence, as a former student and as a friend of Duryodhana, Karna joins the campaign.
14 Ādi Parva 137. In BORI CE (Ādi Parva 128), the retreat/failure of the Kauravas is not explicitly mentioned, whereas both the Gita Press and KMG editions say clearly that the Kauravas had to retreat. However, the victory was due to the Pāndavas—that is confirmed in BORI CE as well, which retains the verse saying 'Ahichhatra (Part of Pānchāl) was given to Drona by Pārtha' (128.18).
15 A sārthi is a charioteer. The role of a charioteer is of prime importance in the war. He is responsible for the safety of the warrior and also for maintaining the warrior's morale. He has to know when to stay and when to turn away. He has to know when to rebuke the warrior and when to comfort. A sārthi is practically a mentor in times of war. In philosophical imagery of the body being a chariot, our intellectual faculty is referred to as the sārthi (*Kathopanishada* 1.3.3).
16 The capital of the ancient janapada of Anga desh. In the present day, the area falls in Bihar near Bhagalpur.
17 Vana Parva 308–309
18 Vasu means gold; hence Vasushena means the one with a golden body.
19 Ādi Parva 131.12
20 Shānti Parva 2.10–11
21 Bhrigu (भृगु) is one of the 'saptarishis', the seven sages born as 'mānas putras' of Brahmā deva. Parashurāma was born in the lineage of Bhrigu.
22 Shānti Parva 2.10–11; Udyoga Parva 62.2
23 Shānti Parva 3.26–33

CHAPTER 7 THE NISHĀDA PRINCE

1 Many interpreters have inferred Dronāchārya's refusal to teach Ekalavya as his caste bias. This cannot be assumed as a fact because Dronāchārya did teach Karna and Yuyutsu who were also of mixed castes like Ekalavya. The Nishādas were known to be great warriors. The text only says, 'तेषामेवान्ववेक्षया'. Therefore, assessing him with consideration to the Kauravas, thinking he is a Nishāda's son, Drona refused. What the consideration was the text doesn't say. It could be his caste, it could be the difference in the background of the pupils or it could be as it said in KMG's translation—Drona's view is that a Nishāda might excel his high-born pupils. Nishādas were known to be great warriors.

2 The gurudakshinā is an honorarium given to a teacher for his guidance and training. Traditionally, a student would offer whatever a teacher asks for. The honorarium could be material or in the form of sevā.

3 Ādi Parva 131.59. The Dakshinātya rendering has an additional verse before this, which says, 'Dronacharya was pleased with Ekalavya's truthfulness and commitment. Hence he showed Ekalavya how to use his fingers to shoot arrows.'

4 Drona Parva 181.20–21

5 Anushāsan Parva 48.12

6 *Manusmriti* 10.8

7 Ādi Parva 1.63–58–61. The text says a fish engulfed the sperm of the king and gave birth to a boy and a girl. The fish was a fallen celestial nymph named Ādri. The author sees this only as an imagery, just like that of the tribe of Nāgas. The fact that she was given away to the fisherfolk community seems to imply the mother was from the fishing community.

CHAPTER 8 THE MARRIAGE THAT TIED

1 The Indian tradition where a woman chose her own husband from the assembled gathering. In some cases, a challenge would be thrown to prospective grooms. The winner would take the lady as his wife.

2 The BORI CE and the note in the Gita Press edition (Book 1, p. 606) suggest Karna tried and failed the

challenge. KMG's translation suggests Karna managed to string the bow but before he could shoot the target, Draupadi announced she wouldn't marry Karna. And he had to retreat. Per the prolegomena to Adi Parva of BORI CE, only 6 manuscripts (including the Nilkanth version, that is, the Gita press version) have this episode of Draupadi rejecting Karna. For compilation of entire CE, a total of 1,259 manuscripts were studied. It appears to be a later interpolation.

3 Ādi Parva 187.4

4 Alms received by Brāhmins and students. Young students, when studying with their teachers, would get food by going around the village seeking for it. They would bring the alms/food back to the guru and everyone would share and eat.

5 Ādi Parva 190.12–16

6 Vana Parva 233. The Gita Press edition has a more elaborate discussion, a summary of which is given here. KMG mentions the discussion in brief.

7 Certain esoteric practices to influence the mind of the 'target' to bring them in one's control.

8 Nitya karmas are daily rituals obligatory for Hindus. These include practices such as Sandhyā Vandana and Agnihotra.

9 Sabhā Parva 52.48

10 Sabhā Parva 165.36

11 Sabhā Parva 59

12 Sabhā Parva 66.4

13 Hari is the name used for God, typically for Vishnu and Krishna.

14 Sabhā Parva 68.44–48. As per the Gita Press and KMG, Draupadi began praying to Krishna to protect her, as he was her only recourse. Krishna became a subtle part of her garment and kept endowing her with additional cloth until, finally, Duhshāsana could pull no longer. In the BORI CE (Sabhā Parva 61.41–42), the references to Hari/Krishna are removed. It says: 'As the garment got pulled, another appeared in its place; it was an extraordinary sight'. The author's take is that the importance here is on the shraddhā (roughly means deep faith and surrender, for the lack of an exact word in English) of Draupadi. When nothing else

works, shraddhā on the divine powers is the only strength of the innocent. The strength of shraddhā and anugrah (divine grace) can make mountains move.

15 Sabhā Parva 67.19–21
16 Sabhā Parva 67.47–48
17 Sabhā Parva 67.50–51
18 Sabhā Parva 68.4–8
19 Sabhā Parva 68.11–24
20 Sabhā Parva 68.89
21 Sabhā Parva 69.1–13
22 Sabhā Parva 69.14–19
23 Sabhā Parva 70.3–4
24 Vana Parva 28
25 Vana Parva 32.2
26 Vana Parva 32
27 Family priest
28 Vana Parva 272
29 Virāta Parva 9
30 Virāta Parva 14,15,16, 22
31 Udyoga Parva 74, 82
32 Udyoga Parva 82
33 Sauptika Parva 16
34 Shānti Parva 4
35 Mausala Parva 6

CHAPTER 9 SĀVITRI

1 Vana Parva 293.1–3
2 Vana Parva 293–297

CHAPTER 10 A FRIENDSHIP OF DOOM

1 Ādi Parva 1.110
2 Pārtha means son of Prithā. Kunti's birth name was Prithā. Hence, all the sons of Kunti could be Pārtha. However, Arjuna was most often addressed as Pārtha.
3 Ādi Parva 136.24
4 Ādi Parva 203.13–25
5 Sabhā Parva 67.2
6 Sabhā Parva 68.27
7 Sabhā Parva 68.35–38

8 Sabhā Parva 71.1–5
9 Sabhā Parva 71.10–12
10 Sabhā Parva 71.13–14
11 Vana Parva 7
12 Vana Parva 247.13–14
13 Vana Parva 250
14 Vana Parva 251
15 Vana Parva 252
16 Vana Parva 302
17 Vana Parva 310
18 Vana Parva 309.13: वसुवर्मधरं दृष्ट्वा तं बालं हेमकुण्डलम्। नामास्य वसुषेणेति ततश्चक्रुर्द्विजातयः ।।
19 Vana Parva 310.38: तथोत्कृत्य प्रददौ कुण्डले ते, कर्णात्तस्मात्कर्मणा तेन कर्णः ।।
20 Virāta Parva 29. The verses are from the Dakshinātya reading of the Mahābhārata.
21 Trigarta, ruled by Susharmā, was a kingdom to the north-west of Indraprastha.
22 Virāta Parva 45.15
23 Virāta Parva 48
24 Virāta Parva 52.4
25 Matsya was also called Virāta Nagar, hence the battle is referred to as the battle of Virāta.
26 Udyoga Parva 74
27 Udyoga Parva 21
28 Udyoga Parva 62
29 Udyoga Parva 127
30 Udyoga Parva 128
31 Udyoga Parva 128
32 Krishna is considered as the eight avatar of Vishnu, the Lord who sustains the universe. Hindus, in general, and Vaishnavas, in particular, believe that whenever forces threatening sustainability and justice on earth get out of control, Vishnu takes birth to restore order and protect the just and innocent.
33 Udyoga Parva 131
34 Udyoga Parva 140. In some translations, Krishna is said to offer Draupadi as a wife to Karna to woo him because of this verse: 'षष्ठे चत्वांतथाकालेद्रौपदुपगमिष्यति ||१५||'. However, the literal

translation is 'in the sixth part (shashthe kale), Draupadi will also come.' The line before this talks of 'the royal men and women doing Karna's abhishek', thus showing him reverence. Hence, to say 'Draupadi will approach as a wife' or 'Draupadi will come to do intercourse with you', as some translations say, is only an assumption, and not something the text states directly. The text has been explicit about 'intercourse' where that has occurred, and has been typically called 'samāgam'. It is possible that Krishna wanted to keep the message ambiguous about Draupadi, hence he only stated that she will come but didn't specify why. The other point is the meaning of 'षष्ठे काले'. The phrase occurs twice in other places within the Mahābhārata as well. In both the places, the implication is related to the time when people ate. For example, Āshwamedhika Parva 90.26 states, 'षष्ठे काले सदा विप्रो भुङ्क्ते तैः सह संवृतः.' This means, 'In the sixth part, the Brāhmin ate with his family.' Then again, Āshwamedhika Parva 57.5 says, 'षष्ठे काले ममाहारो विहितो द्विजसत्तम'. Which translates to: 'The king says, "O Brāhmin, sixth is the time for my food.' Per the Gita Press Hindi translation, as well as the lexicons of Sanskrit scholars Monier Monier-Williams and Vaman Apte, 'षष्ठे काले' has two meanings: i) The sixth part of the day, which is typically mealtime and ii) One meal in three days considering two mealtimes in a day. Therefore, the verse could even mean, 'Draupadi would come to serve you food, either in the sixth part of the day or once in three days.

35 Udyoga Parva 141
36 Udyoga Parva 143
37 Udyoga Parva 145
38 Udyoga Parva 146
39 Shānti Parva 5
40 Shānti Parva 4
41 Sabhā Parva 30.18–30.20
42 This is the hierarchy of warriors who fight from a chariot (rath): Ardha Rathi, Rathi, Atirathi, Maharathi, Ati Maharathi and Maha Maharathi. Maha Maharathi is the most superior.
43 Udyoga Parva 168.3–9
44 Udyoga Parva 168.14–29
45 Udyoga Parva 193
46 Bhishma Parva 122

47 Drona Parva 150
48 Drona Parva 152
49 Drona Parva 158.16–23
50 Drona Parva 158.27–30
51 Drona Parva 158.51–70
52 Drona Parva 159.1–15
53 Drona Parva 183.7
54 Drona Parva 139, 145, 159
55 Drona Parva 148.10, 147.70–147.71
56 Drona Parva 139.94–96
57 Drona Parva 148.11–21
58 Karna Parva 31.42
59 Karna Parva 32
60 Karna Parva 43–45
61 Karna Parva 63
62 Karna Parva 83
63 Karna Parva 89–90
64 The weapon of Shiva.
65 Karna Parva 91
66 Shalya Parva 31–32
67 Shalya Parva 58
68 Shalya Parva 60
69 Krishna's maternal uncle was Kamsa, the king of Mathura. Kamsa had imprisoned his own father as well as sister, Devaki, and brother-in-law, Vasudeva, (Krishna's parents) because of a prediction made that their eighth born would be the nemesis of Kamsa. Vasudeva managed to shift Krishna out of the prison to Gokul, the home of Nanda and Yashoda, where Krishna grew up with lots of love and care. Nanda was a cowherd who supplied milk to the palace of Kamsa. Eventually, the truth of how Vasudeva hid his son was known and Kamsa was killed by an eleven-year-old Krishna. But many people who were jealous of Krishna continued to believed he was a cowherd and not Vasudeva's son, Shishupāla and Duryodhana being among them. Hence, Duryodhana addresses Krishna as the son of Kamsa's slave, out of spite and anger.
70 Shalya Parva 27–39
71 Shalya Parva 39–49

72 Shalya Parva 50–53
73 Tamas is one of the three gunas (qualities) of anything material. These three gunas are sattva, rajas and tamas. Sattva indicates wisdom, discrimination, goodness and virtue. Rajas implies activity driven by desire, greed and anger. Tamas indicates lack of wisdom, ignorance and darkness.

CHAPTER 11 KURUKSHETRA ENCOUNTERS: BHEEMA AND ARJUNA VERSUS DURYODHANA AND KARNA

1 With Bheema: Bhishma Parva 73, 79, 94; Drona Parva 166; Karna Parva 61, 77; Shalya Parva 16, 58. Shalya Parva 58 is the final mace battle of Bheema and Duryodhana. With Arjuna: Drona Parva 103
2 With Bheema: Drona Parva 129, 131, 132, 133, 134, 136, 137, 139; Karna Parva 50. With Arjuna: Drona Parva 139, 149, 159; Karna Parva 91.
3 Drona Parva 147
4 Drona Parva 32; Karna Parva 30
5 Drona Parva 40

CHAPTER 12 A WARRIOR MOTHER

1 Vana Parva 303.19–21
2 Vana Parva 309.15. The reference to Kunti confirming Karna's whereabouts is present in the Gita Press edition and KMG. It has been dropped in BORI CE.
3 Udyoga Parva 90.62–64
4 Ādi Parva 111
5 Ādi Parva 117.18
6 Ashwini Kumars are considered to be physicians of devas.
7 Ādi Parva 162
8 Ādi Parva 62
9 Sabhā Parva 179.8
10 Udyoga Parva 132.5–6
11 Rāja Dharma refers to the duties and responsibilities of a just and righteous king.
12 Udyoga Parva 132.21–22
13 Udyoga Parva 132.31–34
14 Udyoga Parva 133.1–8

15 Udyoga Parva 133.11–15
16 Udyoga Parva 133.15–23, 30, 34
17 Udyoga Parva 133.39
18 Udyoga Parva 134.2–3
19 Udyoga Parva 134.19, 20, 29, 30, 33
20 Udyoga Parva 133.40, 43, 45
21 Udyoga Parva 134.3–7
22 Udyoga Parva 135.1–2,5–6
23 Udyoga Parva 135.19–21
24 Udyoga Parva 137.10
25 Udyoga Parva 137.14–16
26 Udyoga Parva 137.18–20
27 Stree Parva 27.7–29
28 Shānti Parva 7.4–8
29 Āshramavāsika Parva 16.10–16
30 Āshramavāsika Parva 16.26–28
31 As Dhritarāshtra's younger brother's wife, Kunti is the younger sister-in-law. But in Hindu families, the elder brother has a father-like stature. In that sense, it can be said that Kunti served her elder brother-in-law and his wife as a daughter-in-law.
32 Āshramavāsika Parva 17
33 Āshramavāsika Parva 37.31–32

CHAPTER 13 A FRIENDSHIP THAT GROOMED

1 Udyoga Parva 1.13–15
2 Udyoga Parva 25
3 Udyoga Parva 59
4 Ādi Parva 224
5 Vana Parva 15
6 Ban on alcohol and extradition of performers are two interesting measures. Both can delude and confuse. In *Arthashāstra*, Chanakya has extensively written about using actors as spies and honey traps. At the same time, he was careful about how much access the actors got with the common people of the kingdom. Villages were especially a no go for the actors, to avoid any inconvenience and distractions for the simple hard-working village folks (*Arthashastra*, Book 1, Chapter 11; Book 2, Chapter 1).

7 Udyoga Parva 7.35–37
8 Udyoga Parva 154.24–25
9 Udyoga Parva 194
10 Bhagavad Gitā, Adhyay 1
11 Duty and responsibility as a warrior and a prince
12 This discourse is what we know as the Bhagavad Gitā.
13 Bhagavad Gitā 18.63
14 Udyoga Parva 172.19-21
15 Udyoga Parva 192.11–12
16 Bhishma Parva 50
17 Bhishma Parva 106
18 Bhishma Parva 107.77-84
19 Bhishma Parva 108.56–59
20 Bhishma Parva 119.60
21 Drona Parva 12.20–24
22 The name of the Trigarta warriors, or probably their allies.
23 A kind of a celestial weapon possessed by King Prāgjyotisha.
24 The Chakra Vyuha is an army formation representing a labyrinth wheel. Multiple layers of soldiers have to be countered to enter it.
25 Son of Shiva and Parvati, venerated as the commander of the army of devas.
26 Drona Parva 73.46–47
27 Drona Parva 75
28 Drona Parva 79.20–25
29 Drona Parva 91.1–34
30 Drona Parva 94
31 Drona Parva 146.68. The Gita Press edition mentions (as does KMG) that Krishna had a role to play in making the sun disappear and making it appear again to enable Arjuna to kill Jayadratha. The BORI CE does not speak about Krishna's intervention. Both the Gita Press and KMG versions also state that before Krishna intervened, Jayadratha was in Arjuna's line of sight. In fact, all the versions have the incident where, when Arjuna was fighting the 'guarding Kaurava warriors', Krishna tells him, 'Kill him now, the sun is about to set', indicating the sun had not set before that. The darkness might just have been a cloud or dust cover. Some posit that the darkness could have been

caused due to a solar eclipse. That also seems unlikely. See Footnote 35 of this chapter. Nevertheless, intervention or no intervention, the undeniable fact is that Jayadratha was killed by Arjuna before sunset in front of other Kaurava warriors who were rendered helpless before Arjuna's skills. Later in the text (Shalya Parva 61), when Duryodhana, lying on the field breathing his last, accuses Krishna and Pāndavas of using unfair means in the war, he talks of the killings of Bhishma, Drona, Karna and himself, but doesn't include Jayadratha in that list.

32 Drona Parva 146.105–107

33 Drona Parva 146.121–130

34 Drona Parva 173.46

35 The Mahābhārata text has many astronomical observations noted from the time of the war and before. Researchers have used this to date the events of the epic and determine when the war happened. Some claim that the war began on a full-moon (purnima) night. That would mean the fourteenth night was almost a new-moon (amavaysa) night. The moon is observed to rise after midnight closer to amavasya. In that sense, it does fit the verse that 'moon rose just a few hours before dawn'. However, it is still dark on the earth because only a sliver of the moon is visible. A renowned researcher of recent years, Shri Nilesh Nilkanth Oak, in his phenomenal work, *When Did the Mahābhārata War Happen? The Mystery of Arundhati* (Hubli: Subbu Publications, 2011), posits that the war began on amavasya and not purnima. There are references to Rahu eating Surya around the time of the beginning of the war, implying a solar eclipse, which is possible only during the new moon. He mentions many other observations of the Mahābhārata that corroborate his proposal. From that, it follows that the fourteenth night was closer to a full-moon night. That is why, even after sunset, there was enough visibility for the war to continue after midnight. Oak attributes the darkness covering the battlefield to the dust and clouds rather than the absence of the moon. Such descriptions of dust arising out of actions on the battlefield and hindering visibility is mentioned in other parts of the epic as well. He explains

the appearance of the moon a few hours before sunrise as the 'reappearance' after the dust had settled. The description in the text says, 'the moon came and brightened surrounding as if day' ('प्रतिप्रकाशिते लोके दिवाभुते निशाकरे', Drona Parva 184.53; BORI 159.47), which is only possible closer to a full-moon night. In fact, in Mahābhārata as well, when Krishna discloses to Karna the truth of his birth but Karna chooses to remain with Duryodhana, Krishna tells him 'The seventh day from today is Amavasya, the deity of the day is Indra. The war may start on that day' (Udyoga Parva 142.18).

36 Drona Parva 184
37 Drona Parva 60
38 Karna Parva 67
39 Karna Parva 68
40 Karna Parva 69.11–14
41 Karna Parva 69.16–27
42 The story is of Rishi Kaushika and the nuance of dharma (Karna Parva 69.46–53).
43 Karna Parva 69.31
44 Karna Parva 69.57. The root of dharḿa is धृ or dhri, which means to uphold.
45 Karna Parva 69.82–87
46 Karna Parva 70.1–21
47 Karna Parva 70.25–28
48 Karna Parva 70.30–40
49 Bhagavad Gitā 18.78

CHAPTER 14 THE TEN NAMES OF ARJUNA

1 Virāta Parva 44

CHAPTER 15 DHARMA MEETS STRENGTH

1 Dharma in a limited sense here means righteousness and truth. In a broader sense, it means understanding of what is appropriate and what is not in any given situation, especially with respect to administration and governance of the kingdom and society. The eldest son of Pāndu would be the future king of Hastināpur per norms of day.
2 Ādi Parva 194

3 The word used is 'snatak' Brāhmins—those who have finished their education.
4 A conquest mission, which is campaign to conquer other kingdoms to establish dominance.
5 Imperial ruler of the subcontinent.
6 Udyoga Parva 1–5, 73–81, 151
7 Sabhā Parva 58.1–16
8 Sabhā Parva 59.20–21
9 Vana Parva 37.36–37
10 Vana Parva 35
11 Vana Parva 52.26–31
12 Vana Parva 34
13 Vana Parva 36.5–20
14 Vana Parva 37.4–15
15 Vana Parva 258
16 Vana Parva 11
17 Most likely the Himālayan region around present-day Badrinath.
18 Vana Parva 146, 153, 154
19 Vana Parva 160
20 Vana Parva 157
21 Varna, jāti are both translated as caste. But that is not appropriate. Varna is loosely a profession based classification. Krishna explains in the Bhagavad Gitā, 'चातुर्वर्ण्यं मया सृष्टं गुणकर्मविभागशः' ('I created the four varnas based on gunas and karmas.') In essence, the varnas are really about the inherent gunas—the inherent tendencies of a person. These tendencies are mapped to professions. Jāti on the other hand is based on birth. It means the community into which one is born. Here, Yudhishthira is clearly stating that birth in a community by itself doesn't define a person, rather his character and actions do.
22 Vana Parva 180
23 Dharma is used here in the sense of 'fairness'. The actual shloka is 'धर्म एव हतो हन्ति धर्मो रक्षति रक्षितः। तस्माद्धर्मं न त्यजामि मा नो धर्मो हतोऽवधीत् ।।'
24 Vana Parva 312, 313, 314
25 Devas are to be understood as deities as well as powers of nature. The Hindu dharma entails a person to nourish the

ecology so that it nourishes us. Krishna explains the same in the Bhagavad Gitā when he says, 'देवान्भावयतानेन ते देवा भावयन्तु वः।परस्परं भावयन्तः श्रेयः परममवाप्स्यथ'।।3.11।। 'Worship the powers of Nature thereby, and let them nourish you in return; thus supporting each other, you shall attain your highest welfare.' This appears in the translation of the the Bhagavad Gitā by Shri Purohit Swami (USA: Pacific Publishing Studio, 2010).

26 Dakshyam (दाक्ष्यम्) is the word used. It could mean dexterity, ability, cleverness as well as industry/enterprise. The most apt is enterprise because dharma by itself cannot sustain without enterprise. As Rishi Chanakya has also said, 'धर्मस्य मूलं अर्थः'.

27 The Sanskrit word used is 'sadgati' (सद्गति).

28 The verse says 'पञ्चमेऽहनि षष्ठे वा शाकं पचति स्वे गृहे.' This can be 'on fifth day or sixth', or 'on the fifth part of the day or sixth'. Once in five or six days does not seem right because getting to eat only once a week would happen to a very poor person. During the Yaksha Prashna event itself, Yudhishthira says, 'A man in extreme poverty is as good as dead (Vana Parva 313.84). 'षष्ठे काले' is when people ate is evident in other places within the Mahābhārata as well. See Footnote 34 of chapter 10.

29 Purusha here is used in the sense of true existence.

30 Virāta Parva 1.9–53

31 Virāta Parva 6.31–34. The Gita Press edition explains 'the custom' as an indirect reference of the Pāndavas to protecting the weapons—which was definitely done by their forefathers—rather than to the act of tying the corpse.

32 Virāta Parva 13

33 Virāta Parva 16.43–44

34 Virāta Parva 22

35 Virāta Parva 68.36–55

36 Bhishma Parva 43

37 Drona Parva 190.1–17

38 Or was it his own conscience?

39 Drona Parva 191, The phrase 'naro va kunjaro va' is given in the Gita Press edition of the Mahābhārata as an additional quote from the Dakshinātya reading.

40 Drona Parva 192.40–42
41 Sabhā Parva 67.19–21; also covered in the chapter, 'The Marriage That Tied', in the sub-section, 'The Question of Legality'.

CHAPTER 17 THE BLINDFOLDS

1 Ādi Parva 63.112
2 Ādi Parva 109
3 Ādi Parva 114
4 Ādi Parva 138
5 Ādi Parva 139
6 In this context, the word means foreigners or those who lived beyond Bhāratavarsha.
7 Ādi Parva 200.1–3
8 Ādi Parva 202
9 Sabhā Parva 56
10 Sabhā Parva 57
11 Sabhā Parva 74
12 Sabhā Parva 75
13 Sabhā Parva 62.13–16
14 Udyoga Parva 129
15 Stree Parva 1
16 Stree Parva 12
17 Stree Parva 113
18 Stree Parva 114
19 Stree Parva 15
20 Stree Parva 25
21 Stree Parva 26

CHAPTER 18 THE IDEAL OF FETTERS AND FREEDOM

1 Ādi Parva 100.90–102
2 Udyoga Parva 175
3 Udyoga Parva 177
4 Udyoga Parva 178.42
5 Ādi Parva 103.10–11
6 Sabhā Parva 69.15–19
7 Udyoga Parva 172.19–21
8 Shānti Parva 55.15–20
9 Shānti Parva 56.42–46

10 The text mentioned Brāhmins but the concept is different from today's understanding of Brāhmins being restricted to Brāhmins only by birth. Brāhmins were also named by profession and virtues. Like every 'jāti' was tied to a profession, so were the Brāhmins. Trade, war, etc. were restricted from them. Those who did take up the profession of others—for example Dronāchārya, who was a Brāhmin by birth but lived and earned like a Kshatriya not just teaching warfare but also participating in wars—were to be treated like Kshatriyas. The code to not kill, not punish them did not apply to such Brāhmins, though born in the Brāhmin jāti. The idea of the code to not punish/kill was to allow free and honest intellectual development. But Bhishma says, if one is a Brāhmin just by birth but does not display the virtues, then the code doesn't apply to him.
11 Shānti Parva 56.26–31
12 Shānti Parva 57.5
13 Shānti Parva 57.13–14
14 Shānti Parva 80.25
15 Shānti Parva 80.32–41
16 Shānti Parva 86.20
17 Shānti Parva 133.16–17
18 Sabhā Parva 64.16–17: लभ्यः खलु प्रातिपीय नरोऽनुप्रियवागिह |
अप्रियस्य तु पथ्यस्य वक्ता श्रोता च दुर्लभः ||१६||
यस्तु धर्मे पराश्वस्य हित्वा भर्तुः प्रियाप्रिये |
अप्रियाण्याह पथ्यानि तेन राजा सहायवान् ||१७||
19 Vana Parva 4.6–17
20 Vana Parva 4.18–21
21 Udyoga Parva 33.13–14
22 Udyoga Parva 35.77
23 Udyoga Parva 33.16–29
24 Udyoga Parva 33.30.39
25 Udyoga Parva 33.59–60
26 Udyoga Parva 33.69, 33.72
27 Udyoga Parva 33.78–83
28 Udyoga Parva 33.84–85, 89–90
29 Udyoga Parva 33.91–92,105
30 Stree Parva 2
31 Shānti Parva 41.10

32 Āshramavāsika Parva 26
33 Udyoga Parva 34.4–5
34 Ādi Parva 105.29, 106, 107; Vyāsa tells the story of the reincarnation of the lord of dharma as Vidura due to the curse of Rishi Māndavya. The rishi cursed Dharma to be born in the Shudra jāti as a repentance for a severe punishment that he had given to the rishi for a trivial mistake committed when the rishi was still a child.

CHAPTER 19 THE PRODIGIOUS SONS

1 Ādi Parva 211.29; the Gita Press as well as the BORI CE editions mention only this one rule. In the Dakshinātya, another rule of Draupadi spending one year with each brother is also mentioned.
2 Prayer ritual
3 Ādi Parva 213.20
4 Ādi Parva 213.21–23
5 Ādi Parva 214.35
6 Bhishma Parva 90.11–17
7 Bhishma Parva 83.11–23
8 Bhishma Parva 90.18–77
9 Bhishma Parva 47
10 Bhishma Parva 61.2–3
11 Bhishma Parva 100.18
12 Bhishma Parva 100.22–25
13 Arjuna's son
14 Draupadi's sons
15 Bhishma Parva 100.32–54
16 Bhishma Parva 101.8–28
17 Ādi Parva 220.67, Abhimanyu: Abhi (अभि) means unafraid and Manyu (मन्यु), passionate.
18 Drona Parva 34.8–10
19 Drona Parva 48.17
20 Drona Parva 48.24
21 Drona Parva 48.23
22 Drona Parva 48.27–31
23 Son of Duhshāsana
24 Typically translated as demons, these could be forest-dwelling, human-flesh-eating forest tribes.

25 Ādi Parva 154.38. Ghata means pot and Utkacha means bald head.
26 The Pāndavas's next generation; the Pāndavas' sons
27 Ādi Parva 31.71–73
28 The mention of the Rāma Setu is in the Dakshinātya reading of the Mahābhārata. The Gita Press edition doesn't specifically make note of it but it does say Ghatotkacha went to Lanka.
29 Ādi Parva 31.76
30 Bhishma Parva 58.15
31 Bhishma Parva 64
32 Drona Parva 109
33 Another name of Bheema. It means the one with a wolf (vrika) belly (udara), or a voracious eater.
34 Drona Parva 178
35 Drona Parva 156.80–90
36 Another name for Indrāstra.
37 Drona Parva 179
38 Drona Parva 183.27–39
39 Drona Parva 183.42–48
40 A mountain range in Central India.
41 Ādi Parva 220.81, परप्रहरणज्ञाने प्रतिविन्ध्यो भवत्वयम्
42 Ādi Parva 220.82: सुते सोमसहस्रे तु सोमार्कसमतेजसम्. The Soma Yajna is a type of a fire ritual.
43 Ādi Parva 220.83: श्रुतं कर्म महत्कृत्वा निवृत्तेन किरीटिना. Here, Arjuna's son is called Shrutakarma but in Ādi Parva 95.75, Arjuna's son is called Shrutakirti. The meaning of both names, however, remains the same. Later, in the epic, Shrutakirti is mentioned. Shrutakarma is given as the name of Sahadeva's son.
44 The Mahābhārata does not give any order of the birth of Draupadi's sons but it can be safely assumed Shrutakirti was the youngest as he was born after Arjuna returned from his twelve-year exile. Also, when King Virāta offered Uttarā to him as a wife, Arjuna accepted her for Abhimanyu instead of Shrutakirti as Abhimanyu was the elder of the two.
45 Ādi Parva 220.84: शतानीकस्य राजर्षेः कौरव्यः कुरुनन्दनः
46 Ādi Parva 220.85: ततस्त्वजीजनत्कृष्णा नक्षत्रे वह्निदैवते. Here, it says Shrutasena but in Ādi Parva 95.75, Sahadeva's son is

called Shrutakarma, which means actions ordained by Vedas such as yajnas in which Agni is paramount. To avoid confusion, all mentions of Shrutakirti are taken as Arjuna's son and of Shrutakarma are taken as Sahadeva's son.

47 Udyoga Parva 170.1

48 Bhishma Parva 78.26–28

49 Prativindhya: Bhishma Parva 45, 79, 100; Drona Parva 25, 168; Karna Parva 14

50 Sutasoma: Bhishma Parva 45, 79; Drona Parva 25; Karna Parva 25

51 Shrutakarma: Bhishma Parva 45, 79; Drona Parva 25, 108; Karna Parva 14, 85

52 Shatānika: Bhishma Parva 79; Drona Parva 25, 88, 168; Karna Parva 25, 85

53 Shrutakirti: Bhishma Parva 79; Drona Parva 25

54 Shalya Parva 65.35–46

55 Saupatika Parva 1

56 Saupatika Parva 2–5

57 Sauptika Parva 6–9

58 Sauptika Parva 9

59 Sauptika Parva 16.9–12

60 Bhishma Parva 47–48

61 Bhishma Parva 82.22

CHAPTER 20 THE POST-WAR HASTINĀPUR DAYS

1 Practising strict austerities to repent for a sin.

2 Shānti Parva 7

3 Shānti Parva 10

4 Shānti Parva 12

5 Shanti Parva

6 Shānti Parva 33.42–45: कुमारो नास्ति येषां च कन्यास्तत्राभिषेचय। (45)

7 Shānti Parva 24.5–7

8 Āshwamedhikā Parva 3

9 Āshwamedhikā Parva 10

10 Āshwamedhikā Parva 72.23

11 People of Sindhu desh

12 Āshwamedhikā Parva 78

13 Āshwamedhikā Parva 73

14 Somewhere by the coast in present-day Odisha.
15 Ādi Parva 214, 216
16 Horse ordained for the Ashwamedha Yajna.
17 Āshwamedhikā Parva 79
18 Āshwamedhikā Parva 80
19 Āshwamedhikā Parva 84
20 This is the fourth of the yugas (epoch) as per Hindu thought, as creation moves towards destruction before being created again. The death of Krishna is said to mark the end of Dwāparyuga and beginning of Kaliyuga. The yuga cycle has four stages, Satyuga, Tretāyuga, Dwāparyuga and Kaliyuga. The entire Mahābhārata saga happens in the Dwāparyuga. The era of the Rāmāyana was the Tretayuga. The ongoing yuga is the Kaliyuga.

CHAPTER 21 THE END OF AN EPOCH

1 Mausala Parva 6
2 Mausal Parva 3
3 Mausal Parva 4
4 Mausal Parva 6
5 Panchanada is likely to be somewhere close to present-day Punjab–Rajasthana region. Panchanada literally means five rivers. Punjab too is the land of five rivers.
6 Mausal Parva 7
7 Mausal Parva 8
8 Mahāprasthānik Parva 1

CHAPTER 22 THE LEGEND OF THE SCRIPTING OF THE MAHĀBHĀRATA

1 Ādi Parva 62.53
2 Kāvya means a poem. In the story, Vyāsa Muni calls it as a kāvya. Brahmaji tells Vyāsa, 'You called it a kāvya (an epic poem) so that is how it will be known in this world—a kāvya'. The Mahābhārata has been composed as a poem in the anustubh meter. An anustubh composition has eight syllables per quarter, i.e., thirty-two syllables per shloka. For example, the first half shloka from the Bhagavad Gitā is 'धर्मक्षेत्रे कुरुक्षेत्रे समवेता युयुत्सवः।' This has sixteen syllables, eight in each quarter. Even the Rāmāyana is composed in the anustubh meter.

3 Ādi Parva 1.71–79
4 Ādi Parva 1.81
5 In the Gita Press version, this comes in the Ādi Parva after Shloka 1.28.
6 This has been mentioned in the Preface of the Gita Press edition of the Mahābhārata (Book 1, p. 8), quoting Pandit Shripad Damodar Satvalekar, a renowned Mahābhārata researcher.
7 Ādi Parva 1.102–103: चतुर्विंशतिसाहस्री चक्रे भारतसंहिताम् । उपख्यानैर्विना तावत् भारतं प्रोच्यते बुधैः ।।
8 कृष्णद्वैपायनप्रोक्ताः सुपुण्या विविधाः कथाः
कथिताश्चापि विधिवद्या वैशम्पायनेन वै ।
श्रुत्वाऽहं ता विचित्रार्था महाभारतसंश्रिताः ।।
This verse comes from the Dakshinātya recension of the Mahābhārata.
9 Ādi Parva 62.14: इदं शतसहस्रं हि श्लोकानां पुण्यकर्मणाम्। सत्यवत्यात्मजेनेह व्याख्यातममितौजसा।।; Ādi Parva 62.39: भरतानां महज्जन्म महाभारतमुच्यते ।।

CHAPTER 23 VYUHAS: ARMY FORMATIONS IN THE MAHĀBHĀRATA

1 Bhishma Parva 17.38,19, 50, 51, 56, 60, 69, 75, 81, 87, 99, 108; Drona Parva 7, 20, 34, 87.22; Karna Parva 11, 46, Shalya Parva 8
2 The text doesn't clearly say the name of the vyuha, but it mentions the vyuha was the same as the one made on the previous day.
3 While Vyal could mean a snake or an elephant in Sanskrit, to Arjuna the vyuha appears like a huge cloud-महामेघसम (Bhishma Parva 60.7).
4 Pronounced as शृङ्गाटक (ShRangāTaka).
5 Bhishma Parva 94.29. There are two Neels mentioned in the Mahābhārata—one on the side of the Kauravas, the king of Māhishmati, and other on the side of Pandavas, the king of Anup desh.
6 Bhishma Parva 87. The text does not give any other specific name for it. Some other reference texts and websites call in Urmi Vyuha, which means waves of an ocean.

ABOUT THE AUTHOR

Ami Ganatra is an alumna of Indian Institute of Management Ahmedabad (IIMA) and Veermata Jijabai Technological Institute (VJTI), Mumbai. She has over fourteen years of experience in business strategy and consulting, living across four continents and working across a multitude of sectors. In her personal life, she is a devout yoga practitioner and a certified yoga instructor. She is also a student of Sanskrit and Indian knowledge systems. Driven by a deep desire to encourage people to delve into the original shastras, Ami runs weekend reading sessions wherein the participants read and discuss texts on itihās and ādhyātma. An avid traveller, she loves to explore places and cultures. She chronicles her travel experiences and musings related to Indic wisdom on https://dharmorakshtirakshitah.wordpress.com.